The Natural History of Us

RACHEL HARRIS

SPENCER
HILL
PRESS

Library of Congress Cataloging-in-Publication Data
available upon request

Published in the United States by Spencer Hill Press

www.SpencerHillPress.com

Distributed by Midpoint Trade Books

www.midpointtrade.com
Cover design by: Lorin Taylor
Interior layout by: Lorin Taylor

ISBN 978-1-633920-68-2 (paperback)
ISBN 978-1-633920-69-9 (e-book)

Printed in the United States of America

For Megan Rigdon,
whose enthusiasm and heart
influenced every page,

and for Mindy Ruiz,
who inspired such a vital part
of this story.

Thank you both for the gift
of your friendship.

Also By Rachel Harris

Spencer Hill Press
The Fine Art of Pretending

Entangled Publishing for Teen Readers
My Super Sweet Sixteenth Century
A Tale of Two Centuries
My Not So Super Sweet Life

Entangled Publishing for Adult Readers
The Love & Games Series
Taste the Heat
Seven Day Fiancé
Accidentally Married on Purpose

The Country Blue Series
You're Still the One

MONDAY, MAY 12TH

3 Weeks until Graduation

♥ Senior Year

PEYTON

FAMILY AND CONSUMER SCIENCES 1:30 P.M.

They say that once rodeo gets into your blood, you're never the same.

The scent of sunbaked dirt and salty popcorn, the thunder of hooves pounding the earth. Dust circling the air and coating your tongue, wind biting at your cheeks. It becomes a part of your DNA. Supple leather reins leave their mark on your fingertips, and regardless of where you are or what you're doing, you can simply close your eyes and hear the crowd scream as you make that final turn. Ghosts from riders past whisper in your ear, daring you to give it everything you've got, to push yourself to your very limits.

It's exhilaration and devastation. An addiction, really.

Rodeo used to be my entire life, and I was awesome at it. Heck, some even said I was on par to becoming one of the best barrel-racers in our circuit. But that was before. Three years ago, my weak body forced me to admit what I'd feared and fought ever since I rolled out of the hospital a few months before—it was all over.

Well, until now, that is.

As classmates stream through the open door, dropping backpacks and gossip about their fun-filled weekends, I copy the words I just read on Rodeo America's website into my notebook:

> *Barrel racing clinics are a growing trend. Day camps for professionals and fans on the rise. Businesses boasting HUGE profits.*

Those last two words? Yeah, they pretty much glow in flashing neon. In fact, they're the only reason I'm not completely freaking out about Mom's idea, frantically scouring the internet for a different option. *Any* other option.

After a quick glance around the room, making sure no teachers are about, I grab my phone and pull up my messages. Countless conversations about dog food, horse shampoo, and YouTube scroll across the screen. Faith thinks it's absolutely vital to alert me whenever inspiration hits for her popular web channel... even if it's three A.M.

When I find the last group text, my frantic S.O.S. from this morning, I type with shaking fingers: *Crap on moldy toast. This time, Mom's onto something.*

I eagerly wait for a dose of positivity, a little "Hey, this ain't so bad" from the two people who truly understand, who get my fears, and startle when a *thunk* comes from the desk behind me.

"Where were you all weekend? Didn't see you at any parties."

I choke back the retort that jumps to my tongue: *Maybe because I wasn't invited to any?*

My New Year's resolution was to end senior year with less snark, so I spin around, choosing instead to share the fascinating details of Sparky-the-carsick-Doberman dousing me in doggy-phlegm.

"Somewhere better than another *vapid* rager," Lauren Hays replies, beating me to the punch.

Okay, so clearly, Melissa wasn't speaking to me. Evidence being that she never speaks to me, and she's currently staring at Lauren. Usually, prolonged contact with the dance captain/class president/girl-half-responsible-for-decimating-my-heart-freshman-year is something I avoid at all costs, but I can't help grinning at her word choice.

Vapid. Now there's a word that doesn't get enough play.

Lauren catches my smile and curls her lip as if she's smelled something foul, which you'd think would make me look away. It doesn't. I smile wider and she rolls her eyes, leaning back against the desk as she adjusts the waistband of her uniform skirt.

"My sister invited me out to Padre," she says, raising her hem an inch.

At the mention of the elder Hays and former head Diamond Doll, Melissa's eyes go wonky wide. As the two begin rehashing their weekend exploits (who they hooked up with, who saw it happen, and what drama erupted because of it), I turn back around.

My family's broke, we're seconds away from selling our ranch, and the one thing that can save it—save *us*—happens to involve my worst nightmare. Any more drama and my freaking head may explode.

I glance down and stare at my phone, willing it to buzz with a message. I'm in serious need of Faith's balls-to-the-wall confidence and Cade's perpetual optimism. When it stares back, dark and silent, I blow out a breath and clench my hands into tight fists under the desk.

Inhale, two, three, four. Unclench. *Exhale, two, three, four.*

The exercise has become my security blanket. Working my muscles, clenching and unclenching them into submission, reminds me that I'm strong. That I do have some control. Even when it feels as though my life is spinning out of it.

No one admits it, of course, but I'm the reason for our financial crisis. My medical bills cut a bleeding hole through my parents' savings and it's obviously getting worse because they've been at it every night, huddled around bank statements and steaming mugs of coffee. They've talked about selling my great grandfather's land, downsizing the boarding business, even making career changes. But when they brought up the rodeo school last night, it was the first time I heard excitement in their voices. Of course, they had no clue I was eavesdropping. They prefer keeping me in virtual bubble-wrap, not wanting me to worry. But I do listen, I am worried, and I can't let any of those things happen. Not when we can do something about it.

I'm mid hand-clench when the bell rings. Coach Stasi appears and conversations mute into whispers. She begins striding toward her desk, arms filled with papers and a loose shoelace slapping the floor, headed straight to where I am seated dead center in the room. So, naturally, this is when it happens. On my desktop, lit up like a tattling beacon, my phone decides to finally go off—double time.

First Katy Perry and then Hunter Hayes serenade the room in Faith and Cade's designated text ringtones as my feeble fingers frantically fumble with the stupid case. With the collective classroom's gaze upon me, I switch the device over to silent and lift my head to meet my fate. Coach's stare is pointed, albeit slightly amused.

Yep. I'm screwed.

Officially, phones aren't allowed in school. "They are a distraction and a hindrance to higher learning." But we're seniors, the countdown to blessed freedom is on, and in the face of rampant, class-wide rebellion, most teachers have adopted a lax policy. If they don't see it and can't hear it, they don't really care. Unfortunately, in this case, I'm two for two.

Heat infuses my cheeks as Lauren snickers behind me, and I remind myself yet again of my New Year's resolution. *Only three more weeks until graduation.*

Ignoring Lauren, I lift a shoulder and stretch my lips into a wide, cheesy grin. "Oopsie."

Coach shakes her head with a silent laugh then rolls her eyes dramatically before turning to face her desk, needlessly shuffling the pristine stack of papers in her hands on its surface. Thus allowing *me* to check my messages.

I've always said Coach is one of the good ones.

Faith's text is first: *Breathe, girl. No matter what, we got this. *fist bump**

I lift my fist in the air, imagining her fierce scowl of confidence, and switch over to Cade's: *We'll figure something out. Promise.*

Relief floods my veins in a cool, calm rush. This is reason number five thousand and eleven why my friends are made of win. Faith is my voice of reason and fearless counterpart, and Cade... well, *whatever* Cade is, he gets it. Gets me. They're the only two who know about my rodeo fears since the accident, and if they think this is fine, then it will be.

Nodding to myself, almost even believing it, I shift my thumbs to reply when a second text comes in. This one private, just for me.

Cade: *P.S: Love you!*

A wince forms before I can stop it. I'm fully aware this response makes me horrid, and a frisson of self-loathing creeps down my spine. Cade Donovan is everything a girl could want in a boyfriend—he's everything *I* should want. Funny and smart, a great listener. Cute in that pretty-boy, CW actor sort of way, and an ass that fills out a pair of Levis like *whoa*. He's been one of my closest friends since I wore a training bra, my rock the last few years, and in a perfect world, a world where my heart wasn't completely decimated, I'd be ecstatic to hear those words coming from him. Sadly, life is far from perfect.

The truth is, I *do* love Cade. Just not in the way he wants me to.

"All right, kids, settle down."

As Coach Stasi nudges the last few stragglers toward their seats, my friend Mi-Mi hurrying among them, I blow out a breath. With one eye closed, I quickly type the generic (and pathetic) *xoxo*, then power off my phone, stomach churning with guilt.

"We're in the home stretch," our teacher says, causing cheers to erupt across the room. Her smile widens and she nods. "Yep, graduation is just around the corner, and today kicks off our last major project of the year."

Those cheers turn to groans and she laughs aloud, somewhat gleefully. Coach is cool as far as teachers go, but she's also a bit of a sadist.

"I know, I know, Senioritis is rampant," she continues. "But folks, I hate to say it, school's not over yet. Lucky for you, this last section is going to be our best yet."

From the desk beside mine, Mi-Mi turns to face me, wide eyes flared with interest. The two of us are in the same boat, school schedules packed to the max, but for completely different reasons. Mine is overloaded with extra science and math classes prepping for Vet school, while hers are full of every art, music, and theater class our school provides. She's our resident thespian.

Mi-Mi has a love/hate relationship with Family and Consumer Sciences. She prefers classes where she can split eardrums, get messy, and become someone else, but the number of male students in here looking for an easy A makes up for it. As for me? I get my kicks with a good theorem, and centripetal force makes my heart skip a beat, but FACS is my guilty pleasure. It allows my brain to breathe. Projects are easy and we study things we may actually use in everyday life, unlike, say, the mating habits of fruit flies.

Just thinking of last year's Bio II lab gives me the heebie-jeebies.

Coach strides across the floor with a bounce in her step, tapping her fingertips together à la evil scientist. "You kids are gonna be my guinea pigs," she says. "This year, I'm changing things up a bit, combining a few sections, adding a new one. A mini-experiment, if you will. As I'm sure Alyssa can tell you, I love shaking things up."

Aly Reed, one of Coach's volleyball players, laughs from the back. "And it always leads to trouble."

"Nonsense! You're going to like this. Over the few weeks, we're gonna take a close look at issues most of you will face after graduation. Budgeting for the first time. Career and life planning. Possibly thoughts of marriage and starting a family. I decided to combine three units on money, relational skills, and child development into one topical, real life project. It'll count for twenty-five percent of the semester grade, and a co-written paper with your teammate will substitute for a final exam."

A row over, my former nemesis lifts her hand. "What teammate?"

"Ah, glad you asked, Lauren." Hitching her hip onto the desk, Coach pauses for a moment, letting the suspense build. From the look in her eye, this is going to be interesting. I find myself leaning forward, right along with the rest of the class, until she finally announces:

"Congratulations, kids! You're all newlyweds."

Gasps and confused laughter echo around me. Coach grins (See what I mean? Sadist), and immediately, Melissa and Lauren start whispering about who their husbands will be. A mystery evidently high on everyone's minds since a male voice asks from the back, "Do we get to pick our wives?"

Without permission, my head swivels. My survival instincts always suck when it comes to *him*. Yeah, he wasn't the one to ask the question, and I've made it a point never to look back there in almost nine months, but I know he's there. Seated with the rest of the baseball team.

My gaze slides over Drew, our third baseman, and Brandon, our main pitcher. It hesitates over Carlos, the star shortstop and class clown, his hand in the air and a goofball grin on his face. Then it stops on Justin.

Whoosh! Cold flashes the back of my neck. A dull twinge builds behind my ribs, and time turns glacial as my heart seizes in my chest. It's not hate or anger pooling in my gut—*God, I wish it were*. More like humiliation, hurt, and intense regret. Also a dash of loneliness and stupid longing.

How pathetic is that?

"Afraid not," Coach replies and I force my attention back to the front, thankfully before he catches me gawking or I'd be adding embarrassment to the mix. "I'm aware there are several couples in this class, but the project will run the duration of the course. Unfortunately, that's longer than most Fairfield relationships. I think partner assignments are best left to my handy-dandy computer."

With that, she picks up the packets.

As she walks to the far end of the room, she nods at someone peeking through the glass window in the doorway. "Here," she tells Madison in the front row. "Take a stack and hand them back. I have to step out for a moment so use this time to look the project over. All the details about group assignments are inside, including your spouse's name on the last page."

She walks out, the door closes behind her, and laughter breaks out all around.

That's when it hits me.

Why it didn't before, when everyone was whispering and wondering, I have no idea. I blame rodeo. Either way, as the packets make their turtle-like crawl across the room, and the horrific possibility turns more into a sick, twisted, certainty (because, let's face it, that's how my life rolls), all I can do is await my fate and think:

Surely, my luck can't suck *that* badly... can it?

The question's not even fully formed before I'm closing my eyes and chuckling.

Oh, silly girl. Of course it can.

I rock back and forth in my chair, the stiff plastic squeaking as old memories assault me, this time not of rodeo or my weak body, but a particular boy and his wicked grin. The way he teased me, the way he kissed me. The deep sound of his laugh and the haunted look in his eyes.

And the craptastic way I fell for him.

"Peyton." Mi-Mi nudges my arm and I open my eyes. Attempting a smile, I take the packets from her hands and blindly toss five behind me before handing off all but one to my neighbor. "You all right?"

I nod stiffly. "Just a little nauseous."

No truer words have ever passed my lips.

She accepts that with a shrug, and I begin to flip—papers, that is. Funny, I was so desperate to see who my partner is, curious to learn if the universe really hated me that much, but now that the packet is in my hands, and the truth is seconds away, it's like I'm trudging through oil. The room disappears. Lauren's snide giggles float away. My world shrinks until all that's left is the sound of my choppy breaths and the page deciding how my senior year will end: stress-free or in epic misery.

I shake out my hand and exhale, psyching myself up for the big reveal. Then, slowly, *fearfully*, I turn the final sheet and peer at the bottom of the page.

And begin laughing hysterically.

Oh, I feel Mi-Mi's stare. Sense Lauren's judgment. If Coach were still here, she'd no doubt be offering up a pass for the nurse. But no pills and no amount of lying down is gonna stop this crazy train from derailing, because right there, typed in black permanent ink on the final row of the spreadsheet is my name. Paired with the boy who irrevocably broke my heart...

Justin Carter.

JUSTIN
FAMILY AND CONSUMER SCIENCES 1:45 P.M.

"When Gabi hears I'm married to Lauren, she's gonna go ape shit."

Carlos groans and I tear my gaze away from a near hysterical Peyton. My best friend flips his pencil in his hand and feigns stabbing himself in the chest. "Think Coach Stasi will let me switch partners?"

It takes a second to process what he's asking. Peyton's laugh is still ringing in my ears. But I'm a born bull-shitter, so I smirk and say, "Tell her that's what she gets for not taking FACS with the rest of us." Then I steal another glance up front.

I haven't heard it in years, but Peyton's laugh is normally musical. Like, if sunshine, rainbows, and flying unicorns had a sound, her laugh would be it. Or, at least what it is supposed to be, not that hard, cynical, pain-edged shriek she just gave. It's so wrong, so *off*, that I physically wrap my hand around the desktop just to keep from going over to her.

As if she'd want me there anyway.

Carlos shoots me a sideways look. "Kid, how in the hell do you score so many women?" Then he snorts and shakes his head. "Never mind, I answered my own question. You, my friend, know 'Casuals.' Let me instruct you in the ways of 'Commitments.'" He leans across the aisle like he's about to impart some sort of top-secret intel and says, "If I followed your advice, Gabi would cut off my nuts and lock them in her camera case."

"And you wonder why I don't do relationships," I reply with a half-smile, but even I hear that my delivery is off. His smirk falls and he squints in my direction, but I turn my head. The last thing I need is more questions.

A dull ache twinges behind my ribcage and as I fight to keep from staring a hole into the back of Peyton's head, my gaze lands on Aly. She nods at something Brandon says and leans forward to kiss his cheek. I release a breath. It's probably weird to admit since we went out earlier this year, but seeing her with him, happy and smiling, eases the pressure in my chest.

Aly and I weren't right together. She's had a thing for Taylor since freshman year, and as history shows, I suck at commitment. But our blink-and-you-miss-it relationship was the closest I've come to wanting one in years, and ever since we broke up, there's been this itch under my skin. An annoying sixth sense that something is wrong or missing, and nothing I do—not girls, school, or even baseball—feels the same anymore.

Which sucks, since baseball and girls are the only things I'm actually good at.

Carlos's cell buzzes on his desk and I glance over as he drops his head into his hands.

"Shit," he mutters. "Hurricane Gabi is making landfall."

"Someone tip her off about Lauren?" I ask, grabbing a pen. In the corner of my packet, I start sketching a baseball diamond. I'm not Brandon so I can't draw for shit, but it beats the hell out of sitting here psychoanalyzing what's wrong with me.

He nods wearily and I snicker. How people spread shit before Facebook and texts I don't know, but in this case, technology is my friend.

Count on good old Carlos to remind me why I don't do commitment. I swear, he and Gabi invent stuff to bitch about. They're constantly fighting over nothing and spend most of the time driving each other insane. I'm no expert, but that shit ain't normal.

"Carlos, look at me." He lifts his head from his hand and I clasp his shoulder. "Tell me the truth... she's already got you by the balls, doesn't she?" His eyes narrow and I grin. "Blink once for yes and I'll go get help."

His good-natured smile returns as he knocks away my hand and flips me off, which is good since I *am* kidding. Well, mostly anyway.

"What about you, huh?" He picks up the packet and starts turning pages. "What lucky lady got stuck with your punk ass for the next month?"

Since I don't really give a shit I shrug and lean back to study the stained ceiling tiles... until I hear him say, "*Huh.*"

I glance over. "Is that a good *huh* or a bad *huh*?"

He rocks his head back and forth as he replies, "Guess it depends on how you look at it."

I sit up straight and grab the paper from his hand, searching for my name. The fact that I can feel him watching makes me nervous. I've hooked up with half the girls in this class (half the school, really), but none have ended *that* badly. For the most part, they know the score before it even starts—that's the beauty of dating "Casuals." The only semi-weirdness I ever had was with Aly and that's long over. She and Brandon are way too whipped on each other to care about me.

As I near the bottom of the page, Carlos asks, "You two used to hang out, right?" and I do a double-take when I reach the final row.

"Did y'all have a falling out or something?"

"Or... something," I mumble, swallowing hard.

Justin Carter and Peyton Williams.

This at least explains that hysterical laugh.

Slowly, I lift my eyes toward the front of the class. As if she can feel my stare, Peyton turns in her seat, and when her wide blue-gray eyes lock on mine, I completely forget how to breathe.

Guilt, longing, and that damn stupid question—*what if*—hits me square in the chest. You'd think seeing her after three years would get easier. It hasn't. I've just gotten a hell of a lot better at hiding the fallout. Pretending I don't occasionally search her out in the halls, checking to see if she's all right. Wondering what she's thinking, what she's doing, and acting like it doesn't make my whole damn day when I catch her smiling. I used to be the reason for Peyton's smiles.

Now, I'd be thrilled if she didn't glare at me like I was dog shit stuck to her shoe.

"Damn, dude." Carlos whistles under his breath after she spins back around. "That girl is not a fan of yours." He laughs under his breath, ending on a cough when I glare at him. "What in the hell did you do to her?"

"Nothing," I say, wishing that were true. "Just a small misunderstanding."

But it wasn't small, and it damn sure wasn't a misunderstanding. Whether it was the truth or not, Peyton saw exactly what I wanted her to see that day. She believed what I thought she *had* to believe in order to protect her. To protect me. The same thing I've regretted every day since.

Me cheating on her.

Tuesday, January 4th

21 Weeks until Disaster

♥ Freshman Year

PEYTON

FAIRFIELD ACADEMY 7:05 A.M.

So this was high school. Students streaming through every door and lining the walls. Multi-colored fliers and trophy cases, a thousand conversations at once. Mass chaos was what it was, and as I strolled through the middle of it all, wide-eyed and staring like Dorothy in Oz, I couldn't help but gawk. A girl in a uniform exactly like mine walked past and sized me up with a scrunched up nose, and I (thankfully) stopped myself just shy of waving like some sort of socially inept dork.

This. Was. *Awesome.*

Okay, so yeah, starting school on a Tuesday was weird. And I was a semester behind, my uniform was stiff and scratchy, and I was walking the halls with my *dad*. But none of it mattered because it all meant I was here, at Fairfield Academy, and that despite every whispered doubt and liquid fear in my bones, I'd finally gotten my fresh start.

Already I could tell there were things I'd miss. I'd been homeschooled all my life, and with that came certain advantages, such as never having to think coherently before nine A.M. and wearing my ratty pajamas all day. Also, in between learning algebra and earth science, I could bathe a basset hound, watch Days of Our Lives, or ride Oakley after lunch. Most importantly? My stomach never roiled like it wanted to ingest itself. But the fear knotting my gut simply walking through the main door today proved that I was alive, and I was clinging to my new motto like a desperate cowboy on a buck-crazed horse:

"Do what scares you."

"I've missed that smile, angel girl." Dad's gray-eyed gaze softened at my gooberific grin and he watched me wistfully before coughing and glancing away. "Now, the nurse knows your history, and so do most of your teachers. If anything happens—and I mean *anything*—if you feel weak for any reason, or think you need to lie down, you just tell them. They'll understand."

"Yeah, Dad, I know."

"*Or*, we can always delay it another semester." He looked at me again, eyebrows lifted with hope. "There's no shame in waiting until—"

"Dad!" My voice echoed off the ceramic tile and a group of upperclassman stopped what they were doing to stare. *Fabulous.* Twin surges of heat burned my cheeks as I closed the distance between me and my father.

"We've been over this a million times," I said, lowering my voice. "You promised that when I was well enough to walk through the door that I could come here. Well, I just did it. Sans wheelchair and with exactly zero assistance."

Six months ago, that feat wouldn't be so impressive, but today I was flipping ecstatic.

"So yeah, I'm a semester behind," I told him with a shrug. "So what? I've finally gotten through the worst, and I don't care if all the cool clubs are full or the best electives are taken. I'm not wasting another second." When my stupid nose started to burn, I turned away and blinked to clear my blurry vision. "I'm not letting this disorder steal one more thing from me. Not anymore."

My voice wobbled toward the end and I mentally slapped myself for showing weakness. The goal today was to prove that I was strong and tough—that I could do this. Not to break down in the hallway and wind up with the nickname Weepy McNew Girl.

"Besides," I said, knocking his arm with my elbow. "If anything happens, you're here."

That, of course, was my ace in the hole. Coming to the school where my dad taught had always been the plan, and now it just made my argument that much stronger.

Fairfield Academy had an amazing dual-credit program with the local college's Veterinary Technology department. Becoming a veterinarian was all I'd ever wanted... well, other than kicking McKenna's butt in the Junior High barrel-racing ranks. That program alone was worth the price of admission.

Which, technically, *was* a heck of a lot more than homeschooling.

My steps slowed as guilt walloped me in the chest, not unlike the time Oakley got spooked and threw me against the fence. We could have literally wallpapered the den with my unexpected medical bills, so maybe...

"Is this about the tuition?" I asked. "Because if this costs too much—"

"Don't be silly." Dad forced a smile, but it didn't quite meet his eyes. "Faculty gets tuition breaks. Even if they didn't, the money doesn't matter, not as long as this is what you really want..." His voice trailed as we came to a stop outside the office doors, and I nodded vigorously.

"It is," I assured him. *Even if it means dragging my loving, well-meaning, overprotective parents along with me.* "I'm a new Peyton Williams, Dad. A girl ready to rope life and experience it all. The easy, the hard, the safe, and the things that scare me senseless." I winked to show I was (mostly) teasing and injected my voice with enthusiasm. "Let's do this!"

This time, a genuine smile tipped his lips, and he tapped my chin with his finger. "You make me proud, you know that?"

The big lug was such a softie. Biting my lip as tears threatened once more, I nodded, and he exhaled long and slow before opening the door. "Bell's about to ring," he muttered gruffly. "You'll need your schedule."

The heady scent of fresh ink and warm paper hit my nose and my excitement skyrocketed. Nausea, too... but mostly excitement. The spicy tang of peppermint joined the mix a second later and I eagerly bounced in my loafers.

When the office door closed with a *bump*, sealing out the sound of hallway chaos, students sitting in the row of cushioned chairs along the wall raised their heads. Most immediately dismissed me upon appraisal, but a few glanced curiously between Dad and me. Guess I should get used to that.

I followed Dad toward the taupe laminate desk, my hands clenching and unclenching at my sides. I had no room for fear in my life. I could do this. I *wanted* to do this. Beyond the divide, teachers and administrators buzzed about, flitting from mailboxes to the enormous copy machine, reminding me of happy worker bees. Phones rang, people laughed, and somewhere in the chaotic room, a radio played soft jazz. Dad checked his watch and then tapped his knuckles against the laminate, waiting for help, and I closed my eyes to let the frantic energy envelop me.

Here's the thing about GBS (Guillain-Barre Syndrome): it hits you fast and furious. One day, I'd been riding Oakley at the Tomball Junior Rodeo, and the next, I'd become a prisoner in my own body. For weeks, I hadn't been able to talk or move. I couldn't even scream. Nurses and doctors had flowed in and out of my room, checking vitals and talking as if I weren't even there. Guests had stared with poorly hidden fear, holding awkward conversations with my parents about the weather and Texas football. Running home after they left to hug their kids and thank God this hadn't happened to them. I'd been nothing but a silent observer as life happened around me and without me. But those days were over. Now, I *could* walk, I could talk, and I was on my way to becoming a fully functional member of society again.

It felt phenomenal.

Opening my eyes, I released a breath and propped my elbows on the counter next to Dad. I nodded at a few teachers I recognized from our holiday parties and when the principal stepped out of her office to answer a question, I waved and said hello.

"Peyton!" Ms. Gouvas leaned against the doorframe with a warm smile, and from the corner of my eye, I noticed a few students turn their heads. "I'm glad you're finally joining us."

"I'm so excited to be here," I replied, no doubt sounding dorkalicious to the eavesdropping students, but I really *was* excited. So sue me. "Took me longer than I'd hoped, but I'm ready to jump in the fray."

The edges of the principal's smile turned down a bit, a reminder that I wouldn't be *jumping* anywhere for a while, and we both knew it. "Well, I'm confident you'll make the best of your years here, Peyton." She straightened away from the wall and pointed at me. "I'll be keeping an eye on you."

After shooting me a playful wink, she ducked back into her office, and only then did I chance a full glance behind me. As predicted, practically the entire row was watching, a multitude of expressions on their faces. None of them were impressed.

Is being on a semi-first name basis with the principal really that weird?

A blonde who appeared to be around my age snickered quietly.

Yep, it was weird.

"Ah, Dan." A petite woman with long, dark hair and a bright red blouse dropped an overstuffed file folder onto the desk. She blew her bangs off her face and asked my dad, "How are you this crazy morning?"

"Better than I deserve," he replied like always. "But I was hoping you could do me a favor, Kim. Today is Peyton's first day, and I'm running late for a staff meeting. You think you can help her get situated?"

"Of course, it'd be my pleasure," she replied with a reassuring smile, proving that Big Bad Coach Man wasn't fooling anyone. When it came to his baby girl, the man was a teddy bear. "You go along to your meeting now. Peyton here will be in great hands."

Even with that assurance, I could tell he was reluctant. Interesting factoid about getting sick? It de-ages you like ten years in your parents' eyes. Sighing, I wrapped my arms around Dad's stocky body and pressed a kiss to his clean-shaven cheek.

"I'll be fine," I told him, not caring if the other kids were watching. This was my dad, we were close, and if they had a problem with that, well, they could suck it. "I'll find you in the gym after school." When he continued to hesitate, I shoved his meaty shoulder with a laugh. "Go on. Go!"

With a grumble, he finally relented, and my too-wide smile held just until he'd disappeared around the corner. A nervous exhale parted my lips and when I turned around, the woman behind the counter put her hand on mine.

"My younger sister was hospitalized for a month when we were kids."

I shifted on my feet, not sure what to say to that, and she pressed on. "It was pneumonia in her case, but I understand how annoying it is for everyone to treat you with kid gloves like you're helpless. You're not. I know that, and your dad will come around soon enough. As far as I'm concerned though, you're just another student, all right?"

Heart full, chest shockingly light as if the weight of a boulder had suddenly been lifted, I sent her a grateful smile. That's all I wanted to be. *Normal.* "Thank you."

She squeezed my hand as a fierce mama bird look entered her eyes. "But if anyone thinks otherwise and messes with you, you just let me know, all right?"

I chuckled, the last bit of anxiety fleeing. "You got it."

Ms. Kim sent me a wink and opened a folder, withdrawing a white piece of paper. Glancing at it, she raised an eyebrow and said, "I take that back. You're not just a regular student." She lifted her gaze to mine. "You're a very intelligent student with an insane course load. Are you aware that you're in all honors courses and that you're entering school *mid*-year?"

I straightened my spine and replied, "I can handle it."

Her eyes narrowed as she watched me for a long moment, and then she nodded. "Know what? I believe you." She grinned softly and held out her hand. "Here. Your homeroom is listed at the top and first bell rings in ten minutes."

It happened in the span of a heartbeat.

The door opened behind me, her gaze shifted toward the newcomer, and the hopeful bubble I'd been floating in all morning *popped.*

Have you ever had one of those moments when it was as if you were outside your body, watching events and knowing the outcome, but completely unable to stop it from happening? Where everything unfolds in slow motion and you're forced to witness the inevitable ending in silent horror? That's what it was like for me, watching the class schedule slip from her hand, through my weak fingertips, and flutter softly to the ground.

Maybe it *was* too soon.

For the first time since I'd convinced my parents to let me come here, true doubt washed over me. Staring at the discarded schedule, I couldn't help but wonder if I'd pushed for too much, too fast. If I really should sit out another semester.

Mom would be euphoric. If I went home, Dad would dance a jig. I'd be back in virtual bubble wrap, right where they wanted to keep me.

And I—I'd prove that I really was as pathetic as I'd thought.

A dark head suddenly appeared in my vision, blocking my view of my schedule lying helplessly on the brown tile. Blinking away memories of my hospital bed and the sad faces of the nurses, I focused on the gelled strands below me and then the pair of equally dark eyes that replaced them. Eyes that stared into me with a sharp smugness like they could read all my secrets. And see straight through my blouse.

Whoa, hot boy alert!

A slow lopsided grin stretched the boy's mouth, confirmation of his mad mindreading skills. He held up my schedule and asked, "Slippery fingers?"

Friday, January 7th

21 Weeks until Disaster

♥ Freshman Year

JUSTIN

FAIRFIELD ACADEMY BASEBALL FIELD 3:25 P.M.

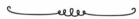

She was back.

I'd been beginning to think I'd imagined her. After rocking my world with her breathy *hi*, her thick strawberry blonde hair, and eyes that stunned me senseless, the girl had just disappeared. She wasn't in any of my classes, I never saw her waiting after school, and as dumb as it was to admit, I'd actually looked. Casually at first, just curious, then more determined when she never showed. I could've asked the guys, but then they'd have known a girl had gotten to me. And that, like a jackass, I'd never even gotten her name, much less her number. But now, here she was. A goddess cheering in the stands, watching as I was about to make the team.

Hot girl was a baseball fan. That worked well for me.

"Friend of yours?"

I tore my gaze away from the bleachers and found a guy smirking above me. He was the same one who always cracked jokes in my math class. "Not yet," I replied, emphasis on the yet, letting him know I had dibs. I switched sides, stretching out my other hamstring and added, "Just laying groundwork for now."

If stalking the hallways counted as groundwork.

Hoping to learn her name, I looked up and casually asked, "She in any of your classes?"

"Nah, I'd remember a sweet face like that." He stole another peek and whistled low. "And into baseball, too? Damn, dude, what is up with you and girls? Every time I see you, you've got another one wrapped around you. You're like the chick whisperer."

I laughed and shook out my legs, muscles warm and ready. Girls were one of the few things that came easily to me. That, and playing ball. "What can I say? I have a gift."

With nothing left to stretch, I pushed to my feet to assess the competition. Sophomore team tryouts started in five minutes, but the diamond began filling with guys about a half hour ago, math-class dude being one of them. It didn't matter, though. One way or another, I was making an impression today.

Fairfield Academy had one of the best programs in the state. They were district champ three years running and bi-district champs the year before that—the year Coach Williams took over. The man knew his shit, he was tough but fair, and I was determined to play for him. I'd even approached him in the fall to see how I could prepare for today.

"Think you got a shot at making it?" I asked, curious what position this guy played. Cool or not, if he was a catcher I'd have to beat him out. No way could he outplay me. And there wasn't a chance in hell this meant more to him.

"Hope so." He hopped up and adjusted his ball cap. "From what I hear, Coach skips playmakers through to Varsity at the end of the year." I nodded, having heard the same thing, and he looked me over, sizing me up before holding out his hand. "Carlos Ramirez, shortstop."

Grinning, I took it and said, "Justin Carter, catcher."

"All right, gentlemen!" At Coach Williams's voice we both turned and then hustled over to the pitcher's mound. "This is how it's gonna go. We have stations set up to monitor your fielding, your ground ball work, and live hitting in the cage. Give me everything you've got today, and I promise, I'll be watching. Results are posted on Monday, and let me just say this now, so we're clear—if you don't make it this round, it just means you weren't ready. We hold tryouts every year, and I hope you'll consider coming back out next January."

His gaze slid over the group, now up to over thirty guys trying out for the same fifteen spots. I couldn't speak for everyone else, but only one thing was going through my mind: one of those spots was mine.

Coach popped his gum and asked, "Everyone ready?"

"Yes, sir!"

My voice was clear and strong among the chorus, and even though I was just one of many, he turned his head and looked me straight in the eye. Nodding once he said, "Let's get to work."

***

"Looking pretty good out there."

I capped my water bottle on the sidelines, a minute into our five-minute water break, and glanced up into the stands. Hot girl was smiling at me. She'd spent most of the last hour reading a paperback or with her face lifted to the sun like a human sunflower. Occasionally she'd cheer for guys who missed at bat or made a mistake, but I only caught her watching me once. I'd made sure to nail it when she did.

"So you *have* been watching me," I replied, smiling wider when she blushed. "Hey now, don't be embarrassed. It's only natural you'd watch the hottest guy out here."

A breathless laugh escaped her lips. "Wow." Setting her book on her lap, she smiled back, an open, sweet kind of smile without any hint of flirtation. "What is it about ball players and egos the size of Texas?" She shook her head and said, "My daddy warned me about guys like you."

"Girl, your dad never *met* a guy like me, because I'm an original."

Honestly, I had no idea where this shit came from. Half the time, I sounded like a total moron—but girls ate it up.

Hot girl scrunched her nose. "Does that kind of line usually work?"

I laughed out loud. "Ninety-nine percent of the time."

Either I had no game with this girl, she had a boyfriend, or she wasn't into hooking up, which was all I did. But still, something kept me from walking. "You got a name, pretty girl?"

That sweet grin returned as she said, "Lord, you're just one bad line after another, aren't you?"

Definitely no game. "Fine, I'll just make one up then."

I squinted up at her, tapping my water bottle against my thigh and feeling that smile all the way down to my toes. Remembering the way she held her face to the sun, I lifted a finger and declared, "Sunshine. Your name's Sunshine."

"Ahh, so I'm a hippie," she said, pursing her lips. They were soft pink, natural, and didn't appear to have any lipstick. Her entire face was makeup-free, and now that I thought about it, she hadn't worn any that first day either. Sunshine laughed softly and tilted her head to study me. After a moment she said, "I'm Peyton."

"See, that wasn't so hard, now was it?" I teased, and she rolled her eyes. "And, since I know you're dying to ask, I'm just gonna tell you. My name is Justin."

"And here I just assumed it was Trouble."

Right there. Any other girl delivering that line and she'd have been flirting. Not this girl, though. She meant it. "I'm hurt, Peyton, really. Making snap judgments when all I've done is give you compliments and hand over your schedule after you dropped it."

A schedule I should've paid more attention to.

For the briefest second, a shadow passed over her face and I wondered what it meant. But then it was gone and she was back to busting my balls. "Exactly. And why *were* you in the front office that day, huh? Called to see the principal on the first day of the new semester." She *tsked* in disapproval and pointed at me. "Trouble."

"Actually, I was there to change my classes around." I didn't know why it mattered so much what she thought. Peyton was fun to talk to and she was definitely easy on the eyes, but it was obvious she wasn't my usual type.

But still...

"I'm gonna make the team today," I told her, "and I need my unstructured period to be the hour before lunch. That's when Coach holds office hours in the athletic department, and I've heard he talks strategy with players who are there."

She raised her eyebrows in surprise. "You're dedicated. He'll like that."

Okay. "And you'd know this—"

A sharp whistle blasted from the pitcher's mound, cutting me off. I turned to see Coach waving us back out and quickly took a final pull off my water.

"Gotta go," I said, recapping the bottle and tossing it to the ground. "See you around?"

She pursed her lips like she wanted to say no, but she nodded. Then, leaning forward on the bleachers, she said, "You know, he's not just watching *what* you do out there. He's watching how you do it. And remember, don't be afraid to sacrifice yourself for the team."

This was the strangest girl I'd ever met. If this was her idea of flirting, she must have a lot of older brothers. Regardless, they were good tips, so I said, "Thanks. I'll keep that in mind."

Touching the brim of my hat, I spun on my heel and jogged onto the field, ready to show the man that I idolized what I could do.

Making this team was everything to me. It meant finding my place in this school, proving myself in front of one of the best catchers to play college ball, and maybe getting Dad to take notice. Baseball was one of the few things he loved more than money, so it was possible he'd make a couple games. And now, even though she was obviously not my normal type, Sunshine had given me one more reason to do well today.

I wanted her to watch me kick ass.

MONDAY, MAY 12TH

3 Weeks until Graduation
♥ Senior Year

JUSTIN
FAMILY AND CONSUMER SCIENCES 1:50 P.M.

"Sorry for the interruption," Coach Stasi says as she walks back through the door and closes it behind her. "While I was gone, I trust that you looked over the packet and found your one true love?"

She says this like it's a joke instead of what it really is—a bloody disaster.

"For those of you who didn't just skip right to the end, you may've noticed the first group date is tomorrow night. Now the school is footing the bill, but I know it's still extremely short notice. A local restaurant has agreed to open their doors early for us and this is the only night they can do it this month."

On the whiteboard, she writes the name Carmela's, a local Tex-Mex restaurant, and circles it. "I realize many of you have practices and jobs, so if for any reason you're unable to attend, just schedule a time to see me with your partner and we'll find another way to complete the first assignment. After all, compromise is what marriage is all about!" She smiles again then points to us with the dry-erase marker. "Write that down."

Coach goes on to talk about other assignments and lessons, and how they will all be used to help write the on-going final paper, but it all goes in one ear and out the other. I can't hear past the echo of Peyton's laugh, or see beyond the furious twirling of her hair. Her foot tap-tap-tapping on the ground. Those old familiar tics cut a gaping hole in my chest and I suck wind to keep from doing something incredibly stupid. Like call out, *Sunshine.*

Damn, I miss her.

"So, any word from the old man about the game?" Carlos asks, and when I look over, he sets his phone down with a relieved smile. Things must be better in Gabi-land. At least for now.

Not wanting to let on how much Peyton has affected me, I strive for casual. "You mean other than the list of training suggestions he slipped under my door, or the reminder that scouts are still watching?" The grin falls from my friend's face, and I shrug. "No, but I'm not surprised."

Saturday night, our team won the bi-district championship. Since my father's company is the team's biggest booster, you'd think he'd have been there. You'd think wrong.

"Maybe he'll show for the area round."

"Yeah, I'm not holding my breath." The last time anyone in my family saw me play was freshman year, and that was only because Dad's boss was in town. *Fake interest in your son's ability while schmoozing the bigwigs.* That's rule one in Mitch Carter's parenting playbook. "Besides, Abuelita screams enough for two of him."

His goofy grin slides back as he says, "More like curses the umpire, you mean."

Carlos is one of the few people who know what a dick my father is and his *loco en la cabeza* family pretty much adopted me years ago. They're the ones who cheer my name at games, hound me about my grades, and relentlessly nag me about girls. And I mean relentlessly.

"She's already planning a graduation party," he says, pretending to write down whatever notes Coach is putting on the board. "The whole family's gonna be there." He pauses a moment, shifts uncomfortably in his seat, then adds, "She, uh, she also said you should bring a girl—as long as it isn't a 'hussy.'"

He lifts his fingers in air-quotes and rolls his eyes in a, "hey, she's my grandmother and she's crazy," sort of way, but I suddenly sit up straight as an idea hits me. That woman's a genius.

Planting my feet on the floor, I grab the packet. I thumb through the long list of group dates, taking note of all the partner-time required (a lot), and a rush of endorphins floods my bloodstream. My heart pounds just like it did when I tagged out Jefferson to win last night's game, and when a relieved exhale parts my lips, I hear Carlos say, "Uh oh."

"What?" I ask distractedly.

"You've got that psycho look in your eyes." I raise my eyes and he waves a finger back and forth in front of my face. "The same one you had before we egged Crestmont High last week. You're planning something."

Adrenaline bounces my knee. "Maybe I am."

My hand beats out a rhythm on my thigh as I realize that *this* is exactly what I'd been waiting for. The answer to the itch under my skin. My extreme restlessness. It's not a new feeling—if I were honest, it's been on a low simmer for years. Being with Aly just brought it to a boil. I've been numb ever since I lost Peyton, and this... this insane project is my chance to finally make things right.

"Tell Abuelita I'll be there," I say, returning my gaze to the back of Peyton's head. "And that I'll be bringing a girl even she can't complain about." From the corner of my eye, I see him stare at me in confusion. "I'm bringing my wife."

Carlos's mouth opens in a mix of shock and doubt and I don't blame him. I saw Peyton's reaction, too. But I have three whole weeks between now and then, and a plan taking shape in my mind.

Peyton may *think* she hates me, but that's only because she doesn't know the total truth. Soon, that'll change—but I can't rush it. I have to start small. Ease into it. Use these dates and outings to show her how much I've changed since I was fifteen and screwed everything up.

But I will do it.

"Mark my words, Carlos," I say, feeling excited about a girl for the first time in a very long time. But then, that's because it's not just any girl; it's *my* girl. She just doesn't know it yet. "I'm gonna be the best damn husband in this entire class."

He looks at me uncertainly, but that doesn't faze me. I won't let it. I know I don't deserve it. Hell, I never deserved *her*. But I'm not letting anything stop me. Not this time. Thanks to Coach Stasi, I'm going to remind Peyton of all the reasons she fell for me in the first place.

And then I'm going to make her do it again.

TUESDAY, MAY 13TH

3 Weeks until Graduation

♥ Senior Year

PEYTON

CARMELA'S RESTAURANT 4:35 P.M.

You know what would rock? A delete button for life. A magical way to erase memories and unwanted feelings. The tingles, the lingering hope. The little things you never thought you'd miss, like simply talking to the boy you once loved, or *not* talking because you didn't need to. You already know all there is to know. Breakups are crappy any way you slice it, but the worst part, even worse than seeing the boy who once owned your heart now happy with someone else, is going from speaking every day, hanging out, and sharing all aspects of your life, to nothing.

Zip, zilch, nada, thanks for playing.

"Remember that night the mariachi band dragged you onstage?" Justin flashes the lopsided grin that still haunts my dreams as he slides across the cushioned bench. "You shook a mean maraca."

Sitting down, I squeeze my eyes shut as the night in question floods my mind, along with a dozen others. Of course I remember it. And, of course, the hostess would choose to seat us in the same booth we sat in that night, our three-month anniversary. I'm at the point where I expect the universe to mess with me now.

"Stop." I lift my hands and shake my head, needing it *all* just to stop. Taking a deep breath, I crack open my eyes and resort to begging. "Please, whatever it is you're trying to do, can you just... not? This is hard enough without your walks down memory lane, okay?"

I've decided that I must have royally screwed someone over in a past life to deserve this twisted brand of torture. Tonight's game plan? Experiencing the "joys of newlywed dining."

When your groom happens to be your ex? Not so joyous.

I keep blinking, waiting to wake up to my Bob Marley alarm and have it still be Monday. I'll walk into FACS, ignore Lauren altogether, and this time, Coach will stick to the normal lesson plan.

So far, all that hoping has gone about as well as Gabi Avila's covert spy mission.

The girl's blue-black mane is speckled with bright, candy-apple-red chunks—her fashion sense rivals that of Lady Gaga—and she's wearing thick, dark sunglasses indoors, yet she somehow expects to hide from Carlos and Lauren behind a peeling menu. She's almost as deranged as I am for agreeing to come out here tonight.

"Look," I say, gaze still glued to the latest "Gablos" drama explosion, "Can we please just stick to the list of questions Coach gave us? That's why we're here, not for whatever weird game you're trying to play."

"Yeah, sure."

Hmm. That went over a bit too easily. Shifting my eyes back across the table, I watch as Justin's smile softens. I pretend the sight does nothing to my stomach.

"Peyton." He lifts a hand as if to cover mine, but, at my raised eyebrow, brings it back to his lap. "I don't want to make you uncomfortable."

I snort, a totally attractive sound, I know. But hey, it's not as if I'm trying to impress him.

That's what I keep telling myself, anyway.

"Moving on."

Yanking out the sheet detailing tonight's assignment, I scan the list of questions, eager to get this horrific show on the road. Maybe if I'm lucky, we'll fly through the suckers and be done before the waitress even appears.

Some of these I already know the answers to, like *what are your feelings on marriage?* What with Justin cheating on me, his never-ending stream of women, and the heartless stunts his dad and stepmom have pulled through the years, I think it's safe to say his stance is a hard "no" on that one.

"What do you think are the components of a satisfying, successful marriage?" I ask instead, setting the paper down so he won't see how badly my hands are shaking.

I avoided the blatantly obvious question, but this one is every bit as pointless. Based on our prior history, it's almost a given he'll say there's no such thing as a successful marriage. Which makes it surprising when he replies:

"Honesty. Commit—"

"Really?" I interrupt with a laugh. "You're gonna start with honesty? *You*?"

Justin leans forward, the paper tablecloth crinkling as he rests his elbows on the surface. With the way he stares into my eyes, it's like he can see straight through to my soul. Maybe Gabi had the right idea hiding behind the menu.

"Yeah," he answers. "I am. Look, Peyton, I know you don't believe it, but people change a lot in three years. I'm not the complete asshole you think I am." I scoff under my breath, and he holds my gaze for another long moment before the thick knot in his throat bobs and he glances away. "At least not anymore."

A twinge of guilt hits my stomach. Which, when you think about it, is so stupid. *He* cheated on *me*! But, luckily, before I can do something even more foolish, like apologize for my well-founded doubts, he turns back and continues.

"Honesty," he says it again, this time emphasizing the word. He holds up a hand and starts listing components on his long fingers. "Commitment. Telling your wife she's the most beautiful girl in the room." He pauses there, three fingers extended, and my hand clenches beneath the table. With a grin, he adds, "Remembering what a lucky bastard you are that she ever chose you in the first place."

That's four, according to the tally, and my pulse picks up speed with each uptick.

"Never going to sleep angry." *Five.* "Getting all your shit out there before it can build." *Six.* "And kissing her every damn chance you get." *Seven.*

He leans back, leaving his hands extended in the air, and I just keep staring at his fingers. I chastise myself—*stupid heart, he's not saying these things about YOU!*—but the longer the fingers remain up, the longer the moment stretches, the more the air around us shifts. The cool tickle of awareness races up my spine, and as I shiver, chill bumps prick my skin.

Justin's eyes dip to my arms. The corner of his mouth twitches and as he curls his hands closed, he shrugs. "That's my opinion, anyway. What about you?"

My opinion? I'm discombobulated.

Before dinner = fully combobulated.

Now = completely and totally without combobs.

"Uh." My head is void of all thought but I clear my throat, grasping to pull *something* out of the air. Another trait to list or quality to check that he didn't already cover.

Since when did the player of Fairfield Academy become a frigging marriage expert?

"Those are good," I say, stalling as I think about my parents who have, hands down, the most incredible marriage ever. They support each other, they listen, and they make room for daily bouts of silliness. Remembering a few of their more gooberific moments I add, "Laughter." Justin looks at me. "I think it's important to laugh with the person you're in love with."

He nods as a small smile plays on his lips. "I like that one. You should write it down."

Oh, right.

We're not just sitting here, dredging up our pain-filled past for kicks. We're actually supposed to turn these answers in and use them to begin our joint paper. Grateful for the excuse to break eye contact, I grab my oversized purse and dig for something to write on other than the tiny margin of the question sheet or the butcher-paper tablecloth. Usually I'm much more prepared.

And much more combobulated.

"Here."

I glance up to find Justin holding out a pocket-sized notebook. The same kind he always used to scribble in, filling the pages with his secret thoughts. Thoughts I once felt honored to read.

He jiggles it, both daring and telling me to take it, so I reach across the table and grab it, meeting his eyes as I do.

"Hey guys, welcome to Carmela's."

I jump, wrenching my hand back.

"I'm Francine, and I'll be your server tonight."

As my pounding heart leaves my throat, the waitress reaches for a crayon. She writes her name upside down and backwards in the middle of the tablecloth along with a drawing of a sun. "Sorry for the wait. They sat you guys all at once."

I give a closed-mouth smile as she grabs an overflowing bowl of chips and bright red salsa from the tray behind her and plops it on the table. This girl has impeccable timing.

Blowing a fringe of bangs from her forehead, Francine reaches into an apron adorned with impressive anime flair. "The school's pre-approved menu is on the insert," she says, hoisting an order pad. "If you want to pay separately, tonight's special is chicken fajitas for two. What can I get y'all to drink?"

I go to answer, but Justin beats me to it. "I'll have a Coke, and she'll have a Sprite along with a glass of water with lemon."

He glances at me, obviously proud at knowing one of my many odd little quirks, and lifts an eyebrow as if to say, "I remember everything about you."

Swallowing hard, I force myself to look away, watching our waitress instead as she grins, taps a black-painted fingernail on the corner of her cute frames, and then skips off for the kitchen with seemingly no more pressing concerns than a bunch of high school kids stiffing her on tips. I stare at the bowl of salsa she left behind, wondering when was the last time I felt *free*.

I snag a chip from the bowl and scoop a large glob of the red stuff. "We should get back to the assignment."

If Justin is disappointed I didn't take his bait with the drinks, I can't tell. He simply reaches over and slides the sheet across the table before reading, "A strong marriage depends on the ability to share with each other at the deepest levels. One of the foundational elements to a strong relationship is to let your partner know you appreciate them. Think of three positive characteristics that your partner embodies and tell them in a statement that says, 'I appreciate...'"

He looks up. "Does this remind you of that time we played three questions?"

I snatch the paper from his hand.

"I'll start," I say, determined to focus on the here and now and take this assignment seriously. Even if it bloody kills me.

My fingers hesitate only for a moment before opening the spiral notebook. It requires Hulk-like strength to beat back the impulse to read the words Justin has tucked within the pages, but I do it, turning to a clean one near the middle.

"Justin, I appreciate what a leader you are on the team," I say, staring at the page and not the confounding boy in front of me. It's been three years since we were together, but some things I can't escape. Listening to my dad praise his favorite catcher and watching the results myself from the bleachers are two of them. "The other guys listen to you, they respect how hard you play, and Dad relies on your work ethic to set an example."

The bench seat groans as he shifts his weight. "It's not that big a deal."

"But it is." I glance up to meet his eyes. For all of Justin's bravado and confidence, he's never been able to take a sincere compliment. And although he's my ex and deserves to roast in the fiery pits of hell, or at the very least a really hot sauna, he's not without his strengths.

When his eyes fill with what appears to be cautious optimism, I quickly look down again and continue. "I appreciate your sense of humor. Even in the most stressful of situations, you can always make people smile."

"Carlos is the clown," he mutters, drumming his knuckles on the table. If I weren't so eager to complete this assignment, I'd sort of enjoy seeing him sweat.

"*Carlos* gets laughs by acting up and pulling stunts," I say, for reasons unknown, needing him to believe I mean it. Clearly, I'm a glutton for punishment. "*You* make a self-effacing joke, say something unexpected, or even flirt, making people feel good. You distract them."

When Justin doesn't argue again, I write down the third and final trait. "I appreciate the way you listen. If someone has your attention, they have all of you." I swallow hard as my eyes bore into the thin paper. "They're the only thing on the planet that matters for those brief precious moments."

Snapshot images flash in my mind. Us talking in his room, at the ranch... in the doghouse.

"You listen without always needing to give advice," I tell him, "but you offer it when asked. You look them in the eye and you remember everything."

Even when it's annoying.

I finish writing and when I have nothing left to do, I lift my head. Soft brown eyes drill into me, almost pleading with an expression that wavers between disbelief and hope. The hope confuses me, and for his sake, I pray the disbelief fades once he gets away from his parents. Either way, I have to force myself to hold still under his scrutiny, not to flinch or look away.

Finally, he asks softly, "Do you really mean that?"

Clenching my hand underneath the table, I nod.

Because the truth is, as torturous as being here with him is and as revealing as that question was, I *did* mean it. And I'm glad I answered. With my own broken heart and embarrassment, it's easy to forget that Justin doesn't have people to tell him these things. There's the guys, I guess, and his brother, Chase. His housekeeper, and my dad... but that's it.

Cheating asshat or not, Justin Carter isn't a completely horrible human being.

He deserves to know that.

We watch each other for the space of two heartbeats until Lauren lifts her voice above the chaos, as if she can sense my weakening resolve. "Baseball players make the best kissers."

I almost roll my eyes. For one, I'm almost certain she just spotted Gabi and said that to annoy her, and for two, there are no words for how dumb that categorical statement is. But I'm grateful for the not-so-subtle reminder. Pressing my shoulders into the soft cushion of the bench, I grab another chip.

"Too bad Stasi didn't pair you with your girlfriend," I say, shooting for levity. I fail miserably since my voice wobbles, but I laugh anyway, even as pressure mounts behind my eyes. I'm nothing if not stubborn. "I'm sure her list would've been much more fun."

"I love *your* list." Justin's voice is gruff and he reaches over, this time boldly and without hesitation taking my hand. I'm too shocked by the contact to pull it back.

"And Lauren's *not* my girlfriend." He stares into me again, never blinking as he says it, and after a slight pause to let that sink in he adds, "She was *never* my girlfriend, and we haven't hooked up all year."

His grip is warm and firm, and panic sets in. I'm not sure what Justin's trying to prove here or what he hopes to gain, but he's messing with my head. The skip down memory lane. The way he keeps looking at me like he can truly see me, all the way down to the marrow. It's as if he's forgotten all the pain and fear and confusion.

Or worse, that he was never into me at all.

"Whatever labels you two want to slap on it," I say, tugging on my hand. Justin tightens his hold, and I narrow my eyes. "I'm sorry it didn't work out."

Honestly? Girlfriend, casual hookup, whatever term they use, it still hurts. Actually, it hurts worse to think that he ditched me for a simple fling.

Justin grunts. "I wasn't gonna do this now." His free hand rakes through his hair and fists the ends in a tight grip. "I planned to wait a few days at least but I can't. Sunshine, you've got to know that there was more to what happened that day. I'm not making excuses, I know I screwed up, but you don't know the full truth."

"*First*," I say, finally yanking my hand from his grasp. "Don't call me Sunshine. Second, as crazy as this may be, I'm great with not knowing the sordid details. Fantastic, even. Believe me, I've imagined every possibility anyway."

"No, that's not what I meant—"

"The details don't even matter," I continue, hearing how my voice borders on hysteria. Licking my lips, I glance around the room and lower my voice to a more discreet level. "The past is in the past. I'm with someone else now, and you're... doing whatever it is you do."

"But I'm not doing anything—" He stops abruptly. "Wait. You have a boyfriend?"

He looks gobsmacked, which is kind of like the icing on the craptastic experience that is this night. *Shocking, other guys find me attractive!* If my self-esteem hadn't been running on empty already, this night would've sent the needle straight to E.

Then Justin nods, his lips twitching into a smirk, and I know he's figured it out. "So, Cade finally grew a pair, huh?"

THURSDAY, MAY 13TH

20 Weeks until Disaster
♥ Freshman Year

PEYTON
FAIRFIELD ACADEMY FRONT STEPS 4:56 P.M.

Gilbert Blythe was a bona fide literary babe. No matter how many times I re-read *Anne of Green Gables*, I always got sucked in, turning each page a bit slower than the last, wanting to prolong the journey. Wishing with everything in me that I were as daring and confident as fellow redhead Anne Shirley, and that a boy like Gilbert would fall head over boots for *me*.

I'd even let him call me Carrots... or Sunshine.

Smiling at my book, I began another chapter, wondering what Anne would do with a boy like Justin Carter. *Not* that Justin was my Gilbert. Two weeks into the semester and I'd already gotten an earful about his exploits with girls—a certain Diamond Doll in particular—and knew that he was way out of my league.

That didn't stop my Gilbert-like crush on him, though. Overinflated ego and all.

As far as the Diamond Dolls went, according to my highly impressive investigative efforts (eavesdropping on hallway conversations and asking my dad), they were a group of girls who pretty much worshipped the baseball team. Some of them were cheerleaders, others were on the dance team, and the rest were just regular students. It was like a weird, non-school-sanctioned version of the Pink Ladies. They wore cute outfits on game day, decorated players' lockers, brought the guys snacks, and sat in a large group at the games, holding up glittery signs and cheering.

Or, according to Dad, "Distracting our boys."

Clearly, he wasn't a fan, and after witnessing a week of their shenanigans, neither was I. The day after the team *officially* welcomed Justin, Lauren Hays *unofficially* assigned herself as his Doll... and all but peed a circle around him while she was at it. It wasn't that I'd fooled myself into believing I actually had a shot at dating the boy. Justin was a notorious flirt, and I blushed scarlet just thinking of a comeback. But the loss of possibility was a bit disheartening.

"There's my Sunshine." At the familiar voice whispered against my ear, I jumped, book to heart, and spun around guiltily as if he'd heard my thoughts. From the devilish grin Justin wore, I wasn't certain that he hadn't. "Whatcha doing, pretty girl? In case you didn't get the memo, school ended two hours ago."

"Oh, is that what the bell meant?" My voice was full of snark, but inwardly I was doing a happy dance. This was the first time we'd spoken since team tryouts and I was secretly thrilled that he remembered me.

Justin was dressed in normal clothes, jeans and a T-shirt, and his hair was wet, fresh from the shower after practice. If I leaned in, I bet I could smell the clean scent of his soap.

"Mom's car is in the shop," I explained, squeezing my book tighter against me. "And Dad is in meetings for another hour, so I'm just hanging out."

His gaze lowered to my hand. "Ah, well, as exciting as reading alone on the school steps can be, what do you say I take you home?"

The idea of being in a car alone with the object of my recent obsession was almost too awesome to comprehend. Then I realized it *was* too awesome. Justin was in my grade, which meant that unless he'd failed at some point, he was fourteen or fifteen at the most.

"You drive?"

"No, but Rosalyn does." He jerked his thumb toward a green Expedition idling near the curb, and my Gilbert-like hopes deflated like a sad, old balloon. Le sigh.

"That's all right," I said, honestly having zero interest in riding backseat to him and one of his many female admirers. "Thanks for the offer, but I'm sure y'all would rather be alone anyway."

Justin cocked his head and squinted at me as if I were a science experiment. A look I'd unfortunately grown used to getting from my classmates. Who knew it was weird or uncool to answer questions in class? Or to ask them when you were confused. Wasn't that supposed to be the point of learning?

"Rosalyn is my housekeeper, Peyton." He made a squicked out face that resembled a pained fish. "I'm sure she's capable of some sweet, sweet loving, but she's forty. And like my mother. Seriously, that's revolting."

Oh.

My cheeks warmed yet again, a common occurrence around this guy. On the upside, as long as he was around, I'd never have need for blush.

Laughing, Justin bent to pick up my bag and then lifted his chin toward the car. He started walking toward it and, like a brainless dope, I followed.

"You know, you're not as innocent as you look," he said over his shoulder. "I'm starting to worry about my virtue here.

I won't have you corrupting me, Sunshine." He shot me a wicked grin and I laughed.

Me, corrupt the infamous player Justin Carter? Riiight.

Amused at the thought, and giddy at his use of my nickname, I hip-checked him and said, "Yeah well, I promise to be gentle."

My next step faltered.

Had that just come from me? Out of *my* mouth? I swear, the words fell out of their own accord. I'd opened my mouth to say *not likely* and out popped that... innuendo. How or why or what that was even supposed to mean, I had no earthly clue, so I simply stood there, frozen in place, my jaw shocked unhinged.

Was I flirting?

Justin stopped, too, and turned his body to face me. "That was, hands down, the sexiest thing I've ever heard."

Yep, I was flirting.

"Yeah, I seriously doubt that," I replied, rolling my eyes. I breathed a sigh, feigning like I wasn't flustered, and trapped my bottom lip between my teeth—but nothing could hide my gigantic smile. Or stop it from breaking free. So I tromped past him, grinning like a dope, my previously inner happy dance transforming into a full-on Thanksgiving Day Rockettes number, complete with jazz hands.

Feeling brave, I spun around and said, "Just don't get used to it, Carter."

Justin chuckled as he began walking again and the sound melted my insides into warm, sticky syrup. At the curb, he ducked his head through the passenger window to speak with the driver.

My hands were clammy so I rubbed them down the sides of my uniform skirt, hoping I hadn't gotten my hopes up for nothing. It was only a ride. Yet, somehow, it felt like more. When Justin turned and waved me over, I withheld my shoulder shimmy and typed a quick text to my parents. Then I hopped inside.

"Thanks so much for the ride," I said, headed to the third row bench Justin pointed to and scooting all the way over. He followed behind me and closed the door. "I really appreciate it."

"It's no problem at all." The driver turned around in her seat, a wide smile on her face. Her voice held a slight accent and her cropped brown hair was shot through with silver. "I'm just glad Justin saw you before it got dark. It's too cold to be sitting outside."

The concern was sweet, but honestly, the weather didn't bother me. If I'd wanted, I could've waited in the athletic department while Dad had his staff meeting. It's just that I'd spent far too many days locked inside as it was. I preferred being outdoors, feeling the sun on my face, even with the cooler air.

Explaining that didn't exactly make for sexy banter, however, and people tended to get weird when they learned about my illness. I wanted Justin to think I was fun and hot. Not a pity case.

After Rosalyn entered my address into the GPS, she adjusted the radio so that the music was blaring up front. Thus giving us in the back a semblance of privacy (eep!). We pulled away from the school and as the sign for Fairfield Academy whipped past my window, I couldn't help but smile.

I was doing it!

It was hard to explain to my parents exactly *why* I needed to come here. Sure, the Vet program was a plus, but that elective wasn't even available until senior year. And the school had dual-credit options for homeschoolers, too. The real reason was more... indescribable. A feeling deep down that my recovery depended on me being here. It sounded strange even to me, so it wasn't something I could ever tell them. But, after everything I'd been through, I needed a drastic shift to mark the end of that chapter. Something big to start a fresh one, to experience new things. Begin living out loud.

Sitting in the backseat with Justin Carter? That counted as living.

BIG time.

"You realize you're smiling every time I see you, right?"

I curled my lips around my teeth and tore my gaze away from the passing trees. Justin's mouth kicked up in his own lopsided grin.

"What's your secret?" he asked, leaning in. "Are you laughing at the rest of us? Plotting our destruction?" I shook my head, trying desperately to suppress my smile and failing miserably, and he added, "Singing along with Barney in your head?"

The purple dinosaur reference almost got me. Out of nowhere, the motivational quote from my physical therapist's office floated in my mind and I said, "A smile doesn't always mean you're happy." I shrugged and looked away. "Sometimes it just means you're ready to face whatever comes."

"Huh?"

"Nothing." From spouting innuendo to quoting inspirational posters in a matter of minutes. At least I was unique. "Just something I read somewhere."

We drove in silence for another block, but the quiet wasn't awkward. It was comfortable, exciting. I stopped short of calling it *normal*, as this was the first time I'd sat so close to a boy I was crushing on. Not that surprising since I was a crush-virgin—unless you counted Gilbert Blythe, Theodore "Laurie" Laurence, and the hotties on Supernatural. But being this close to Justin felt nice.

Yes, I realized testing my innocent heart on a boy like him wasn't my smartest move. It was sort of like trying to eat a gallon of Ben and Jerry's in one big gulp—you're more than likely gonna regret it. And walk away with a brain freeze. But wasn't that what this new chapter in my life was all about? Doing what scared me, stepping out of my comfort zone?

I stole a glance at him, watching the way his lips tightened, how his forehead furrowed and his chest stopped moving like he was deep in thought. Suddenly, sharing a car ride with this boy wasn't enough; I wanted to know everything I could about him. What he liked, what he hated. How he felt about a certain Diamond Doll.

"Hey, I've got an idea." I slid my foot beneath me and turned to face him on the bench seat. He quirked an eyebrow. "Have you ever played three questions?"

"Uh, is that a thing?" I nodded eagerly, and he laughed. "You've just got, like, surpluses of energy, don't you?"

I winced. "Ah, pretty much."

Would I ever stop being such a weirdo? Here he was, fresh out of practice and no doubt exhausted, and I was like an exuberant puppy with a chew toy. *Way to be hot and fun, Peyton!*

Justin touched my hand and I lifted my eyes. "I like enthusiasm."

For once, his wicked grin was gone, replaced with something softer, sweeter. Sincere. Then he linked our fingers together. My heart stopped in my chest. It was the first time a boy had ever held my hand. "How do you play?"

Blink. Blink. "Hmm?"

"The game?" he asked with a small laugh. "How do you play it?"

"Oh! It's simple." *Don't let go of my hand, please don't let go of my hand.* "Uh, I pretty much ask you any three questions I want and then you get to do the same. No judgment, no worries, we just say the first thing that comes to our minds."

48

The warmth from his skin spread up my arm and into my chest, leaving me breathless, rambling, and giddy as heck. I swallowed and attempted to tone down the crazy. "Are you in?"

For the length of three passing cars, he just looked at me. No words, no face change, and I'd never wanted to be a mind reader more than I did in those moments. It wasn't fair that he held all the secret powers in this... friendship? Relationship? Gah, whatever *this* was.

Justin's firm lips twitched. "Sure. Why not?"

Victory!

"Great!" Too late, I remembered my goal of tempering my puppy-like enthusiasm, and I fiddled with my school skirt. "Um, want me to go first?"

He nodded, once, and said, "Remember, you promised to be gentle."

Oh, dear heavens above. "You never stop, do you?"

He chuckled. "Nope."

As Justin glanced up front, presumably to make sure Rosalyn wasn't paying attention, I forced my mind onto the game. I was on a mission, after all, and while I doubted his housekeeper could hear a thing anyway, threat of a potential audience wasn't about to stop me. Who knew when I'd get another chance to be alone with him—*if* I'd get another chance?

Lolling my head casually against the seat, I asked, "What's your favorite book?"

Justin laughed. "Seriously? You know there's a huge divide between being gentle and a softball-question like, 'what's your favorite book,' right?"

"Yeah, well, maybe I'm working up to the hard stuff," I suggested. "Ever thought about that?" Really, I was just a huge book nerd who loved raiding people's bookshelves. But he need not know that.

"All right," he replied. "*Moneyball.*"

Challenge rang from his tone and from his craned eyebrow, it was obvious he expected me to tease him for his choice. But that's not how this game worked. Plus, Dad had read that thing like a gazillion times, too. And I was fluent in Brad Pitt movies.

I gave an approving nod. "Good one. Now it's your turn."

"That's it?" When I nodded, he seemed surprised. "That was easy enough."

I stayed quiet, simply smiling, as a sudden case of nerves ping-ponged in my gut. Would *his* question be easy, too?

How did I not think this through? What if he asked about my occasional slight limp? What if he'd caught me staring at him in the hallways and wanted to know why I was such a stalker?

Why on earth had I thought this would be a good idea?

Justin's left eye closed slightly more than his right as he pondered his first question, and I was certain that I was toast. "Biggest pet peeve?"

I released a grateful sigh, thanking my lucky stars, and replied easily. "Entitlement."

"What do you mean?"

I shrugged. "I'm just tired of people taking things for granted. Thinking they're owed something. Throwing a fit or acting a fool when they don't get their way. Nothing in life is a guarantee, you know? Every day that we wake up and get to throw off our covers is a freaking gift, and we can either appreciate that, be grateful for what we have and work hard for what we don't, or we can choose to wallow and complain and expect someone to just hand it to us."

The last bit was punctuated with a *smack* as my free hand slapped my thigh, and the noise jolted me off my soap box. 'Fun and hot' was slipping further and further away.

Taking a breath, I snorted at my own dorkiness and concluded, "I guess I just think we could all stand to be a little more grateful, is all."

Smothering a sigh, I mumbled an apology, and Justin gave me a crooked grin. "Don't be sorry. I like seeing you get all feisty like that." He leaned close and whispered, "Who knew Sunshine had a hidden edge?"

Ha! The words, of course, were typical Justin flirtation, but when he leaned back, the look in his eyes said he meant it. They'd gone soft, like melted chocolate, and the combined effect of the expression, his words, and his proximity turned me into a sticky puddle of Peyton goo. Mentally, I doodled our names together in linked hearts and fantasized about him giving me his letterman jacket in front of the entire school.

I frowned. Or did that only happen in old movies?

Sitting taller in my seat, I said, "So, it's my turn again."

The goal for this round was two-fold: shift the attention away from me, and crack Justin's impenetrable shell. I grinned when the perfect question came to me and I leaned in close. "Secret love?"

"What?" Eyebrows shot heavenward as he snapped his head back, banging it with a thump against the window. He glanced at Rosalyn, still jamming out to Rod Stewart, before asking, "You mean like girls or something?"

"No, nothing as horrifying as that," I teased.

Note to self: avoid all uses of the "L word" in the future.

Ignoring my tingling spidey-senses, I said, "What I mean is, what gets your heart racing? Or, just the opposite, what calms you down? What's the thing you enjoy doing more than anything else in the world but no one else knows about?"

When Justin shifted uncomfortably, I gave him one final nudge. "Hey, you're the one who said I'd soft-balled you before."

At my teasing smile, he huffed. "Yeah, well, remind me never to correct you again."

He dropped my hand and rubbed the back of his neck, the skin around his mouth growing taut. When he shifted in his seat, tugging on the leg of his jeans, I took in his narrowed eyes and dropped my mouth open in surprise. I'd actually gotten to him.

The unflappable Justin Carter was flapped!

I watched, gape-mouthed, as he turned to face the window, and I figured that was it. Game over. Either that or he was preparing to toss out another flirty one-liner. What I hadn't expected was hearing him clear his throat and mumble, "I like to write."

The words, spoken softly, hung almost visibly in the air between us.

That he had answered... and then *how* he'd answered... left me so stunned, so speechless, that I just sort of sat there. Writing obviously encompassed any number of things—something as simple as keeping a diary to writing full-length novels. But the literary geek in me was awake and swooning hard.

Justin glanced at me from the corner of his eye and barked a laugh. "Jesus, Peyton. I'm not a total dumb jock." He stretched out in the seat, picked at a nonexistent piece of lint, and just like that, his bravado was back, slipping on like a well-worn pair of Nikes.

Quickly, I said, "No, of course not. It's just..."

It's just that I want to peek inside your brain and learn ALL the things. What makes you tick, what prompts you to write, how it started. And maybe sniff you some more while I'm at it.

"Write how?" I asked. "I mean, in what form? Can I read any of it?"

"Hell no," he shot back, eyes wide. He laughed again, sort of breathless, and that along with his borderline vulnerable smile softened his words. "I believe it's called *secret* love for a reason," he said, bumping my shoulder with his. "As for what kind of writing, well, that'll cost you your last question."

Oh, the boy was good. Giving in was tempting, so very, *very* tempting, but for now, other things—*relationship* things—were equally as important.

"Nah, I'll let you keep your secrets." I grinned and silently added, for now.

He flashed me a smile. "That means it's my turn again."

I nodded, already plotting how I could steer the conversation back to his secret bookish side, and Justin tilted his head. "Your name. Don't get me wrong, I think Peyton is damn sexy on a girl—"

"But you're wondering if I'm named after a football player," I finished for him.

Justin lifted his shoulder. "I heard someone call you Manning in the hall."

I banged my head against the seat. "Our teacher in homeroom is obsessed with roll call," I explained via way of complaint. "Manning is actually my *middle* name, but she refuses to remember that. After the first day or two, it was easier just to go with it." Truth was, I liked my name. The family tradition around it, the uniqueness.

"Manning's always been one of my dad's favorite athletes, even back when he played in college," I went on. "The University of Tennessee is his alma mater. But Dad's equal opportunity when it comes to sports. My oldest brother, Jesse, is named after Jesse Owens, and Lars is named after Yogi Berra." I grinned. "Lucky for him, Dad went with Yogi's real name, Lawrence."

"Wow." Justin nodded, impressed. "Your old man's some sort of sports nut, huh?"

"That would be an understatement," I agreed with a laugh.

We came to a stop and I glanced out the tinted window. We were at the light in front of the railroad tracks near my house, which meant we were about five minutes away depending on traffic. Time to bring in the big guns.

"Final question." I paused as the ending notes of one song faded and a new one began, then watched Justin carefully as I said, "You've got quite the reputation with girls."

His smile was slow, confident, and amused. "That's not a question."

I shot him a look that said, "you're hilarious," and urged the butterflies flapping in my gut to chill. That crooked grin of his so wasn't helping.

Clearing my throat, I scooted closer, lowering my voice as I said, "Word on the street is that you hook up with tons of girls—"

"Word on the street?" Justin's smile grew, and I rolled my eyes. I would not be deterred!

"—But that Lauren Hays is your girlfriend?"

I leaned back, proud that I actually got that out, and of my wordsmith skills. Part statement, part question, I was ninety-two percent sure he couldn't tell my very happiness depended on his answer. Even if he could, though, it wouldn't matter. My obsession demanded answers.

"Definitely not." Justin's lip curled with disgust, and my belly did a flip. A bit prematurely, I discovered, when he added, "I don't do the whole girlfriend thing."

Ah. His eyes met mine, hammering the point home, and I strove to keep my face neutral. "Good," I replied, light and breezy. See, no skin off my nose, la la la. "I don't do the whole boyfriend thing, either."

Easy to say when I'd never been given the chance, but whatever.

We fell silent after that declaration, Justin searching my eyes, looking to see if I was sincere, and me desperately trying to shield my emotions. Not the easiest thing to do when you're straight up lying, or staring into the face of the boy of your dreams.

"What about you?" he finally asked. "What's your story?"

I released a pent-up breath. "Is that your final question?"

He nodded, and I shrugged. I'd already decided against sharing details about my illness, but GBS was the only semi-interesting thing that ever happened to me. "Not much to tell."

"Cop out."

Justin's patient, expectant look pinned me to the seat and I sighed in defeat. "Well, I was homeschooled up until this semester," I said, playing with a loose thread on my skirt. "And before you ask, yes, I miraculously gained an acceptable level of social skills, and no, I didn't just sit around and watch television all day."

I'd lost count how many times I'd answered those questions over the years.

"My mom taught me, and we spent our days reading books and challenging ideas. I loved it," I told him honestly. "But this year I was ready for a change."

"Were your parents upset?"

Yes and no. "We'd always planned for me to go to Fairfield for high school," I said instead, keeping it simple. "Besides, as you'll see when we get to my house, we still spend plenty of time together. Life on a ranch provides lots of family bonding moments."

...And there was the wide-eyed look I was used to.

"*Ranch*?"

"Yup. Five horses, a cow, and a dozen chickens," I said proudly. "The Texas stereotype personified. We even teach horsemanship and riding classes, do birthday parties and scouting events, fun stuff like that." Justin looked a bit shell-shocked, so I figured why not bring in the big guns? "Actually, the ranch is also kinda like a dog-version of Disney World."

"Disney World," he repeated, his forehead going all wrinkly. "For *dogs*?"

This was where I often lost people. "We run a grooming and boarding business on site, too. That's actually where I've been working ever since—" My eyes widened as I realized what I was about to reveal. "Well, that's where I've been helping the most lately."

The expression on Justin's face said he wanted to ask, that he knew I'd left something out from my story. Luckily, before he found the words, Rosalyn stopped at the callbox.

"Enter nine twenty-eight," I told her, watching eagerly as she input the code. The gate swung open, she drove ahead, and I turned my attention back to Justin.

I loved seeing people's reactions the first time they saw the ranch. Our life here was far from typical; while people seemed to believe all Texans ate hayseed and raised cattle, the truth was that most have never even stepped foot on a ranch, much less been on a horse. But this was all I'd ever known.

Our house sat on fifteen acres, a private oasis just a few miles from your standard cookie-cutter neighborhood. When I was younger, I used to visit friends for playdates and get jealous over how close their neighbors were. Mom had me in lessons and homeschool co-ops, and kids were always coming in and out of the ranch, but I never knew the ease of having someone to play with who lived just a few feet away.

On the flip side, *they* never knew what it was like to wake up and have horses a few feet away. They didn't have acres and acres to run around on and hidden areas to create pretend kingdoms. They didn't have trees to climb, land to explore, and animals to love and spoil. As soon as I was old enough to realize my friends were all jealous of me, I learned to appreciate this place that much more.

Rosalyn stopped at the top of the path, in front of the main house, and Cade turned to watch from the paddock.

Justin shook his head. "It's like we just traveled back to the Old West."

I laughed before elbowing him in the ribs. "Wanna meet Annie Oakley?"

JUSTIN
SWEET SERENITY RANCH 5:25 P.M.

"You seriously named your horse Annie Oakley?"

"Yup," Peyton said. "After the toughest chick in the Old West." She cleared her throat and glanced up front through the windshield, then clutched the pendant around her neck as she asked again, "Want to come meet her?"

The look Rosalyn gave me in the rearview mirror clearly read, *say yes.*

Here's the thing: Sunshine was dangerous. Case in point, that little game of hers in the car. Not only did she get me to play along, but when she slid me that sweet smile and asked about my writing, it was like I physically couldn't deny her—and I'd gotten damn good at refusing girls.

No one knew about my writing. There was no point. The poetry and lyrics that filled my notebooks wouldn't ever amount to anything, but like she'd said, it calmed me down. Helped clear my head of the white noise. And whenever I found the perfect word to describe how I felt, it was incredible. Not that I'd admit that to anyone. But for some reason, Peyton knowing about it wasn't so bad. In fact, I kind of liked it. Which was exactly why she was so dangerous.

When I didn't respond right away, Rosalyn did it for me. "I just remembered I have an errand to run. It's no problem to swing back by in an hour if you want."

Did I want?

When it came to Peyton, the answer was yes, regardless of the question.

The issue was more if I *should*.

This couldn't go anywhere. Sunshine had to know that as much as I did. We were two different people, wanting two completely different things. She may've said she didn't do relationships, but she didn't strike me as the laid-back, casual hookup type either. Yet despite that, I couldn't deny the pull she had on me. Just being around her made me feel good, and obviously, she must've felt the same way if she wanted me to hang around.

It'd be dumb to deny ourselves something we both wanted, right?

Cracking my knuckles, I swung my gaze from my housekeeper's silent urging to Peyton's quiet hoping and finally admitted defeat. As if I'd ever stood a chance anyway.

"Sounds good," I replied. I hoped like hell I knew what I was doing.

We got out of the SUV and the moment I shut the door behind me, Peyton took my hand. She wouldn't meet my eyes, and a low vibrating hum came from her throat, but she laced her thin fingers between mine, and I swallowed hard.

Confidence in a girl was always hot, but watching this shy, almost awkward beauty taking charge was even hotter. I grazed my thumb over the smooth skin of her wrist and electricity shot up my arm.

I was so screwed.

Rosalyn honked her horn as she pulled away, and I could've sworn I saw her laughing. After the red taillights faded down the long strip of driveway, I turned to Peyton. "Guess I'm all yours."

That cute blush that shouted "innocent," and "not for you," crept up her cheeks as she bit her pink bottom lip. She looked at me through thick lashes and asked, "Ever ridden a horse before?"

"Uh, no." I glanced at the barn in the distance and imagined the beating my junk would take on the back of a horse. Wincing, I added, "That would be an emphatic no. And, no offense, but I've got no plans on changing that, either."

A smirk tilted her lips as she said, "We'll see about that." I grumbled, loving the smile but hating the reason for it, and she tugged on my hand. "Come on, City Slicker, I'll introduce you to everyone."

Whoa now... everyone? Digging the heels of my sneakers into the soft dirt, I asked the obvious. "Who's everyone?"

"Oh, Mama," she said offhand, like meeting a girl's mom was no big deal. News flash? It totally was. "Cade and Faith. Trevor's probably around here, too."

As she tugged me toward a smaller-sized version of the main house, I glanced longingly at the driveway. Rosalyn was long gone, and Peyton's small hand was in mine, so I guess I didn't really have a choice. But, for the record, I'd signed on to meet a *horse*.

"All right then," I said, resuming walking. How hard could it be? "Give me a quick rundown then. Who the hell are all those other people you mentioned, and are any of them relatives?"

See, sisters were easy. All I had to do was smile, say their hair looked good or some shit about their clothes, and they were putty in my hand. Younger brothers just had to hear I played ball and that was usually enough. It was older brothers, male cousins, and—God forbid—*fathers* that were a different story. They tended to take one glance at me and get suspicious and overprotective. Not that I could blame them.

Still, it was best to be prepared.

"Faith is my best friend," Peyton replied. "She goes to Fairfield High and is pretty much my complete and total opposite. But she's my rock. She's also an amazing dancer and has her own YouTube channel with an *insane* amount of subscribers." From the look on her face, you would think it was Peyton's channel.

"Cade's been around forever," she continued. "His family owns a ranch on the other end of town, which is where he goes to school, but he works here two to three days a week. He's great with the horses and helps me teach a lot of the lessons."

In other words, Cade had the hots for Peyton, had somehow gotten himself friend-zoned, and was patiently biding his time. Got it.

"And Trevor..." She laughed, stopping just short of the staircase leading to the house. "Well, Trevor is an original. He's brilliant—like *literally* brilliant. He's also a golf prodigy and one of the top ranked junior golfers in Golfweek Magazine."

At the pride in her voice, I suddenly felt like a dumbass.

How did this girl have me so turned around? I watched for her in the halls like a lovesick jackass, played back our one conversation at tryouts for hidden clues, and she had a *boyfriend*? I'd known she was the relationship type. Obviously she'd just been blowing smoke when she said otherwise in the car. What I couldn't figure out was what the hell she was doing with me.

"Unfortunately, he's terrified of the horses," she continued with a shrug. "So he spends most of his time in the doghouse."

A shocked laugh expelled from my lungs. Well, all right then. Not only did Sunshine have a man, but she obviously wore the pants in their weird, Old West style relationship. Seriously, who was this girl?

Releasing her hand, I stepped back, confused even more when she frowned. "Not that it's any of my business, but if horses mean that much to you, why even date him?"

The blue-gray eyes formerly focused on my hand shot to mine. "Date who? *Trevor*?"

I lifted a shoulder to say, "well, yeah," and she asked, "Why on earth would I date Trevor?"

Now I was... well, whatever the hell emotion came after confused.

Hadn't she just been bragging on the dude, going on about how brilliant and famous he was? To me, that was a pretty damn big clue. If she wasn't dating him, then why show off?

Scrubbing a hand across my face, I tried again. "Okay, so if this Trevor guy's *not* your boyfriend, then why the hell is he in the doghouse?"

The squiggle on her forehead faded as my words sank in, and then, she began to laugh.

I'm talking total, full on belly-laughter, hand slapped across the mouth and tears springing to her eyes. Normally, a chick laughing at me would equal sayonara with a quickness. But Peyton's laugh was so free, so freaking happy, that I couldn't help but join in. Even though I had no clue what we were laughing at.

"God, I've gotta remember to tell Mama that one." She wiped under her eyes and smiled as she took my hand again. Did it make me a total pussy to admit that I liked her need to keep touching me? "Sorry, Justin, I guess I should explain. *This* is the doghouse."

She lifted her chin, indicating the house behind me, a standard, modest-sized home you'd find in most neighborhoods. I glanced from it to her. "Huh?"

"This is our boarding and grooming business."

This girl lived to confound me. "So you're saying this whole house is for *dogs*?"

"Pretty much," she confirmed, still laughing at herself. "Weird, right? We have eighteen rooms—suites as we call them. There's a master, you know, for humans, but I don't think Mama's ever made Dad sleep in it. And if she has, I really don't want to know about it. It's more for emergencies or if we get really, really busy."

I nodded, because what else was I going to do? A house for dogs. Sure. Why not?

Following as she pulled on my hand, half-feeling like I'd entered some sort of bizarre, altered universe, I climbed the first weather-beaten step. The wide porch was just as worn, the light gray paint on the landing cracked and peeling in spots. But small touches, like potted plants and even a double swing, made me feel welcome. Comfortable.

And it was for *dogs*.

Peyton stopped short on the landing, hair blowing in the wind. "Please tell me you're not allergic."

I couldn't help myself. I reached out and freed the strand stuck to her mouth, and while I tucked it behind her ear, her gaze collided with mine. "Allergic to meeting moms, yes." I swallowed hard as I slid my finger across her silken skin. "Allergic to dogs, no."

Cheeks pink, she ducked her head away, though I caught the edge of her smile. "Dork."

I chuckled quietly and waved her ahead. Peyton threw open the screen door and a second later, I followed...

And entered the "Dog Zone."

Statues of basset hounds stood guard on either end of the door. Paintings of Dalmatians in top hats and fedoras playing cards lined two of the walls, dog treats, food, and toys were on display in every corner and crevice, and, I kid you not, "Who Let the Dogs Out" was playing overhead.

The entire back wall consisted of two large whiteboards filled with different colored ink. A calendar of sorts showed who was checking in and who was checking out and listed a detailed schedule of grooming, training, and play times.

Behind a makeshift desk, not really more than a fold out table really, sat a girl with her gaze glued to a laptop. Tufts of bleached-white hair curled out from beneath a turquoise cowboy hat, and her black studded T-shirt read, "Get in Line, Bub."

"I'm almost done," she said, not shifting her eyes from the screen. "The cutest Pomeranian came in for a grooming today and the owner let me video her. I'm making it look like she's shaking it to Taylor Swift."

Peyton bit her lip and glanced at me with an unreadable expression. "Uh, Faith, can that maybe wait a second?"

Click, click. The girl continued typing, but heaved a dramatic sigh. "Geez, where's the fire? Something happen at school? Another failed run-in with Baseball Stud?"

Peyton choked and sputtered beside me, but Faith continued despite her distress. "I already told you what you have to do. Find out whichever locker is his, stake it out, and when that Diamond Doll floozie leaves his side, offer to be his bat girl instead."

She giggled as she said it, wiggling her eyebrows for innuendo, and Peyton's face blazed five shades of red. I couldn't wipe the smile from my face if someone paid me to.

As Peyton's mouth opened and closed like a fish, I leaned close to her ear, inhaling the intoxicating scent of sunflowers, and murmured, "I'd *love* it if you did that."

My low voice must've carried because the clacking stopped and Faith suddenly lifted her head. When her dark eyes met mine, they widened like saucers. "Holy crap!"

Time to turn on the charm.

Best friends are vital when you're into a girl. Knowing that, I put on the crooked smile known to make girls loopy and said, "Hi, I'm Justin." Then, unable to help myself, I shot Peyton a sly grin and added, "Or, as someone people like to call me, Baseball Stud."

Peyton's eyes narrowed as she fought back a smile, and I gave her an innocent look in return. Faith watched our interaction with ever-growing delight before sending Peyton a nod of endorsement. "I completely approve."

"Oh, no. We're not... It's not..." Peyton lifted her hands in the air to explain, realizing as she did so that she was still clutching one of mine. She dropped it like a hot potato. "It's not what it looks like."

Faith snickered. "Sure it's not."

Amused, I watched as Peyton smashed her lips into a hard, thin line, which only caused her friend to smirk more. The two entered that silent communication thing girls do where they hold an entire conversation in nothing but eyebrow lifts and facial expressions. After a few moments, Faith winked, Peyton exhaled, and then, they both glanced at me.

"Anyway," Peyton said, her smile at once embarrassed and exasperated. It was adorable as hell. "I thought I'd give Justin a quick tour of the place. Is Mama in the back?"

"She's in the salon with Buster." Faith tipped the rim of her rhinestone cowboy hat up with a pointer finger, sizing me up one final time. "My girl was right about one thing, though. You are pure eye candy." She shot me a playful wink as Peyton gaped beside me. Oh, this girl was fun. "You know, if you read the top ten fashion trends of the season, my views would go through the roof!"

I chuckled and shook my head. "My apologies, but the only video I do is game tape."

Grinning, she took that in stride and said, "Let me know if you change your mind." Then she blew Peyton a kiss and went back to her work.

When I turned to face Peyton again, I expected her to be red-faced. Embarrassed that her friend spilled so much, worried that I was going to use it against her. But she wasn't. If anything, she appeared more confident than I'd ever seen her, shoulders back and a serene expression on her face that seemed to say, "oh well, whatcha gonna do?"

"Come back and say hello with me?"

Saying yes meant meeting her mom. Willfully doing that was the stress-ball equivalent of suggesting Coach let me squat behind the plate without a mitt. But, as I'd already established, logic flew straight out the window when I was around this girl. Especially when she looked at me like I was the answer to every question ever asked.

With Peyton, there were no games. No hiding her emotions. She wore them openly like a sign for everyone to see, for *me* to see, and for some reason, it made me want to be near her that much more. Unfortunately for me, it also made disappointing her impossible. Forcing a smile, I nodded and motioned for her to lead on.

"We mainly board dogs," she told me, this time taking my elbow as we walked down the hall. She rapped her knuckles on the whiteboard listing the *salon* schedule. "Grooming and training sessions are included with every stay, but some dogs come in just for those things. Except for days when we're really slammed, Mom handles the salon while we exercise the dogs."

About halfway down the corridor, she stopped in front of a window overlooking a pond and fenced-in field. A cool breeze blew in through the opened glass, lifting the loose strands of her hair and bringing with it the sound of incessant yapping.

"That's Trevor," she said, nodding toward a figure in the center of the chaos. I narrowed my eyes, curious about my competition.

The guy appeared to be around my age, maybe a little older, leaning back in a Houston Texans folding chair. His head bopped to the old-school rap floating in the air, his lips moving in complete unison to the words. Some sort of cartoon character was ironed onto his oversized black hoodie, his hair was a muddy brown mop on his head, and his tennis shoes were two different colors—neon yellow and magenta.

Peyton pressed her chest against the windowpane. "How's Mitzy today?"

Without turning around, Trevor stopped singing and scooped a black poodle onto his lap. "The little beauty's got it now!" he called back.

"Sweet!"

After executing the cutest victory dance imaginable, Peyton went on to discuss various training methods, treats, and even dog poop with the dude. I'm talking frequency, color, and even consistency. The least sexy topics known to man—and the guy didn't check her out once. By the time she waved goodbye and continued our trek down the hall, it was safe to say any insecurities I'd had were obliterated.

Honestly, though, now that I knew where I stood, I was actually impressed with the guy. His style was wacked, but he clearly knew his shit when it came to dogs, and his rank in Golfweek Magazine spoke for itself. That was the other sport, apart from baseball, Dad loved. Half his business deals were held on the fairway and he took an annual trip to Scotland and Ireland to play with his colleagues. I, on the other hand, had never held a club. He'd never bothered to teach me.

At the end of the hall, Peyton stopped in front of a closed door marked Salon where a low buzzing emanated. A woman's voice lifted over the hum.

"Baby, let me be. Your loving... teddy bear."

Eyebrow quirked, I exchanged a glance with Peyton.

"Put a chain around my neck... Uh huh."

The improvised musical stylings trailed off into a series of melodic grunts and finger snaps, accompanied by excited doggy yaps. It appeared Elvis was in the building. And that he enjoyed a good grooming. Peyton closed her eyes and hung her head.

I grinned and bumped her shoulder. "Wouldn't "Hound Dog" be a better choice?" I mused aloud. She shot me a look through a veil of strawberry blonde hair. "No, seriously—"

"Who's a good boy?" the woman's voice asked in baby-talk from the other side. "Yeah, who's a good boy? That's right, you are. You're a good boy."

Peyton groaned and knocked her head against the door once, twice, three times. The disembodied voice invited us inside.

"Mama, we've got company," Peyton said as she pushed open the door. A half-shaved chocolate lab stood on a table with a leash around its neck and a woman in front of it, facing away from us. "Is there any way we can try to tone down the crazy, at least until he leaves?"

"Never hide what you are, dear," she replied with a disapproving *tsk*.

It was such a mom thing to say, or at least what I'd imagined a mom would say, that I laughed as I leaned against the doorjamb. Peyton eyed me with a traitorous expression. "Sorry, Sunshine, but I've got to go with your mom on this one. Besides, I like crazy."

The buzz from the clippers stopped and the woman turned around. She was an older version of Peyton. "Oh, I like that. Hello there, I'm Grace, Peyton's weirdo, crazy, embarrassing mother. And you are...?"

"Mama, this is Justin," Peyton answered for me. "He's the one who brought me home today and he's hanging out while his ride runs an errand. I thought I'd show him around and introduce him to Oakley."

The light, easy smile suddenly slipped from her mother's face, replaced by a strange, borderline fearful expression. She glanced away and swallowed. "Do you ride, Justin?"

Confused, I pushed away from the doorframe. "Uh, no ma'am," I told her. "The closest I've ever come to a horse is on a hayride when I was eight. Don't really have an interest in getting much closer, either."

That answer seemed to please her, which was strange considering she owned a ranch. "Oh, well that's good." The clippers buzzed back to life as she turned back to Buster. "I better finish this up for Mrs. Murden. You two have fun."

That was... odd. Peyton wouldn't meet my eyes while she walked past, snagging my hand as she did. I followed her out the room, down the hall, and past a curious Faith who waved at us with her pointer finger, right through the door and onto the front porch. The moment the screen door closed behind us, she let go of my hand and leaned against the wall.

Her breath was labored, her eyes shut tight, and she looked so vulnerable it took everything in me not to tug her to my chest and wrap her in my arms. Peyton was confident and shy, open yet confusing, and so far out of my league it wasn't even funny. But hell if I was going anywhere just yet.

"So where's this badass horse I was promised I'd meet?"

Slowly, her eyelids opened and her eyes found mine. I wouldn't push her to talk if she wasn't ready. Hell, if she were ready, I wouldn't know what to say anyway. Touchy-feely crap wasn't my forte. Distraction, however, was another story.

I glanced around the wide horseless porch and gave a bored sigh. "Well, Sunshine? I ain't getting any younger here."

Clamping her lips together, she stifled what appeared to be a grin before lowering her gaze to the floor. She inhaled deeply and let it out. When she raised her head again, her smile was almost blinding. "Well, come on, then."

The barn, as it turned out, was pretty much what you'd expect. Light gray wood, bales of hay, and tools. Four horses stood in their stalls, watching me quietly as I walked by until we came to a stop in front of number five.

"This is Oakley," Peyton said, her voice soft and sort of reverent. The horse was a warm chestnut color, all but for a long white stripe down her nose. She gently ran her hand along the slope.

"She's a sorrel quarter horse," she continued, and I nodded as though I had a clue what that meant. Pressing her face against the horse, she breathed in and wrapped her arms around Oakley's neck. Then she turned her head and gave me a small smile. "You should see her cut on a turn. She's amazing."

"When do I get to see you ride?" I asked, my voice low. It felt like if I spoke too loud, too quick, it would ruin... something. The moment. The look in her eyes.

But then a voice broke in, ruining everything anyway.

"Hopefully within the next year." A dude stepped out of the shadows, running his hand along Oakley's nose right behind Peyton. Practically caging her in with his body. "CC's amazing out there."

He smiled down at her and my eyes narrowed. I knew this game. Hell, I wrote the damn playbook. What I didn't know was who this guy was or why he was playing it with me. "CC?"

"Just a silly nickname," Peyton mumbled. She ducked out from under the guy's hold and leaned against a beam near the stall. The guy turned to me, dropping his smile.

"Can chaser," he explained. "It means she's a barrel racer." He took in my unlaced tennis shoes, a far cry from his roughed up cowboy boots, and his eyebrows lifted behind his wire-rimmed frames. "Are you here for lessons?"

With the way he kept glancing back at Peyton and the dust covering his clothes, I guessed this to be Cade. "Nah, Sunshine's just showing me around," I replied with a smile, showing I had my own nickname for CC.

Like I'd said, I knew this game.

But then something he'd said before finally registered and I dropped the smirk. "Wait, why hopefully within the year?" I turned my gaze to Peyton. "Why not now?"

"Because it's too soon," Cade cut in, answering for her again. Seriously, this guy needed to back the hell off. He stared at me as if I'd suggested she take a flying leap off the town water tower. "She needs to stick with the program."

The program. Something about the way he said it struck me as odd. Just like that weird moment inside with her mom.

"What am I missing here?" I asked, keeping my focus on Peyton, wanting *her* to answer. She nibbled some more on her bottom lip and shifted her gaze between the two of us. Cade, the little shit, stayed silent for once, but his hands did find her shoulders, rubbing them gently like in comfort. My back teeth clicked. "Why can't you get up there now and show me a thing or two?"

Peyton's shoulders drew in slightly, and she looked so deflated, so fragile, that I felt like the biggest ass for even asking... which made no sense. Wasn't this her thing? Wasn't that why she brought me here?

When she opened her eyes again, the emotions swirling inside nearly crushed me.

"I guess you'd find out eventually," she said, stepping away again from Cade's side. He frowned, and despite my confusion, I fought a surge of satisfaction. She sucked in her lips, then released them. "I had GBS."

There was so much pain and fear in her voice, and her shoulders curled slightly into her chest. Cade shifted protectively, and although I had no clue what she was talking about, I realized that whatever this was, it was big. "GBS?"

"Guillain-Barre Syndrome," she clarified, looking away. "It's a disorder that affects the nervous system. It's rare. No one really ever talks about it or even knows how or why some people get it. But it's not contagious or anything. I was in and out of the hospital and rehab for the last year..." She shook her head and formed a tight smile. "But I'm fine now."

Cade scoffed. "I'd say it's a little more than that, CC."

Peyton nailed him with a glare. "Fine. So I'm not exactly completely healed, but I will be."

Her chin tipped up, as if she was daring either of us to disagree. I for sure as hell wasn't. Her shoulders were squared, her back straight, and I figured she could do just about anything she wanted to. She stepped up beside me, that sunny smile struggling for a comeback even though it didn't quite meet her eyes. "Want to come see my room?"

It was obvious there was a lot she was leaving out, parts of this disease that were still messing with her, and I wanted to know. God help me, I wanted to ask more and be this girl's protector. But then she took my hand again, clutching it almost desperately, and I found another way to do exactly that.

Then Cade made a noise in his throat, and when I looked over, I found him staring hard at our linked hands. Call me a dick, but that made my entire day. Win-win.

"Sure thing, pretty girl," I replied and watched as a genuine smile, one that *did* reach her eyes, curved her mouth. The expression of complete gratitude trumped any scowl Cade could've thrown my way.

Peyton wrapped her other hand around my elbow and said, "See ya later, Cade."

As she led me out the barn, I couldn't help but glance back. "Yeah, later, Cade."

His gaze met mine and I smirked.

THURSDAY, MAY 22ND

2 Weeks until Graduation

♥ Senior Year

JUSTIN
SWEET SERENITY RANCH 5:20 P.M.

Stepping foot on Peyton's ranch is like coming home again. Well, coming home if you live in the Old West, wear giant belt buckles to dinner, or, you know, have people who actually want you there.

Welcome or not though, I close my eyes and breathe deep. The earthy scent of kicked-up dust, sweet hay, and faint manure fills my head and I lean back against my Jeep, my knees suddenly weak. It's crazy that this place, more than the clean, sanitary, Pine-sol scented structure I've lived in my entire life, makes me feel like this—content and happy, like a puzzle piece finally locking in.

Peyton's ranch is the only spot in the world—other than the baseball diamond—that I've ever felt like I belonged. Where I'm welcomed, just as I am, without expectation. It's like a black-and-white sitcom where moms give hugs and bake apple pies, dads pass the potatoes and ask how your day was, and the girl of your dreams holds your hand beneath the table, a curtain of strawberry blonde hair masking her smile.

No more screw-ups, Carter.

Dinner at Carmela's was a shitastic disaster. I got cocky and threw it all out there too soon, banking on the old Peyton sitting across from me, the one who was shy and unsure at times but always went after what she wanted. She was fearless because she had to be.

That wasn't the girl who showed up to the restaurant.

This new Peyton is skittish, like one of the wary horses in her barn. At least around me. To even have a shot at winning her back, I'll have to stick with the game plan from here on out. Take things slow, start with being her friend, and not push whenever we work together on the project. That's what I've been trying to do since the dinner. I've got her sitting next to me in class, meeting me in study hall, even emailing the paper back and forth, and that's a hell of a step from where we were a week ago. Now I just need to prove that she can trust me again.

Like that'll ever happen.

As I kick myself yet again over my appallingly poor choices in the past, the musical notes of Peyton's laugh float toward me on the wind. I turn away from the paddock and find her standing on the porch of the doghouse, her head tipped back with a smile bigger than Texas on her face. That's the Peyton I remember. A grin makes its way to my mouth before my gaze shifts and I discover the reason for that smile. Cade is right beside her, an expression of pure reverence on his face, watching her like he's freaking king of the world.

I can't even blame him. I used to look the same way whenever I made her laugh like that. But seeing her hand on his chest and the smile she used to send me directed at him almost makes me lose it. And when his arm slides around her waist, tugging her close, I finally do.

Slam.

Peyton's eyes snap to mine as my closing door echoes across the field. Cade turns, too, and when his eyes meet mine, that King of the World expression turns to complete and total loathing.

Bring it on, horse boy.

"Hey, hot stuff. Long time since you've come around here." Faith steps out from the barn, a few feet away from where I'm standing. She drops a bucket and blanket on the ground then glances toward the doghouse. When she turns back, her eyes are twinkling. "As you can see, no one's been pining in your absence."

Okay, I deserve that. It doesn't make hearing the truth any easier, but I get it. Once upon a time, Faith and I used to be sort of friends. We hung out at the front desk whenever Peyton was out back bathing a dog—occasionally I'd help out with training, but washing and grooming mutts wasn't my thing. Faith would talk my ear off about her vlog, I'd pretend to follow along, and once, she even got me to read off the season's fashion trends. She still owed me for that one. But with all that behind us, I expected a warmer welcome. Then again, that was all before I screwed everything up so royally.

Swallowing my pride, I shove my hands deep into my pockets. "You let her go out with that spineless weasel?" I ask, nodding back toward where Cade and Peyton are now talking heatedly. It's almost enough to put the smile back on my face. "What kind of best friend are you?"

It might not look like it, what with me insulting her, but I know what I'm doing. Getting the best friend on my side, buttering her up, is crucial... and to play the game right, you have to know the other players.

Faith is an original. Snarky, with a true heart of gold. Fiercely loyal and protective of Peyton, but also the devilish voice in her ear, whispering to let loose and be spontaneous. She was my biggest ally when Peyton and I were together, and I'm counting on that support again. But first, she has to know that I want in.

Faith sizes me up and answers, "The kind that watched you destroy her three years ago."

That knocks me for a bit of a loop, just as she knew it would.

"It's not what you think," I tell her, taking a step closer. "I messed up and I'm not denying that, but I did what I did to protect her. I let her believe the worst but I promise you, I didn't cheat. Not really."

Faith scoffs and glances over her shoulder again where Peyton and Cade appear to be getting into it. "Don't go pulling some crap about Diamond Dolls not counting or being in different zip codes—"

"I never touched her."

I can't say it any clearer than that and I need her to know the truth. I need at least one person on my side.

Faith pins me with a, "do you think I was born yesterday?" look, and I shrug.

"Not then, at least. Look, Lauren and I hooked up, but not until junior year. I never said I was a saint. Just..." I shove my hand through my hair and squeeze the back of my neck. "Just not a cheater. I did what I did because I thought it was best." I hesitate before adding, "For everyone."

I don't know how much Peyton shared with her best friend. If Faith doesn't know everything that went down back then, it sure as hell isn't my place to spill. Besides, it'll only make Peyton run faster.

My hands slap against my thighs as I growl in frustration. This is fucking pointless. The evidence was damning—I should know, I planned it to be that way. And hell, I *did* hook up with Lauren eventually. Maybe this whole plan is doomed for failure. Maybe I should let Peyton go. Let her be happy with Cade.

Even the thought tastes like bile on my tongue.

Looking past Faith, I watch my girl slowly make her way toward me. She and Cade evidently sorted out their shit, and now confusion and anger battle it out with something else in her eyes. Something that dares to give me hope.

"For her sake, I hope you're not shitting me," Faith mumbles. Before I can wonder if she noticed that same expression, she turns back, pinning her gaze to mine. "Look, I know what happened back then—*everything* that happened—and the last thing that girl needs is you swooping back in to break her heart again." She tips up the brim of her rhinestone cowboy hat, targeting me with an intense stare as she lowers her voice. "You're a master bull-shitter, Justin, and you can't kid a kidder. But for some reason, I believe you."

That flicker of hope? It blazes into a damn forest fire.

Faith looks back and then lowers her voice even more. "I never really believed you cheated. I didn't doubt my girl, but I figured there was more to the story. I saw you with her, I saw the two of you together, and you suddenly pulling that kind of crap didn't sit right. But here's the deal—you should've come back sooner. You should've fought for her or fixed the mess you made. Cade's my boy, and he's been here a hell of a lot longer than you have. He was the one here when things went to shit, he's done his time. He's good for her."

My jaw clenches as I target horse-boy with my eyes. Good for her? He's a chickenshit who waited until she was heartbroken to go after her.

Faith snaps her fingers in front of my face. "But that doesn't matter because Peyton's heart isn't really in it. Not like it was with you. Now, you did not hear that from me, all right?" She waits for me to nod, which I do, my heart pounding in my chest. "But if you're gonna be here, you better *really* be here, and if you're honestly trying to do this, you should know you've got your work cut out for you."

"Got it." The first full breath I've taken since Peyton dropped the boyfriend bomb at dinner fills my lungs as she and Cade stop a short distance away.

"Got what?" she asks, narrowing her eyes at Faith. Her best friend shrugs innocently.

"That I can't go around slamming car doors," I reply easily. "It'll spook the horses."

Peyton looks dubious but she doesn't question it. Instead, she rocks back on her heels. "What are you doing here?"

Ouch. "Now, Sunshine, when you say things like that, you make me believe you don't want me around."

The truth? I use the nickname for a couple reasons. Mostly because I like it and because I know she secretly does, too. She just won't admit it. The fact that her new boyfriend hates it so much is simply a bonus.

"Why would she want you here?" Cade asks, sliding his hand around her waist and resting it possessively on her hip. "You got lucky being paired with her for an assignment, but that doesn't mean she wants you anywhere near her outside class."

The hand on Peyton's hip flexes and Faith chokes on a laugh. Seems along with growing a pair, horse boy found some spunk. Clearly, he doesn't want me here and isn't afraid to show it. Unfortunately for him, things like that don't stop me. If I only ever went where people were glad to see me, I'd never go home.

But this does mean I have to adjust my strategy on the fly. I'd hoped Peyton wouldn't have told Cade about our project. That she'd be so confused over the time we've spent together lately that she would've hidden it, at least for a little while, and the advantage of surprise would be mine. His knowing proves how close they really are, and frustration churns in my gut.

Leaning against the Jeep, my gaze drops to the hand clamped around her waist and then away toward the main house. "Actually, as much as I love seeing this pretty girl's face, I'm here to see my father-in-law."

"He's not here." When I turn back, Peyton is stepping out of Cade's grasp, a subtle shift of her feet. I'd be lying if I said that didn't make my damn week. "We're out of feed pellets for the horses so Dad went out to get some. You actually just missed him." She folds her arms across her chest and kicks the dirt with her boot. "You're welcome to wait if you want."

An innocent offer, one I've accepted a number of times over the years. I normally tried to show up late whenever we had a team meeting or party, hoping to avoid an awkward conversation with Peyton, but I've certainly not been a stranger to the ranch. For some reason though, hearing her invite me to stick around feels different. Like gaining ground. Something that Cade obviously doesn't like.

Glaring at me, he asks, "What do you need with Mr. Williams?"

I don't owe this dude a damn thing. It's no skin off my nose if he doubts me—but I enjoy rubbing my relationship with Peyton's dad in his face. Cade has always hated the way he treats me like a son.

"I ran into the area scout for the Rangers last night at The Zone," I say, referencing the local batting cages. "It seems the rumor I could go high in the draft has actual legs and I'd like his advice on a few things."

"You'd really give up A&M?" Peyton's expression gives nothing away, but it doesn't have to. That she knows about the letter of intent has to be a good sign. Perhaps sensing that, she quickly adds, "Dad mentioned it at dinner one night."

"I haven't decided anything yet," I tell her with a shrug. "Hell, that scout could be blowing smoke up my ass for all I know."

Don't get me wrong, I'm good. *Damn* good. But I gave up optimism a long time ago, right around the time I stopped believing people kept their promises.

"A&M is still a definite possibility." I meet her eyes, wondering if I'm making a mistake when I say, "The plan can still happen."

Peyton's eyes widen, seemingly shocked that I remember. As if I'd ever forget.

Back when we were together, our plan was College Station, me for their baseball team and her for their top-ranked Vet program. Even though we broke up, and the idea of her taking me back hadn't seemed impossible, another college had never been an option.

"You can major in creative writing," she says, needling me the same way she always did.

"I could major in kicking ass," I reply, giving it to her right back.

This right here proves my strategy is working. Strange, considering Cade is practically breathing down her neck and Faith is unabashedly watching us. Quietly, too, which is a shocker for Faith... and means she's capturing every detail.

"He wouldn't seriously give up the chance to go pro, CC," Cade says, driving me batshit crazy with that nickname. "If he's drafted high, the money they'll throw at him will be outrageous."

Which shows how truly little he knows me. Money has never been a factor. I've got enough of that already and all it's ever done is bring me problems. I don't go into that, though. One, because it's none of his business, and two because Peyton's mom steps out from the main house. Phone pressed to her ear, eyes shielded with her free hand, she spots us by the Jeep, and her smile gets even bigger.

Peyton's parents never knew we were together. I'm sure they suspected, but we didn't confirm it, and when we suddenly stopped hanging out, the teasing comments and amused glances stopped. The one thing that didn't was how they treated me—proof that Peyton never told them a thing. If they knew, they'd definitely hate me.

As Mrs. Grace makes her way toward us, she nods vigorously at whoever is on the phone. "Yes, sir. That's an amazing opportunity and we thank you for thinking of us." She nods again as if the person on the other end can see it. "Sounds perfect. Thank you so much. Uh huh, we'll be in touch."

The moment she hangs up, she grasps Peyton's hand. "I have news!" Tugging her daughter toward the Jeep, she wraps her other arm around me in a tight hug. "Justin, it's always good to see you. You don't come around here enough, son."

Dust kicks up in the slight breeze, making my eyes water. I return the hug awkwardly and step back, clearing my throat. When I glance up, Faith is watching me.

"You just missed Dan," she continues, "But you should stick around. In fact, supper's almost ready—"

"Mama, you said you had some news?"

Peyton's mom blinks and then shakes her head, that enormous smile creeping back. "Oh, right! That was Jerry with the Round Rock Kick-off to Summer Rodeo. I'd put a call in to ask about sponsorships for our new school, and get this. Opening day, they're holding public demonstrations for the crowd and they want you to exhibit for barrel racing!"

Pure terror washes over Peyton's face. It's gone in an instant, but it was there.

"Me?" Her voice wobbles and Cade takes her hand. If I hadn't seen that expression on her face, I'd almost believe she were excited.

Mrs. Grace must think exactly that because she says, "Yes, isn't that great? It's the perfect opportunity to get the word out about our new riding school!"

Peyton opens her mouth to speak and I notice the tremble in her lips. I push away from my Jeep, wanting to help, even though I have absolutely no clue what is going on, but Peyton stops me with a look.

"But I haven't trained in forever," she says casually, or at least that's what I think she intended. To me she sounds scared shitless. Her refusal to look me in the eyes confirms it.

None of this makes any sense. Peyton loves horses, loves to ride, and she'd been desperate to get back to rodeo. That's all she cared about when we were together. Riding Oakley again in the circuit and proving herself after her illness.

I turn from Peyton's trembling lips to Cade's protective hand and Faith's quiet concern. Her friends seem poised to intervene while her own mother is acting like she won the damn lottery.

What in the hell is going on?

PEYTON
SWEET SERENITY RANCH 5:43 P.M.

"Don't worry about that," Mama says, brushing aside my lack of training like it's nothing, when it's actually everything. It's a symptom, a clue, not to mention my only excuse to get out of this... well, other than my abject fear.

But she doesn't know about that.

"There's tons of time before the rodeo," she goes on, happiness practically shooting from the top of her head. "Barrel racing is in your blood, sweetheart, and you said you've been practicing. An exhibition ride will be a piece of cake. Besides, I'm sure the others will help take a few of your shifts."

She glances expectedly at Faith and Cade who both mumble halfhearted agreement. Faith offers me a shoulder shrug and Cade squeezes my fingertips.

"It's not like a full on rodeo," Mama continued, completely unaware of my dilemma... or the fact that I *lied* about practicing. "There's no competition. You won't have to outrace anyone, just ride well and wear the ranch's name on your back while you do."

Oh, is that all?

Mama stops her endless march and taps my chin with her finger. "You've put so much on hold the past few years, baby girl, getting healthy and then helping us here at the ranch. This is your chance to do what you love again. To get back out on the circuit."

The smile she sets on me is so full of life and hope that it's impossible to argue without admitting the truth—that I took advantage of their faith in me.

A couple years ago, I was given a clean bill of health, both from GBS *and* the accident, and my doctor gave me the all-clear to ride. My parents expected me to jump right back on Oakley and never look back. It made sense. My obsessive need to ride again had led to me getting injured, after all. They sat me down, said they loved me, and told me they were proud of how far I'd come. They *praised* my newfound patience with therapy, and through tears they confessed the last thing they wanted to do was hold me back from something I loved. Something I was *born* to do.

That was the killer.

How could I admit my fear and disappoint them? I couldn't, not after the pain I put them through in the hospital and then with my long recovery. Not when they finally looked so hopeful again. So, I did the next best thing. I hugged them both, thanked them for being so great, and then promised to start right away. Each week I gave fake status reports when they asked, putting on a smile and creating a million and a half different reasons why it wasn't a good time for them to come watch. With help from Faith and Cade, who I swore to secrecy, it really wasn't that hard to do. Of course, their preoccupation with our struggling finances certainly didn't hurt.

And just like that, I'm reminded why I need to do this.

"You're right," I say, toeing the hard ground with my boot. I can't look at her and lie again. "It sounds great. Really. I just, uh, have to check my school schedule..."

The jubilant hug she envelops me in nearly lifts me off my feet. "This is going to be fantastic, just you wait and see!" Releasing me with a squeeze, she spins on her heel and walks away, a bouncing skip now in her step. "There's so much to do. The rodeo is the day after your graduation, which means we only have two weeks to prepare... not even!"

Two weeks.

No one says anything, no one even moves, until the screen door slams behind her. When it does, Cade tugs me into his chest. I go willingly, my arms at my sides, my head resting on his solid shoulder.

"You don't have to do it, you know," he says, running his hands up and down my back reassuringly. "You can always tell her the truth."

"And then what? Lose the ranch?" I step back and shake my head. "I can't do that, Cade. It's my fault they need the money. My medical bills did this, and the riding school is our golden ticket. You saw the research. Even with schools being a dime a freaking dozen in Texas, only a handful of them specialize in event training, and none of them for barrel racing within a fifty-mile radius. The school is smart business, pure and simple."

But why did that mean *I* had be a part of it?

Pushing the selfish thought away, I say, "Riding in the exhibition will put the new clinic and day camps on the map. I have to do it. It's not like anyone else can ride in my place."

A quick glance at Faith confirms my suspicion. She lifts her hands in the air and takes a giant step back. "Sorry, girl, but you know I don't do the fast stuff. Rodeo Queen? That, I'm all over. But chasing cans and racing?" She shakes her head again with a grimace. "I love you something fierce, but put me out there and I guarantee no one will be signing up for classes. They'd be running for the exits after I spew my lunch."

"And you know I'd do it in a heartbeat if I could," Cade says, looking frustrated and helpless. When the proverbial shit hit the fan three years ago, he was the one to pick up the scattered pieces. Jumping in and saving the day is kind of his shtick, but in this case his hands are tied. "Though it would be one way to get attention for the ranch..."

"It's just not quite the kind we're shooting for," I finish with a laugh.

Guys aren't exactly welcome in this event, and while Mama may've been a pole-bender and show jumper in her day, that was a long time ago. That only leaves me.

I smother a sigh and scrub a hand across my face. "I'll figure something out."

"Seriously, what in the *hell* is going on here?"

At Justin's annoyed, borderline angry tone, I squeeze my eyes shut behind my hand. Of course he'd be here for this.

I've avoided looking at him since Mama went inside. Seeing her hug him again, not having a clue how he'd broken my heart, not even knowing we dated at all, was hard enough. Seeing the way her touch affected *him*? I just don't get it.

Justin acts as though he misses me. Like our time together actually meant something. If that were true, though, he wouldn't have thrown it all away. Now he's back, screwing up my life two short weeks before freedom hits. And he's discovering all my secrets.

When I don't answer, Justin takes hold of my elbow. He tugs, and in spite of myself, I turn around. "What am I missing here?" he asks, and the question is so similar to what he asked on his first visit, the day he learned about my illness, that I laugh once and throw my head back.

Lord. Life is nothing but a string of crazy, wrapped up in a giant ball of what-the-hell.

"I got hurt riding," I admit to the sky, knowing he won't drop it until I do. "Years ago. I don't do it anymore."

Of course, I saddle up for birthday parties. During lessons, I hop on to demonstrate a particular skill, and I even get up to a trot along with the student. But I don't ride free, I never go fast, and I refuse to go anywhere near barrels.

My cheeks flush as I remember the way my body failed me, and when I lower my head, Justin's eyes are flared with concern.

No. He doesn't get to look sad for me. Not when *he* hurt me first.

"You can take that pity in your eyes and shove it," I bite out, poking him hard in the chest. "I don't want it or need it. I'm doing just fine the way I am."

Instead of looking put in his place, or hell, even guilty, the jerkoff smiles. The nerve.

"You're right." He folds his arms as that dang disarming grin grows. "You don't need my pity. The girl I remember was strong and could do anything she set her mind to. A setback wouldn't get in the way of anything she wanted. Anything she *believed* in."

Damn him. He emphasized the perfect word to get under my skin, and he knows it, too. Despite my fears, I do believe in this new school, in its ability to resurrect our finances and put the ranch back in the black. But that doesn't mean he gets the final word.

"Oh yeah? Well maybe what I want has changed since you knew me," I say, leaning back into Cade's chest. He tenses behind me and wraps a protective arm around my waist. My gut clenches beneath the embrace.

I. Am going. To Hell.

Picking a fight, deflecting the truth, and using Cade's feelings for me to do it is wrong, so wrong, on so many levels. What makes it even suckier? Justin sees right through it.

Nodding slowly, he stares at the hand resting just above the snap of my jeans. "Maybe." Then he raises his eyes to mine. "But you haven't changed the person you are deep down inside."

The intensity in his gaze rocks me to my soul. He's just a guy, a jerk-face half the time, but I swear it's like he can read every thought in my head.

Maybe I'm that transparent.

Maybe he did know me, and our relationship wasn't a *total* lie.

But none of that matters. The only thing that does is how we ended.

Misreading the sudden stiffness in my arms, Cade's grip around me tightens. "Don't you have anyone else to annoy right now?"

Justin continues undeterred. "I get it, okay? I hurt you. I made a mistake three years ago that I desperately regret and I have to live with that. But, Peyton, I know you. Right now, you're scared as hell. You're telling yourself that you're scared of the horse, of failing, or even letting down your parents, and hey, all that might be true," he says before I can jump in. "But what you won't admit is what *really* scares you."

Showing just how weak I am, I fall right into his trap. "And what's that?"

86

Justin grins like he won some kind of battle and the effect does insane things to my belly.

"What really scares you," he says, "is the huge part of you that so badly wants to do this. Wants to push herself again and prove to everyone that she can."

His gaze holds me entranced as breaths saw in and out of my chest. Fear pools with what dangerously feels like excitement in my core, shooting out through my body until it reaches my fingertips. My mouth tumbles open in an exhale, unable to contain it, and that wicked grin detonates into a full-on devastating smile.

Beside me, Faith whispers, "*Hot damn.*"

Justin releases me from his stare but he doesn't swing it to Faith. He targets Cade as he delivers his final blow. "And I, for one, believe in you."

Cade sucks in air, staggering a bit as if he got the wind knocked out of him, and I snap out of the trance. What in heaven's name is happening here? Have I learned *nothing* from the past? Justin is persuasive and charming. He's proven time and again that he can sweet-talk the pants off any girl he wants, flooding the school with victims of his smile. That doesn't mean he gets to work his magic on me. Not anymore.

Standing tall, I throw my shoulders back and stare into his smug, all-knowing eyes. "Yeah, well, it's too bad I stopped caring what you think the day you broke my heart," I tell him with a bitter smile before turning on my heel and walking away.

FRIDAY, JANUARY 28TH

18 Weeks until Disaster

♥ Freshman Year

JUSTIN
JUSTIN'S HOUSE 8:49 P.M.

"*Kid* are you sure your old man won't check his stash?"

I lifted my eyes from my phone and smirked at Carlos, each of his hands wrapped around the neck of a bottle from my father's liquor cabinet. "Even if he did, it wouldn't matter," I replied. Hell, if he did happen to notice and thrash me around, at least he'd remember I existed.

Carlos squinted at me but went back to moving all the liquor to the living room, and I returned to staring at Peyton's text.

Dandelion and Oakley think you should stop back by sometime :)

Who the hell named their pit bull Dandelion? Evidently, the same girl who named her horse after a tough-ass gunslinger, quoted inspirational posters, and had a smile sweeter than honey. And damn it if all those things didn't make me want her that much more.

Two weeks had passed since the day at her ranch. Two weeks since she'd told me about her illness and showed that inner-fire. When I got home, I'd looked up GBS on the Internet.

She was right—it was rare. Even crazier, no one seemed to know how people got it. It wasn't genetic. Sometimes it was preceded by a cold or the flu, but not in every case. Often, healthy people, athletes even, went from walking around and living life one day to lying immobilized in a hospital bed the next.

I still couldn't believe she'd gone through that and came out the way she had. Positive. Determined. If I'd been in her place, losing the ability to move and control my body, just lying there helpless without any answers, who knows what I would've done. Most likely complained and given up.

More than attraction, I admired this girl. Which honestly pissed me off.

Peyton was off-limits. I knew that. I just kept forgetting why.

"Do you guys mind if I fast forward through this crap?" Brandon asked, already skipping ahead on the video. I pocketed my phone without replying to Peyton's message. "We're behind time and I want to get to the action."

"Hell yes I mind," Drew replied, snatching the remote from our pitcher's hand. "I like the human interest shit. If I'm gonna watch two dudes beat the shit out of each other, I want to be emotionally *invested*."

He glanced at me and grinned, rewinding to the beginning. I shrugged, honestly not caring either way. As long as I wasn't alone, they could do whatever the hell they wanted.

Dad was traveling again, and Annabeth had taken my brother to her parents' house. Rosalyn always had weekends off, which meant I'd have the house to myself until Monday. Most people think this would be awesome—visions of Tom Cruise dancing in his underwear in that old movie flash through their mind. But the truth is, being alone sucks. The walls close in, the silence is deafening, and you can only play so many video games before you slowly go insane.

Unfortunately, my usual distractions weren't appealing, so I'd invited a few of the guys to watch the fight on Pay-Per-View.

"The personal stories are all fluff," Carlos replied, settling down with a bottle of Jim Beam. "But if you fast-forward through the octagon girls, I'm gonna have to hurt you."

I shook my head with a laugh. Carlos, I'd quickly learned, was all talk. Pushing to my feet, I headed to the large cooler in the corner as the announcers began discussing the title fight.

"Did you guys watch that dude on Ultimate Fighter last season?" I asked, pointing at Alex Ryan's face on the screen. Taking out an ice-cold beer, I twisted off the cap. "Broke his damn toe in the middle of the first round and kept on attacking. This match is gonna be a bloodbath."

Drew turned up the volume and we all fell silent as we listened to Joe Rogan make his predictions. A video package started, showing Alex and his opponent training in their home gyms and wrapping up their previous fights. They'd both bested the most insane competition ever to enter the octagon, proven themselves when and where it counted, and made it to the top. Win or lose tonight, they deserved their spots.

That's all I wanted at the end of the day— for people to say that about me. That *I'd* beaten the best and earned my spot. That I belonged there... wherever *there* was. I hoped it was baseball, and so far, Coach seemed to agree. He'd already pulled me aside a few times after practice, gave me tips during unstructured period, and was even nominating me for an invite-only catcher showcase, despite the fact that I was only a freshman. Things were trucking along exactly the way I wanted them to. I just had to make sure it stayed that way.

"Now there's my honey right there," Carlos said as a girl with a deep tan, long dark hair, and a huge rack strutted away from the cage. She sat back in her chair and winked at the camera. "That girl wants me."

I waved away the tequila Brandon held in my direction and plopped my ass on the couch. "Man, if a girl like that ever came at you, you'd piss your pants."

The guys cracked up laughing, and Carlos scoffed. "False." Then, after thinking about it, said, "Actually, truth. But only because her muscle-head boyfriend would kick my ass. I'm really more of a lover than a fighter."

Brandon shook his head, holding back a smile. "From where I'm sitting, I've got to say... I don't think you're much of either."

"Have you not seen Ashley Walsh all over my junk?" he asked indignantly. "She thinks I'm the shit."

"You mean your *Diamond Doll*?" Drew threw his head against the back of the sofa. "Jesus, dude. I bet you'd think strippers like you, too."

I choked on my beer, and Carlos flipped us all off. "Screw you guys."

I slapped him on the shoulder and he shoved my hand away. "We're just fucking with you, man."

"Yeah, well, what the hell do I care why she's with me? Have you seen Ashley? Her ass is smoking, and her Rice Krispie treats taste like tiny bits of heaven." He raised a shot glass full of whiskey in salute. "If she's with me because I'm on the team, then all I can say is, 'bring on the games.'"

He downed the shot, Brandon followed, and Drew caught my eye.

I didn't know much about the dude, other than he played third base and seemed to be a good guy. Didn't talk a lot of shit, mostly kept to himself. He didn't even appear all that interested in Bethany, the hot cheerleader that trailed his ass since they'd announced he made the roster.

"I don't know," he said. "Don't y'all think the whole Diamond Doll thing is a little stupid? I mean, the only thing those girls care about is that we play ball. If I weren't on the team, I doubt Beth would give me a second look." Around a mouthful of popcorn he mumbled, "And she's not exactly my type, either."

"Ah, okay, so your type isn't hot blonde." Carlos nodded seriously. "Gotcha."

"What I mean is," Drew said, beaning him with a kernel, "casual isn't really my thing. I prefer one girl, a sweet, normal, cool girl I can be with, not a bunch of meaningless hookups."

"And I'm the exact opposite," I replied, even as a pair of blue-gray eyes and a shock of strawberry blonde hair flashed in my mind. After witnessing my dad and step-monster's joke of a marriage, I'd learned relationships were a waste of time. "I don't do commitment."

"Too bad girls don't come with some sort of label, huh?" Brandon asked. "A name tag that said if they wanted a relationship or are cool with just hanging out. Nothing serious. Just..." He glanced at Drew. "Casual."

Onscreen, the first fight of the night began. The guy in the red corner was a huge favorite, not much of a matchup. We watched the fighters size each other up, and Carlos said, "Maybe we should make a list for ourselves."

"Huh?"

He lifted a shoulder and said, "We've been going to school with most of these girls for years, some since kindergarten. Odds are at least one of us has a good read on them, knows what type of relationship they're looking for. May make it easier on the rest of us, you know?"

Brandon looked at Drew. Drew glanced at me. I turned to Carlos and said, "I'll be right back."

In my room, I headed straight for the bookshelf. Although several private schools fed into the high school, mine had been just down the block and was where the majority of the students came from. My eighth grade yearbook would have at least half the girls in our class.

When I snatched it off my shelf, the corner of the book hit the stand holding my baseball. It rolled under my bed and I quickly stooped to get it. Palming it, I stood back up and glanced at Larry Dierker's name. Everything about that day flooded over me. Dad taking me to the game. Standing beside me in line while we waited to meet his favorite player. Larry signing my ball and showing me a proper grip.

I tossed it in the air, caught it, and put it back on the stand. Then, grabbing a legal pad and a pen, I left the room.

"Back," I announced, brandishing the yearbook like some sort of answer key. "This should help with that list."

Cracking open the book, I quickly flipped to the eighth grade photos and tossed the pad to Carlos. He drew a long line down the center and at the top wrote "Casual" on one side and "Commitment" on the other.

"Gabi Avila," I read, looking at the tough chick from English class. "Huh. You know, I can't get a read on this girl at all. I've gone to school with her for a while but haven't said like two words to her."

Carlos glanced over and I held up the book. "Hot," he announced. "And my luck, a 'Commitment.'"

"She's friends with Aly Reed, so I'd say that's probably right." Brandon pointed at the right side of the legal pad. "I've known that girl for a long time and she's one of my closest friends. I can tell you she's absolutely a 'Commitment.'"

As Carlos jotted down both names, I flipped to the end of the class photos and found Aly. She was cute. If I remembered right, she played for the volleyball team. In her picture, she was laughing instead of smiling, and something about the way her eyes crinkled reminded me of Peyton.

"I think it's safe to say most of the Diamond Dolls are 'Casuals,'" Carlos said, already writing Ashley's name. "They seem cool with just hanging out and having fun, not trying to call any of us their boyfriends or anything, right?"

The other guys nodded in agreement. I wasn't sure what Lauren wanted from me, but she'd never brought up labels. She left notes in my locker before games, cheered for me in the stands, and saved me a seat at lunch—basically the same things all the Diamond Dolls did. She also ignored me the other six days of the week, openly flirted with the other players, and kissed random dudes in the hallway. I'd say that was probably the definition of "Casual."

"What about that new girl?" I asked. "I think her name is Peyton?"

Carlos side-eyed me, having seen her that day in the bleachers, but he didn't out me.

Drew scratched his chin. "Who?"

"You know, the cute girl who started this semester. Strawberry blonde, kind of quiet, spends most of her lunch break reading a book?"

From the way all three of them turned to stare at me, it was clear my attempt for nonchalance missed by a mile. Carlos smirked, but replied, "Yeah, I've seen her around a few times. She came to the game the other day, didn't she?"

Yes, she had. And I'd felt her watching my ass from behind home plate.

"The girl who screamed bloody murder at the umpire for missing that call?" Brandon asked, and I nodded, fighting a smile at the memory. It had been a horrific mistake, almost cost us the game, but hearing Sunshine yell so loud, and seeing her face turn red while she did it in the stands, had made it damn hard to stay angry.

The guys looked at each other for confirmation before saying in unison, "'Commitment.'"

I went to argue. I wanted to believe Peyton could be a "Casual." If she didn't want anything serious, then there would be no problem with us hooking up, having some fun, and hopefully getting her out of my head, since nothing else seemed to work. But, I knew the guys were right.

Carlos glanced at me, the pen pressed to the paper. I released a breath and said, "Yeah, she's totally a 'Commitment.'"

And completely off limits.

SATURDAY, JANUARY 29TH

18 Weeks until Disaster

♥ Freshman Year

PEYTON
JUSTIN'S HOUSE 4:20 P.M.

"Peyton?"

Justin blinked at me in confusion as he raked his hand through a severe case of bedhead. He fisted the ends, causing them to stand straight up, clearly not a hair product in sight, and I decided this was my favorite look on him by far. Sleep-rumpled, almost innocent, and completely off-guard.

"Did I wake you from a nap?" It was late in the day so while I'd been prepared for a slew of potential scenarios, Justin sleeping hadn't been one of them. My determination waffled. "Maybe this is a bad time..."

"Nah, it's fine," he replied on a yawn, bringing his hand down to scratch his stomach. The hem of his white T-shirt lifted, exposing a strip of tan skin. *Definitely worth it.* He shook his head as if to clear it, then squinted at me. "But what are you doing here?"

"Uh." My gaze wandered from that strip of skin, over his ratty sweat pants, down to his bare feet. My mouth flooded with saliva. Why was that so hot? Dragging my eyes back to his, I stuttered, "I, uh, I was bored... at home... and thinking of you, and I decided that was rather silly." I beamed up at him.

"Why sit there all alone when I could swing by here and see you in person?"

Amusement and wonder washed over Justin's face and I rolled onto the balls of my feet. "So... mind if I come in?"

Smiling indulgently, he tugged the door open wider. Victory coursed through my veins as I turned, suppressing a shimmy, and waved goodbye to Mama.

"I know I should've called or even texted," I said when I stepped inside the grand entrance. I took in the marble tile, soaring ceiling, and three-level staircase. Impressive. "But if I'd done that, then you could've said no. I'm much harder to deny in person."

Justin laughed and the rich sound gave me goose bumps. "Anyone ever tell you you're crazy?" I frowned at that and he tugged a strand of my hair. "Good crazy. You say whatever you think, whatever you feel. You don't hold back." He craned an eyebrow. "I like that. But it doesn't make you normal."

"Normalcy is overrated," I replied, although normal was exactly what I'd longed to be. Unfortunately, after almost a month of being the freshman class nerd-slash-weirdo, I was discovering ordinary might not be in the cards. Hard to be heartbroken, though, when Justin Carter smiled like that "It's all part of my new life philosophy: Do what scares you."

He leaned against an ornate side table. "Was coming here scary?"

"Are you kidding?" I huffed a laugh. "You could've told me to get lost, laughed in my face, or been busy with your friends." *Not to mention another girl.* "Of course it was scary!"

"What about me?" he asked and his firm lips twitched. "Do I scare you?"

"Justin, you terrify me."

His smile was slow and dangerous and full of every wicked thing I'd ever fantasized about. Sweet baby Jesus. Biting my lip,

I spun on my heel before I attacked him, and escaped down the hall, following the familiar opening notes of Sports Center.

Today, I was on a mission of cute-boy discovery. I'd learned lots of little things about the mysterious guy trailing me over the last few weeks. Scraps of intel pieced together from text conversations, stealthy spy missions, and hours of focused pondering. Unfortunately, that was all I really had since we never spoke much in school. We didn't share any classes, and I had zero interest in duking it out with Queen Bee Barbie at the lunch table. Lauren still held court as his Diamond Doll and she made sure everyone at Fairfield knew it, too.

Strangely enough, I was content with our *secret* friendship. Oh, sure, I daydreamed about him grabbing me up in the cafeteria, unable to deny his feelings anymore, and kissing me senseless in front of God and everyone. But it's what would come *after* the kiss that kept me from truly wanting that to play out. The constant stares, the endless questions, the confrontation with Lauren... that, I wanted no part of. I was still getting my feet wet with not being homeschooled, and shooting to instant fame was not on my to-do list.

Besides, other than simple flirting, Justin gave no signs he even *wanted* to kiss me. Some days, he barely acknowledged we were friends, letting two, three days go by without a single text, and I'd wonder if he'd had his fill with me. But then, out of the blue, he'd reach out again. Mostly at night, a few texts even during school hours, and they always sucked me back in. They also hinted at a hidden loneliness, a need for connection, something I understood perhaps better than anyone. I wanted to be the one who gave that to him.

Also, let's be real—I had a mad crush on the guy. There was no use in denying it. I was falling for him. Hard.

The hallway opened into a sunken living room with a huge television, plush sofa, and lots of baubles that looked über expensive and breakable. Other than a soft blanket sitting in a heap on the sofa, the rest of the room actually felt extremely... cold. Desolate. I frowned and glanced at the enormous kitchen visible just beyond.

"Your house is beautiful," I said, because, really, it was. Uncomfortable, yes, but it was like HGTV had exploded and dropped all things posh and overpriced in the Carter house. Justin shrugged, looking a bit uncomfortable.

"Thirsty?" He lifted his chin toward the kitchen and I nodded, not really thirsty, but not really knowing what else to do with myself. I followed him through the arched entry and butted my hip against the granite countertop. "Okay, we got water, OJ, Sprite—"

"Sprite would be perfect," I said, noting the tense line of his shoulders.

He made a noise of agreement and snagged two cans from inside the door. The fridge, like the rest of the room, was gleaming silver and flawless, but when he closed it, I noticed a crude drawing tacked in the center. Justin handed me the soda and caught me staring.

"Nice work," I said, smiling at the picture. "Artist as well as a writer?"

The frown he shot me said he wasn't impressed with my memory. "That's my little brother Chase. He's obsessed with baseball right now."

"Easy to see why," I murmured.

The picture was clearly one of Justin. He was drawn in his uniform with a roughly sketched (and hugely disproportionate) catcher's mitt on his hand. A bright green diamond was in the background, the yellow sun shone bright, and he wore a larger than life cheesy smile. The obvious idol worship was completely charming. From the sudden tender look in Justin's eyes, the affection went both ways. "Do you have any other brothers or sisters?"

The soft look hardened and his grin fell away. "Nope."

Hmm. That was strange. Even stranger, the longer I stood in his house, gawking at this beautiful, flawless kitchen, the more sure I became that something was... off. Missing, somehow, which seemed impossible since the Carter family manor had every upgrade known to man. I just couldn't put my finger on what was wrong.

Interest piqued, I looked around again and realized at least one thing that was weird—no one else was here. The house was like a tomb, creepy quiet... well, other than Sports Center, that is.

"Where is everyone?"

I lifted my can and took a long, syrupy sip while Justin shrugged. He dropped his gaze to the floor and his shoulders deflated on an exhale. When he spoke, his voice was so low I wasn't sure he even meant for me to hear him. "My family's not like yours, Peyton."

Pain and longing filled his voice and I had a sudden and intense urge to hug him. But, before I could, he pushed away from the fridge and nudged my elbow. "Come on, I'll show you my room."

Curiouser and curiouser. With a final glance at his brother's sketch, I followed in his wake.

Everywhere my gaze touched as I followed Justin down the hall screamed money, sophistication, and "hands off." I tried to take it all in without appearing as if I was scoping the place, but for the life of me, I couldn't imagine a little kid living here. Or a teenage boy, for that matter.

At the end of the hall, Justin nudged a door open, and I quickened my stride to catch up. With my mind still back with the secrets of the kitchen, I distractedly glanced at the open door on my left, and came to an abrupt stop two steps later when I realized what I'd seen.

It was a museum. Not a museum like the rest of the house in that it *felt* untouchable, it was, like, an actual museum. Glass cases lined the walls, filled with black and white team photos, various memorabilia and pennants, and stands displaying signed balls. A dozen at least.

Above the cases, framed baseball cards and action shots hung beside plaques and complete uniforms. A signed bat held pride of place in a protective case all its own. I took a step closer to try and read the signature and a hand on my arm halted my progress.

"This is my dad's room." Justin's eyes were guarded as he gruffly added, "No one comes in here."

"Oh." I looked around, confused. Why have all this stuff if no one else could see it? It made no sense, but it was clear Justin meant it. He glanced behind him, like he was worried we'd get caught. "Sorry, I didn't..."

I trailed off, not really sure what I was apologizing for, and he shrugged. He took my hand, message received, and walked back out. Not wanting to push, I took one final glance around the room and followed.

Justin's bedroom, however, was a different story. Here, I unabashedly stared. The purpose of today's visit was to learn more about him, to discover what made the boy tick, and this was the place to do it. His inner sanctum.

Seeming to finally relax, Justin left me to my snooping and dropped to the bed with a small bounce. *Soft*, I thought, wondering if I had the guts to join him. His dark eyes lit with an unspoken challenge and I quickly looked away.

"Impressive collection." I trailed a finger along his bookshelf, noting his worn copy of *Moneyball*, along with a few biographies of players. The expected classics from English class. Trophies from sports. A framed photo of the team. What I didn't see were pictures of him with any girls. That made me stupid happy.

"Told you I wasn't a dumb jock," he teased.

"I stand corrected," I replied with a backwards wink. Next to the bookshelf was his desk, holding a laptop, fancy printer, a yellow legal pad, and a spiral-bound pocket-sized notebook. The notebook was closed, but the pad had distinctive writing—what appeared to be two lists.

Biting my lip, I glanced at him and caught the ticking muscle below his eye.

Jackpot!

We both bolted forward. Even though I was standing *right there*, he miraculously beat me to them, snatching both the pad and notebook up before I could process he'd even moved, and holding them high above my head with a burst of laughter.

"No way." Eyes sparkling, he peered down at me and said, "Not on your life, Sunshine."

His free arm wrapped around my waist, pinning me tight to keep me from reaching the paper. My struggles were only halfhearted. While I desperately wanted to read what he'd wrote, I wanted to move even less. A side benefit of our current position was my head being pressed solidly against Justin's chest. His very *nice*, smells-like-manly-soap, chest.

Yeah, I wasn't going anywhere.

"Your writing notebooks, I take it?"

"Possibly." His voice held evidence of his smile and I lifted my eyes. I was addicted to Justin Carter's grins. This was one I'd yet to see before—this one was happy, free, and almost embarrassed. "Guess you'll never know."

With us standing this close, Justin towered over me. His chin, if he chose to do so, would tuck perfectly on the top of my head, my nose fitting the center seam of his chest where I imagined his heart racing as fast as my own.

Just like that, I forgot about today's mission. I forgot about being fine with our secret friendship. And I forgot that right before I came here, I'd chowed down on a thick slice of pizza, heavy on the onions.

Grasping his hips, I gripped the soft cotton of his shirt with my trembling hands. Usually, it was a reminder of my weakness, my body's lingering failure. Right now, it was a sign of my excitement. "Justin...?"

My voice sounded breathless and Justin's eyes darkened. I'd read about that phenomenon in my books, imagined what it looked like in real life, but had no real clue. Now I did. And I liked it. A lot. As anticipation, anxiety, and wonder roiled in my gut, only one thought rushed through my head: *Is this it?*

In the hospital, I'd convinced myself I'd die a kiss-less virgin. Before I got sick, I'd never had a boyfriend, and during my worse days, I imagined I never would. Back then, there was no way I would've believed I'd one day be here. In Justin Carter's bedroom. In his arms. Being stared at like I was beautiful.

A tingling sensation zinged across my scalp as the rough pad of his thumb ghosted across my cheek. He flicked his gaze between my eyes, slowly bent his head, and a swarm of butterflies began the cha-cha in my gut. Yep, this was it.

Clenching my fists, I closed my eyes, waiting for the moment when our lips would touch. The moment that would change me, take my kissing V-card. It never came.

His hands left my skin, cool air rushed in, and I pried my eyes open. Justin watched me, his hands clutching the legal pad and notebook and his expression torn. Over what? Had I done something wrong?

Nodding his head as if he'd come to a decision, he took a step back. He turned his back, placed the notebooks high on top of his bookshelf, and I battled an overwhelming wave of disappointment. *Silly girl.*

Not wanting him to know how much the near-kiss affected me, I forced a smile. "I'll read them one day, you know. Every writer deserves an audience."

Justin didn't react. Instead, he twisted back around and pressed his lips together in a thin line. "Can I ask...?" He shoved his hands into his pockets and shifted his weight. "I mean, if it won't upset you or anything... could you tell me about your illness?"

Like a magic pill, any trace of sexual tension in the room evaporated.

GBS, the instant mood killer.

This was why I hadn't said anything before. Now it was all he saw when he looked at me. Not a girl to flirt with, or ask out, or kiss passionately next to his bookshelf, but someone who was sick once.

"What do you want to know?"

I settled on the edge of his bed with a plop and Justin walked over to his desk across from me. Away from me. He pushed up to sit on the surface and ducked his head, lifting a shoulder as if he were embarrassed.

"I looked it up online," he admitted to the carpet. "I watched a few videos on YouTube, too. But I guess I wanted to know what *your* experience was like." He raised his head. "I can't imagine what you went through, how terrifying that must have been... but I'd like to know. If you want to tell me."

It didn't come across as pity or even mild curiosity. Justin appeared genuinely interested and concerned. Caring. The warmth of that feeling spread through me like wildfire.

Smiling gently, I told him, "I don't mind talking about it. I mean, I hate it when people hear and assume I'm weak or a charity case, but I don't mind sharing my experience."

He scooted back until his back reached the wall, and I blew out a breath, preparing for story time.

"I never really thought about things before I got sick. I took it for granted when I could tell someone how I was feeling, what was wrong. The ability to write a friend a letter or send a text. Heck, to brush my own dang teeth. But those were the things that kept circling my mind in the hospital. How I wished I could do something so simple, you know?"

He nodded, letting me know he was listening, and I shifted to lay belly down on his mattress. I'd been right before; it was soft.

"It started with a weakness in my legs," I told him. "I thought I'd overdone it riding that day. But by that night, it was so much more than that. My parents took me to the ER, but no one seemed to know what was wrong—other than it looked like I was dying. That's what Mama kept whispering over and over: That her baby was dying."

I swallowed past the painful memory lodged in my throat. Those words still haunted me at night.

"Within hours, I couldn't breathe on my own. I couldn't swallow, so they had to put in a feeding tube. I was lying there, in excruciating pain, and I couldn't tell anyone. I couldn't even point to one of those stupid rating charts with the round faces. You know what I'm talking about?" Justin nodded again.

"People talked and moved around me for days, no answers, no nothing. Just fear and pain. I couldn't even lift a hand to wipe away my own tears. My entire world boiled down to the constant swoosh of the respirator. The beeps of the alarms on the machines. Lights flashing when it was time to draw more blood. It was like a thin curtain blocked me from the rest of the world. The worst part was that anyone could've come into my room at any time, and I wouldn't have been able to do a thing about it. Not scream, or even flinch."

Justin closed his eyes and inhaled deeply through his nose. I lowered my gaze and noticed his hands clenched around the desktop. His knuckles were blanched white.

"Things got a little better once we had a diagnosis," I quickly assured him, hating that he was in distress. Which was odd since we were talking about me. But it meant everything that he cared.

"Doctors and therapists started coming in around the clock. They taught me how to communicate again. I couldn't talk right away, though, so they had me blow into a straw whenever I needed the nurse. Slowly, I learned how to roll over and sit, how to feed myself and go to the bathroom." I paused there and shuddered. "You have no idea how humiliating it is to be a teenager and need someone to wipe your own ass."

Justin opened his eyes. "No, I don't." His voice was scratchy and he shook his head. His mouth curved into a smile as he said, "I don't know how you did it. You're incredible, Sunshine."

Justin Carter knew how to rock a smile. Flirty grins, mischievous smirks, even vulnerable pouts. The smile on his face now, though, was filled with wonder, respect, and true affection. It was easily my favorite of them all.

"Not incredible," I replied. "Just a survivor. A stubborn one. Once I started making headway, I was determined to be the best patient ever, to kick the thing's ass, you know? It wasn't easy. At first, I didn't have any muscle tone. Within days of being admitted, I could see all the bones in my hands. But I never gave up, I kept pushing, and I did everything my therapists told me. Sometimes I pushed too hard too fast and set my recovery back." I sighed in frustration. "I'm not one hundred percent yet, but I will be. One day."

I fell silent and rested my head on my arms. As I lay there, quiet, simply staring back at Justin, a peculiar sensation crept over my skin. I was no mind reader, and my knowledge of boys was limited to my older brothers and my string of book boyfriends, but I could've sworn pride shone in Justin's eyes.

Being from an athletic family, it sucked having everyone waiting for me to relapse and telling me to slow down. Second guessing every move I made. The doctors said they'd never heard of patients having a relapse; sometimes people suffered residual weaknesses, but they were generally older, and I was expected to make a full recovery. But no one ever knew for sure. Too much was still unknown, and it made me feel out of control and helpless.

But through Justin's eyes, I didn't feel weak. He looked at me and saw someone who could accomplish anything. *Do* anything. I liked that feeling. A lot.

Outside, a dog barked, and suddenly, as if waking from a stupor, Justin blinked his eyes. He cleared his throat and he pushed off the desktop, onto his feet.

The spell was broken. Story time was over.

Confused by the abrupt change, I clamored to sit up as well. Had I said something wrong? I rolled off the mattress, found my balance, and then stood awkwardly in front of him. He wouldn't even look at me. The comfort and ease of the last few minutes was gone, erased, replaced with restless feet and darting eyes.

I frantically glanced around the room, desperate for something to talk about, and that's when I saw the ball.

A level lower than I'd looked before, it was on a stand on his bookshelf. I walked up to it and recognized Larry Dierker's signature. "Ah, nice one."

Justin moved in behind me. Taking the ball off its stand, he stared at it, palmed it, and admitted almost to himself, "It's my only decent memory from childhood."

This was huge. Out of everything I'd discovered from my hours of Justin research, I knew one thing without a shadow of a doubt: The boy was Private with a capital P. Worried *he'd* remember that, too, and stop talking, I clamped my mouth shut.

"The only thing Dad loves more than money is baseball," he said, this time with a definite edge. "Not his own family, not even this stupid house. This place is more like a hotel."

He scoffed, playing the tough-guy role he probably thought he'd perfected, but I heard the loneliness behind it. I wanted to turn around and hug him, tell him I was sorry, but I knew he wouldn't want that. So, I stayed where I was, clenching and unclenching my hands.

"Anyway," he continued, "when I was a kid, one of Dad's vendors had tickets to the game where they retired Dierker's jersey. I never really knew why, but for some reason, Dad let me tag along."

"2002," I murmured without thinking.

"Yeah. How did you know that?"

I blew out a breath, cursing my stupid mouth for interrupting. Turning around, I found Justin gaping at me and I shrugged. "Sports fanatic for a father, remember?"

"Oh. Right." He frowned at that, then shook his head and glanced back at the ball. "I got to meet Larry that day. He signed this and even showed me a proper grip."

Justin stretched his arm back, miming a perfect throw, and the harsh lines on his face faded away, transforming into a boyish grin. He dropped his hand and sighed. "Baseball's been my life ever since." He waved the ball in his hand. "And Larry, my favorite player."

I smiled. "He's one of my dad's favorites, too. I'm actually shocked he didn't name any of us after him, but then, that'd be pretty weird whenever we saw him over at the house."

Justin's eyes cut to mine. "What do you mean?"

I lifted a shoulder. "Dad's friends with him and he comes by the house sometimes. Mostly after a school visit to go over drills with the team. Dad brings him home for dinner. As you know, he's really active in supporting local youth athletic teams."

As I spoke, every muscle in Justin's body turned to stone. I scrunched my nose, clueless as to what I could've said to make him catatonic, and waited five, maybe six heartbeats before he closed his mouth and then asked, "Team?"

Now I was really lost. "Well, yeah."

He had to know... right? I thought back over all our conversations, at school, at the ranch, and over text, and realized I'd never specifically said anything. I also never told anyone at school. The teachers knew, of course, but it never came up in class, and it wasn't like I wore a neon sign over my head that said I was the Coach's daughter. I'd just always assumed Justin knew.

Judging from his current frozen form, I wasn't so sure.

Will this matter? Praying it didn't, I tucked my hair behind my ear. "Justin, you know my dad's your baseball coach, right?"

A giant step back and a harsh, cynical laugh gave me my answer.

SATURDAY, MAY 24TH

2 Weeks until Graduation

♥ Senior Year

PEYTON
SWEET SERENITY RANCH 1:35 P.M.

"Hey girl, you ready to ride?" Annie Oakley's wise eyes peer at me from her stall, saying more than she could even if she could speak. Everything I've already been thinking myself. "Yeah, I know. It's been a while."

The ranch at least is quiet today. Dad already left for the ballpark and Mama is out buying supplies for the business. Trevor has a golf event, Faith and Cade are inside working, and I'm out here, trying to resurrect an old dream.

"Don't worry if you're scared," I say, gently tugging Oakley toward the barrel course Cade and I laid out just last week. "That's perfectly normal. In fact, if you want to know a secret, I'm pretty scared, too."

Her soft whinny makes me smile and I comb my hand through her long, chestnut mane.

It's not as if the two of us haven't ridden together since the accident. We've gone on walks around the pasture, even made it up to a slow trot. Easy instructional things with the kids. But slow and easy ain't gonna cut it for the exhibition. It's time for me to put on my big girl panties.

We make it out to the course way too soon. A quick check around the field is enough to know we're still alone. I can still back out if I want to. Walk away, give Annie an apple, and pretend this never happened. No one would be any the wiser. But even as I think it, I know that's not true. I would know.

Justin is a hell of a lot of things, but one thing he's not, at least in this case, is wrong. There is a huge part of me that lives beneath the fear that wants to do this. Wants to break out of the steel prison of anxiety and feel the wind slap across my face again. My heart rate picks up speed just imagining it.

A question bubbles to the surface, the same one that's taunted me for years. *What if?*

What if I really can do it again? What if I can find greatness, find that missing piece that's been absent for so long, and be whole again?

What if I've wasted my best years on the circuit for nothing?

Obviously, the "what if" game is a double-edged sword. Not only the back and forth of doubts but the chance that things can go horribly wrong. I could fall again, get hurt worse than I was before. Or I could find out, once and for all, that it really is all over.

That certainty is something I'm not sure I can handle.

A strong breeze, unusual for this time of year, slaps my face, and I breathe deeply. "Enough navel gazing," I mutter, channeling my dad. I take the reins and cluck my tongue. "Come on, girl. Let's do this."

Luckily, the mechanics of riding still come naturally for me. After I mount Oakley, it's easy to steer her toward the opposite end of the course. Easy in theory, at least. From the way my heart pounds, you'd think I was doing a heck of a lot more than a slow walk.

Breathing through the anxiety bunching my stomach, I tell myself everything is fine.

"Nothing we haven't done before."

Oakley's ears twitch at my voice and I close my eyes, visualizing success. As I rock back and forth in the saddle, I remember everything I need to do. The steps, the posture... the confidence. I open my eyes, exhale the fear, and glance at the doghouse one last time.

With a cluck of my tongue, I nudge Oakley's flank.

Wind lashes my hair back as we pick up speed. My clucks continue, my spurs nudging us onward, knowing we'll need to go much faster than this at the event. Hooves pound the earth beneath me as the first barrel approaches, so much slower than I ever remember, but that doesn't seem to matter, because suddenly and without warning... it's all too much.

My heart racing impossibly fast.

My chest squeezing with each pulse.

I can't. Catch. My breath.

Fear coats my skin and I tremble as I push my heels out and forward. Self-loathing churns my stomach as I slide myself back in the saddle. My eyes slam shut and I pull on the reins, somehow finding enough air to force out one pathetic word. "*Whoa.*"

Silence.

The absence of wind.

Only me, my hammering heart, and Oakley.

And the answer to, "What if?"

Fighting back tears, I soak in the moment of defeat. Saturate myself with it. In case I need further proof, I open my eyes and see where we slid to a stop, right in front of the first barrel. A humorless laugh breaks free, along with a blasted tear. We never made it beyond a slow freaking lope. If that doesn't count as a failure, I don't know what does.

"Peyton!"

I curse at Cade's frantic voice, the rhythmic sound of his close, thumping footsteps telling me that my covert ride wasn't nearly as secret as I'd hoped. Quickly, I swipe the telltale evidence of my tears and put on my game face mere moments before he rounds the fence in front of me.

"Are you all right?" His eyes are wide behind his black frames. I hate that I scared him. Even more that I disappointed him. We both know that I'm far from all right, but I answer the only way my pride will allow. I roll back my shoulders, cluck softly, and nudge Oakley forward, around the first barrel.

Cade watches, leaning his arms against the fence post as Annie and I walk—not trot, not lope, and certainly not gallop—around the second and then the third and then straight out of the ring. It's not until we are headed back to the barn that I look back and meet his worried gaze.

"It's time to go to the game."

JUSTIN
FAIRFIELD ACADEMY LOCKER ROOM 2:00 P.M.

"Gentlemen, we're almost there."

Coach Williams stands before us like the god of baseball that he is, a clipboard in one hand and pride in his eyes. The air feels charged, electric. Like the calm before the storm. The storm, of course, being us kicking Newfield Prep's ass.

"Today is just one more step to glory," he says, looking around the room. "After today, we move on to the Semi-finals, and then, hopefully, the Regional Championship. For you seniors, that'll be the curtain call for your time on this team. Some of you will go on to play college ball. Others, potentially drafted." He swings his gaze to me and I freeze. "I for one am eager as hell to say I coached you when."

A moment of understanding passes between us. This man has been more of a father to me than my own. It's his opinion I value, his respect I crave. The thought of losing that in a few short weeks scares the hell out of me, and, perhaps sensing that, Coach holds my stare just a moment more before nodding and glancing away.

"Until then, though, *this* is your team. This is your family."

I make eye contact with Carlos, Drew, and Brandon.

"The stands out there are already packed. Parents and girlfriends, your classmates, they're all here waiting to cheer for you. Scouts are here, too, ready to see what you've got. You should be proud. You've *earned* this respect and attention!"

It's impossible to explain to someone who's never played a team sport. For someone who's never put their faith and trust in their brothers, knowing they'll have your back. To someone like that, this kind of speech can seem lame. But as I look at my teammates, the determination that blazes hot with every word our coach speaks, I know the truth. Moments like these are powerful.

Coach lifts his chin and smiles. "You boys remember that when you take the field and show those suckers why the Hoakies own the diamond!"

Boom. The entire team rushes to stand, lifting our voices as one in a raucous roar. If we didn't want it before, we do now. We're taking this win. We're taking it for us, for our school, and for Coach, who deserves it a hell of a lot more than we do. He brought us here and it's him we surround now, chanting and talking shit, acting pumped. Hell, it's not acting. We *are* fucking pumped.

The room swells with energy, and the strangest feeling floods my chest. It's not painful, not really, but it's intense. I drop my head, fighting to hold everything in. The emotion, the reaction. The *words.*

My head is still down when Carlos finds me on the bench near my locker. "You nervous, man?"

I raise my eyes and huff a laugh. "Do I look nervous?"

His left eyebrow cranes, his right one drops, and I follow his pointed gaze to my bouncing leg. He lets it slide. "So the whole family showed today," he says. "Got Gabi sitting with them, too."

He crosses himself and points to the sky, eyes closed in petition, and I give him the laugh I know he wants. It rings false and Carlos drops the constant grin.

"Guess the old man's traveling again, huh?"

"Guess so."

I don't know why I'm surprised. I lift my shoulder in a half-hearted shrug as someone somewhere turns on our game day tradition: Outkast's "Hey Ya!"

Why this song is our anthem, I have no idea. If I had to guess, I'd blame the fool sitting next to me. But right now, I couldn't be more grateful for the distraction. Superstitions exist for a reason, and there's not a player on this team who'll dare hit the field before shaking it like a damn Polaroid picture.

I exhale confusion and anxiety, breathe in eagerness and a sense of belonging. Carlos jumps to his feet, sticks out his ass, and begins popping it in the air like Beyoncé. Our first baseman beats on the lockers as Brandon and Drew leap on top of the benches. Everyone starts outdoing each other in how horrifically bad they can dance—and no doubt, it's damn awful.

The familiar tune works its magic and I bop my head, preparing for what is to come. Only one of us has any rhythm at all, and wouldn't you know, he's on a mission to cheer me up. Carlos grabs a discarded shoe as his microphone, rolls his hips in a circle, then bats his eyelashes like a chick before blowing me a kiss. I throw my head back in a laugh.

"'You think you've got it. Oh, you think you've got it.'"

My best friend is certifiable. Not a shrink in town will tell you any differently, but he's my boy, and other than my girl, he's probably the only one to ever get me to genuinely smile. But when he breaks into the Carlton, and does a piss poor impersonation, I decide it's time I step in.

He can never do it like me.

By the time we're all shaking our Polaroids, I'm over the shit with my dad. Screw him. I didn't need him to show up anyway. To Mitch Carter, fatherhood is paying bills and shoving training suggestions under the door. I don't need those either. I've already got my partial ride to A&M, and if the season plays out, there's a decent chance a pro team will draft me. Yeah, the salary will suck, but the signing bonus will be sweet, and my trust fund from my grandparents kicks in the day I graduate.

College or pro... it doesn't matter. I'm out of here the second I get my diploma. I'm leaving home and I'm not taking another cent of my father's money. He thinks love is a fat bank account, well he can take his overstuffed checkbook and shove it.

The playful music fades to silence and I turn with the team, breathing hard, as we look to our captain. The smile on Brandon's face is cocky as he lifts his hands and yells, "Who's ready to kick some ass?"

Adrenaline surges through my blood stream as I scream with the chorus. This is ours to lose. Today, I'm not holding anything back. I'm leaving it all out on the ball field. Because those scouts out there watching in the stands, waiting for a good show?

They're my ticket to giving my old man the big F-U.

***

The look in Carlos's eye when he enters the dugout clearly says, *don't start*. After three swings and a miss, it's safe to say the boy is off his game. Grumbling, he tosses his gloves and helmet in the cubby, slides his cap back on his head, and falls on the bench beside me.

Not taking my eyes off the field, I tell him quietly, "It'll come."

The tension is getting to everyone. It's another Texas scorcher and the stands are packed with anxious fans sweating it out on broiling metal seats. It's the bottom of the fourth and we're two runs ahead, not nearly the sort of margin our team is used to. But we'll find our rhythm. Of that I have no doubt. Losing today isn't an option.

Knowing that Carlos needs to work it out on his own, I sit next to him without saying a word, drinking tepid Gatorade. A low buzz behind us signals an incoming text and it doesn't take a genius to guess who it's for. Reaching back with a sigh, Carlos grabs his phone and unlocks it, then grins like the whipped dope that he is.

I lean over to get a look at the screen. It's a picture of Gabi blowing him a kiss. No message, no words of wisdom. Just her showing her unique brand of unconditional love. I had that once.

Nudging his arm, I say, "I know I talk a lot of shit, busting your balls and all, but that girl's good for you."

Carlos nods and types out a quick reply. "I know it."

As my best friend finds comfort with his woman, I stretch my arms out, casually glancing out into the stands. Far left, third row, right next to the dugout, to be exact. Otherwise known as Sunshine's seat.

Ever since freshman year, she's sat in the same exact spot. She never misses a chance to support her dad. Once there was a time she came to support *me*. With her attention focused on Drew out at bat, I push to my feet, preparing for my turn, and simply watch her.

I love everything about this sport. You can't fake it in baseball. It's pure and honest and demands excellence. Another reason why I love playing it, at least at Fairfield Academy, is the uninterrupted excuse to watch the girl who owns my heart. Every time I grab my helmet and gloves from the cubby at the end of the dugout, I get to look at her. Every once in a while, I even catch her looking back. *That* makes my whole damn day.

Now, as I tug on my gloves, I know she feels me staring. A slow flush rises on her peaches and cream skin, and her legs suddenly move with a restless twitch. I smile. Despite what she says, her body can't hide how much I affect her. How much she still wants me. It gives me hope for an entire thirty seconds—until I spy Cade shuffling down the bleachers.

I glance away before he sits. I can't watch him take her hand or make her smile. Not when that hand belongs in mine, and those smiles are meant for me. Instead, I glance at the coin in my hand, remember a different day, and use that memory to center me for my turn.

I take a deep breath, feel the calming weight of Peyton's coin in my palm, and place it in my sock before heading out onto the field. I'm ready.

SATURDAY, FEBRUARY 12TH

16 Weeks until Disaster

♥ Freshman Year

PEYTON

FAIRFIELD ACADEMY BASEBALL FIELD 3:12 P.M.

My confidence lasted as far as the parking lot.

The diamond behind the school was most definitely Justin's turf. He had his areas in the school, I had mine, and rarely did the two meet. Sure, I sat in the bleachers, watching practices and games, but the two of us didn't talk. Heck, we barely made eye contact. Up until now, our friendship had been kept completely separate from our everyday lives, away from prying eyes, and if things had continued as they were before, it probably would've stayed that way indefinitely. But ever since the day Justin discovered who my father was, things had been awkward. Stilted. Strained. I didn't like it.

My plan for today involved stepping up my new life philosophy, doing what scared me, with the total acknowledgement that I'd likely get burned. If Justin was that uncomfortable hanging out with me because of my dad, I wouldn't force him to be my friend. And if being seen with the coach's daughter/nerdy new chick embarrassed him around his friends, well, I could take a hint. But he was worth at least a fight.

"Hey, Carter, you got a sec?"

He was standing alone a few yards away from the dugout, beyond the short fence, shaking his legs out before the game. I figured this conversation was best done minus an audience.

Justin glanced over and his entire demeanor changed. "Peyton." His eyes brightened with his smile... though I didn't miss the cursory glance he gave toward the dugout. "What are you doing here?"

Suddenly, the speech I'd rehearsed for close to a week flittered out of my mind. I *knew* I should've written it down.

"Ah, I wanted to wish you luck," I told him, bouncing up on my toes. "Or, you know, if you're one of those superstitious types, break a leg!"

Gah. I winced as my exuberant voice carried. Could I be any more of a freak?

Justin wrapped his hand around the back of his neck and glanced at the ground. *Riiight.* That was my cue. "Anyway, I'll let you get back to stretching then. I'll be cheering for you."

Mortified, I turned around and squeezed my eyes shut. Loneliness and sadness flooded my chest. Just when I thought I'd made a real connection at this school, a friend... with possible benefits... I realize how alone I really am. And I'd actually let myself think Justin Carter could like me.

A firm hand on my elbow stopped me. "Wait."

Justin tugged my arm, gently guiding me back around, and bent at the knee to look at my face. "You're not smiling," he murmured with a slight frown. "What's wrong?"

I hesitated, considered my options. On one hand, I could deny, deny, deny and carry on with the way things were, no doubt looking back later and wondering what would have happened had I been brave enough to try. Or, I could live my new motto, listen to my heart and follow its lead, and see where the journey takes me.

Here goes nothing...

"Listen, Jutsin." I released a breath and straightened to my imposing five-foot-four frame. "I know I'm not your normal type. I'm not cool or popular or beautiful." His frown deepened at that and I rolled my eyes. "I have no delusions here, okay? I'm not a Diamond Doll or mindless groupie pretending I don't know how to throw a frigging ball. That's not me."

"I never said—"

My finger jumped across his lips, silencing him. I think I surprised us both. "It's just..." I took a calming breath and admitted, "I like you. A lot. I guess I just thought you should know that."

Bafflement. I'm pretty sure that was the only word to describe Justin's reaction as emotion flooded his eyes and a puff of warm air escaped his lips. I jerked my finger back as if he'd burned it.

Justin shook his head. "But... *why?*"

I squinted my eyes. Was he joking?

"I'm serious, Sunshine. I don't get it. What could someone like you possibly see in a guy like me?"

Someone like me. Those three words repeated in my brain, wounding me with their simplicity. But the crazy thing was, the longer I studied him, reading nothing but total sincerity in his eyes along with an almost boyish vulnerability, I realized this wasn't some player move or some strange attempt to feed his ego.

Justin Carter actually wanted to know how *I* could swoon over *him*.

"Um, well, your passion, for one," I said. "Every time you step out onto that field, you kill it. You refuse to settle for less than your personal best, and everyone around you follows your lead."

His nostrils flared with an inhale and his hungry gaze clung to mine. Could this beautiful boy seriously not know how special he was? A zing of confidence shot through me at the knowledge that this was something I could do for him, something no one else had. Smiling, emboldened, I pressed my chest against the fence.

"I also like the way you make people laugh," I told him with a smile. "I think your obsession with Larry Dierker is freaking adorable. You get all soft and gooey when you talk about your brother, and I love that your ears turn bright red when I ask about your writing."

Justin's lips twitched, the tips of his ears flashing a vivid crimson, and I laughed aloud.

"Yep, sorry to break it to you, Carter, but you're busted. There's so much more to you than the world sees, but my blinders are off. You're not hiding anything from me."

It was weird, admitting all that to the boy I liked. He could totally use it against me, make fun of me, take the heart I'd clearly just attached to my sleeve and smash it. But I trusted him. Even if he did choose to hurt me, I was glad I told him how I felt. He deserved to know.

"Yo, Justin!"

At the loud call, we jerked. Drew Jamison stood a few feet away, eyeing us both. The game was about to start.

Justin nodded and yelled back, "I'll be right there!" while I reached in my back pocket and grasped the present I'd brought for him. When he looked back at me, I grinned.

"Hold out your hand." At the expression on his face, I rolled my eyes. "Just do it." Cautiously, as if I was going to put out a cobra or something, he uncurled his fingers and lifted his palm. I dropped a small silver coin in the center. "For luck."

Wonder warred with confusion in his gorgeous brown eyes and my heart melted.

"On this side there's a horseshoe," I said, my cheeks warming with a blush. "You know, the universal symbol for luck... and a small reminder of me."

I bit my lip, hoping he didn't think that was too corny—or that it revealed too much.

I flipped the coin over, exposing the other side, and my fingers slid across his rough skin. My breath caught. When I lifted my eyes, I found him watching me with so much intensity, so much *heat*, that an actual shiver rolled through me. Just like in my favorite books.

Huh. So that was what smoldering looked like. Good to know.

I swallowed hard and noticed him do the same, and nothing could hold back my giddy smile. Justin glanced down and laughed. "Kick some ass!" he read, skimming his fingernail over my initials.

"I figured..." I cleared my throat. "I thought you could hide it in your sock or something," I said, unable to tell if he liked the gift or not. He just kept staring at it. "If it's dumb, you don't have to—"

"No."

He'd said it so quietly I almost wasn't sure he'd spoken at all. But then he closed his hand around the coin and raised his head. Time ceased to exist as Justin's eyes trailed across my face. I held my breath waiting and a sweet smile crossed his face.

"Damn." He shook his head softly. "You've done it now."

"What?" I asked, hoping whatever it was that it was a good thing. "What did I do?"

Justin merely shook his head again and smiled. "Wait for me after the game." Shifting his gaze to the old concession stand, he took a step back and said, "Over there, okay?"

When I nodded, excitement lodging in my throat, making it impossible to speak, he winked and then took off to join his teammates. As I watched his cute butt in those uniform pants run across the field, a giddy grin found my lips.

JUSTIN

FAIRFIELD ACADEMY BASEBALL FIELD 5:12 P.M.

The coin in my sock felt weighted. It was as if every doubt, every reason I shouldn't do what I was about to do clung to its polished surface, bearing down on my ankle and preventing me from moving forward.

If the guys had known what I was planning, they'd crucify me. We'd just made the "Casual/Commitment" list, all agreed on what side Peyton landed, and here I was ignoring the truth. Or acknowledging it and doing it anyway.

Sunshine could get hurt. Truthfully, this was the only consequence that gave me any pause. Before anything happened, I'd have to make it clear who I was, exactly what I could offer her, but if after that, Peyton wanted me anyway, I was hers. I was done fighting it.

Coach would burst a freaking blood vessel. No dad wanted to open the door to their daughter's guy and see my face on the other side, especially not him. He knew exactly what we were like, had heard it with his own ears in the locker room. Besides that, I'd seen the way he watched her from the dugout. I saw the fear that still glazed his eyes. She was his baby, his princess, and I was the evil ass who'd inevitably break her heart.

Any *one* of those reasons should've had me headed back to the locker room, celebrating the day's victory with my teammates. Forgetting the way Peyton's eyes lit up when I asked her to meet me after the game. Added together, well, I was a damn fool for pursuing her. But, call me a dumbass or a selfish prick, I *needed* this girl in my life. Her joy, her optimism. Her warm smile and honeyed laugh.

I rounded the corner, and Peyton's eager eyes met mine.

And maybe, just maybe, she needed me, too.

"Hey."

Her voice was soft and shaky as it floated on the stiff wind. Along with her bouncing foot, it was obvious she was nervous. What was crazy was that for the first time in my life, I was, too.

"Hey," I replied. I didn't stop walking when I reached her, though. I took her hand and pulled her back behind the painted green brick building, away from any spying, gossiping eyes. Concessions stopped being served during the fifth inning, so the two of us were alone... well except for the oppressive smell of buttery popcorn and chili dogs. But it was better safe than sorry.

The second we cleared the corner, I dropped Peyton's hand. I still got off on the feel of her smooth, satiny skin against mine, but there was no way I'd get through this if I continued to hold her. She was too tempting. I took a step back, closer toward the chain-link fence, and said, "You know this is a bad idea, right?"

She craned an eyebrow. "What, talking?" she asked with a sarcastic smirk. "Sure, I mean, I've heard open communication can totally be hazardous to your health, but somehow, I think we'll survive."

I huffed a laugh as I laced my fingers behind my neck. Her sass was adorable. Almost as cute as her innocence.

But thoughts like *that* were what got me in this mess to begin with.

"Listen, Peyton, you've gotta know I suck at relationships." Too wound up to stay still, I started down the short path behind the building. "Even I've heard the rumors about me, and believe me, they exist for a reason. I'm no good at that touchy-feely crap girls like. I don't do emotions. They're messy and annoying and I don't have time for that shit."

I made it to one end of the path and began retracing my steps. "You deserve to be with a guy who'll bring you flowers and take you out. Who'll show you off in front of his friends and introduce you to his parents." I stopped in front of her but had to look away as I admitted, "That'll never be me."

Owning the truth hurt, but it had to be said. She *did* deserve better than me, and if telling her that helped Peyton to realize it, then all the better. Not better for me, obviously. I still wanted her. But it would be a hell of a lot better for her.

I should've known, though, that she wouldn't do what I expected. She hadn't since the day I met her, so why start now? Instead of walking away like she probably should've done, what most girls in her place *would've* done, Peyton rolled her shoulders back, shook her head, and said, "I don't care. I don't need any of that."

"Yes," I told her. "You do."

She opened her mouth to argue, again, and I tapped a finger against her lips. "And I wish that I could be the guy who gave it to you. But I'm not. You saw my house. It's cold, it's heartless, and it's my life." I laughed a humorless laugh, and shrugged like it didn't bother me. "I'm Mitch Carter's son. I don't know the first thing about healthy relationships."

Peyton rolled her eyes. "That's bullshit."

The crude word in her sweet voice got my attention. "Excuse me?"

She stepped toward me and lifted a hand as if to touch the side of my face, then dropped it somewhere between us. I couldn't tell if I was grateful or disappointed.

"You forget, Justin, I saw your brother's picture," she said. "I saw the look in your eyes when you told me about him. I'm not saying your home life isn't strained, or your parents aren't sucky, egotistical jerkoffs. From what I've gathered, they wouldn't know the meaning of unconditional love if it hit them square in the face. But your brother? Chase? He's amazing." Her eyes softened as she took another step closer. "And it's clear that boy loves you like crazy."

My ribs squeezed. She was right, actually. Despite my many fuckups, Chase was like my mini-me. We were only half-brothers—a fact his mother reminded me of daily—but that never seemed to matter. Chase followed me around, dressed to match, and begged me to play trucks with him every chance he got. At night, whenever he threw his short arms around my neck and told me he loved me, I vowed to one day become a man he could be proud of.

Up until this year, he'd been the one good spot in my life. The one person who made me feel like I belonged.

"Dad says you're an incredible leader and the most skillful player he's seen in years," she continued. "In fact, Mama and I are getting pretty sick of him bragging about your 'natural talent' at dinner."

She pulled a face as she made air quotes, then smiled to show she was teasing. I couldn't help but grin. Our eyes held for a moment before she took the final step forward, erasing the distance between us.

"And you've got me," she whispered. "I care about you, Justin. More than you know."

I swallowed thickly. She was missing the point. "But that's just it. If this goes south," I motioned between the two of us, "and we both know I'll find some way to ruin it, then I'm out. I lose you, and I lose your dad's respect. I can't do that, Peyton. I just... can't."

In that moment, I loathed myself. The guy I'd become. A spineless wimp grasping at a grown man's approval. But I needed it. God, I needed it like air. Dan Williams wasn't only the best high school coach in the state, he was a man of integrity. A true family man who cared about other people.

Who saw something in *me*. That meant everything.

"Then we won't tell anyone." Peyton squeezed my shoulder and I raised my head to look at her. "I mean it. If that's what's keeping us apart, if telling people bothers you that much, then we'll keep it a secret. It's no one's business but ours anyway."

The time to keep my hands to myself was over. Reaching out, I grasped her hips and said, "You don't mean that. You can't. This isn't middle school, Peyton. People don't have secret boyfriends and girlfriends. You deserve—"

"Jesus! Will you stop telling me what I want and deserve?"

Frustration widened her eyes, sparking them with fire. "I don't want to be with you so I can write our names together on a bathroom stall, Justin! I don't care about popularity or rubbing it in girls' faces. I want to be with you because you make me laugh. Because you're confident and smart and you actually see me." When she heaved a sigh, warm breath fanned across my lips. "Because when I'm with you, I remember how it feels to be *alive*."

Out of everything she could've said, that did it.

Peyton Williams would be the end of me. I felt the truth of it in my bones. But there was no more stopping it or sense in denying it—I was done for. I'd sooner cut off my arm than refuse this beautiful girl the chance to feel alive, not after what she'd been through. And hell, knowing I was the one who made her feel that way made me feel unstoppable.

I'd said my piece, done what I said I would. I'd given her an easy out. Now it was time to take what was mine. "Good," I said, tucking a strawberry strand of hair behind her ear. Honesty and vulnerability stared back at me, and God, she smelled incredible. "I like being the guy who makes you feel that way."

Peyton's mouth fell open, eyebrows furrowed, and I almost laughed. Yeah, I was giving myself whiplash, too. Time for a new plan. I was more of an action guy, anyway.

Dragging my fingertips across the soft cotton of her shirt, I found the hollow of her spine and tugged her against me, swallowing her small gasp of surprise. When I began lowering my mouth, she stuttered, "I... I'm confused."

I touched my forehead against hers. "And I'm yours." Her hands left my shoulders and skimmed hesitantly over my back. "I mean it, Sunshine. You deserve better, but if you still want me even after knowing what a disaster I am, then I'm all in. I'm too selfish to walk away." I leaned back. "But don't say I didn't warn you."

The smile began in her eyes. Blue-gray glowed with an inner light, then the smooth skin around them crinkled. When I grinned in return, letting her know I was for real, that this was for real, the full force of it broke through. It was like watching a sunrise.

Peyton's grip around me tightened, her chest became flush with mine, and I chuckled when her cheeks turned light pink.

"Consider me warned," she replied. Her smile was playful and sexy without trying to be, just like her, and I released an exhale of relief. Denying myself what I wanted sucked. No wonder I never did it.

I ducked my chin again, eager to taste the lips I'd been dreaming about for weeks...

"Ah!"

...and ended up grazing cheekbone.

Peyton flinched, *not* the reaction I was going for, and I loosened my hold on her hips.

"Uh, okay." Frowning, I fought the impulse to laugh it off or make a joke. Instead, I said, "I'm sorry. Did I... read this wrong?"

This hadn't happened before. Usually, I was the one turning girls away, not the other way around. She shook her head vigorously and the pink of her cheeks flushed a bright red.

"No! No, no, no." Peyton squeezed her eyes shut and laughed at herself, a strained sound that turned itself into a snort. Groaning, she dropped her head to my shoulder. "This is *all* me."

She mock-sobbed, a strange reaction I found cute as hell, and I raised an eyebrow. "I'm just gonna say straight out that I have absolutely no idea what's happening here." I dipped my fingers beneath her hair and kneaded the muscles that had turned to stone. "But hey, you're calling the shots here, all right? We don't have to do anything you don't want to do. You hear me?"

"But I *do* want to," she insisted, or rather, I thought she insisted. Peyton's voice was muffled against my shoulder, so I nudged her chin up with my thumbs. She let out a sigh. "It's just that... well, it's the *first time* I've ever wanted to."

Her eyes widened, imploring me to read between the lines, but the pink swipe of her tongue distracted me. Sue me, I'm a dude. But then, a few seconds longer than it should have, her words sank in, and I jerked back like I'd been electrocuted. "*Oh*."

Not my smartest move.

Peyton winced and her head fell back against my chest, hiding her face, and if I could've kicked my own ass in that moment, I would have.

"Hey, listen." Gently lifting her chin again, I bent my knees so I could look into her eyes. "I'm glad you haven't done this before." She scoffed at this, and my smile grew smug. "No, I'm serious. I'm damn proud to be your first. You think I don't love knowing I beat out all the other dudes with their heads up their asses?"

"Ha, yeah, cause there was a real line forming, let me tell you." Peyton rolled her eyes. She really had no clue how amazing she was.

"Maybe you didn't notice," I said, sliding my thumb over

her lips. "But guys were watching. Trust me. How could anyone see this mouth and not go insane wanting a taste?"

Evidently, this was better. I was bound to say the right thing eventually.

Peyton's lashes lowered as a soft smile curved beneath the rough pad of my thumb. Something heavy moved inside my chest.

"Well, it's hard to be kissed when you're in and out of hospitals for a year," she said, latching onto my wrists. "Before that, there were guys in my homeschool co-op, and I was around a bunch at rodeo events, but there's never been anyone I was really interested in."

"Until me," I clarified because I was an arrogant ass. Also because I wanted her to smile again. She didn't disappoint.

A musical laugh sprang free, her happy smile trailing behind, and I was in heaven. "Until you," she agreed. She squinted one eye and added, "Though you should know, I'm probably gonna be really, really bad at it."

The expression on her face said she honestly believed it, and I couldn't wait to prove her wrong. I leaned close to her ear and whispered across her skin, "That's impossible."

Peyton's breath caught in a gasp, and I angled back to see her face.

That's when the moment changed.

Sounds of the emptying baseball field fell away. The cool air around us kindled. The soft smile on her face faded as she looked into my eyes, shifting her gaze between them to see what I'd do next. Part of me wondered the same thing.

I'd kissed dozens of girls before. Some I wanted, others purely because I was bored. But I'd never felt anything like this. Anticipation. Want. Fear. Unlike any other kiss I'd ever shared, this one needed to be epic. Girls remembered their first kiss for the rest of their lives, and I had to leave Peyton with something good to cling to later... when I inevitably screwed everything up.

Gauging her reaction, I slowly lowered my head and watched her soft lips part. Adrenaline surged through my veins at the swipe of her tongue. She nodded once, silently giving me permission, then closed her eyes.

Inhaling the scent of sunflowers, I kissed her.

Soft and sweet. Those two words defined this girl. She tasted like sugar and her sigh was addictive as I brushed her mouth with mine. Again and again. I couldn't get enough. Her hands clenched my wrists, tugging me closer. I could've lived in that moment forever.

My restless hands memorized the curve of Peyton's spine, the dip of her waist. Hers slid down my arms and around my back, fisting my shirt before slipping underneath. A jolt of electricity ran over my skin. When her nails raked down my spine, I jerked and groaned into her mouth. She was a fast learner.

I kissed the corners of her triumphant smile, licked the bow of her top lip, and nipped at the bottom one. She sighed again and sank in my arms, matching me kiss for kiss, playful tug for playful tug. And still, I needed more. I'd probably always need more.

Tilting my head for better access, I grazed her cheeks with my fingertips. Traced the seam of her mouth with my tongue, silently asking for what I wanted. Hoping like hell she'd open up. Her answer was one shy flick. The shiver reached my toes.

No girl had gotten to me like this. Burrowed under my skin, held my interest, or had me thinking about tomorrow. Wishing I could be that guy. I lost myself in the strawberry taste of Peyton's mouth, the sweet sounds in her throat, and I didn't fully emerge until hours later. When I did, it was with one thought circling my brain:

How long until I mess this up?

SATURDAY, MAY 24TH

2 Weeks until Graduation

♥ Senior Year

PEYTON

FAIRFIELD ACADEMY BASEBALL FIELD 3:30 P.M.

"It drives me insane the way he stares at you." Cade's voice is low, meant for my ears only, but that doesn't hide the edge of possession in his tone. And there's no need to ask who he is. "Shouldn't he be concerned with, oh, I don't know, the game he's in the middle of?"

"We're ahead by two runs," I say, watching Drew's follow through and pretending not to feel Justin's gaze on my cheek. "Plus, Justin's ranked 25 in ESPN's top 100 high school players. He could hit off this guy in his sleep."

Sometimes, I seriously need to think before I speak.

What Cade wants to hear right now is, "God, you're right, he's so annoying." Or, "Who cares? Let him look. It's not like he's got a shot with me anyway." Or even, "Justin could stare at me all day long and it wouldn't touch us at all. We're solid."

What my current boyfriend definitely does *not* want to hear is a frigging fangirl report on my ex's stats. Normally, I'm much more accommodating. Today, my brain's just muddled.

Can you blame me? Between my epic fail at the ranch, the pressure on Dad for his team to win, the constant memories of Justin, the tension with Cade (and not the romantic, sexy kind, either), finals, graduation, and college on the horizon—it's amazing I'm not checking myself into the looney bin.

A muscle in Cade's jaw flinches. "You were able to spit that out pretty quickly."

I lift a shoulder and shrug but hold my tongue before anything else stupid can fall out.

The truth is, I've always been aware of Justin. It's never stopped. I know about his game, I see him in the cafeteria, and I sense when he's near me in the hall. Other than Cade, he's the only boy I've ever dated, so I always just assumed this behavior was normal. Sure, things are different with Cade—there's no itch under my skin, or desire to be around him constantly—but Justin was my first love. It made sense that my body reacted differently with him.

Only, why *don't* I feel that way with Cade? And why do I still feel it with Justin? One boy hurt me beyond repair, the other stitched me back up. Cade and I have been together for almost a year. There should be no confusion here. My heart shouldn't be so torn.

I steal another glance at the dugout and find Justin watching me again.

The sick pleasure I get from it warms my toes.

The problem is *this* Justin is so different from the boy I once knew. Well, in some ways he's different... in other ways, the best ways, he's exactly the same. He's still charming and easy to talk to. Crazy determined and driven. From the little I've seen and heard over the last few weeks, he's also still surprisingly introspective and protective. But there's a confidence there that wasn't before. Justin as a freshman was cocky and arrogant for sure, but this new self-confidence is quieter. Deeper. It's like he knows what he wants now and isn't trying to hide it.

A few feet away, his gaze sharpens as if he can read my thoughts.

What he wants now is me.

"Thank God this project's almost over," Cade mutters, and I blink and look away, breaking eye contact with Justin. "The sooner we get that loser away from you, the better."

My tongue is going to be sore tomorrow from all the biting. "Uh huh."

Usually, Cade is the least jealous guy I know. He doesn't act like a caveman or like those possessive jerks I read about in some of my books. He's actually really chill. It's just that Justin Carter has always been his kryptonite. To this, I can relate.

A pop fly is caught for the second out and Justin heads to the plate. I loop my arm through Cade's, feeling guilty for making him insecure, and lay my head on his shoulder.

A few minutes pass, enough for Justin to hit a double, and I think the subject is dropped. But then Cade says, "The whole thing is stupid anyway. If anything, I should be the one doing this project with you, not him. I'm the one you're gonna be with in the end."

Cade has our whole future planned. After we're married, we'll continue working both ranches, my family's and his, until the day we take over and merge the two together. Most of the horses will then relocate to his land, along with the future riding school, while my family's land will host all the birthday parties, scout events, and, of course, the dog boarding business.

Where exactly running my own veterinary practice fits in the middle of all that, I'm not really sure, but I'm sure we'll figure it out. This is Cade, after all. He's a problem solver.

"What sort of things do the two of you talk about anyway?"

I tear my gaze away from the field. "Huh?"

Cade gives me a patient smile, the one that drives me just the tiniest bit batty, and says, "For the project. You said it's mostly answering a bunch of questions and writing the paper. What sort of things do they want to know?"

Hmm. This sounds like the beginning of a slippery slope if I've heard of one. Warning signs practically blind me with their flashes. But answering does seem like the better of two evils, the other option being to say nothing or change the subject, and let Cade imagine the worst. That would not end well at all. So, I give him an example.

"Okay, here's one of the questions we went over in class yesterday." I turn slightly to face him on the bleachers. "If we only had $1,000 and three days for a honeymoon, where would we go, and what would we do?"

Cade makes a scoffing sound in his throat and I withhold a sigh. "It's about learning how to live on a budget and compromise," I explain, wishing we'd never started this to begin with. "You said you wanted to know."

"Yeah, well what's he know about living on a budget anyway?" He motions to Justin who is taking the field with the team and my hackles rise. Cade's family is loaded too, almost as much as the Carters, so his attitude is completely ridiculous. But I say nothing.

"Do you want to answer the question or not?"

Cade exhales, shaking off whatever he'd been thinking, and sits up straight. "Three-day honeymoon and only a grand, huh?"

I nod in confirmation, more than slightly annoyed, but also extremely curious to hear his answer.

"Easy," he says. "Stay home."

He shrugs as if this is the most obvious choice, and my mouth parts in confusion. "We'd throw most of it towards your student loans," he explains. "It wouldn't make a huge dent or anything, but every little bit helps, right? Besides, we don't need a big, fancy vacation. We've got each other. If anything, maybe we'd take a couple hundred and go down to Galveston, invite Faith and whoever she's stringing along at the time, and make a party out of it."

Right. A party with my bestie at the beach. Because nothing spells romance like a group date and smart financial planning.

I school my expression as best I can because, I mean, I get it. Thanks to those medical bills, it's pretty much a given that my college experience will be funded by the good old folks at Sallie Mae. But must Cade always be so stinking practical?

Unfortunately, my acting job apparently sucks because he catches my reaction and says, "All right then, what did Mr. Baseball suggest?"

Something a lot closer to my answer. "Well, he suggested a small weekend getaway to the mountains," I say, trying to ignore the couple to our left hanging on our every word. "Rent a cabin, hike a few trails, sit by the fire, that sort of thing."

Actually, Justin's exact words were that money didn't equal happiness, but if ever there was a time to be frivolous, a wedding would be it. Then he spun his romantic version of a honeymoon which seemed to be plucked right out of my own head. It was almost eerie.

Justin didn't know about my cousin's recent vacation to Tennessee. He didn't see the pictures of the big roaring fireplace, the cute little chalet, or the gorgeous waterfalls nearby. He didn't hear me say that I'd love to go there some day, too. But Cade did.

"Of course he said that." He huffs with laugher and removes his glasses, closing his eyes as he squeezes the bridge of his nose. "Peyton, why can't you see—?"

If there is an end to that question, I don't hear it.

Along with most of the crowd, my attention turns to the ball field. Specifically, to the runner rounding third and sprinting for home.

I've never believed in female intuition. To me, sixth sense is merely a weird Bruce Willis movie. But as I watch the runner drop his head and charge ahead like some sort of enraged bull, every hair on my body stands on end. Justin moves into position on homeplate, prepared to catch the ball and tag him out, and a scream builds from somewhere deep within my belly.

The *smack* of the hit as they collide. The roar from the crowd as we surge to our feet. The cry that rips from my throat. It feels like it takes an eternity.

In reality, it all happens way too fast.

WEDNESDAY, MAY 28TH

1 Week until Graduation

♥ Senior Year

PEYTON

SWEET SERENITY RANCH 4:22 P.M.

Justin swings the driver's side door closed with his right hand, his left one hanging limply from a sling. It's been several days since the accident, and I've seen him at school, but I can't stop staring at his arm. Remembering my mad dash to the field when he didn't immediately get up. The confusion on Dad's face when he gently pulled me away, assuring me that Justin would be fine. The hurt simmering in Cade's eyes.

"Looking good," I tease, wanting to break the tension. Only, it works against me when that slow, confident smirk forms and I flush to my toes. "How ya feeling?"

He lets out a sigh. "Useless." Resting his hip against the hood of his Jeep, he gazes out at the paddock. "Your dad's ban from practice is slowly driving me insane, Sunshine. I can't even think about them playing the semi-finals without me."

I know how hard this is for him. Justin lives and breathes baseball. He's a damn good player, and he's a leader on the team. Dad only wants to protect him, keep him safe—a concussion and shoulder sprain are nothing to joke about, and it could've been so much worse. When he finally sat up, dazed and confused as to what happened, and later threw up after staggering off the field, I thought it was.

Waiting to hear how bad the injury was had been terrifying. I know how much the sport means to Justin. If he'd torn a ligament and couldn't play again, it would crush him. In the end, he got lucky. The shoulder was sprained, not dislocated or torn, and the concussion mild. Scouts making their final decisions have already seen Justin play. They know these types of injuries and, more importantly, they understand the need to be smart. Missing one game, even the semi-finals, is nothing compared to his future. We're expected to win anyway, and pushing now could lead to a much greater injury. With adequate rest, combined with cold therapy and eventual light stretching on his shoulder, Justin will be healthy and set to play in next week's Championship when it counts.

Unfortunately, knowing that doesn't make sitting out now any easier.

Walking down the porch steps, I smile and say, "So, what, you decided to come by and drive me crazy instead?"

"I thought we could work on our project," he replies with a smile. A real one this time, not one of his player ones. "We have a few questions left to answer and the next section of our paper to nail down. Besides, I couldn't spend another second in that empty house."

I nod because I get it. I've heard how quiet that huge place gets when no one else is there. Plus, if I'm being honest, I'm going a little stir-crazy, too. Cade is at his own ranch today— he's been giving me some space since the game this weekend. Faith has dance practice and Dad, well, he's at school doing the very thing Justin wishes he was right now. It's only me, Trevor, and Mama here today.

As if my thoughts summoned her, Mama comes flying out of the house, arms out for a hug. Luckily for Justin, she slows before she reaches him.

"Oh, I'm so glad you're all right," she says, eyes misty, hands looking for a place to settle. Like he's made of glass. She finally decides on his face, cupping it between her palms and shaking his chin a little as she says, "I was so worried when they told me what happened, that boy slamming into you like that. I can't imagine. If I'd been there..." She takes a breath and moves her hands to his shoulders. "How do you feel? Does your shoulder hurt? You want some cookies?"

I hide my laugh behind a smile. That's Mama for you. Never lets you get a word in, but never leaves you guessing how much she cares. Cookies are her love language.

As I watch Justin stare back at my mom, pressure builds behind my eyes. Our childhoods were so vastly different. He didn't get chocolate chip cookies when he fell and hurt himself. Didn't have a parent coddle him when he was sick. I wonder if his parents even know he was injured. Or, if they do, if they worried about him at all.

"Thank you, Mrs. Grace," he finally says, though his voice is husky. "Cookies sound amazing."

Mama, the old softie, clamps her lips together as her eyes fill with tears. She nods, pats the side of his face, and gives a close-mouthed, trembling smile. "I'll be right back."

Justin watches her walk away, inhaling deeply through his nose. I both love and hate that his only real moments of parenting seem to come from my family. Did he have anyone filling that role since we broke up?

The screen door closes and he turns back to me.

"Let me go grab my binder," I say cheerily... perhaps a little *too* cheerily.

He nods. "I'll be waiting at the table." He heads toward the large picnic table we have set up near the barn, and I dash inside for my schoolbag, trying desperately to hold onto my previous anger.

Three years is a long time to hold on to hurt. To convince yourself you hate someone, never want to see them again, wish they'd suffer a disgusting ailment. You'd think it would take a lot more than a few conversations over the course of a few weeks to make it all disappear. But that's exactly what's happened, because when I try and dredge up the old feelings of resentment and pain I've clung to over Justin, all that remains are smoldering embers of sadness.

What did Justin mean when he said there were things I didn't know about that day? I knew plenty, witnessed it with my own eyes, and let my imagination fill in the rest. If you'd asked me a month ago, I'd have said I was content never learning specifics. But his words continue to poke me.

Would knowing the full truth really make a difference?

"Got it," I announce when I appear back at the table, slightly out of breath and more confused than ever. I take a seat across from him and follow his gaze to the barrel course.

Justin motions toward it. "How's it going?"

"Ah, well, it's going," I say before exhaling in frustration. "I got out there with Oakley last Saturday actually." His eyes widen with curiosity and pride, and I douse it. "Couldn't even make it past the first barrel."

I open the binder to avoid the way Justin looks at me. Like he sees so much more than just my face or the expression I'm wearing, past my thoughts and into my beliefs. My fears. My truth. Chewing on my bottom lip, I thumb to the latest page of questions Coach gave us, grab a pen from the handy pouch I keep inside, and only then do I lift my gaze.

"It'll come," he says.

"I wish I could be as confident as you," I reply with a small laugh.

"Then I'll be confident enough for the both of us." Justin smiles, another one of those real ones, and my breath catches in my throat. "You said you got hurt before. Do you mind me asking how?"

I hesitate. Justin has always been easy to talk to, and a big part of me wants to share all the details about what happened. I like that he isn't automatically shutting me down, assuming I can't do this. If he knows the truth, maybe the doubt will enter his eyes, too. Just like it does with Faith and Cade.

Another reason, of course, is the circumstances *around* the accident.

Best to keep it simple.

"I pushed too hard too fast," I say, sealing myself off from the pain of that day. Now is not the time to get into it. "Haven't really ridden hard since, though Mama doesn't quite realize that." He lifts an eyebrow in question, and I wince as I admit, "I've sort of lied to them about it. Not to hurt them," I quickly add. "The opposite actually. They were finally stepping back, loosening the reins, and they were so proud of how far I'd come. I couldn't take that away from them. So, I implied that I was practicing more than I was, and avoided their attempts to watch."

Although my eyes are on the table, I can feel Justin watching me. He knows how close I am with my parents. He used to tell me how he wished his were more like mine. Is he judging me for lying to them... half as much as I'm judging myself? I blow out a breath. "Basically, it was one huge game of misdirection, one that only worked because they trust me so much, and now it's about to all blow up in my face. I can't keep putting it off. I'm gonna have to tell them the truth soon because I just don't see a miracle happening before next week."

Justin sets his sling on top of the table and leans toward me. "Let's finish the homework assignment, and then I want to try something."

"Try something?" I repeat, smiling as I match his posture. There's no judgement in his eyes, only determination and understanding. I didn't know how badly I needed that. "Why, that sounds mysterious, Mr. Carter. Whatever do you have planned?"

Yeah, I hear the flirtation in my voice, too. Even as I chastise myself for it—I have a boyfriend, and this one lied and cheated on me—I can't find the energy to regret it, either. It's like a stone has been rolled away, lifted from a place inside my chest. For the first time in a long time, my smile doesn't feel so forced.

Maybe it's because we're practically strangers now. Maybe it's the hint of magic Justin always seemed to hold, his ability to charm the pants off me. Whatever it is, I feel... happy. Selfishly, I want to cling to that feeling for a little bit longer.

Justin's gaze dips to my lips before returning to my eyes. "Do you trust me?"

JUSTIN

SWEET SERENITY RANCH 4:30 P.M.

Peyton freezes and I mentally kick myself.

Why did I ask that? She's finally talking again, looking at me like I'm not the devil incarnate, and I ruin everything with four short words. *Do you trust me?* Seriously? For all Peyton knows, I broke her heart and never bothered to look back. If I were her, I damn well wouldn't trust me.

Smooth, Carter. Real smooth.

Refusing to watch the playful light fade from her eyes, I reach over and slide her FACS binder to my side of the table. My stupid mouth should come with a warning label.

"Yeah." Peyton's voice is soft, hesitant, and I slowly raise my head.

She swallows visibly and nods, eyes tight with emotion. "I think I might."

Just like that, I have hope. More than I've felt in a long time. My chest swells with it, inhaling a deep breath, and chills dance down my arms. The anxiety over my shoulder, about missing a game and possibly watching my future fall apart disappears, and everything in me screams for me to jump, to tell her the truth now before she changes her mind. Before I can, she winces.

"Or at least I want to," she admits, and a shaky laugh escapes her lips. "And that scares me to death."

I didn't think it was possible to hate myself more than I already do, but there you go.

Three years ago, doing what scared her used to be Peyton's thing. Diving into it, seeking it out, not letting fear win. It was one of the things I admired most about her. More than her not riding, this shows how much she's changed. How much I've missed. How badly I hurt her.

The thing is, though, she's still a fighter. Courage still exudes from her pores. I see it more and more every day, and I'll make it my mission to help *her* see it, too. But not now. Right now, the important thing is to keep her talking.

Looking at the page in front of me, I read, "Both sets of in-laws want you to come home for Thanksgiving dinner." Peyton gives me a tight-lipped, grateful smile, and I return it with a wink. "How can you avoid hurt feelings and resolve the issue?"

"I don't know," she says with a shrug. "Two turkeys sounds like a plan to me."

"Ah, but you forget these are *our* in-laws," I say, craning an eyebrow. "My family doesn't do holidays, remember? They're never home. Dad travels and Annabeth takes Chase to her parents. Thanksgiving for me is whatever Rosalyn leaves wrapped up in the fridge. Or whatever Carlos's abuela whips up after taking pity on me." I hide the embarrassment of that truth behind a smile. "So I guess one turkey it is."

Sadness washes over Peyton's features. She leans over, takes my hand, and says, "You know you've always got a seat at our table."

I roll my eyes, trying to distance myself from the pity in hers. She tightens her grip.

"I'm serious. Look, I know things have been crappy between us, but I'd never want you to be alone on the holidays. And don't you dare say this is pity, either, because you know how much I hate that."

She widens her eyes and looks at me until I nod, because I do know. She hated it when people felt sorry for her after the accident, so I should know better than to think she'd do that to me. I guess that's easier to believe though, than that someone actually cares.

When I reluctantly give in, she grins. "Besides, it wouldn't be the first time you celebrated a holiday with my family. You remember Easter, don't you?"

I blink at her in shock. My heart freezes inside my chest before it pounds. "Do *I* remember Easter?" Is she serious right now?

Peyton nods, almost hesitantly, gaze locked with mine. A pretty blush steals across her cheeks and it reminds me so much of another blush, a blush I once traced down the slender column of her throat to where it spread across her bare chest. My fingertips tingle in response.

Air ignites as the memories pass between us. The spark of challenge she'd held in her eyes. The impossible softness of her skin. My awkward, inexperienced fumbling.

The pained wince that shifted into a euphoric smile after I entered her.

I inhale a sharp breath and release it. "Hell yeah, I remember."

THURSDAY, APRIL 21ST

7 Weeks until Disaster

♥ Freshman Year

JUSTIN

JUSTIN'S HOUSE 5:18 P.M.

"What the—?"

Behind me, the front door closed. Bags and suitcases filled the entryway, lining either side of the foyer with a random assortment of toys thrown in the middle. Peyton frowned as she nudged a Spiderman rolling backpack with her shoe. "Y'all going on a trip?"

I almost laughed. It was cute how innocent she was. How wholesome and sweet. In her *Full House* world, it made sense that a family vacation would involve, you know, the entire family. But that wasn't my world.

"Nope," I replied with a tight smile. "*We're* not going anywhere."

God, I hated that this shit still got to me. I'd lost count how many times I'd come home to discover one or both of my so-called parents jetting off to parts unknown, so this sort of thing shouldn't have phased me anymore. In this case, I blamed the timing.

Usually, Easter was the one weekend a year I could count on Dad actually being around. It wasn't that my family was religious or anything. Lightning would probably strike

Annabeth dead if she ever set foot inside a church, and Dad, well, he worshipped at the altar of money. But he faked it well for his shareholders. It came with the job of CEO in the Bible belt. Holidays, holy days of obligation, and St. Edward's annual spring carnival of gluttony were prime elbow-rubbing appearances. This year he must've somehow gotten a pass.

"Well, someone's going somewhere," Peyton muttered, eyeing an expensive looking designer suitcase with distaste. She made a face like a disgruntled bunny. "They seriously didn't tell you about this?"

"Are you seriously surprised?"

For her sake, I forced a playful smile, trying to act like it didn't bother me. I should've known better. Concern flooded her eyes, proof of how off my game I was, so I dropped the smile and tugged on her hand. "Come on. Let's go to my room."

As we made our way through the living room, I prepared myself for the inevitable.

This was what I got for inviting her here. When Peyton found me after practice, another book in her hand and a sweet smile on her face asking for a ride, I couldn't say no. The best part was that I didn't have to, now that we were... whatever we were. She'd suggested we hang out at the ranch but I knew Cade would be there, sniffing around like a dog in heat. He had it bad for my girl. Thankfully, Peyton either had no idea or had no interest, and I planned on keeping it that way. So, like a dumbass, I'd invited her here, knowing Rosalyn would give us our space and expecting the rest of house to be relatively quiet.

The sound of Annabeth's nasal yap shut that down.

Tugging harder on her hand, I increased my pace, wanting to get to my room before the step-witch figured out we were here. That was just what I needed. For her to see Peyton, and find some new way to humiliate me. Next to me, Peyton hurried her steps, sensing my unease.

A half a foot away from my bedroom door, my brother darted out of his.

"Justin!" Chase launched himself into my arms and I dropped Peyton's hand to catch him. "Did'ja hear? Did'ja hear? I get to meet Mickey! I'm gonna meet Mickey!"

Huge brown eyes stared at me with liquid joy and my anger melted. I'd kill for this kid. Readjusting his light weight on my hip, I gave him my full attention. "Mickey, huh? Man, that's awesome. Someone must love you a lot."

He beamed at me. It was a game we played. Whenever anything remotely good happened, he'd run into my arms and I'd remind him how much he was loved. How special he was. Lord knows he wasn't hearing it regularly anywhere else.

"Think he'll give me any *cheese*?"

Just the thought had Chase's smile bordering on the slightly manic and I had to choke back a laugh. Peyton chuckled quietly behind me.

"You know, bud, anything's possible. But if he gives you any, you better save me a piece, okay?" When he nodded, he did so with his entire body, and I ruffled his hair before setting him on the ground.

"I'm pretty jealous," I told him, only half-way teasing. Honestly, I could give a rat's ass about a six-foot cartoon character, but I hated missing this experience with him. "You're gonna have a blast in Disney World."

Like most ankle-biters, my brother lived and breathed Disney. Seeing his face when he met Mickey or Goofy or whoever else floated around that place would've been cool. Not that I was surprised by the lack of invite. I was just the unwanted step-son.

As Chase ducked back into his room, screaming the theme song from Jake and the Never Land Pirates at the top of his lungs, I raised my voice so he could hear, "Make sure you take lots of pictures!"

"Oh good, you're here." At the nasal voice floating down the hall, the smile fell from my face. Begrudgingly, I turned to confront the spawn of hell.

Annabeth *click-clacked* toward me in four-inch heels, typing away on her phone. "Your father got added to a panel in Orlando at the last minute, so we're joining him there for a little vacay. We leave in a few hours."

At her fast and loose use of the word "we" I couldn't help but say, "Oh yippee! Guess I better run along now and pack, huh?"

My stepmother rolled her eyes. "Please. Like you want to spend Easter break with a talking rodent."

When she finally raised her head to glare at me, Annabeth noticed the girl at my side. Shock filled her face before her lip curled, and after giving Peyton a cold once over, she said, "Besides, with us gone you'll have the house to yourself to... *do* whatever you want in peace." Turning up her nose with thinly veiled disgust, she added, "Do try not to burn the place down."

And with that helpful nugget of parental wisdom, and a final scathing look at my girl, Annabeth exited the hall. It took everything in me not to kick a hole in the wall.

"Holy crap." Peyton's mouth hung open, eyelashes blinking. "That... that..."

Her eyes narrowed as her hands fisted at her sides, and if this had been a cartoon, fumes would be rising from her ears. She was seconds away from going nuclear. To tell you the truth, it was sexy as hell. But when she tucked her chin and leaned forward, clearly ready to take off after my stepmother, I grabbed her hand and hauled her into my room.

"Damn, you're feisty," I said, shutting my door with a low chuckle. She'd gone a little crazy the day I'd finally told her about my dad and messed up upbringing. Peyton might've looked sweet and innocent, but she rocked a hardcore inner fire. "Just ignore her, Sunshine. I know I do."

"But you shouldn't have to!" Throwing her hands in the air, Peyton walked the length of my room. "That woman is a mother? *Seriously*? That should be illegal! And that poor adorable little boy... how in the hell is he so sweet with that... that *monster* providing half his genes?!"

Feisty and protective was a sexy combination.

Biting the inside of my cheek to subdue my smile, I replied, "He takes after his kickass brother, obviously." Then, plopping said ass on the bed, I patted the mattress beside me. "Seriously, baby, I'm fine. Who needs Disney World? I couldn't go anyway. With school out, your dad scheduled a practice for tomorrow, and I'd never let him down, so see? No big deal."

Only, I couldn't seem to force my face to match my words. I was used to quiet. Most days, it was better than Annabeth flitting around, spending my father's money and pretending she was mother of the year. But school didn't start back up until *Wednesday*. That was a whole lot of quiet.

Peyton growled, not buying my act for a second, and jutted her hip against my bookshelf. Eyes narrowed, she mumbled curses under her breath—or what passed as curses for her—and I turned on my side to face her. She was seriously pissed.

Nobody had given a shit about me, not really, not since I had lived with my grandparents. That was years ago. That this sweet girl was so worked up over me boggled my mind. But I liked it. Probably too much.

"Why don't we put all that aggression to use?" I suggested, trying to get things back to a normal footing. I didn't do serious—but I rocked at casual hookups. I patted the mattress again. "I'm sure there's something we can do to distract ourselves..."

I raised my eyebrows and Peyton laughed like I was a dork. Not the result I intended. But when her peaches and cream cheeks warmed with a blush, I counted it as a win. Rolling her eyes, she tromped over and went to give my shoulder a playful shove, but I reached out and snaked my fingers around the delicate bones of her wrist, tumbling her onto the bed.

"Oomph!"

Peyton's blush deepened as she wiggled on the bedspread beside me. Curiosity widened her eyes, but the underlying affection was what got me. And with her wild hair spread out over my pillow, I swore she'd never looked hotter.

"Listen, it doesn't bother me, okay?" I smoothed the hair away from her face, addicted to the feel of her skin, and her eyes searched mine, obviously not believing me. Damn, she was smart. And loyal. And way too good for me.

My mouth lifted into a smile, this time a real one. "I'm used to it by now. As long as you come by and see me a couple times, I'm all good. I promise."

Peyton frowned, and I swear, it was like I could hear the wheels turning in her brain. I already knew she was stubborn, determined, and on a mission to save me. Knowing she was planning something... no lie, it made me nervous. When she bolted upright, nearly knocking me out with a head butt to the chin, I figured I had every right to be.

"Oh, you'll see a lot more of me than that," she declared, pushing up to her elbows.

Say what?

"Uh, Sunshine, not that I don't love where your head's at right now—because I totally do. But we don't have—"

A pillow to the head shut me up.

"Not like *that*," she said with an amused sigh. "God, you're such a horn dog!"

"Guilty as charged," I said with a laugh, and threw the pillow near the headboard. "But there's a pet name for me. Sunshine and Horn Dog. Has a certain ring to it, I think."

My dirty little secret: making Peyton laugh was my new favorite hobby. I preferred it even to baseball, so when she

RACHEL HARRIS ♥

tossed her head back, musical notes combining with groans at my ceiling, the crap with my parents flittered away.

This, right here, was all I needed.

Mumbling about boys, hormones, and one-track minds, Peyton tramped over to my closet. She yanked the door open and I watched, amused, as she pulled out a duffle bag and began throwing random shit inside.

"Just curious," I called from my prone position on the bed, "but what exactly are you doing?"

"Packing," she called back, like it should be obvious. Which, I guessed it was. I must've missed something.

"And why are you packing again? You heard me say I don't care about Disney, right?"

"Oh, you're not going to Disney."

"Uh huh." Women were weird creatures. "Then if I'm not going to Disney... can I ask where it is I am going?"

In response, Peyton tossed the opened bag on my bed, placed her hands on her hips, and smiled so wide I feared her face would crack. "Yep. You're moving in with me."

PEYTON

SWEET SERENITY RANCH 8:55 P.M.

The clock on the wall was broken. Useless piece of junk. I'd been standing by the window for an eternity, staring out into the quiet, car-less night, yet the stupid digital read-out claimed only two minutes had passed since I last checked.

I called shenanigans.

154

"Relax, honey." Mama smiled a secret smile and stole a glance at my dad. She didn't know Justin and I were together, but it was pretty obvious she thought I had a crush. Her side of the bookshelf was stuffed full of red-spined romances, and knowing her, she'd be in matchmaking mode this weekend. I'd have to remember to warn Justin.

Sliding another cookie onto the tray, she asked, "Justin likes chocolate chip, right?" Spatula in the air, she frowned at the cooling rack of goods. "Or maybe I should've gone with chocolate chunk?"

The woman and her baking. It was a wonder I wasn't the size of a hippo.

"I told you, Mama, we're friends. How am I supposed to know his favorite cookie? You act like I know the guy's shoe size."

Size 11. That tidbit was obtained when I'd packed his bag earlier because, as we'd already established, I was a borderline stalker when it came to Justin Carter.

Mama so didn't need to know that.

"Cookies are cookies," I told her, softening my words with a smile since it wasn't her fault the dang clock was broken. "He's a growing boy so I doubt he'll care either way. If it's edible, he'll devour it."

Dad snorted his agreement and I turned back to the window.

Where is he?

When I'd left Justin's house two hours ago, Rosalyn had promised she'd drop him off on the way to the airport. He'd chosen to stay behind and help Chase finish his packing, which made me happy for two reasons. One, because watching him with that adorable little boy made my cuteness-meter explode. And two, because I needed extra time to prep my parents.

It'd never really been a question that they'd agree. Mama was a total softie and if she was on board, I knew Dad would be, too. He normally went along with whatever she wanted—'happy wife, happy life,' he often said. Wise words to live by.

So, once I'd gotten home, I'd casually asked if we'd have room at the table for Easter, dropping the fact that a friend was going to be all alone for the holiday. As expected, Mama pounced on it and invited them to stay the entire weekend.

That was when I'd dropped the friend being a *boy* part of the scenario.

Strangely enough, it didn't much seem to matter. Mama had heard all about Dad's skilled catcher over countless dinners, she'd met him a few times here at the ranch, and most importantly, her big, bleeding heart couldn't stand for anyone to be lonely. Hinting at how horrible his parents were, without going into any specifics of course, had cinched the deal.

For Dad's part, he'd been suspicious at first. Hesitant after that. But thanks to my Oscar-worthy performance, proclaiming my relationship with his catcher to be strictly platonic, he'd approved the plan with flying colors.

My latent guilt was growing palpable.

"I'm proud of you, angel girl," Dad told me now, hugging me to his side. "I appreciate you watching out for my boys."

I nodded as my stomach churned, shame settling like a rock. But Justin was worth it.

"Team Williams sticks together, right?" I replied, fighting for a smile. He beamed back at me and it fell with a thud. This officially sucked. "Besides, I was glad to help. Justin's a good guy."

A hotter than hot, incredibly-gifted-at-kissing good guy. Something told me Dad's feelings would change in a heartbeat if he knew that, though, so with the familiar warmth of a blush heating my cheeks, I peered back out into the night...

And jumped about a foot when two bright lights pierced the dark.

He was here. *Finally*. Arguably the hottest guy in school, at the very least the freshman class, would soon walk through my front door with a duffle bag... a bag I'd packed for him no less... and then live with me for *four whole days*.

My euphoria was matched only by my trepidation.

Naked baby pictures were hidden, the main bath had been cleaned of tampons, and I'd made Mama vow on her prized Elvis statue that she wouldn't do anything over-the-top insane. But I'd yet to get anywhere near that far with Dad. I'd been too busy watching the stupid, car-less view out the window.

I latched onto his hand. "*Please, please*, for the love of Easter bunnies, don't embarrass me this weekend."

"Would I do that?" he asked, his face a picture of innocence. I didn't buy it for a second. "I'm thrilled that you're friends with Justin. He's one of my best players. And I'm happy he'll be here with us instead of alone." Outside, a car door slammed and his eyes sharpened to steel. "But you should know, I will be watching."

Boom! The parental gauntlet had been thrown. Two seconds later, footsteps pounded up the front stairs and a knock sounded on the door.

Mama set the tray of cookies on the coffee table. "Peyton, would you like to get that?"

"Mmhmm." I swiped my sweaty hands down the sides of my jeans, fighting a telltale blush. Okay, so, apparently neither of my parents were fully sold on the platonic song and dance, and now they'd both be watching us like crotchety old nuns at a first boy-girl dance. That didn't mean we couldn't still have fun. Right?

Another knock pounded the door and Mama gave me a knowing look. "Want me to—?"

"No, I got it." I needed to chill. My hesitation only fed their suspicions.

Determined to be the embodiment of calm, breezy, and totally unaffected, I rushed toward the door, forgetting my lingering balance issues, and the fact that I was in bare socks. The cotton was no match for our laminate wood. I skidded across the floor, managing to stub a toe, knock over a coat rack, and bang my elbow against the wall with a muted *oaf*! before throwing open the door with decidedly *unchill* flair.

Justin's eyebrows shot to his hairline. "Uh, hey there, Sunshine."

My heart knocked like a giddy bird inside my chest at his lopsided grin. Looking behind me toward the living room, Justin quickly dropped the smile and straightened his shoulders.

"Coach," he said with a brisk nod. "Mrs. Williams. Thanks for letting me stay with you."

As I fought to regain normal breathing patterns, he stooped to pick up a potted plant at his feet, an Easter lily, Mama's favorite. Yep, he'd just achieved gold-star status.

"It's not much," Justin said, handing the plant over to my mom. He shoved his hands deep in his pockets. "But I know how much my being here is a hassle. I'll do anything I can to pitch in. Wash dogs, muck stalls, whatever you need, put me to work. I'm happy to do it."

I had a hunch *happy* was overstating things, considering he'd never once mucked a stall. Or tried to bathe a hundred pound Doberman. But I couldn't help but smile. Bad boy Carter was a parent charmer. Who knew?

Mama, charmed as all get out, ushered him inside as she held her flowers tight. "This is so thoughtful, Justin, really, but it's no hassle at all. We're happy you're here. Though in all fairness, we should warn you... it's gonna be a mad house."

Her thin shoulders slumped, as if she'd fully recalled how busy Easter weekend was for the boarding business. Mad house didn't begin to cover it—we were chin deep in four-legged fur balls!

With a heavy sigh, as if she could exhale that exhausting reality away, Mama set the lily on the table and took up the tray of deliciousness. "Justin, would you like a cookie?"

His gaze fell to the tray of homemade treats and his boyish smile changed.

I wasn't sure if it was the endearment or the snack. Couldn't really read the emotion behind it. But as Justin stared at the collection of misshapen, oozing chocolate cookies in my mother's hand, something in him altered.

The knot in his throat bobbed with a swallow and his eyes glazed as he reached out with a slightly trembling hand and took the nearest one. "Thanks, Mrs. Williams."

"You're welcome, hun," Mama replied softly, concern creasing her forehead. But she didn't push. She'd raised my two brothers, and always said, "boys only talk when they're ready." Instead, she gave him a genuine smile and said, "And please, call me Grace."

Justin nodded and nibbled a corner of the treat, his pain palpable. Wishing I knew how to fix that didn't make it any better, either. Thankfully, as he chewed, he found a different sort of help—the kind that came from my mother's kitchen. The woman didn't win awards for nothing.

"These are really good," he said, snatching another one, and for a moment, the mood lightened. We all laughed and grabbed a cookie of our own, even Dad, and snacked in somewhat comfortable silence until Justin dusted his hands of crumbs. "So, where should I put my stuff?"

Crap. Just like that, good feelings vanished and embarrassment and utter awkwardness took their place. Something told me it wouldn't be the only time that happened this weekend.

"Right. About that." Here came the only drawback of my master plan. "You're actually… kind of staying in the doghouse."

Justin's jaw dropped. "Kind of?"

"Okay, you're totally staying in the doghouse," I clarified with a sigh. "Apparently Dad thinks you're gonna try and steal my virtue."

My father choked on his cookie. Crumbs flew as he sputtered and coughed, beet red, though I spoke the God's honest truth, and Mama pounded his back as she fought a fit of giggles. She found amusement in all life's challenges.

"Oh, that's not it," she told him with a smile, then tilted her head as she reconsidered her words. "At least, that's not the *only* reason you're outside."

The giggles won out, Mama's eyes twinkling like she'd shared the punch line of a joke, and I smacked my palm against my forehead.

Justin looked mortified. He turned to me with wide eyes and I shook my head at his silent question. Nope, I hadn't told my parents a single thing. Our platonic pact for the parentals was still in effect. Mine were simply old-fashioned worry-warts who distrusted any non-related Y-chromosome who waltzed through the door.

Perhaps noticing Justin's slightly green complexion, Mama had the decency to appear sheepish. "We trust you both," she assured him, as if reading my mind. "But we converted our sons' bedroom into an office last year, and there's already a comfortable guest room set up in the doghouse."

She winced a bit, only now seeming to fully grasp how weird this was. Asking our holiday guest to sleep with a bunch of dogs. Luckily, she rambled when she got nervous.

"You'd honestly be doing us a huge favor," she went on, no doubt making it worse. "We have a solid security system and have increased staff for the week, but it'll give me so much peace of mind having you out there, keeping an ear out. We've got a packed house with all the families leaving town and needing to board their babies..."

Mama trailed off, but her mouth stayed open like she was wishing the words back inside.

Justin laughed humorlessly. "Then I'll fit right in."

My heart squeezed. More than anything, I wanted to hug him, wanted to wrap my arms around his neck and tell him everything would be all right. That his parents sucked and none of this was his fault. But I couldn't do any of that. Not with our two adult-sized shadows looming over us.

I bumped his shoulder with mine. "Let's go get you settled, huh?"

Justin gave me a tight smile and Mama thanked me with her eyes. As he shouldered his bag and snagged the half dozen cookies my mom shoved at him, I pushed open the door. When Dad mentioned tomorrow's practice and what time they needed to leave, I silently crept out onto the porch, needing a moment alone.

Outside, stars punched holes into the dark. The air was still and warm, but I folded my arms against my chest anyway, feeling a chill in my bones. I took a deep breath, inhaled the scent of pine, and leaned against the porch rail.

What was it about the night? The dark always made things appear so much bigger, so much more intense. This was the first time I'd really stopped moving or thinking since I'd concocted my plan at Justin's house, and now that I had, I realized I was terrified.

I was about to be alone with Justin for four whole days. No Diamond Dolls, no watchful teammates or lunch room politics. Just me, the boy I was falling for, and my well-meaning, overprotective parents... who might have had a hint, but really no clue just how much he meant to me.

I closed my eyes and rested my head against the post.

Would anything happen while he was here? Did I want anything to happen? The tickle low in my belly screamed yes, especially when it came to more earth-shattering kisses, but there were things... tons of other things... still yet to be explored. I may've been sheltered for a large part of my life, but I wasn't dumb. I watched television, listened to conversations in the bathroom. Swiped Mama's books when she wasn't paying attention. Curiosity was a living, breathing thing, and intuitively, I knew Justin would be up for anything. Did I dare go for it?

Do what scares you.

My motto hadn't failed me yet, in fact, it had done just the opposite. It brought me my first kiss, my first secret boyfriend, and more excitement and hope than I'd ever felt before. The nervousness in my gut was like a beacon, leading the way. And it was steering me now.

Behind me, the door closed with a muffled thump and goose bumps erupted at the sound of heavy footsteps drawing near. Funny how I didn't need to look to know it was him. My body had become a Justin Carter tracking system.

Alert, alert! Severe hottie approaching! Batten down the hatches and gird your loins!

"Ready?" he asked, voice low and at my ear. I had the sudden urge to lean back against him. Feel the strength of his body against mine. But fifteen years with my parents taught me that they were watching, so I restrained myself and turned to face him.

"Are you?"

Under the soft light from the moon and distant flood lamp near the barn, Justin looked different. Less guarded, more relaxed. The ghosts that haunted his eyes earlier were gone, replaced with more of that wicked smoldering I'd seen once before.

"I'm always ready," he said in reply, and the left side of his mouth kicked up in a devilish smirk. Suddenly, the porch light flicked on, bathing us both in bright yellow light like a spotlight. My shoulders shook with a whine.

Justin chuckled, which only made me want to kiss him more. "Don't worry, we'll find a way to be alone. I can be creative when I need to be," he promised. "Plus, I hear doghouses are total aphrodisiacs."

I laughed aloud, even as a small shiver ran down my spine. Thus was the power of Justin Carter. I looked into his eyes and said, "With you there, hell yeah they are."

I think I surprised him.

I *know* I surprised myself.

My mouth fell open, and his trademark smirk transformed into a full-fledged grin. Evidently, I was getting better at this whole flirting thing.

As his eyes grazed over my face, almost reverently, like he was memorizing every detail, I couldn't help wondering what it was that he saw.

Justin shook his head and stepped back, making a production of it like if he didn't, he'd ravage me on the spot. *Promises, promises.* "I swear to God, woman," he said, his voice low and thick, sending a thrill across my skin. "You're gonna be the death of me."

Wild horses couldn't stop my smile.

This boy was it for me. It was as simple as that. Even crazier, it seemed like I was it for him. I was certain I was stuck inside some wonderful dream and would wake up any moment back inside my hospital room, but I refused to pinch myself. If I was dreaming, I was happy to stay that way forever.

Heaving a sigh, Justin linked his pinkie finger with mine. "Well, come on then. Show me to my room in the dog palace."

He smirked and I rolled my eyes at his teasing. Then, listening to the butterflies in my gut, I followed him down the front porch steps.

SUNDAY, APRIL 24TH

7 Weeks until Disaster

♥ Freshman Year

JUSTIN

SWEET SERENITY RANCH 4:05 P.M.

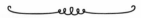

Peyton's family was weird. They were very nice, extremely welcoming, and over the top supportive of each other.

Like I said, really weird.

They'd treated me like one of their own all weekend—much to the chagrin of that horse boy, Cade. The dude had it bad for Peyton, that much was obvious, but he'd been too much of a chicken-shit to step up to the plate. Now I was here, and too bad for him, I owned the plate. And Coach loved me.

I'd been his sous chef, whatever the hell that was, at the annual fish fry on Friday. He taught me his secret trick to keep the batter from falling off. Then this morning, he had me join him behind the grill, prepping the big family Easter meal.

And by big, I meant *big*.

Who knew someone could have so many relatives? Since my grandparents died, it'd just been Dad, Annabeth, Chase, and me. There were no cousins or aunts and uncles running around. No close family friends wearing the honorary title, either. Peyton, though, she had it all. Brothers, sisters-in-law, nieces and nephews, aunts and uncles, cousins like you wouldn't believe. Both sets of grandparents, and even a set of great-grandparents, were sitting off in the shade.

What would it have been like to grow up with that much love around you? What would it feel like to know that many people had your back?

It was unfathomable to me.

Even weirder than the legions of relatives taking over the dining and family rooms were the Williams' family traditions. Apparently, Mrs. Grace was from south Louisiana, and there it was common practice to smash brightly-colored Easter eggs for fun in some type of battle royal. They called it *pocking*. I called it strange.

Peyton's great-grandfather had been the first to rumble, squaring up against her three-year-old nephew Baylor. The two got all serious about it, too, going squinty-eyed and lining up the pointy end of the chosen eggs in their hand. Then, at some unheard cue, Baylor smashed his egg against the old man's. Since his egg wasn't cracked, he'd been declared the victor.

I couldn't make this stuff up.

My Easter tradition? Waking up, spoiling Chase rotten with chocolate, then helping him into a monkey suit for church, so Dad could make his annual appearance. Afterward, I'd lock myself in my room for a nap. At some point, Rosalyn would swing by fresh from her own family's celebration and leave me a covered plate of food.

"Justin, what's it like playing ball for my old man?"

I blinked away the memories, and focused on Peyton's brother Lars. "It's awesome," I told him honestly, and Peyton squeezed my thigh under the table. "The man knows his shi—" I quickly glanced at the young girl across from me and corrected myself. "His stuff."

Lars's wife Susan smiled at me as she scooped potato salad on little Eva's plate.

"He's one of my best players," Coach interrupted from the head of the table. "Justin's on JV, but I can already tell, the boy's gonna be unstoppable."

The tips of my ears grew warm and I stared down at my plate. Normally, I got off on praise. God knows I never heard stuff like that from my own Dad, and making Coach Williams proud was what I lived for these days. But here, surrounded by Peyton's family, it sort of made me uncomfortable. Which made absolutely no sense.

"One of my friends played for Dad back when I went to Fairfield." This came from Jesse, Peyton's other brother. "He ended up getting drafted and got to play a few years in the majors. Think you'll want to go to college, or try pro straight out of the gate?"

I shifted in my seat, mutilating the linen napkin in my lap. Despite the chaos of bodies, the *clink* of silverware, and the soft music in the background, it seemed like all eyes were on me. Waiting to hear what I'd say.

"Well, I—"

"He'll have his pick," Coach predicted for me. "As long as he listens to instruction, as he's been doing, and keeps working hard, he's got the stuff. I can feel it."

He met my gaze with a proud smile and a weird sensation tightened my chest.

"On the field, scouts look at two things," he said, lifting a hand and counting them off on his meaty fingers. "Field position and batting average. But what happens off the field is just as important. Keep your grades up, stay out of trouble. No problems with the law or too much disciplinary crap in school, stay away from drugs and alcohol." His wise gaze sharpened. "And stay the hell away from steroids."

"Dan!" Mrs. Grace scolded, swinging her widened gaze toward the children. "Language."

Not wanting to laugh, I rolled my lips between my teeth. *Hell* was probably the least offensive thing I'd heard slip from his mouth when he got going, but I wasn't about to bust him for it. Seeing his sweet wife put the tough old man in his place, however, was classic and I wished the guys were here.

I looked at Coach nodded, letting him know I heard what he'd said.

Steroids were no secret around sports, especially baseball. There'd been talk around the locker room, but so far, I'd yet to see anyone actually dope up. I was glad, too, because that shit was stupid. One of the best things about baseball was how pure the sport was. Unlike everything else in my life, it was straightforward, honest, and fun. Drugs had no part in that.

"I'm sure Justin doesn't want to be beat over the head with sports talk," Mrs. Grace said, sliding me a wink. "You boys do enough of that at school. Today's a holiday, for Pete's sake, one celebrating the season of redemption and life, and this year, we have a lot to be thankful for."

She swung a pointed look toward Peyton and the entire room took a collective breath.

Beside me, Sunshine clenched my hand.

I was no expert on women. Sure, I knew how to get their attention, how to make them blush, and how to turn them on. But I didn't pretend to understand what made them tick. Peyton, though, I was starting to know her.

She hated being the center of attention, especially because of her illness. She hated looking weak. Maybe it was because I hadn't known her before she got sick, or when she was in the hospital, but the girl I saw was far from fragile. The Peyton I knew was strong. She was beautiful, smart, and carried herself with grace, even with her occasional limp. When she cared about someone, she did it with her whole heart.

Even when they didn't deserve it.

Trapping her hand on my thigh, I linked our fingers and gave them a squeeze. Her eyes met mine from beneath her lashes, her long strawberry blonde hair masking a grateful smile. It was like a jolt of Red Bull to the heart.

"Who's ready for volleyball?" Sandra asked suddenly, and Peyton glanced away.

I frowned at Jesse's wife as a dozen folding chairs screeched across the wooden floor. "Volleyball?"

"Yep. Another fun Williams' tradition," she answered with a grin. "We sure do have a lot of them, huh?"

"That's an understatement." I tossed my napkin on an empty plate and turned to Peyton. "Did I miss a volleyball court somewhere on the ranch?"

"Nah, only sissies play on a real court," she teased, her pink lips curving in a smile. "We don't even use a regulation ball. We play with a blown up Dora the Explorer beach ball and the only rule is to keep it airborne for as long as possible. We don't even use a real net or keep score."

"How do you know who wins?"

Peyton laughed and poked me in the ribs. "It's not always about winning, you know. Besides, it's hard to worry about that when everyone's playing, including my toddler nephew and ninety-year-old great-grandfather. It's just fun, Justin. You do remember fun, right?"

What was the point of a game with no winner... and why would anyone want to play it?

Coach's belly laugh trailed behind him and I shook my head in wonder. The man was even more competitive than I was, and he actually agreed to this? Sure enough, when we walked outside, there he was, standing out on the pseudo court wearing a big happy smile and holding a fluorescent pink beach ball in his calloused hands.

If the guys could only see this.

The makeshift net was a tree branch, and the family broke into roughly equal numbers on either side. I ended up with Peyton, her dad, her brother Jesse, her nieces Eva and Jennifer, and her seventy-two-year-old grandmother, Velma, who I quickly learned was a feisty old woman with a wicked serve.

I tried my best to stay in the moment. I truly did. I volleyed. I served. I even laughed at the complete ridiculousness of the game. When the huge ball came toward Eva, I hoisted her up and helped her nail it right in her dad's face. He wasn't real impressed, but she giggled like a banshee.

But, after about twenty minutes, it got to be too much.

Fourteen years of lonely Easters rushed over me. Christmases and birthdays with a card, a few hundred dollar bills, and one year even a new Jeep, one that I couldn't even drive for another two years—but no hugs, no laughter. No love. Nights spent lying awake cursing Hollywood for the happy family crap they sold each year. Knowing it was a scam just to make a buck.

How was I to know that it wasn't? That the whole time, Peyton and her family had been here, living that reality.

I couldn't wrap my brain around the unfairness of it all. *Every* kid should have this. Families who spent time together. Who had traditions and memories and laughed at inside jokes. Families who celebrated holidays and didn't leave for vacation without one of its members... or if they did, they at least missed that person while they were gone.

Everything hit me at once. My chest squeezed so tight, my ribs ached. I couldn't breathe. My pulse began a painful tattoo inside my head, my temples felt like they were caving in, and I realized... I was about to cry.

Like a bitch, I was about to totally lose my shit in front of Peyton's entire family.

Without a word, I took off.

"Justin!"

I couldn't look back. No way could I face her like this. A pitiful excuse for a guy sobbing over stupid shit. It was embarrassing, it was painful, and it wasn't her fault—but right now, I needed to take it out on someone, and I'd die before I let that be her.

I waved a hand at the question in Peyton's voice and screamed, "I'll be back."

That's all my thick throat allowed before it closed on a sob... a fucking *sob*... and I bit my lip until it bled. With my shoes slapping the earth, I fled as far away from the perfect, happy family as I could get.

God, I was pathetic.

PEYTON

SWEET SERENITY RANCH 5:45 P.M.

"Oh, thank God," I whispered, releasing a heavy breath. I'd covered every inch of the ranch, starting with the doghouse, and hadn't been able to find Justin anywhere. It figured he'd be in the last place I looked—not that I would've kept looking after I'd found him. I never had understood that expression.

Not wanting to spook him, I padded quietly past Oakley's stall to my favorite spot on the entire property. It was fitting I'd find him here.

"I've always loved the way the sunset reflects on the pond," I murmured, coming to a stop just behind him. Justin's spine tensed and I added, "It's peaceful."

Eyes wary, he glanced at me over his shoulder. "Yeah. It is."

Pursing my lips, trying my best to keep the vomit of questions I had for him contained, I strolled around the picnic table and hopped up to sit on its surface. Close, but not too close, in case he still needed space. Quietly, we watched the colors in the sky grow warm.

When he'd taken off like a bat out of hell earlier, I'd stood frozen for a full minute, paralyzed by indecision. Should I follow him? Did he want me to? I wasn't even sure what had happened. One moment we were laughing, playing my family's silly game, and I was thinking how awesome it was that I'd gotten to share it with Justin. The next, he was gone.

Had he hated it that much? Had he been bored? He'd seemed to be enjoying himself... but what the heck did I know anyway? Boys in general were still a mystery, but I'd thought I was getting to know this one pretty well. Bolting like a spooked horse, though, was weird.

"Sorry." Justin sighed and scrubbed a hand across his face. "I just... needed a minute."

"I get it," I told him, scooting slightly closer. "Hey, my family is a lot to take. Now, the secret's out: I'm a geek who hails from a nutcase family. I don't blame you for running while you still could. There was gonna be an initiation after the match."

A hint of a smile played at his lips. "Geeks aren't so bad. Haven't you seen *The Big Bang Theory*? Nutcases are all the rage these days."

At his teasing chuckle, I slid over again, removing the distance between us. Our shoulders bumped and I noticed for the first time a small spiral notebook in his left hand. The same kind I'd seen in his room. Justin noticed where I was looking and turned back to the pond.

"Had to clear the white noise," he explained, tapping the notebook against his thigh.

So many questions flooded my mind, but I promised myself I wouldn't push. So, against every curious-cat instinct I had, I asked, "Do you want me to go?" *Please say no, please say no.*

"Nah."

Justin beat the notebook on his leg again, eyes unfocused on the water, obviously lost in thought. I felt so helpless. He was so much more sensitive than anyone knew, and while I wanted to wrap my arms around his neck and hold him, I didn't know if I'd be welcomed. Instead, I decided to try and lighten the mood.

"You're lucky I'm not swiping that book and running for the hills," I said, leaning into his body. "If I recall, I did vow to read your stuff one day, and here you are, flaunting it in front of my face."

I grinned to show I was teasing and he glanced at me from the corner of his eye. Then, shocking the ever-loving hell out of me, he handed it over.

My mouth tumbled open in shock. "*Really?*"

Justin lifted his chin in a nod and glanced at the water. Hesitantly, with trembling hands, I set the notebook in my lap and took a breath. This felt huge. Monumental. I was about to get a peek inside the secret musings of the undisputed bad boy of Fairfield Academy.

If not for the constant rubbing of his fingers, the increased rise and fall of his chest, I'd have no clue this bothered him. That it did, and he was letting me read it anyway, warmed my heart. I made a promise to myself right then and there— whether his writing was good or bad, I would praise him.

I turned the cover.

And fell even deeper in love.

Lyrics that clearly meant something to him. Notes on how he played a particular day, what he wanted to improve. And poetry. God, the poetry!

Short phrases and lines like: "Head down. Work Harder. Don't let them see that you care."

And longer ones, obviously about his dad. I stopped at one about half-way through the book, and tears filled my eyes.

Man I Need to Be
Hey, look at me!
Am I everything I'm supposed to be?
Do you even care?
Do you see the burden I bear?
Hey, look at me!
Am I the man I need to be?
You are never there.
Maybe I never really had a prayer.
HEY, look at me!
You look, but never really see.
Time with me, not a second to spare.
A kingdom of loneliness and I'm the heir.
HEY, LOOK AT ME!

The tears fell silently and I brushed them away, not wanting Justin to see. Not wanting them to fall on the page and ruin these beautiful words. Not beautiful because they painted a pretty picture... beautiful because finally, I was getting a glimpse of the real Justin. The lonely, sad, heartbroken boy who desperately wanted to be loved.

I turned another page.

Bottled Up
I toss out another lie and a smile that's just for show.
I'm bottled up and hidden, but you'll never know.
Your oblivion is my only crutch.
Close your eyes so you don't see too much.
I've never been the guy with his heart on his sleeve,

But you don't always have to see to believe.
I open up and you shut me down.
I feel like a prince who has lost his crown.
But I'm fine, and it's okay.
It never fit right anyway.
I've never been one to beg...
So, go ahead and knock me down another peg.

It felt almost wrong, reading these words. Seeing the pain he kept hidden so well behind his flirtatious smiles and teasing words. But I was addicted. I was a girl obsessed, hooked on discovery. Reverently, I flipped the page and came to his latest entry. The words Justin wrote after hightailing it away from my family. I sniffled and curled forward, hoping this final poem gave a hint in how to help him.

Empty House
I'm a pawn and your life is a game.
Nothing real, just a picture in your frame.
This cold, empty house is all an act.
It's really just broken and cracked.
Hang me like a trophy on the wall.
Use me to show how you have it all.
I've seen how a family should really be.
And you're nothing but a pretend father to me.

"I'm no Whitman or anything." Justin's timid voice snapped me back to the moment, and I raised my head, realizing just how long I'd been reading.

Overhead, the sun was giving its last hurrah, bathing the sky in deep orange, purple, and red. Its reflection on the pond's surface along with the scattered trees and old, weathered dock painted a picture of total peace and contentment.

The juxtaposition of the image and his troubled words themselves was sort of poetic.

"You have to know how incredibly talented you are," I murmured, not wanting to break the spell that had fallen. Justin had let me into his secret world. Showed me what a deep, sensitive person he really was. The thought that he'd now close up or regret sharing his words with me terrified me.

He'd already told me about his absentee dad and horrid stepmom. My bad opinion had been confirmed when I finally met her a few days ago. I knew his father lived on the road, and that when he was younger, he'd been raised by his grandparents. He'd shared these things like they weren't a big deal. Obviously, they were.

"I never met my real mom." Justin reached over and took the notebook from my hand. His eyes and smile were hard as he said, "Annabeth wants nothing to do with me—not that I want anything to do with her, either. Dad's never home, my grandparents are gone. The only person who cares about me, other than a three-year-old who needs help brushing his teeth, is paid to do so." He barked a cruel laugh and I winced. "How pathetic is that?"

"It's not *you*, Justin. You know that, right?"

He leaned back and shoved the notebook in his pocket, a scoff on his lips.

"I'm serious. That's on them... it's their problem. If they can't see how amazing you are, then I feel sorry for them. Really." I hopped off the bench and came to stand in front of him. "I'm so sorry if being here this weekend hurt you. I wanted—"

"No," Justin interrupted. "Don't feel guilty, Sunshine. I love that you're close to your family, okay?" He put his hands on my hips and tugged me between his open legs. "I'm grateful as hell that you let me be here. I would've been climbing the walls at home, writing even more horrific crap I pretend to be poetry." When I went to argue—his writing is *amazing*, not crap!—he silenced me with a finger across my lips. "But being here is hard, too."

"I know," I told him, my lips brushing against his skin. His eyes fell to my mouth and he swallowed thickly before moving his hand to cup my cheek. "I mean, I don't *know*, but I can sympathize. I'm so glad you shared this with me, Justin. You can tell me anything. You know that, right?"

He lowered his gaze and nodded, and I wrapped my arms around his neck. "I feel closer to you now," I admitted, and he raised his eyes again. "Is there anything you want to know about me?" I'd already told him about the hospital, but I figured putting myself on the hot seat might make him feel less vulnerable.

Justin seemed to think for a moment, then said, "Tell me about your recovery."

I sighed. "My therapists are great. They are. They know I'm into horses so they worked them into my therapy from the beginning. While I was still in a wheelchair, I brushed Oakley to build my shoulder strength and endurance. When I progressed to a walker, they had me brushing her while holding onto a post, or feeding her carrots. That helped increase my control and stamina. Later, I braided Annie's mane for finger coordination, and cleaned the tack—Mama loved that, of course. Less work for her," I said with a chuckle.

"Eventually, they put me on a machine that mimics a horse's movements, and finally, they let me on Oakley. But I still can't ride like I used to. Not yet anyway." Even admitting that aloud made me feel weak. I hated that feeling. "My grip is different, my balance is off. Even now, over a year later from when it all started."

I stared past him, toward Oakley's stall, regretting sharing so much. Now I felt exposed.

Good plan, Peyton.

"You really are incredible."

I smirked. "I don't know about that..."

"You're a fighter," he said. "The strongest person I've ever met, in fact."

"I just did what I had to do." I shrugged as a blush from his praise lit my cheeks. "Anyone would've done the same."

Justin tipped up my chin with his finger and said, "You're far from just anyone, Peyton. You're impulsive and fearless. You're stubborn and curious. You drive me *insane* with your millions of questions. And your heart... Sunshine, it's the most beautiful thing I've ever seen."

I wanted to look away. Hearing compliments was hard for me, I never really believed them. But when it came to Justin? God, I wanted to believe them so badly.

He brushed his thumb across my jaw. "Instead of giving up in the hospital, like most people would've done, you walked away optimistic. Grateful, even. I'm in awe of you." Justin looked deep into my eyes and said, "Peyton, you make me want to be a better guy. I want to deserve those sweet smiles of yours. I—"

I leaned forward and kissed him.

Words wouldn't express what he did to me. My heart felt heavy, so overflowing with love for this wounded, insecure boy that I couldn't contain it all. So I put it in my lips. In my mouth and in my tongue and in my small gasp of surprise when Justin yanked my body flush against his.

I gave myself over to emotion, threading my fingers through his thick, dark hair. Deepening the kiss and tangling my tongue with his. Dizzying desire whipped through my body, fogging my head with want, and settling in a warm pool of tingles in my belly. Goose bumps danced across my skin as the cool, crisp taste of mint exploded on my tongue.

"Baby..."

Wow. The word set off a flame in my blood. It was a claiming, every bit as much as his lips as they ravaged my mouth, taking over control, possessing me. And I *wanted* to be his. Completely, in every way I possibly could.

Justin was wrong before. I wasn't strong or incredible. I wasn't anything special. But he made me feel as though I was. If I'd learned anything living post-GBS, it was that life was short, and when you found happiness, you grabbed on with both hands and never let go. I had no intention of loosening my grip.

"Uh..." Justin groaned as he tore his lips from mine. "We can't." He pushed my hips back, but kept his hands clenched around my waist and leaned forward to brush another kiss against my swollen mouth. His heavy-lidded gaze fell on his handiwork. "Your dad... your whole family... they'll see us. We have to..."

That he was so breathless over me was a thrill of its own. I grinned up at him, taunting his inner battle by raking my teeth across my bottom lip, and he swallowed hard before inching closer to the edge of the bench. Closer to me.

"We need to slow down."

"No, we really don't." Setting my palms against his chest, I pressed my lips to his jaw. "No one ever comes back here but me." He moaned as my lips traveled higher, closer to his ear, and he tugged me back between his legs. "Besides, they're too busy with my grandparents to—"

"Peyton!" At my father's disembodied voice calling from a not too far distance, Justin's eyes grew wide with fear. "Justin! Where are you, son? Jesse wants to watch you catch."

There goes that plan.

Sighing the sigh of the sexually frustrated, I bowed my head and stepped out of the warmth of Justin's arms. "We'll finish this later," I promised. Then, with a final nip of his lips, I called back, "Coming!"

When Justin didn't immediately follow, I turned back in confusion. "I think I need a minute," he told me with me a rueful smile. I frowned in confusion and he sent a pointed look toward his lap. "Tell your dad I'll be right out."

What the... *Oh.* "Sure!" A strange mix of pride and embarrassment flushed my cheeks, turning my face what had to be five shades of red and I stuttered, "T-take your time. Really. However long you need. You know. Until things get, uh, back to normal."

Justin chuckled at my inane mutterings, and I quickly spun on my heel, heading back toward the main house before I could say anything more idiotic. Could I possibly be a bigger virginal nitwit? But, make-out-newb or not, as I rapped on the post outside Oakley's door and waltzed out the barn, there was no fighting my Cheshire-cat-like grin.

WEDNESDAY, MAY 28TH

1 Week until Graduation

♥ Senior Year

PEYTON

SWEET SERENITY RANCH 5:10 P.M.

Walking back out onto the doghouse porch, I can't help remembering that Easter all those years ago. What on earth possessed me to bring it up? We were having a good, mostly uncomfortable, innuendo-free time, and my brilliant self just had to go and throw *that* into the mix.

In times like this, I seriously consider wearing a muzzle.

Sure, the thought of Justin being alone again for another holiday hit me solid in the chest, and I reacted purely out of instinct, wanting to make him smile. But the truth is, he's probably spent *every* holiday alone since our breakup. And that... *God*... that sucks.

"Hey." Metal chains clank together in a funky melody as Justin stands up from the porch swing. My gaze falls to his sling and an unwanted shiver racks my spine. *I was so scared...* "All set?"

"Yep." I shove my hands in my back pockets and direct my gaze toward the grass. A midnight blue extended pick-up roars to life and the owner, Mr. Hamilton, waves a goodbye.

"Sparky's eating a pig's ear in her deluxe accommodations as we speak," I say, watching the truck's taillights disappear down the worn path.

Cade has a truck similar to Mr. Hamilton's. Dark blue, lots of room to store and transport ranch equipment. He loves that truck. Even though his parents are well-off, Cade worked his fingers to the bone, taking extra shifts and saving every penny he made so he could buy it himself. I'll never forget the pride in his eyes the day he cut the check to the dealership.

A fresh wave of guilt comes with the memory.

How can I even *think* about that Easter? I have a boyfriend—an incredible boyfriend—who, yeah, has been getting on my nerves a bit lately, and his jealous comments aren't exactly attractive... but obviously, his feelings are justified. If our relationship was as solid as it should be, as I used to *think* it was, memories like that spring night wouldn't keep popping up. And Cade wouldn't feel so threatened.

So really, this is all my fault. *Surprise, surprise.*

"You okay?"

Justin touches my elbow to gain my attention, and electricity shoots up my arm.

Cade, Cade, CADE.

"Yeah," I say, twisting slightly away from the touch. Ignoring the way his eyes darken. "Just thinking is all."

Justin shifts back on his feet and studies me. Either he reads my thoughts or decides against asking because instead of pushing for details, he says, "Guess it's time for our experiment."

Huh? "What experiment?"

A small smile forms on his lips but he doesn't answer as he walks past me silently, down the porch steps and back out toward the barn. Since I want answers, I have no choice but to follow.

As I rush to catch up, I remember him saying something about an experiment once we finished our FACS assignment. We'd been talking about riding just before then... oh crap.

When I'm still a few steps behind, he says over his shoulder, "Tell me what went through your head while you were riding Oakley."

I groan, realizing exactly what the so-called experiment is about, and he glances at me with an apology in his eyes. "You said you didn't make it past the first barrel, but I'm curious what you felt before that? When you walked Oakley out on the course."

My insides squeeze painfully as I mentally step back onto the barrel racing course. "I don't know... nervous, I guess. Curious if things would magically be different this time. Mostly doubting they would be. But, you know, for a split-second there," I shake my head and huff a humorless laugh, "I actually fooled myself into thinking they might."

Justin frowns at this and pulls me to a stop just inside the entrance to the barn. He blinks to adjust his eyes to the dim lighting, then leans a shoulder against the beam. "What changed?"

I shrug. "I mean, at first it felt great. It felt like it used to. The wind whipping my hair, Oakley's hooves pounding the earth—it brought back every memory of every race we'd ever done together. But then..." I swallow down the rising panic. "The memories, the bad ones, got to be too much. I lost control, let the fear win over, and I flat out freaked." Shame and weakness saturate my skin as I close my eyes and relive the sensation of failure. "It was a complete disaster."

"Was anyone with you?" His voice is so soft that I open my eyes, finding his filled with compassion. I shake my head, once, and he asks, "Not even Cade?"

"Not watching, no. I didn't want anyone to see," I confess, humiliation burning my cheeks. Oh, how I loathe my fair skin. "If I let everyone down again, and I knew I would, I couldn't—"

"See, right there," he interrupts, and I jerk my head back. "Sunshine, you didn't have a prayer. From the second you entered that course, you were already defeated. You can't do that—you have to believe in here," he moves close and brushes two fingers across my heart, "and in here," he says moving them over my temple and keeping them there, "that you *will* succeed. That you have what it takes. You've done it before, it's all muscle memory by now. Oakley knows what's what. But until you believe it yourself, push past that fear and doubt, you'll never do it."

Justin's palm gently cups to cradle my cheek as he stares into my eyes. His golden brown irises are intense with emotion, more than I ever remember seeing before. "Victory starts in your head, Peyton. You know that."

As an athlete, Justin's heard a million pep talks, most of them probably from my dad. But this seems to go so much deeper than that. I can't help but wonder if perhaps, with his recent injury, this speech of his is as much for *him* as it is for me.

"You also did it alone," he scolds, ducking his chin and raising a sharp eyebrow, reminding me of Mama when she's in über-serious mode. I bite the flesh of my cheek to hide my smile. "When are you going to see that you're surrounded by people who want to help? Who love and care about you?" Any comment I would've made flies right out of my head when his thumb begins tracing the shell of my ear. "You might not want to hear it, but I'm one of them."

This is when you should push him away.

Instead, my hands find their way to the soft cotton of his T-shirt and grip.

Justin takes another step closer and places his hands on either side of my head, caging me in against the wall. "Next time you do something huge like this, or even something small, I want you to call me, okay? You have to know I'll always come running. You snap your pretty little fingers," he says and a *click* sounds near my ear, "and I'm here. Just like that."

My chest rises and falls with increased breaths and I shift my gaze between his eyes. Is he serious? Up until a couple weeks ago, we didn't even make eye contact, we avoided each other for years... and now I'm supposed to *call* him? Trust him to help me?

But then, a lot has changed in two short weeks.

Slowly, sneakily, in ways I didn't always catch, but happened regardless, things shifted. My defenses toppled, the wall I thought I'd built so high in order to keep from getting hurt again: obliterated. Justin bulldozed his way right through every obstacle I lay in his path—almost as if they never existed.

"Stop overthinking it, Sunshine," he murmurs. His fingertips caress my cheek as he slides a strand of hair behind my ear. Tingles shoot across my scalp. "I see those wheels turning. You're just gonna have to accept that we'll be together again one day. Once you stop fighting it so hard, you'll see what I see."

I lick my dry lips and ask, "And what do you see?" though my voice is suddenly so breathless I doubt he understands me. Somehow, he must, because his smile grows.

"Inevitability," he replies, and a rush of sensation curls through my body.

It begins at the nape of my neck, forcing my head back against the wood. It courses down my spine, straight through to my toes. Excitement, disbelief, a hint of anger, and an even stronger dose of an emotion I'm too afraid to name zings through me as my eyes lock on his. My rapid breaths bring with it the sweet scent of hay and the clean scent of boy—soap, a hint of mint, and Justin. He has an intoxicating scent all his own. It was once my addiction.

Our mouths hover just a hairsbreadth apart, and every instinct, every desire screams at me to close the gap. Just as I concede the fight, a screen door slams in the distance. I squeeze my eyes shut.

This is wrong. So wrong. Even having this conversation is wrong. It's not fair to Cade, and the emotions Justin's words have stirred within me make me feel as guilty as if I'd actually done the deed. Cade has been my rock for so long, and Justin... he *destroyed* me freshman year.

Why do I keep forgetting that?

When a cool rush of air replaces the heat of his body, my eyes snap open. Justin is standing a few feet away, his face a mask of calm, collected, confidence—and he's wearing a smirk like he'd just won a freaking Championship.

"But for now, what do you say we get you up on that horse?"

I swear, it's enough to give a girl whiplash. But, he is giving me an out from the conversation, and, like it or not, I *do* need his help if I want to save our ranch. So, ignoring the hand Justin holds out to me, I nod and waltz past him.

"We can try," I reply, ignoring the possible double meaning to his words.

It's not truly until Oakley's ready and it's time to head out for the course that nerves explode in my stomach. What if Justin can't help? What if the same exact thing that happened last time happens again? A repeat may just break me.

"Hop on," Justin instructs with a tap of his fingers on the saddle. "I'll walk you out."

My body freezes with one boot in the stirrup. "You're not going anywhere... are you?"

He smiles gently. "No, Sunshine, I'm not going anywhere. I'll be right here until you kick my ass to the curb. But let's take this one step at a time, all right?"

I nod, swallowing hard, and swing my other leg over Oakley. Gripping her with my knees, I lean down and lay my cheek against her chestnut mane. "We've got this." She whinnies softly in reply and I say, "Forget about last time. Or the time before that," I add, stopping that flashback before it can even begin. "Today's a new day."

Please, Lord, let it be a *successful* new day.

As Justin begins leading us outside, I go through a mental checklist of what I need to do. It's heartbreaking in so many ways—what used to feel as natural as breathing, and every bit as necessary, has somehow turned into this... an obstacle to conquer. As we approach the barrels, I almost can't bring myself to look at them, but eventually I do. I can't let the fear win out this round. Not with Justin's too perceptive gaze so hot on my left cheek.

"See," he says, lifting his chin toward the barrel course. "Nothing to it, right?"

I want to roll my eyes, but don't since I know he's trying to help. Of course there's nothing to this yet. All we've done is step out onto the field. It's everything that remains that's the challenge here... but this is where, yet again, Justin surprises me.

When we enter the pen, he doesn't just let go and push himself up onto the top fence post like I expected him to do. No, he keeps right on leading us, walking both Oakley and me down the unmarked path toward the first barrel. And then, around it.

"What... what are you doing?" I ask, and Annie's ears twitch.

"Helping you get comfortable," he replies, a proud glint in his eyes as he looks over. "Letting you find your rhythm again. You know Oakley can sense your anxiety, and that's not helping anything."

This time, I let the eye roll fly. "Oh, so now who's the horse whisperer?" I ask with a grin. Justin laughs at one of his old nicknames for me, then clucks his tongue softly, guiding us past the second barrel.

"Listen, I just figured instead of jumping in feet first, we warm up a little, that's all."

I have to admit, he has a good point. I've always been an all or nothing sort of girl. I've never really been able to do things halfway or in stages. That's what got me in trouble the first time I tried to ride again, pushing too hard too fast, wanting to be back to normal immediately instead of understanding the small steps my therapist suggested for what they really were—time to heal.

When I stay quiet, Justin once again fills the silence. He's become quite the chatterbox since we dated. "Whenever we have a stressful game coming up, Carlos and I take a cooler out to the field the night before." He steers us around barrel three. "We visualize the game, talk about our opponents, breakdown their strengths and weaknesses. Sometimes, Brandon and Drew join us, and the four us throw the ball around, preparing ourselves for the battle." He looks over at me. "That's what this is, Peyton. *Your* battle. We just need to get you prepared."

My first thought is that I *am* prepared. This literally isn't my first rodeo. I've done this hundreds of times before. But, this *is* the first time I've tried, truly tried, since that day three years ago, so maybe he's right. Maybe I'm not as prepared mentally, physically, or emotionally as I should be.

The fear that lives beneath the surface of my skin? It pretty much proves that I'm not.

So, that's what we do. We prepare, with Justin leading us through the course again and again, each time with my chest allowing a bit more air into my lungs, until the third complete rotation when he circles back to the beginning and comes to a stop.

"Want to try a slow lope?" he asks.

I'm smiling too big by this point to comment on his sudden and proper use of riding slang. I wouldn't want to ruin the moment anyway. I'm breathing deep on the back of my horse, unencumbered by anxiety or memory, and the only response I can give is an honest, "I think I'm ready."

The pride in his eyes brings hope and confidence to my soul. I don't know what it is. Maybe I *did* just need to prepare better. Take it bite by bite. Maybe it's just the magic of Justin. Whatever the reason, I feel a sense of calm in my core. Justin pushes himself up onto the fence, his eyes never once leaving me, and I turn to face the first barrel.

My heart begins to race, but this time, not in fear. It's excitement that hums through my veins. Justin believes in me, he thinks I can do this. I intend to prove him right.

"Let's show him, girl," I tell Oakley, nudging her flank as I cluck my tongue. "Ride!"

Wind, my old familiar friend, kisses my cheeks and tangles my hair as Annie and I take off. Her hooves pound a rhythm as old as time and a smile crosses my face as we near the first barrel. For a split second, doubts enter. Fear has stolen this moment from me twice before, and as we approach the turn, I close my eyes, hoping instinct and memory take over.

When I open them again, we're headed toward barrel two. "Yeah!"

Justin's scream of approval echoes through my ears and I laugh aloud.

Holy crap! We actually did it!

The second and third barrels go just as easily, just as naturally, and by the time I come to a giddy stop in front of Justin again, I can barely feel my fingertips. I'm simply one huge, numb ball of shock and awe. No, I didn't race nearly as fast as I once did. But, I did do it. Oakley and I both did. Thanks to Justin, that is.

"Hell yeah!" he yells again, and his feet barely touch the ground before he's running toward me, a smile as wide as the Texas sky on his face. I shake my head at the sight. The whole world, or at least the population of Fairfield Academy, only ever sees the bravado, the mask he wears to disguise the tender, vulnerable heart hidden inside. Oh, there's no denying that Justin Carter can be a touch overconfident at times. He's a showboat to end all showboats. But in this case, *damn* did it work in my favor. "I knew you could do it! Didn't I tell you that you could do it?"

My smile matches his when I reply, "Yeah, yeah. You may've mentioned it."

His enthusiasm is contagious and I bite my bottom lip, so many emotions now surging through me that I feel restless. I want to cry. I want to laugh. I want to hop off Oakley's back and tackle Justin to the ground—but *that* would be highly inappropriate. So, instead I rock back and forth in the saddle, feeling more alive than ever before.

Justin watches my exuberant display and chuckles. "Let me guess, you want to go again?"

"Again, and again, and again," I answer, a swell of gratitude rising within me. This is how it feels to get a part of your life back. There are no words in the English language powerful enough to thank him for this. "Justin, I don't know how to—"

He places his hand over mine, silencing me. For once, I don't try to move it. "You don't need to say anything." His eyes betray his words, as they're filled with so many things left unspoken between us. But instead of giving them voice, he squeezes my hand and says, "Just ride, pretty girl."

And that's exactly what I do.

JUSTIN

SWEET SERENITY RANCH 7:35 P.M.

The loud crunch of gravel smothers Peyton's laugh and the toned muscles of her thigh turn to stone beneath my palm. My dopey-ass grin falls. Shielding my eyes against the glare, I turn to see who's barreling up the road behind us, thinking my luck's about run out.

It's not Coach; there's not a shot in hell he called practice early, not two days before the Semi-finals. He won't come home until at least ten, spending the night surrounded by empty pizza boxes and scrutinizing game footage, and normally, I'd be right there with him. Instead, thanks to my injury, I found myself here, listening to Peyton's laugh and hoarding her smiles like they're Cadbury cream eggs at Easter.

And damn if it doesn't feel like I'm exactly where I'm meant to be.

"Nut burgers."

Peyton's voice is pitched low and sort of breathless, so I glance at her before looking back out at the road. A dark blue truck roars past us, jerking to a stop in the field next to the barrel course. I catch her hand clenching in my periphery, another one of her anxious tics, and when I raise my eyes again, I watch as her gorgeous smile slips from her face.

Fuck that.

"Hey." I squeeze her hip and her gaze darts to mine before flitting away. It doesn't take a genius to know who it is... or what she's thinking. "Baby, you did nothing wrong. There's nothing to hide here, so there's no reason to feel guilty."

Her head bobs distractedly and I cover her fist with my palm. "Peyton, you just kicked major ass out there. Hold onto that." I stop myself just short of saying *please*.

Selfishly, I admit a part of me wants Cade to walk up and find her happy with me. But more than that, I want this for her. What she just did out there was amazing. She conquered a fear—no, she smashed it to hell. Peyton owned that barrel course and right now, she should be on cloud fucking nine, not gnawing on her lip like some cracked out rabbit.

I pry the fingers of her clenched hand loose and Peyton's eyes finally settle on me. Her mouth lifts in a wan smile, lip still trapped, and I growl with the need to free it. If she weren't perched so high on Oakley's back, I'd do exactly that. I'd tug it free and soothe the tender flesh with my thumb... before following with my mouth.

But that's only if she let me, and the chances of that are slim to none.

Sure, we shared an incredible day. We laughed, we smiled, we worked together like a team. But she's still not mine. She's his, and if she rejected my touch after the last few hours... I'm not sure I could handle it.

We could fill a book with the words left unsaid between us. My plan was to tell her today, after we brushed Oakley down, the truth about what happened freshman year, the way I feel about her now. The way I've always felt. Guess that plan's shot to hell.

Cade's door slams. You'd think, after how long he's been sitting in his truck, he'd at least *pretend* not to care that I'm here. You'd think wrong. Whatever little pep talk he gave himself didn't do a damn thing because he's glaring at me like I'm horse shit under his boot.

The feeling's mutual, kid.

Peyton's low hum yanks me from our silent show down. She rocks in the saddle, back and forth, watching Cade storm up the trail in his stupid cowboy boots, taking in Oakley, the barrels we obviously just left, and me, standing right beside her.

When he comes to a stop in front of us, a tight smile a poor mask for his tension, he asks, "What'd I miss?"

Jesus, what a loaded question. One I'd love to answer, too, but Peyton beats me to the punch. She hops off Oakley's back before I can even form a word. *Smart girl.*

She hesitates only a second before running and jumping into his arms. "I did it!"

Gone is the apprehension and guilt, replaced with pure excitement and energy. Though it kills me that she's looking at *him* the same way she looked at me not five minutes ago, at least she's smiling again. That's an improvement.

"Can you believe it?" she asks, face lit with awe. "I actually did it! I didn't even freak out this time."

Cade glances at me, so quick she probably misses it, before running his hand down her back. "Of course I believe it, CC. I didn't doubt you for a second."

I try and fail not to make a gagging sound. Cade shoots me another one of those horse-shit looks as Peyton steps back from his embrace.

"Justin helped me complete the course at least a dozen times," she says. "I don't have to tell Mama to call off the expo. We can still save the ranch!"

This is the most enthusiasm I've seen out of Peyton in weeks. From Cade's reaction, it's the most he's seen, too, and from the expression on his face, he's clearly torn between loving it and loathing that I had anything to do with it. If he had his way, I'm sure he'd stick with the status quo—me being the royal fuck-up, and him the white-hat hero.

Finally, he says, "That's amazing," though his tone implies he's anything but amazed.

His fingers glide through her strawberry blonde hair, mussed by the wind and riding, and he cradles her face to press a kiss against her forehead. His dark eyes meet mine.

I've never been an overly violent person. Aggressive, maybe. Protective, absolutely. Like any other guy, I've gotten in my share of fights, but it's not like I search them out. I don't relish the thought of cracking skulls or watching someone bleed. But this little shit is getting to me. He's standing in the way of what's mine, and it takes every memory of Peyton's smiles to keep me from going after him, right here, right now.

I won't ruin her day with my bullshit. But soon, Cade and I are gonna have a talk.

Dismissing me with a glance, Cade tips her head back and continues. "I have to say, though, I wish you would've come to *me*."

The words hit as intended, and Peyton winces, that inner-light dimming again. If I had no other reason, I'd hate the guy just for that.

"I know." She steps out of his arms and folds hers tight across her chest. "But if you or Faith or Mama saw me fail again... I couldn't deal with that. Too much is riding on this. I had to do it on my own."

"But you didn't." He presses his lips together, then lifts his hand as he accuses, "You turned to him."

Peyton's eyes blow wide. "No, I didn't!" She moves like she's gonna take his hand, then thinks better of it, and rubs her palms down her thighs. "I swear, Cade, it wasn't like that at all. Justin asked how the barrel riding was going, and when I told him about my epic fail the other day, he..."

"He volunteered," I finish for her, my jaw aching from clenching. He's doing it again. Taking a moment that should be awesome, about *her*, and making it about himself. "I'd think you'd be happy for her. What she did today was incredible and, I don't know, maybe I'm wrong, but I think that's what's important. Not who was here to watch."

I shrug, innocent as can be, knowing as I do that I'm driving him bat-shit crazy.

Peyton bites out a warning, "*Justin...*"

"No," Cade says, "he's right."

Releasing a sigh, he removes his glasses and pinches the bridge of his nose. I almost feel for the guy. When he replaces them, a heavy look of defeat coats his expression, and a hum of victory buzzes beneath my skin.

"I'm sorry, CC. I'm being a jealous ass," he admits, reaching out and taking her hand. "But that's on me, not you. It doesn't matter who was here to help, just that you did it, and I'm proud of you. Really."

Damn. This is *not* how I saw this going.

"I guess I just don't understand why he's here," Cade continues, offering her an "aww, shucks" grin. "Shouldn't he be out on a diamond somewhere?"

"*He* can hear you," I grit out, "and I'm benched for a week." I wave my slung elbow like a stupid flag and go for the joke. "Apparently, my head's not as hard as we thought."

The truth is, my head was in a fog the first two days, and my sleep has been shit. Concussions suck and it's made my life miserable. But today... today made it all worth it. If it brings Peyton back to life, I'll gladly get knocked on my ass every game.

Peyton frowns at my sling. "He stopped by to go over our project, and when we were done, he suggested I try a different approach on the course. It ended up working."

We both know it was more than a new outlook. Peyton succeeded because she was born to ride, her instincts are strong, and because we worked together, just like we used to. But I won't push it. I've already gotten my win for the day.

Cade huffs a laugh under his breath. Then, shaking his head like what he's about to do is against his own better judgement, he holds out a hand. "Well, then I guess I should say thanks. Peyton belongs in that ring. I'm grateful you helped her find her way back there."

Like an idiot, I stare at his extended appendage for a few more beats before accepting it.

Our handshake is awkward as hell, not only because I'm forced to use the wrong hand, and as we lock eyes, we hold an entire conversation in a glance.

Thanks for helping... but she's still my girlfriend.

You're welcome... and not for long.

Cade drops the act and shoves his hand back into his jeans pocket. "So, when does this assignment end anyway? Isn't graduation in a week?"

"Uh, this is the last week," Peyton says, staring at the patch of air where we shook hands. A strange squiggle forms between her eyebrows. "Today wrapped up the marriage unit—"

"And tomorrow we become parents," I finish for her, wanting to get a rise out of Cade.

But, as soon as the words leave my mouth, I realize my mistake.

Instead of Cade flushing in a jealous rage, Peyton's fair skin turns ghost white. Her shoulders bow like she's been hit, and a strangled sound emits from her throat.

I bite back a curse as memories assault me. How can I be so stupid? Cade narrows his eyes, like he's not sure why he should lay into me, but he's ready to do it anyway—and he should. He damn well should. Because while I don't know what he knows, or even *if* he knows, what I just said was heartless.

I want to drop to my knees. I want to curse my stupid mouth and tell her I didn't mean it. But if Peyton hasn't told Cade anything, I can't. I can't make this worse than it already is.

When Peyton speaks again, her voice is small. "Coach Stasi gave us a budget spreadsheet." She forces a smile, pretending like I haven't gutted her, and I stare a hole in the side of her cheek. "Tomorrow we have to meet at Walmart and price out baby items, then extrapolate that over a year." She makes a face and laughs a little. "Your math nerd brain would be in hog heaven."

Cade laughs at that, a real laugh this time, and I watch as they share a small smile. It's worse than yelling at me or showing me how much I hurt her. She's ignoring me. Desperate to turn the tide and interrupt their bonding moment, I stupidly say:

"Nothing says romance like a date at Walmart."

Are you shitting me? That's what you come up with?

It's amazing I've gotten any women at all.

Shockingly, my dumbass comment does the trick. The goo-goo eyes stop and Cade shoots me a look like he'd forgotten I was even here. Fat chance. Peyton scratches her elbow. "We pick up our electronic baby Friday morning and have to keep it for the weekend."

And that reminds me of the other reason I stopped by.

Grateful for the shift in subject, I go for my best panty-melting grin and say, "Oh, hey, I almost forgot. A bunch of us are going out to the beach house this weekend. A weekend-long baby-shower–slash-misery-loves-company kind of deal." I glance at Cade, including him in the invite with strong, *strong* reluctance. "You're both welcome to come along."

Friday's a school holiday, a teacher in-service or some bullshit, so we have a three-day weekend once we pick up our babies from Coach Stasi. Which means I'll have close to sixty hours with Peyton if she agrees. Anything can happen with that much time. This is my last shot, so I'm holding out for a miracle here, even if Cade *does* tag along.

Besides, I have a few tricks up my sleeve.

"What do you say?"

Peyton hesitates. "Well... it *would* be easier if we're both there with the baby." She turns to Cade and explains. "We're supposed to share responsibility. The babies will be programmed to shut down sometime Sunday, which leaves us just enough time to get over sleep deprivation before exams on Wednesday." She sighs, like she's already exhausted thinking of it, and adds, "If a bunch of us go through it together, it might suck less."

I try not to show how much this means to me, but it's so damn hard.

Then she says, "While we're in Galveston, we can also stop by Pleasure Pier."

This is directed at Cade, and an underlying tone in her voice tempers my excitement. From the way he's smiling, I know I'll regret asking... but I do it anyway. "Pleasure Pier?"

"It's our spot," he replies, tucking Peyton against his side. "It's where I took her for our first official date."

Well fuck my life.

Why can't anything ever be easy? Just one small thing? I'm working my ass off here, trying to win back the girl I'm in love with and atone for my horrible mistakes of the past, and just when I think I'm finally catching a break, shit like this happens.

Cade brushes a lock of Peyton's golden hair aside and whispers something in her ear, looking like he thinks he's won. But I hold tight to what I know:

Cade Donovan may be a good guy, but he doesn't know Peyton like I do. He doesn't challenge her. He doesn't see through the mask she shows the world that hides the scared yet resilient heart beneath. He couldn't, or she wouldn't be doubting herself so much. She'd know how amazing she is. That she can do anything because she's strong, stronger than anyone I've ever met. And because she'd be hearing it every damn day.

Everyone knows I'm not good for much, but I was made to love this girl. I'm good for her and I'm good *with* her. It may've taken me three years to fully realize that, but I know it now.

Soon, she will, too.

"I'll have to rearrange some things back home," Cade says, his cocky grin implying that this is over. That the weekend will be some kind of romantic weekend escape for two. He should know better than to doubt me by now. "But, sure. We're in."

Peyton smiles, although it doesn't quite reach her eyes. Those beautiful peepers are swirling with curiosity and a dash of apprehension. And rightly so.

Horse boy has no clue what he's up against.

FRIDAY, MAY 30TH

1 Week until Graduation

♥ Senior Year

PEYTON

GALVESTON BEACH HOUSE 10:52 A.M.

When we get to the Carters' beach house, Cade makes a scoffing sound in his throat. It grates on my nerves, but I can't really blame him. It's the biggest one on the block, not that I expected any less, and of course it's smack dab in the middle of the ritziest section of Galveston.

But see, Cade is only looking at the surface.

Sure, colorful flowers line the drive, providing the perfect contrast to the mansion's stereotypical all-white façade. A wraparound terrace and fancy gazebo add that touch of southern sweetness and sophistication. The whole shebang screams money and entitlement and everything I've come to associate with Mitch and Annabeth Carter.

But I've peeked behind their oh-so-perfect curtain. I know the danger of judging a book by its cover. So as I set my sandal on the flawless, paved driveway, and stare up, up, *up* to the top of the house, all I can think is that it feels lonely.

How sad must it have been to vacation here as a kid? My parents never had a lot of money, even before my insane medical bills, but they always filled my summers with sticky treats and pure silliness. Justin's beach house is the *opposite* of silly. It's pristine, enormous, and lacking any trace of true comfort. It makes me hurt for the little boy he once was.

"Nice place," Cade says. Sea gulls squawk overhead and waves crash against the shore behind the house, but his sarcasm is unmistakable. "Think it's big enough?"

Somehow, I withhold my groan. *Is it Sunday yet?*

The trip only just began, yet it already seems to be dragging. The ride down felt like it took days instead of a couple hours. Cade's constant snide little digs at Justin made my molars ache.

News flash? I don't need reminders of how badly he hurt me in the past. Every second I spent with Justin, every up and down, is seared into my memory. *Cade's* the one that doesn't know all the details.

But, I understand.

Even before my ex steamrolled his way into my relationship, Cade and I hadn't clicked in a while. Not like we did in the beginning. The very things I loved and found refreshing in the beginning now started to irk. His response to the honeymoon question was a perfect example of that. But, that's Cade. It's not fair to suddenly change the rules on him when he's been consistent and loyal the whole time.

That's why we're here, or at least it's one of the reasons. My hope was that if we got away from the stress of the ranch, snuggled on the beach, and reconnected at the Pier, that we'd rekindle the feelings of last summer. Relive the incredible memories we made together.

Unfortunately, my stellar plan isn't turning out so stellar.

"It's gorgeous," I agree with a tight smile, choosing to take his words at face value. New plan? Distract, distract, distract. Lowering my voice to a flirtatious level, I bump my shoulder against his and ask, "You know what the best part is?"

Cade shifts his gaze from the four-story home. "What's that?"

"Pleasure Pier is right down the road." I extend a finger in the opposite direction we came, knowing from my Google Maps check that it's about a ten-minute walk from where we stand. Technology is my new bestie.

Dark lenses shield Cade's expressive eyes, but a small smile plays upon his lips. *Finally.*

"Is that right?" he asks, casually leaning against his truck. "Huh. You know, if I remember correctly, I still owe you a funnel cake."

"With extra sugar," I confirm. "I won that puppy fair and square, and just because I was too stuffed to eat it then doesn't mean you're off the hook." Playfully, I poke him in the arm and say, "I always collect my debts, Mr. Donovan."

A tiny dimple pops in his cheek as his entire smile ignites. "And *I* always honor my promises, Miss Williams." He covers my hand with his, and hope fills my chest.

This is what I wanted. Cade literally swept me off my feet on our first trip to the pier. He was romantic and sweet—well, up until he tossed me in the waves, but even that was fun. He made me laugh, something I did far too little up until then, and was everything my stupid heart once wanted Justin to be.

We splashed in the waves, napped on the beach, and rode every single ride they had. Cade won me a stuffed elephant at ring toss, and later bet me a funnel cake over free throws at Big Shot Hoops. The silly boy really should've known better. I do have two older brothers, after all, and one seriously athletics-crazed dad. But he completely charmed me.

That trip marked a turning point for us. For three years, he'd been one of my best friends. We'd known each other even longer than that. I'd sworn off dating after Justin, having lost all interest in the prospect, but that day, touched by Cade's affection and sweet attention, I let him kiss me in the back row of the Sea Dragon. When my tummy dipped, it had nothing to do with the freefall and everything to do with taking another chance.

Cade's patient tenderness healed my scarred, battered heart, and under a full moon, accompanied by childish giggles, excited screams, and the hypnotic lull of the waves, he promised he'd never break it. Trusting him that he wouldn't, I took a leap.

That's why we're here.

"The pier's not the only thing this place has going for it," he says, gently brushing his thumb across the pulse point in my wrist. It jumps in response... even as a weird sinking feeling enters my stomach.

"It's not?"

"Nope." He shakes his head with a slow grin then lifts his chin toward the house. "As huge as this place is, I'm betting there's lots of space for privacy. Hidden corners, doors with locks. Even with your baby project and a full house of guests, we should get plenty alone time." The edge of his nail rasps the tender skin of my wrist and his teeth sink into his lower lip. "Especially at night."

My breath catches, and my heart loses its rhythm for a beat. Feeling the change beneath his fingertips, Cade's eyes sharpen.

He doesn't know about... *before.*

From the look in his eyes, he has his theories, and I'm sure they're not that far from the truth. But he's never asked and I've never told him. I don't know, that's probably pretty telling in itself—couples share things, solid couples at least, and part of me wants to tell him some of it. But it's not that easy.

Sometimes... sometimes things happen that are too painful. The very thought of putting them into words, speaking them out into the universe, tears a piece of your soul.

My secret with Justin is one of those.

Cade's seductive grin slips and he releases my hand. I wrap it against my chest, guarding against a sudden chill, and watch him grab our bags from the truck.

"Who else is coming?" He shoulders his duffle and lifts the handle on my rolling case, then takes off for the tall staircase. Feeling a headache mounting, I fall into step behind him.

"I assume some of the guys from the team," I say, scoping out the cars and trucks already parked on the driveway and in the street. An F150 with huge tires tells me Dad's pitcher is here. "Brandon, Drew, and Carlos are in our FACS class, plus they're Justin's best friends. They met up at school this morning to pick up our robot babies. Also my friend Mi-Mi should be here since she's Brandon's partner for the project."

His girlfriend Aly is in our class, too, so she's a definite. That makes me happy. We only ever shared a class or two but she's super sweet and Dad adores her. Plus, her baking skills are legendary. I admit I was a *tad* jealous when she hooked up with Justin last year; she was the first girl who made him smile like he used to—not the fake one he wears in the halls, but the real one that reaches his eyes.

Unfortunately for Justin, they never had a chance. Anyone with eyes knew Aly and Brandon were inevitable.

"And what do you see?"

"Inevitability."

I lose my footing on the stairs and grab hold of the railing.

In the barn, Justin seemed so sure that we belonged together. That I'll forgive the past, drop my boyfriend, and run back into his open arms.

Why is he so confident? Will what he's hiding really make *that* much of a difference?

I honestly don't know what I hope for more—that it will, or that it won't. That scares me.

We reach the top of the staircase, where the large terrace overlooks the Gulf, and Cade pops his neck, rolling it like he does whenever he's nervous. Not the best start to our weekend.

"Hey." Reaching up, I slide off his sunglasses and find his dark eyes troubled. "Thank you. I know you don't want to be here, but you came anyway... for me. I appreciate it."

I lean up on my toes and press a kiss across his mouth.

Cade exhales against my lips and presses his forehead to mine. "You're worth it."

The way he's looking at me says he means much more than just this weekend. I nod, unsure of what to say, and he touches his lips to my nose. With a sigh, he turns and knocks on the door.

Considering how many people are here, I expected the door to instantly fly open. When it doesn't, he raps again, then tries the knob only to find it locked.

"Maybe try the bell?" I suggest, rocking back on my heels.

He presses it, sending a series of twinkling sounds into the air, and a nervous flutter tickles my belly. I always hate being late to a party. People stare and they whisper. It reminds me too much of my illness.

From inside, a female voice screams, "*Coming*!" and my heart jumps into my throat.

A BMW is parked below. It was the first car I spotted when we arrived, my eyes trained to seek out Lauren before I could be ambushed. Justin told me she was invited, so I knew about it coming here. She's Carlos's *wife* for the project, after all. But my plan is to avoid her at all costs. If she answers the door, that won't be avoiding. It'll be in my face. And nothing screams bad omen like an awkward door greeting by the other woman.

Thankfully, when it opens, a cute, tiny redhead appears.

"Awesome!" Aly pulls the door wider and waves us in eagerly. "Peyton, your timing rocks."

"Uh, okay." At Cade's questioning glance, I lift a shoulder and say, "You're welcome?"

Aly laughs as I step inside what suddenly feels like a cloud—or a home for the Stay Puft Marshmallow Man. Everywhere I look: white, white, white, white, white. The sofas—white. The walls—white. The rugs—you guessed it—white. I shake my head, wondering who would invite a bunch of crazy teenagers to a place so painstakingly immaculate, but then roll my eyes as I answer my own question.

This is Annabeth we're talking about. If things get messy, she'll just refurnish the place.

"I just finished a batch of brownies," Aly says, wrapping her arm around my elbow like we've been friends forever. "The two of you are my new taste testers. Since the guys took the first baby shift, they're all down by the beach. Already we've had diaper changes, feedings, and burping. Plus, these things breathe, Peyton. I'm calling it now, y'all. They're gonna drive us crazy by tomorrow."

Then to Cade she says, "Just leave those bags there for now, because dessert awaits!"

He gives her an amused smile and does as she says, sending me a subtle wink. Already things feel lighter between us… and I have Aly to thank for it. Releasing a relieved breath, I smile at my new friend and follow my nose into the kitchen.

Of course, it's beyond ridiculous. Marble countertops, stainless steel appliances, and more snacks than I've ever seen at one time. Aly's mom is a caterer, so I shouldn't be surprised, and as I said, the girl is known for her snacks. I spy the tray of brownies in question on the stovetop and my stomach grumbles.

Dropping my arm, Aly slides over to the goods. "Justin put me in charge of all things snackage this weekend since it's my thing, and I want you both to give me your honest opinion."

She selects two giant squares and sets them each on a napkin. "Tell me if they're too bold or too much."

"I feel like those two words will never apply to chocolate *anything*," I confess and accept the gift of fudgy goodness.

The brownie is moist, that's obvious just from looking at it, and when I lift it to my mouth my fingers sink into the soft texture. My taste buds prep themselves for a happy dance. Then the rich scent of cocoa hits my senses and I close my eyes in bliss.

"Holy crap!"

A surprising burst of orange hits my tongue and I moan, taking another bite, hoping my sprung-open eyes tell Aly everything she needs to know, because I refuse to stop eating for something as silly as words. Seriously. Roll out a sleeping bag, call it a day, I'm good to go camping in the kitchen.

"You like it?"

I exaggerate a head nod, and Aly bounces on her sneakers. "Really? See, normally, I'm a brownie purist. Cookies, cupcakes, tarts; I go wild with those, but brownies are my religion. But the other day I saw a recipe on Pinterest and it sparked my imagination." She raises an eyebrow and says, "That site is addictive... for realz."

"They're incredible," I mumble, mouth filled with orange-flavored chocolate. "What's in here? How did you get it to taste like this? I swear it looks like a normal brownie."

Aly leans in with wide eyes. "The secret is orange marmalade. Fun, right?"

I nod my agreement and gather every possible crumb, pressing my fingertip into the moist morsels and licking without shame. I consider tonguing my napkin, too, but decide that may be too weird, so instead I break the edge off Cade's remaining sliver and smile around my bite. He laughs and hands the whole thing over, blowing me a kiss.

He's good people.

Aly watches our exchange with happy yet curious eyes, and I can't help wondering how much she knows. She and Justin parted as friends, surprising since other than me, I never knew him to have friends who are girls.

"These are delicious," Cade tells her, and she smiles in gratitude.

"Thanks. When you have a wicked sweet tooth, you learn how to bake pretty quickly."

Male laughter floats through the open window and Aly glances outside. She pushes off the marble counter and says, "We better get y'all settled. Girls take over parenting duty in thirty minutes. You ready to be a mommy, Peyton?"

No. No, I'm not... "I can barely contain my joy."

Cade links our fingers as we follow Aly back toward the door to get our bags.

"Is your baby-daddy here for the weekend?" he asks her, shocking me with his teasing. I'm almost positive if Justin referred to himself as my "baby-daddy¬," Cade would go ballistic.

"Yep," she says. "Drew's on the team with the guys."

Catching her smirk I ask, "How's Brandon handling you being *married* to his best friend?"

"About as well as Gabi's handling Lauren," Aly replies with a snort. "He knows nothing is going on, but sometimes, hmm, how do I put this..." She scrunches her nose and squints one eye. "Brandon's jealous tendencies tend to overrule his common sense."

Somewhere inside a voice screams, "I so get that," even as another voice yells out, "so not the same thing!"

Our situations are completely different. One, Drew and Aly never dated. Two, Drew is in love with his girlfriend Sarah, and Aly and Brandon are Fairfield's super couple. Three, Brandon and Drew don't try and send ocular laser missiles whenever they're within two feet of each other.

And four, I'm sure Aly doesn't get butterflies every time she thinks Drew's name.

Gah. I'm so screwed.

"The rooms on this floor have been taken," Aly says, motioning toward the second level as she continues up the enormous staircase, "but there's two still open on the third. The fourth is for his parents and is off-limits. Every floor has three bedrooms, two baths, and one central hang-out area." She looks over at me and grins. "It's a pretty sweet setup."

When we reach the third level, I stop on the top step to get my bearings. The space is dominated by a cozy nook in the center with a plush sofa, and bedrooms on either end. The two rooms to the right of the landing share a bathroom, and the larger bedroom on the left has its own.

"That's where Justin is staying," Aly says, pointing to the master. "And Cade, you're over here." The room she ushers us toward is large, with the same white driftwood walls as downstairs and two twin beds.

A black suitcase with clothes tumbling out already sits on one, next to a guitar case.

Cade looks at the bed, looks at me, and then frowns.

Aly glances between us. "Did Justin tell you the house rules? No couples are rooming together... girls are staying with girls, boys staying with boys." She shakes her head and says something under her breath. "He really didn't tell you?"

"No," Cade says, the scowl emerging again. "He conveniently left that part out."

He tosses his bag on the empty bed, his posture saying louder than words how he feels about the setup. Ignoring Aly's watchful gaze, I turn to the window and pretend to be fascinated with the view.

Waves break and foam on the beach, boats bob in the distance. And on the sand just below us, a group of guys cradling babies like footballs stand around laughing. As if he can feel my stare, Justin turns and looks up, finding me standing in the window. His player smile falls for just a moment, revealing the sweet, vulnerable one he seems to only reserve for me.

My heart kicks in my chest.

Oh, he's smooth. Justin Carter suddenly has a problem with co-habitation? *Please*. We both know the reason for his sudden modesty—Cade does, too, and I have a suspicion so does Aly. But I can't quite summon the energy to be angry. In fact, I'm grateful.

I'm not ready to sleep with Cade. Not the way that he wants. So, as crazy as it is, and whether he realizes it or not, in this case, Justin's selfish motives actually work for me.

"You're rooming with Carlos," Aly says, snapping my attention away from the window. "Heads up, he's a bit of a slob, but hopefully his wicked guitar skills will make up for it. Peyton, you're right across the hall."

"See?" I say, trying my best to steer this ship of positivity. "We're still close. Besides, you'll be so exhausted at night that you won't even notice you're not rooming with me."

The look Cade shoots me says, "nice try."

We head across the hall, but Aly makes a sudden stop in front of the bathroom. Biting her lip, she gives the closed door a look before leaning in and lowering her voice. "I hope you don't mind, but right before you got here, we had a little switch up. Originally you were going to room with Mi-Mi, but once Kara saw who she was paired with, she sort of claimed your bed. If you have a problem with it, though, she said she'll totally move back."

She winces slightly and bounces on her feet, clearly anxious but giving me a hopeful look, and dread hits my gut like a rock. I already know where this is going.

"We just figured if anyone could handle *her*, it's you. Somehow, you've survived our entire high school experience without once clashing heads or getting on Lauren's shit list."

I almost laugh aloud. It's true that most of Lauren's former victims are well-known. Added that to the fact that no one at school knows Justin and I ever dated, much less what happened with him and Lauren right after, of course Aly would assume this wouldn't be a big deal. I'm Peyton Williams. The quiet senior who barely has any friends, much less enemies, and miraculously avoided all the Fairfield Academy drama.

Ha!

Obviously taking my silence for agreement, Aly knocks on the closed bedroom door and an annoyed voice within says, "*Yeah?*" Immediately, cold chills creep down my spine. A sudden case of the giggles hits me and Cade gives me a worried look.

A minute ago, I was worrying about fighting with my boyfriend about sex. Now, I'd gladly trade that problem for this. Aly rolls her eyes toward the door, mumbling under her breath, and turns the knob, and I steel my spine before following her into the room.

The blonde bombshell near the dresser spares me a glance before returning to her unpacking. "I claimed the bed by the window because it's better. Also, I'm gonna need the whole dresser."

Cade's eyebrows lift and then his jaw clenches, clearly picking up on the tension in the room. I squeeze his hand, letting him know it's fine. There's no point in arguing over her theatrics. I'm used to her bitchiness, and really, it's only two days. How bad can it be?

I force my lips into a smile I don't feel. "Whatever you say, Lauren."

MONDAY, APRIL 25TH

7 Weeks until Disaster

♥ Freshman Year

JUSTIN

SWEET SERENITY RANCH 11:58 P.M.

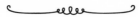

Soft whines, muffled yaps, and low scratching didn't exactly equal a lullaby, but I'd eat nails before I ever complained. Noise meant I wasn't alone. It reminded me that someone, a whole family, actually, cared about me. And the cloying scent of bleach stinging my nose... well, it gave me something to focus on *other* than the hard on from hell that wouldn't go away.

Flipping on my stomach, I punched the pillow and slammed my face against the cotton.

Peyton was taunting me. Walking around in those little short shorts, finding excuses to touch me whenever she passed. Flushing pink and sending flirtatious looks my way whenever her parents weren't watching. That kiss at the pond shifted things. Made me feel things I never felt before. Think things I never thought I would. Like what a future with her would be like... and asking her to be mine, officially. Introducing her to my friends, telling the whole damn school I was taken. Because I was.

Official or not, Peyton Williams owned me.

But that was where it got dangerous. With Sunshine, it wasn't about the chase. It wasn't even about the possibility of sex. I'd been turned on before, I was used to the pounding heart, the restless itch under my skin, the need for physical connection. This went beyond that. As hot as other girls had gotten me, I'd always been able to walk away. So much so that, despite my impressive reputation, I'd yet to take a girl to my bed.

I wasn't claiming to be a saint. I'd hooked up plenty, and rounded three of the bases. Multiple times. But technically, if you wanted to get picky about it, I'd never made it to home. Something had always turned me off before it reached that point.

Turning *off* wasn't even a possibility with Peyton. Every kiss, every touch, was fucking fantastic. She got me on a level that blew my mind. Honestly, it scared the hell out of me. I no longer knew which way was up, and the only thing keeping me from sneaking over to the main house, finding her bedroom, and seeing if she wanted me as badly as I wanted her was knowing how perfect she was. How innocent and pure and too damn good for me.

Plus, I owed Coach way too much to disrespect him like that.

I groaned into my pillow. I closed my eyes but the image of her kiss-swollen lips still burned my mind. Seeking relief, I tilted my hips and pushed deeper into the mattress.

One more night of this madness and then I'd be home. One more night and I'd be away from temptation, away from those short shorts, tan legs, and perky little—

A loud, angry bark pierced the fog of lust and stilled my movements.

"What the hell?"

A muted *thump* came from down the hall. My head snapped up, and I stretched my hearing, not even breathing so I wouldn't miss a sound. I knew every door was locked, I'd checked them myself, so there was no way a dog was loose.

Another *bump*, this one closer, and the Doberman across the hall went nuts. I shot to my feet, reached for the baseball bat sticking out of my bag, and inched closer to the door. My chest felt like it was about to explode.

Holy shit. Someone had broken in and was trying to steal the dogs.

Who *did* that?

I popped my neck and tightened my grip on the wooden bat, the familiar feel centering me for the fight. No one messed with Coach and his family. Not when he trusted me with patrol. I inhaled a breath and reached for the doorknob, bracing myself as I leaned toward the door... just as it swung open for me.

"Shit!"

"Holy crap!"

The Doberman howled again, and I grabbed Peyton's wrist, yanking her inside.

"Are you trying to give me a heart attack?" I asked, whispering like a dumbass even as the dogs went crazy around us. The baseball bat dropped from my fingertips and I slapped my hand over my thundering heart. "What—what the hell are you doing here?"

Through the faint light of my bedside lamp, I saw the rosy glow in her cheeks. Peyton tugged on the hem of her long tee, drawing my gaze to her bare legs, and I swallowed hard.

"Well—" the Doberman snarled again and she swiveled her head to hiss, "*Nein!*"

Miraculously, that shut the dog up.

The other ones fell quiet in quick succession, no longer being instigated by the large animal. The lone holdout was a little yappy dog that continued to yelp for another twenty seconds. I kept expecting Mrs. Grace to dash through the door in her bathrobe and slippers. Kept waiting for Coach to storm in and find me with his daughter. That would go over about as well as telling Annabeth her expensive skincare crap got discontinued—he'd flip.

When tiny Napoleon finally went silent, Peyton parted her lips and I shook my head, trying not to breathe, scared to make a sound, and listened for their approach.

"My parents aren't coming," she said after a minute, taking a step closer. She placed her hand over mine, right over my heart. "You'd be surprised how soundproof this house is."

"But aren't..." I swallowed again and tried to catch my breath. It felt like it was trying to pound out of my body. "Aren't they worried about people breaking in?"

Peyton smiled, a small one that said she thought I was adorable. I wasn't adorable—I was protective. I was strong. I was her freaking hero. I *wasn't* adorable.

"We have an alarm and we lock the doors," she said, telling me like I didn't already know. I did know; I just, well, I'd forgotten about the alarm. "Plus we have the code at the gate. The likelihood of anyone getting in here is pretty slim. So, Dad insulated the crap out of both houses to keep us from getting woken up every night."

My ears heard what she said. My thoughts were just too scattered to grasp them right away. When I did, the relief was almost paralyzing. My knees went weak, the fear of the last few minutes fully catching up with me, and I blindly reached back for the mattress, tugging her with me onto the bed.

"Oh, thank God."

For the next few minutes we just sat there, holding each other, letting my racing heart match its rhythm to hers. I wasn't cut out for this shit. Fifteen years of living pretty much by myself, only having to look out for myself, messed with my survival instincts. Thankfully, the longer the dogs stayed quiet, the more my breathing relaxed.

Slowly, I became less and less focused on the excitement of the last few minutes... and more and more aware of the girl in my arms.

I inhaled naturally, easily, the tightness of my chest easing, and the floral scent of her skin mixed with coconut shampoo hit my senses.

"Christ, you smell amazing." I took another drag and locked it in my lungs. She always smelled amazing—like the perfect summer day. Breathing her in, my head clouded and my skin blazed hot. I felt drunk, drunk on the scent, drunk on *her*, and the craving I had just before she got here—that I've had ever since I met her—stirred again. My fingers clenched at the thin cotton of her shirt.

We were alone in the near darkness. Her parents were asleep. And Peyton was in my bed.

I repeated my question from before. "What are you doing here?"

I softened my words by cradling her cheek, but I needed to be sure. My control was hanging by a thread. She shivered in my arms and her neck tilted back, lifting her eyes to mine. They shimmered with want.

Calmly, deliberately, she untangled herself from my arms. She stood from the bed, and I panicked, grabbing for her hand, thinking she was leaving. But she wasn't. She came closer and nudged my knees apart.

Peyton's long, smooth, completely bare thighs, exposed by her flimsy tee, slid between my legs, light next to dark, and I looked down, realizing for the first time what *I* was wearing. A pair of nylon basketball shorts—that did jack to hide my current condition—and that was it.

"I'm here," she whispered, eyes steady on me, "because I need you to make me feel alive." As she watched me absorb her words, her hands drifted toward the hem of her shirt.

"Are you..."

My voice disappeared as she whipped the top over her head.

Peyton's hair fell wildly around her shoulders and moonlight danced across her soft skin. My hungry gaze was the only thing covering her, and it devoured. As shadows chased each other over the planes of her body—and my eyes recorded the curves to memory—every last drop of my blood pooled south.

"You're beautiful." My words came out like a prayer. She was perfect. Absolutely perfect. Any image or fantasy my overactive imagination had conjured the last few months paled in comparison. It almost hurt to look.

"Make love to me, Justin." Peyton's voice, although shaky, sounded sure. She stood in front of me naked as the day she was born, completely confident in her own skin, and my body responded—

Holy hell, did it respond.

Lust surged like a freaking missile, ready to launch me right off the bed, and I fisted my hands in my lap in a desperate attempt to keep from grabbing her hips.

I'd been selfish my entire life. Shit, I was a Carter, that's what we did. It was our legacy. I did what felt good, said screw it to the consequences, and took whatever I wanted. Regardless of the fallout. But Peyton deserved better than that. She deserved better than *me*.

"I want to... God, you've got to know I want to," I said throatily. I licked my lips and pleaded with her to understand. "But I don't want to hurt you. Your first time should be with someone special. Not some pathetic shmuck his own parents don't want."

I couldn't believe what I was doing—I was telling the girl of my dreams *no*, when everything in me screamed *yes*—but it was the right thing to do. I knew it was, and so help me, I would do right by Peyton. Even if it killed me.

A pained sound left my throat and my hand shot out without permission, grasping the curve of her hip. I was weak, but I could give myself that much. That one touch. Her skin felt like heaven and my fingertips dug in, trying to keep it at just this.

But Peyton had other plans.

Wrapping her hand around mine, she guided it higher until it lay flush against the petal-soft skin of her stomach and said, "The only way you'll hurt me, Carter, is if you say no."

I shuddered, fighting the desire to give in to what we both wanted, and she moved closer, close enough that if I leaned forward, I could kiss a path across the underside of her breasts.

"This feels right," she whispered, her long fingers sliding through my hair. Her nails raked over my scalp and a shiver traveled the length of my body. "Don't you think it feels right? I don't want anyone else, Justin. I know you'll make it incredible. I trust you, and I want my first time to be with someone I—"

She cut off abruptly and my gaze shot to hers.

Distantly, I heard an internal warning bell, an alarm sounding trouble ahead. But then she was kissing me... and I thought, fuck the bell.

Every good intention I'd had flew out the window when her hands landed on me. If Peyton was sure she wanted this, wanted *me*, then I was hers for the taking.

Grabbing her hips, I spun us around until she was lying below me on the bed, her hair a cascade of gold across my pillow. She was so gorgeous my chest ached. I took a mental picture, wanting to remember this night, the look in her eyes when she looked at me lying over her, forever. She reached out and trailed a gentle finger down my cheek. Her mouth tilted in a smile and I took it in a kiss.

I threw everything I had into the kiss. Every pent-up frustration, every secret longing, every hidden fear. I was shit with words in person. Without a notebook, I couldn't express myself worth a damn. But I could show Peyton how I felt. How crazy she made me. How amazing she truly was.

My lips trailed downward, sucking at the tender skin below her chin, and she tossed her head back in a moan.

"*Justin.*" I grinned against her neck, loving the sound of my name on her lips.

I let my wandering hands get their fill. Her gentle curves fit them like a dream, and I relished the feel of her bare skin. Where I was hard, she was silk. I'd never get enough. I could count on three fingers the times in my life I'd felt worthy of affection—my grandmother telling me on her death bed that she was proud of me, newborn Chase wrapping his tiny fist around my finger, and this moment, with Peyton giving me everything she had to give. I never wanted to leave this bed.

Beneath me, Peyton grew restless. Her leg hooked around my hip and her mouth sucked at my neck. When her tentative hands reached down to touch me, a fire set loose in my blood.

Soon, my shorts were gone. They were lost in a blur of eager hands and seeking mouths. I did my best to prep her, my trembling hands finding her and making her squirm. In this way, my past was useful. I knew how to get a girl off with my fingers. Earning their sated smiles momentarily eased the loneliness I always carried within me. But it never lasted. The void always came back.

It wasn't until Peyton clutched my shoulders, her head thrown back in a scream, that I entered her. Her wide eyes squeezed shut on a wince.

I instantly stilled. "Baby, you okay?"

I held my breath, held my muscles tight, ignoring how incredible she felt. How complete *I* felt. In that moment, all that mattered was that she was there with me, still wanting me with no regrets. I swallowed hard and waited, hoping like hell that was the case.

"I'm good," she croaked, eyes still shut. I needed to see her eyes. "Just need... a second."

My arms shook, beads of sweat rolled down my face, and my body screamed for me to move. I fisted the sheet in my hand. "Sunshine, I need you to look at me. Please. Can you do that for me, baby?"

Peyton released a shaky breath and the mask of pain shifted on her face. As relief seeped through my veins, I allowed myself a quick inhale and watched as her mouth relaxed, the tension disappearing from her forehead.

A moment later, her eyes opened. Emotions swirled within the blue-gray depths, awe, fascination, a lingering of pain, and a few I was afraid to name. Then she smiled and four words I hadn't heard since my grandfather died, four words that would change my life forever, passed her lips.

"I love you, Justin."

SATURDAY, MAY 31ST

1 week until Graduation

♥ Senior Year

PEYTON

GALVESTON BEACH HOUSE 3:02 A.M.

"Hey."

I blink my bleary eyes and attempt to focus on the fuzzy form in front of me. It doesn't work. It's been a long night of trying to figure out what this robot wanted. Most recently, that was a bottle and a diaper change, followed immediately by another bottle and burping. Do real babies eat and poop this much? I only just got the thing to settle down. I'm exhausted, stressed, and partially deaf. My ears won't stop ringing from the crying.

Yawning, I gently prop the blessedly silent baby in a borrowed car seat, dig my fists into my eyes and rub, then try again. A sleep-mussed Justin materializes with a tired grin.

"How ya doing?" He whispers the question, almost like it's a real baby and not a robotic demon, and for some reason, it makes me smile. The annoying little sucker sure cries like it's real.

"Peachy." I heave the slightly off-hinge laugh of the sleep deprived, and scratch the skin on my wrist beneath the sensor bracelet. "He's woken up twice so far, and the last time was just brutal. Lauren's off baby-duty tonight, and threatened to shake ours, so I figured I'd come hang out here." I lean my head against the impossibly soft sofa cushion, my heavy eyelids half-closed before a worrisome thought comes to me. "God, I didn't wake you, did I?"

"Nah." Justin shifts his weight, almost looking nervous. "I just figured you could use a pick me up." He glances down and for the first time I notice a movie-sized box of chocolate almonds and a twenty-ounce bottle of Sprite near his hip. My greedy eyes widen with excitement. "I'm hoping I got the candy right."

"Please. Like you ever get anything wrong," I tease, making grabby hands at the gift of chocolate like it'll be my last meal. Sugar rushes are the cure-all to exhaustion... well, at least until the eventual crash. But right now, I'm all about the instant gratification.

A sad expression washes over Justin's face. "Sometimes," he says softly, his gaze dropping to the floor. "Sometimes I get things horribly wrong."

An awkward silence descends.

I'm not sure how I'm supposed to respond to that, so I rip into the shrink-wrapped plastic of the candy. A strange urge to comfort him tenses my arms. The truth is, whether there's a miracle detail that'll somehow change things between us or not, he did get it wrong freshman year. He hurt me—no, he destroyed me. There's never an excuse for that.

Releasing a heavy sigh, Justin pads over to the sofa. With the car seat on the cushion near the wall, I'm sprawled out in the middle... which leaves only one cushion left. The one right beside me. Glancing at the empty seat, it suddenly looks as if it's shrunk during our short chat.

Justin sits and my senses instantly go on high-alert. Phantom tingles explode across my thigh, and I inhale, needing to calm my nerves. The sharp scent of mint clouds my head, almost making me dizzy. Mint is forever linked with Justin. It's his scent. For about a year after we broke up, a mere whiff would send me into hysterics. Now, it just leaves me feeling confused. And a bit sad.

"Thanks for this," I say, shaking the box in his direction. "You want some?"

He nods and I pour a few decadent morsels into his extended hand. A really fat one plops in the center of his palm, the holy grail of chocolate—the magic twofer—and he laughs, a low rumble of a chuckle that causes the fine hairs on my arm to stand on end.

"Here." Justin scoops up the piece and hands it over with a grin. "You know you want it."

For a nanosecond, I debate not accepting it… but, of course, I do. Come on, it's a twofer! It's like snagging one of Wonka's Golden Tickets.

"You rock." I pop the candy into my mouth and close my eyes, moaning my gratitude. When Justin chuckles again, I elbow him in the side. "You know, you can head on back to bed. I've got this now. This should keep me happy through the next crying fit. Besides, you're on overnight duty tomorrow." I peel open my eyelids and smirk. "Best be storing up that beauty sleep."

Justin lifts his arms in a long, exhausted stretch and kicks his feet onto the coffee table. Nope, no need for beauty sleep on his end. I glance down at my frumpy pajamas and sigh.

"I'm good," he says. "I'm up anyway. I'd much rather be out here keeping you company."

His gaze drifts toward the closed door of the other bedroom, and I know what he's thinking. But Justin's wrong. I don't mind that Cade's not out here with me. He probably didn't even hear the baby crying—Drew passed out earplugs at dinner. Besides, it's not his project anyway. Cade doesn't even go to Fairfield Academy. He's strictly here as a favor to me, so I can't really blame him for wanting to sleep through it.

Justin shifts his hips, turning slightly on his side, and our eyes lock.

But the thing is, *he* heard, and he didn't want to sleep through it. He's here. With candy... and soda... and a listening ear, and quiet company, something I didn't realize I even wanted or needed until he appeared.

The air-conditioning unit clicks on with a low hum, muffling the other noises of the house—the slight snores, the muffled sounds of other baby cries, whispers that prove we're not as alone as it feels. Justin's hand twitches, his pinkie finger moving a hair closer than it was before, and it would be *so* easy to stretch mine out to touch. My finger itches with the urge to do it. But it would be wrong. Incredibly wrong.

I curl my hand into a fist and shove it under my thigh.

"So, the draft's coming up," I say, snapping my eyes back to his. They're filled with longing and sadness and I don't even want to know what he sees in mine. The thick air around us feels magnetic, like it's trying to pull us together, but I refuse to give in. "Have you decided what you want to do?"

Justin draws a deep breath and lowers his gaze to his hands. The sling is off now, not needed anymore, but he's on strict orders not to overdo it. As reckless as he can be, I know he won't risk it. Baseball means everything to him.

"No. Not really." Justin flips his hand over and stares at the grooves in his palm. "Coach says the injury won't be a problem. As long as I'm a hundred percent for the next game, and I will be, then I still have a good shot."

"That's not what I asked." I match his body posture, shifting on my hip to face him. "I asked what you *want* to do. The choice will be yours, I have no doubt about that. But at the end of the day, what path will make you the most happy—college or pro?"

He huffs a laugh. "What'll make me the most happy has nothing to do with baseball."

My breath catches at his meaning, and Justin's eyes burn into mine. An emotion stirs in my chest, a feeling akin to hope and happiness, and I lock it down quick. This isn't about me.

I quirk an eyebrow, giving him a look, and Justin sighs.

"You know the rules, Sunshine. If I play for pay, I can't go back later. I can't change my mind and decide to try it in college. I mean, I can get a degree, but I can't play ball." Frustrated, he rakes his fingers through his thick, dark hair. "But then, if I decide to let it ride and go to A&M, what happens if I get hurt? My career would be over before it even started."

"Maybe," I admit, knowing what he needs from me is honesty, not to be coddled. "But so what? If that happens, you'll do something else... You're more than just baseball, Justin. You know that, right?"

He doesn't say anything, which means *no*, he doesn't. Sadly, I'm not surprised. It's always come down to this. His family did a real number on him. I curse them for the millionth time in my head and pull my knees up onto the cushion.

Justin won't listen if I push. He'll clam up, stubbornly telling himself I'm being nice. Polite. Even flirtatious. But I want him to feel a real connection. Even after everything that went down between us, I feel an overwhelming need to protect him. Shifting closer, I hesitantly reach out and place my hand on his. He doesn't waste a second flipping his over.

Eyes on our joined hands, Justin says, "If I sign with a team, I'll be constantly traveling. Living on the road, practicing all the time. Eating crap and forgetting what city I'm even in. I'd barely ever see... the people I care about." His hand squeezes mine, leaving no mistake who he means.

The thick knot in his throat bobs, and Justin raises his eyes.

Three years of questions and regrets pass between us. I want to run from the room every bit as much as I want to stay,

224

to confront them. For a moment, I think, *this is it*. He's finally going to tell me what really happened that day. What detail I supposedly missed.

Instead, Justin looks at the sleeping baby beside me and asks, "Do you ever wonder?"

TUESDAY, MAY 31ST

Disaster Imminent

♥ Freshman Year

JUSTIN

SWEET SERENITY RANCH 5:25 P.M.

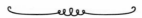

One thing I'd learned in my short life of being a secret boyfriend—you came when your girl called. When she called you in tears, you booked ass.

Practice ended not fifteen minutes ago, and I was already at the ranch, having begged an upperclassman for a ride. It would be my luck that today was the one day Rosalyn had to stay late at Chase's daycare, needing to help him rehearse for tomorrow's parent recital. I didn't begrudge my brother his moment of attention; I did, however, hate the curious look in Pete Langley's eyes when we pulled past Coach's gate. The senior was notorious for talking shit, but he'd been my only option for a ride. Hopefully, the twenty bucks I slipped him would shut those flapping lips.

I squinted against the abrupt light change inside the barn and called out, "Sunshine?"

Oakley stood in her stall, chomping happily on hay, but there was no sign of Peyton. I scratched my head and grabbed my phone, checking to make sure she'd said to meet her here, and that's when I heard it. A broken sob.

Blood turned to ice in my veins, but I followed the sound, past every stall and Coach's ridiculously huge riding lawn mower, right through the back door. She was there, lying on the picnic table that had changed everything. It'd been seven weeks since the weekend she'd read my notebook and snuck into the doghouse. Seven weeks of perfection. Being with Peyton, earning her smiles, it gave me the peace I'd never had before. Being inside her made me feel invincible.

But, for some reason, I'd yet to tell her I loved her.

I didn't know why. She told me every chance she got, so it wasn't like I didn't have the opportunity. But something about those innocent eyes filled with hope, trust, and more love than I'd ever seen directed at me before always held me back. I was afraid to tip the scales.

Peyton's quiet, constant affection had healed every broken memory, every doubt, every fear that I was like my parents. Those insecurities vanished when I was with her. She deserved to know that.

Maybe today would be the day. Maybe knowing would fix whatever hurt her now.

Leaning down, I picked up her curled body and sat down on the bench with her in my arms. The smooth surface of the pond rippled, reflecting a distorted image of the cloudy sky.

"Tell me what's wrong."

I pressed a kiss against her hair and, like always, it smelled like sunflowers. Peyton's body shook with silent tremors and I tightened my hold around her. "I can't fix it unless you tell me what's wrong. You're obviously upset. You called and told me to get down here, and now I'm here. Tell me what's going on. Whatever it is, we'll figure it out. Together."

Tears splashed my neck as she buried her face in the crook near my shoulder. She mumbled something, half words, half wails, but I couldn't make out anything that sounded like English. I pressed my back into the table, stroking her hair away from her wet cheeks so I could look into her red-rimmed eyes. My heart thudded in agony. "I'm sorry, baby, but I couldn't understand that. What's wrong?"

Fear and desperation flooded her gaze and the hair on the back of my neck stood on end. Whatever it was, it was bad, but I was here now. I would walk through fire if she asked me to.

Then Peyton's mouth formed two short words: "I'm late."

I kept waiting for more.

Late for what, I wanted to ask. School was almost out for the year, her job was here at the ranch. I had no clue what she could possibly be late for...

Then, it clicked. And my body turned to stone.

"Justin? Did you hear me?"

Peyton climbed up my body and straddled my hips, grabbing my face so she could stare into my eyes. My arms fell loose around her. "Say something."

I couldn't. Speaking would've required brain power that I didn't possess at that moment. Every synapse I had misfired at the word "late."

The faint scent of charred wood wafted through the air, and I imagined it was the scent of every dream or plan either of us had for our lives going up in smoke.

Was this how my father felt when he heard those words? Sixteen years old and soon to be a father? A malicious laugh echoed inside my head. Be careful what you wish for. I'd vowed to never become like him, and look at that, I succeeded—I was worse. Hell, I beat him by a whole year.

"Tell me what you're thinking."

Peyton grabbed my shoulders and shook them. I felt the bench beneath me, her soft weight on my lap, and the sun beating down on my head. But I wasn't at the ranch, not really.

I was back in my childhood home, overhearing a conversation I never should have.

Gramps and Gran raised me as their own. They protected me from the truth as best as they could, but I was a curious boy. When the man who I normally only saw in pictures, the man they said was my father, came home late one day, of course I had to sneak downstairs. What I overheard that night gave me a stomach ache.

Gran had refused to talk about it when I asked the next morning, but Gramps, he'd understood my need for answers. That afternoon over two fly fishing rods, he'd done his best to give them, putting the truth in words a seven-year-old could grasp.

"My mom had me when she was sixteen."

My voice came out robotic, and Peyton's eyes widened with surprise. Tears still clung to her lashes, but the sight no longer affected me. It was like a wall had fallen, shutting me off from the world, sealing me away from feeling anything painful.

"Turns out, being a teen mom wasn't high on her to-do list. Put a crimp in her perfect pageant world, but I guess I should be grateful she had me at all. I guarantee my dad pressed for an abortion. Mom's parents kicked her out—evidently, having a pregnant teenage daughter didn't look good to voters, either—but Gramps and Gran took her in, took care of her, and after I was born, took care of me."

A bird dove down and snatched an unsuspecting fish from the pond. Peyton's gaze stayed steady on me, waiting for me to continue, but I couldn't look at her. It hurt too much.

"My dad was pissed. He wanted a kid about as much as good old mom, and she at least got free after signing the papers. But dad... he was stuck. Gramps used to say, 'A Carter owns up to his mistakes,' and I'm my father's biggest."

I flashed her a grin. "After graduation, Dad joined the family business, earning his degree at night, learning how to be a man in his father's eyes. Of course, that meant he had no time to see me, and that was just fine by him. I saw him maybe three or four times before Gran got sick. She died when I was seven, Gramps when I was nine. After that, Dad's luck ran out."

Peyton's cool hands cradled my face, forcing me to look at her. "Justin, I... I don't know what to say. I'm so sorry you went through that."

I shrugged a shoulder. "It is what it is," I said. "You know the rest. Dad hired Rosalyn, and she's pretty much raised me from then on. Eventually, he married Annabeth, and Chase was born. Effectively replacing me. Hey, it sucks, but it's my life. What are ya gonna do?"

I exhaled a breath and felt the fight leaving me. Damn, I was pathetic. Throwing my head back, I stared at the gathering clouds.

"A long time ago, I made myself a promise. If I ever had kids, I'd be different. I'd do it right. I'd let them know they were loved, I'd take care of them." I laughed at the sky. "I swore I'd never become like my father."

"But you're not!" Sunshine's response was so immediate, so forceful, it was almost funny. "You're nothing like him. You'd never do the things he does or act the way he did."

I lowered my head and sighed as I glanced at her flat stomach. "I just did. History is repeating itself right now."

Self-loathing coated my skin like a thick layer of sweat.

We'd been so careful. The day I went back home from Easter, I stopped at the drug store and bought out an entire row of condoms. I'd pulled out that first night and it almost killed me. Peyton hadn't yet figured out how to ask her mom for birth control, but once she did, we'd do that, too. But we were smart. We were safe, every time.

Every time but the first.

"We don't know that," she said, and I raised my eyes. Hurt was evident on her face, yet she still tried to comfort me. It somehow made it worse. "I'm late, and it freaks me out, but we don't know I'm pregnant for sure. I'll take a test in the morning, before school, and then we'll figure it out, okay? This is probably just a false alarm."

She looked away and I sighed, knowing better than to let hope win out. This was me we were talking about.

"Can you get it?" she asked, squirming on my lap. "I'd ask my parents, but..."

"No, I'll get it." No way did I want Coach hearing about this until we knew for sure. "I'll get it tonight and bring it with me tomorrow. We can use the bathrooms on the second-floor," I suggested. "Detention kids are the only ones around before seven-thirty, but it's better to be safe than sorry. Upstairs, no one will even know we're there."

I'd slipped back into robot talk, but I couldn't help it. Shutting down was easier. Feeling was what hurt; it was what got me in trouble. Peyton's acceptance tricked me into thinking I wasn't a fuckup. Opening up now could only harm me. Letting myself wonder, imagining what would happen. I couldn't do that, not yet.

One thing at a time.

As gently as I could, I lifted Peyton from my lap and placed her back on the bench. Then I stood and shoved my hands deep into my pockets, keeping her from reaching out for them. Stopping *me* from reaching for *her*.

I kicked at the frame of the picnic table and raised my eyes, allowing myself one last look at her stricken face. "I'll see you tomorrow."

Numbly, Peyton nodded, her rapid breaths rocking her body, and I turned away.

I'd done that. I'd caused her pain. My weakness, my mistakes. My legacy.

I retraced the steps I'd taken here, walking all the way down the gravel path to the gate near the highway. Once there, I headed south and grabbed my phone, sending a text to Rosalyn to meet me at the strip mall a few miles away.

The long walk there in the unforgiving heat would be good. It'd keep my mind busy. Hopefully, it'd wear my body out. As it was, I doubted I'd see a wink of sleep that night.

Or, depending on the test results, ever again.

SATURDAY, MAY 31ST
1 Week until Graduation
♥ Senior Year

PEYTON

GALVESTON BEACH HOUSE 9:45 A.M.

Cade huffs as he shoves a pair of shorts in his open bag. "I'm not an idiot, Peyton, I know what I saw." As I try to find a way to explain, the bedroom door swings open and Carlos steps inside, his ever-present goofball grin in place. I try to warn him to escape when Cade, his back to the door, continues with his rant. "You slept with him, dammit!"

Carlos's eyes go buggy wide, almost like a cartoon character, and he backpedals out the door, shutting it quickly with a bam. Cade turns at the sound, then forgets it just as quick, looking at me with anguished eyes. "How could you do that to me?"

"I know it looks bad." I push off from the wall and hold my hands palm up. "But nothing happened last night, I swear."

After Justin and I talked, our electronic infant woke up again, *twice*, and sometime around five A.M. we must've crashed. When Cade found me this morning, my head was on Justin's lap, his hands were in my hair, and Justin Jr. was cooing contentedly beside us. Understandably, he wasn't happy...

"Don't you trust me?" I ask him, hating myself. It's a cowardly question, one I'm frankly afraid to hear the answer to. Cade sighs, sinking onto the mattress, and my fear spikes as I sense my concern is warranted.

"I love you," he says instead, an amazing response... but not to the question I asked.

Cade's face is open and honest; knowing he loves me should make me happy. But it's his eyes that do me in. The bleak look in them tears at the healing hole inside my heart.

"I've loved you for years, CC, you know that. But trust?" He shakes his head. "I wish I could say yes, I really do. But when it comes to him... you just don't think clearly."

I take a step toward the bed. "Listen, you have to believe me. Last night—"

"Was nothing more than a repeat of the same old pattern," he finishes, a humorless laugh lifting his shoulders. "What surprises me is that I'm even surprised. I've played second fiddle to Justin Carter for years. Now... now I see that's all I'll ever be. Even though I treat you better than he ever will. Even though I *love* you more than he ever could. He's who you want." Cade drops his head into his hands. "I'm so damn tired of pretending otherwise."

His posture slumps in defeat and everything in me says to go to him, to hold him tight and deny, deny, *deny* what he's saying. But I can't. As much as I hate it, as much as I loathe what it says about me and my messed up priorities, he's right. Justin is who I want. Who I've always wanted.

I'm seriously a glutton for punishment.

Tremors quake my hands and I fist them under my arms. This feels like an ending.

"Are we... are we breaking up?"

I whisper the words so low, I wonder if he even hears them. Cade stares at the floor for a long, heavy beat, and I assume he didn't. It's a relief because hearing would make it real. He'd have to answer. But then, slowly, he nods.

"Yeah." Cade's voice breaks, and my heart crumples right along with it. "I think we are."

It's not until he stands and grabs his bag that I lose it for real.

"Wait. Where are you going? You don't have to..." I trail off as he gives me a look.

"Home," he answers. "I'm going home, Peyton. I think I've overstayed my welcome."

Heaving the bag onto his shoulder, he removes his glasses and scrubs a hand over his face, looking uncomfortable as hell. Like he can't wait to get away from me. And that... that hurts more than the breakup.

"You can come with me if you want," he offers, always so damn polite. I hesitate, swallowing past the painful lump lodged in my throat, and he laughs. "Yeah. That's what I thought."

Cade rocks back on his heels, and slaps his palms against his thighs. With a decisive nod, he turns toward the door. Numbly, not knowing what else to do, how else to stop this from happening, I fall in step behind him.

I pad out the door and down the stairs, arms wrapped tight around my chest as I watch my best friend leave. Leave the house or leave my life, I'm not sure, and that terrifies me. But I don't ask. The potential answer is more terrifying than the question.

We make it outside, and the briny scent of the Gulf floats on the breeze. If I stretch my hearing, I imagine I can hear the bells and rings of Pleasure Pier. Maybe it's good we never made it back. Better. If we were destined to break up anyway, I'd rather keep those memories between us untainted. A perfect snapshot of what we once were. Or could have been, had my head and heart not been owned by Justin Carter.

I stop at the base of the stairs and Cade tosses his bag in the bed of his truck. He stops near the driver's side door, his

Adam's apple bobbing in his throat. This is goodbye. We'll see each other at the ranch, around the rodeo circuit, but it will never be the same. It'll be tainted. Tainted with loss, sadness, and regret.

For a moment, I let myself wonder what it would've been like had things been reversed. How different our lives would be had Cade brought me to the pier *freshman* year, sweeping me off my feet before I even met Justin. It's impossible to know for certain, but I'd like to think we'd have been great. Because Cade Donovan is an incredible guy. He'll find his other half one day. He has way too much love to give not to.

Wrapping one hand around the stair railing as an anchor, I lift the other in a wave, knowing he needs me to be strong. If I ask him to, even now, he'd stay. He'd come back and pretend some more, but I can't ask him to do that. Not anymore.

Cade nods slowly and his mouth lifts in a small, heartbroken smile. Then, he yanks open the door. The engine fires and I wince, feeling the finality of that sound.

As I stand there, watching the rapidly disappearing taillights, a shadow falls across mine on the pavement. "I know it doesn't feel like it now, but it's for the best."

I give Aly my best attempt at a smile. "Speaking from experience?"

There's no point in pretending she doesn't know exactly what just happened. We weren't exactly quiet, Carlos isn't known for keeping his mouth shut, and, as I saw yesterday, Aly Reed is sneakily perceptive.

"Yep," she confirms. She sets her car seat on the ground and lays her head on my shoulder. "It hurts, I know, but in the end, it's always best to follow your heart. The sooner you do that, the less pain is involved."

We stay like this, her head on my shoulder, my heart in my throat, for what feels like forever. The house is quiet. Sometime between Carlos peeking inside our bedroom, and Cade and I leaving it, the baseball team headed out. Well, the team minus Justin. Dad asked him to stay behind, knowing how hard it would be for him to sit in the dugout and not play in the Semi-finals. One bright spot is that by staying here, he was able to take care of Justin Jr. while my relationship imploded.

Aly breaks the silence by saying, "I'm here if you want to talk. I understand we're not close, and I don't know everything that went down, but Justin's told me enough. He mentioned that you two were together once... and he told me that he loved you."

I must gasp because she lifts her head and studies me. "He never told you?"

"Uh, no," I stutter, torn between wanting to believe and doubting, and Aly rolls her eyes.

"Boys are stubborn creatures," she says with a sigh, "and Justin is one of the worst. He's stubborn and a flirt, but Peyton, I've never known him to lie. He said that he loved you and I believe him." She covers her eyes with her hand, shielding her face from the sun. "Though, from the way he said it, I'm guessing things didn't exactly end well. He implied it was his fault."

I shrug, neither confirming nor denying her assumption, and look off into the distance. "In some ways, it was both our faults."

It's true, too. I was a mess back then. I was impulsive and daring, looking for ways to prove I was alive. That GBS hadn't won. I took all the energy I normally reserved for barrel racing and put it into challenging myself, rushing through steps and pushing past fear. Pretending I had none.

Man, did that bite me in the ass.

Aly brushes sand off the bottom step and takes a seat. "Probably so, but from talking to him, it's obvious Justin blames himself. I'm not gonna sit here and blow smoke up your skirt, claiming he won't ever mess up again. He will. But

I *can* promise you this—Justin's a different guy than he used to be. He's different than he was when we were freshmen, he's different than he was when I dated him in the fall, and he's changed even since this project began."

Leaning back on her elbows, she squints into the sun. "It doesn't take a genius to know that last part is all you. He's in deep. He cares about you a lot, and as his friend, it's my duty to be nosy and ask you... how do *you* feel about him? Because, at the end of the day, it's on you. That boy ain't going nowhere. So what is your heart telling you?"

What is my *heart* saying? It's saying I just destroyed my best friend. That I'm standing here getting advice from a girl I barely know, as an electronic baby coos at her feet, and that I need to find the nearest gallon of ice cream and dive in head first. But even as I think it, I know I'm not being completely honest.

My heart... it's screaming at me, loud and clear.

I kick at the railing. No wonder Cade left me; our relationship isn't cold, it's barely even reached room temperature, and I'm already thinking about Justin. Wondering if, now that I'm free, he'll tell me the rest of the story. If after he does, it'll make a difference. If the timing is *finally* right for us.

How can my heart be so fickle? It should be in mourning. Hell, after the beating it took with Justin three years ago, it should be curled up in the fetal position.

Do what scares you.

The long-forgotten motto roars through me like an old friend, like a lion waking from its slumber. But look what happened when I followed that philosophy before. It backfired miserably. I've spent the last three years doing the exact *opposite* of that, avoiding the sport I love and keeping my heart locked up safe and tight. Yeah, it's been boring, but it's also been beautifully tear-less.

My heart whispers, "But Justin helped you face your fear, and you kicked the barrel course's ass. Maybe it's time you let *him* back in, too."

Gah. My heart is so damn nosy.

Excitement and anticipation surge though me with such force I practically vibrate on the steps. Aly beams up at me, clearly a mind reader, and I exhale the toxic fear. "I need to find Justin," I say, and she nods at me.

"My work here is done," she replies. "Last I saw him, he was heading out to the beach with Justin Jr."

My feet have already spun, guiding me down the walkway to the private strip of beach behind the house. I'm halfway down the path before I even realize it, and I quickly turn and call out, "Thank you!"

Aly waves me on, holding a thumbs-up, and yells out, "Go get your man!"

Laughing at the absurdity... and possibility... of Justin Carter being my man, for real this time, I take off for the beach. Hope flutters in my heart, an odd yet familiar sensation when it comes to him, and I my press my open hand over my skin.

The steady *thump, thump, thump* against my palm pushes me on.

Part of me realizes I need to grieve my relationship with Cade, to take stock of what happened, and find a way to salvage our friendship—and I will. He deserves that, and I can't lose him from my life completely. He was a huge part of my past. But right now, I need to chase my future.

I check either side of the beach, holding onto the rope railing as I search for Justin. The walkway climbs over a sand dune and I smile as I crest the hill, somehow knowing he's waiting on the other side.

A few steps away from the top, I call out, "Justin?" too eager to wait, and hear a muffled shuffling in response. I always knew my body was attuned to his. Smiling, I rock back and forth on my heels and wait for him to duck out from behind the dune, still amazed that I'm actually doing this.

"Peyton?" Justin appears in front of me, just on the other side of the railing, with the robot baby in his arms and a strange expression on his face. "What are you doing here? Is everything okay?"

"Yeah." I shake my head a bit, hoping to shake off the sudden weird vibe, and say, "I think so. I mean, Cade just left... We, uh, we broke up."

Joy lights his face before he quickly checks it, replacing it with a look of concern. I stifle a grin. "I'm sorry to hear that."

"No, you're not." I laugh as a swarm of hyped-up butterflies takes flight in my gut. "But that's not why I'm here. Not really. I came to find you because, well, I talked to Aly, and I think... I mean, if you are, I'm ready to..."

My voice fades as the scene plays out like a bad teen movie.

The slight breeze off the Gulf of Mexico carries a sharp, salty scent, and with it comes the past. I'm here on the beach, but I may as well be back at the concession stand at Fairfield Academy. The players are the same, the shock just as real.

The slap of stupidity every bit as embarrassing.

How insane can I be? Will I ever learn? I'm standing here with my heart in my hands, prepared to hand it over to the very guy who once cut it to shreds, and out comes the girl who once held the knife.

Lauren struts out from behind the sand dune, the same one Justin was just behind, and flashes me a smile as she fixes the bottom of her impossibly tiny bikini. I stagger back, my gasp echoing in my head, and Justin holds out his hands as if to catch me.

"Sunshine?" He looks back and discovers Lauren waiting behind him, Carlos Jr. in a bedazzled carrier by her side, then twists around with eyes blown wide. "Shit. Baby, please, it's not what it looks like. You have to let me explain."

"Explain?" I repeat, my dumb eyes filling with hot tears. "Explain what? What a fool I am? That I actually thought..."

The lump in my throat refuses to let me complete that thought. Instead, I spin on my heel.

Shame and embarrassment threaten to push my tears over the edge, but I can't let them fall. Not where they can see. The two of them have gotten enough tears out of me.

Warm sand kicks up beneath me as I jog down the path, Justin's voice chasing behind me. He can't take off and risk jostling the baby's neck, so if I keep moving, maybe I can outrun him. If I move a little faster, maybe I can outrun the pain, too.

A girl can hope.

WEDNESDAY, JUNE 1ST

Disaster

♥ Freshman Year

JUSTIN

FAIRFIELD ACADEMY 7:05 A.M.

The mental tapes played the entire drive to school.

So... baseball's not the only thing you and the old man have in common. A baby in high school. Maybe you should compare notes.

You knew you were never good enough for Peyton... and this only proves it.

Just when she's getting her life back, you have to come along and ruin it.

That last one hurt the most.

Peyton Williams was a fighter. Her determination to literally get back up on the horse and ride Oakley blew me away. In the short time I'd known her, her progress was incredible, and her therapists believed that by the end of the summer, she'd be back to kicking rodeo's ass.

But you can't ride horses at breakneck speeds pregnant.

The one thing my girl loves the most—the thing she's been *killing* herself to get back to—may very well be stripped away from her again. All thanks to my stupidity. Some secret boyfriend I'd turned out to be.

And then... that was just how this affected her. What about me?

Yeah, I was a selfish prick for thinking it, but this didn't only involve Peyton. My future was on the line, too. Baseball was the one thing I was good at. The diamond, and my team, the one place I ever belonged. Coach Williams was the first man since my Gramps who ever saw anything in me, *believed* in me. Would that faith be shot to hell once he found out how I betrayed his trust? Would he kick me off the team?

From the very beginning, I'd told myself to stay away. Peyton Williams was a *Commitment*. She was declared off-limits, so I had no right sniffing around her.

But I couldn't—or didn't want to—tell her no. Which led me back full-circle:

This was all my fault. As such, it was up to me to fix it.

When Rosalyn pulled up in the circle drive in front of the school, Peyton was already there, waiting on the front steps. I'd jokingly named it 'Sunshine's stoop,' so the sight was familiar, only this time she wasn't furiously turning the pages of one of her books—another sign of how being with me had changed her, and not for the better.

I closed the door behind me and she pushed to her feet, smoothing the wrinkles of her uniform skirt. "Hey." She waved goodbye to Rosalyn with a small smile that didn't reach her eyes, then turned to glance at the brick building behind us. "Like you said, it's dead right now. Only a few admins and a couple upperclassmen in for detention. We should have the entire second floor to ourselves."

"That's good," I said, feeling awkward as hell. Questions and uncertainty hung between us, making the already oppressive Texas heat heavy. I hiked my backpack higher on my arm. "I've got what we need, so let's do this."

Peyton bit her lip, relief obvious in her eyes. She hadn't been sure she could count on me. I couldn't blame her, since the last time she saw me, I'd been borderline catatonic, but the lack of trust hurt.

I tugged open the main door and waved her inside, making sure our skin didn't touch. It was dumb and probably juvenile—we'd touched a lot more than hands to find ourselves in this mess—but it felt necessary. Like, one touch from Peyton could break the carefully constructed façade of calm I'd erected overnight.

Peyton padded inside, eyes on the floor, and waited for me to join her. Then, she began filling the silence with chatter.

"Dad thinks I'm here to help Mi-Mi clean out her locker," she said, hanging a right into the stairwell. Her voice echoed in the corridor and she quickly lowered it. "He was so glad to hear I'd made a friend that he didn't even question it. I mean, how much crap could Mi-Mi possibly have in her locker that she'd need me here this early, you know? But he bought it hook, line, and sinker. I lied to him, straight in his face, and he didn't even blink."

Guilt cracked her voice, and the pressure in my chest grew tight. Peyton and her family were close. So close it freaked me out, to be honest, because I never had that. Knowing she lied to them, that she probably felt even more alone because of it, triggered those mental tapes again.

You made her lie. You brought her down to your level. Soon, she's gonna hate you.

At the top of the stairs, I placed my open palm on the door, keeping her from opening it. "Let me check the hallway first." The smooth skin between her eyes furrowed as she studied me, confusion and a trace of hurt in her eyes. "What?"

Peyton stepped back, shaking her head. "Nothing. Go ahead."

A part of me realized I was handling this wrong. I was snippy and standoffish and frankly, losing my shit. But I was in survival mode. I had no clue how to let her in without leaving myself more vulnerable.

Luckily, when I stuck my head out, the coast was clear. I pulled the door open wider and lifted my chin. "Come on."

The women's bathroom was located in the middle of the hall. We booked it down the path, feet slapping against the linoleum, and I wrapped my hand around the door handle, ready to duck inside. Peyton stopped me cold with her hand.

My skin burned at the contact.

"I should probably go in first," she said, eyes trained on the spot where our skin touched. Her tongue glided across her bottom lip, and I wondered if she felt the heat, too. "Just in case. The last thing we need is one of your many admirers to see you in there."

Slowly, she raised her eyes to mine. They pleaded with me, seeking a connection, wanting to know that she wasn't alone in this. And she wasn't—I was *right here*. But the words to tell her that were locked inside my head. Behind a fake, crumbling wall of indifference.

"Fine, but hurry," I said, taking a step back and severing contact. The hopeful light in her eyes dimmed. "We don't have much time."

Peyton nodded and slipped inside the bathroom, and I banged my head against the wall. Too many questions, too many unknowns swirled around us—and I was a guy with no answers. Sunshine needed me to be strong, to get her through this. I needed to stop being such a dickhead.

The door opened a crack and she whispered, "All clear." With a final glance down the hall, I snuck inside.

The women's bathroom smelled a lot better than the men's. Looked different, too. I locked the door behind us, realizing just how weird this was, then slumped against the wall near the sinks. Peyton rolled on the outsides of her feet and raised her eyebrows.

"Oh, right."

I opened my backpack and pulled out the box I'd spent a half hour in the aisle at the drug store trying to choose. Why the hell did they have so many kinds? Each of them different, too. I'd been terrified I'd get the wrong one and mess things up—well, worse than I already had—but thankfully, a clerk took pity on me. She reminded me a lot of my Grams. After I explained our dilemma, she handed me this one.

Peyton's fingers trembled as she took the box from my hands. "Thanks. Uh... think you can turn on the faucet?"

I frowned in confusion. "I don't think you need to add water or anything," I said, and she shook her head with a small smile.

"Shy bladder." Her cheeks turned pink, and the ice around my heart thawed the tiniest bit. After everything we'd been through... everything we'd *done*, she was still self-conscious.

Returning her smile, I turned on the water.

Peyton chose the stall farthest from me and the actual act of peeing on the stick didn't take very long—not that I was surprised. Out of the whole process, that part was pretty basic. It was the waiting that sucked.

She set the test on the sink as I set a timer on my phone. Three minutes to go.

"Should we talk?" Peyton asked, twenty seconds in. "You know, about what will happen—?"

I shook my head. "No point worrying until we know for sure."

The truth was, I couldn't let myself think too far ahead. If I did, I'd panic. Ever since she told me she was late, I'd been living moment to moment. First, it was getting to the drug store. Then, finding the right test. The rest of the night was spent checking and double checking my alarm, making sure I woke up on time, and making up a bullshit excuse about a team meeting.

Two minutes.

The *drip, drip, drip* of the leaky faucet filled the silence, and my anxiety ratcheted with each plop. The seconds ticked so slowly that I knew they were messing with me, trying to drive me insane. I heaved an impatient breath, and my knuckles blanched white as I clutched the basin.

"Justin, I just think you should know, that regardless of what it says, I—"

"Please, Sunshine. Can we please just... wait?"

Forty-five seconds. I couldn't listen to her speech for another forty-five seconds. If she blamed me then, she had every right to do so; if she didn't, well, she damn well should. But until that stick declared our fate, I couldn't handle anything else.

Evidently, Peyton could. "Seriously?" She folded her arms against her chest. "That's how you want to play this? You know, I'm every bit as scared as you are. It's not like I planned for this to happen. But it is, we're here, and it'd be a hell of a lot easier if you..."

She glanced down where the indicator sat on the sink and her shoulders slumped.

Oh shit. Positive. This was happening. We were about to be parents.

I stared at my reflection and firmed my jaw. It was time to man up.

"Okay." My voice was rough and I coughed to clear it. "I'll find your Dad. I can tell him, or we can do it together..." I stopped talking when Peyton raised her head, eyes filled with tears, but a smile of relief on her face.

"It's negative." She grabbed the stick, fisting it like it would run away or suddenly change responses, and said, "I'm not pregnant. Holy cow, I'm not pregnant!"

The stone walls echoed her scream and she slapped her free hand over her mouth, laughing and crying at the same time. "Can you believe it? It was a false alarm. Maybe... maybe it was just stress from exams? Oh, who the hell cares, I'm not pregnant!"

The tackle hug took me by surprise and my back slammed against the wall.

"Thank you," she said, wrapping her arms around my waist. "Thank you for being here. I couldn't have done it alone. I was up half the night, wondering what we'd do, how I'd tell my parents." Another laugh escaped and she leaned her head back to look at me. "What a relief, right?"

I nodded in agreement. I'm pretty sure I even smiled. My limp arms slid around her shoulders as the words "not pregnant, she's not pregnant," repeated over and over in my mind.

What the hell was wrong with me?

Why wasn't I laughing like a maniac, too, or squeezing Peyton tight in celebration? We narrowly escaped a fate neither of us wanted. And here I was, standing like a zombie.

Peyton slid her arms to my chest and pushed back, studying me again. "You're okay, right? I mean, this is good news... isn't it?"

"Oh, yeah, awesome news," I replied, trying to snap myself out of it. "I guess I'm just in shock. But yeah, definitely good news." And now I was a robot zombie.

Worry replaced joy as she watched me and she said, "Today's only a half-day. Just a bunch of B.S. assemblies and weepy goodbyes. If you want, we can skip... maybe grab some breakfast and hit up a movie?"

"Nah. The team has a meeting after school, so I should hang around." I took her hands in mine, gave them a gentle squeeze, and then pushed away from the wall. "But maybe later, yeah?"

Peyton nodded, face blank of emotion, and I knew it was my fault. I was acting bipolar, but hell if I could help it. My head was a mess, my chest felt like a block of ice, and I suddenly wanted to punch my fist through a wall. I wanted to talk to my grandparents, but they were long gone. The only other person I could talk to now stared at me like I had two heads.

I had to get out of here.

"Listen, I'm glad you're all right," I told her, grabbing my backpack from the floor. "There's something I have to do before school starts, but let's talk after, okay?"

Then, like Satan himself was after me, I bolted from the room.

***

"Hey, gorgeous, you gonna miss me this summer?"

Sometime between January and now, Lauren Hays's voice became like nails on a chalkboard. Chills, and not the good kind, crept down my spine whenever she stopped to say *hi*, or stalked my locker to flirt, like she was doing now. It was annoying as hell, but, ready to get my ass out of here, I put on a fake smile.

"You know it, beautiful. But you know what they say, absence makes the heart grow fonder." With a disgusted grimace, I shoved a binder in my backpack.

This was why I needed to go home. I'd been saying dumb shit all day. My brain clocked out right around the time we got the results, and now, a shot of Dad's tequila was seriously calling my name.

First step, getting past Lauren.

"Well, hopefully your heart's already fond because guess who's gonna be your Diamond Doll next year?" She bounced on her toes with a huge grin, and when I didn't jump to answer, she did it for me. "Me! I thought we made an awesome team this year, so I requested to keep you as mine."

The territorial smirk was straight out of *Fatal Attraction*. It creeped me the fuck out, but the point was to get out of here so I just nodded and stuffed a wad of junk in my bag. How did all this shit accumulate in one year? It was disgusting. Forgotten protein bars, ripped-out notes, and sweat-stained socks. Lauren peeked inside and wrinkled her nose.

A loose paper was lodged in the corner and as I yanked on it she asked, "Anything I can do to help you today?"

I shook my head, prepared to say no, *hell no*, when I flipped the paper over in my hand. It wasn't old biology notes or a discarded syllabus—it was a picture of me and Peyton, taken around Easter. She must've printed it out and shoved it in here, because underneath the smiling photo she'd written: "Aren't we cute? Thanks for an amazing time."

Of course, Peyton meant the entire weekend... but the conclusion Lauren was drawing wasn't wrong. Her jaw dropped and her eyes narrowed, and any chance of our relationship staying a *secret* was over.

Lauren loved gossip even more than she loved her designer shoes, and I'd heard her talk enough about that shit to last for years. I needed a distraction, quick, or the truth would be spread around school sooner than an ump could call foul ball.

That was the last thing either Peyton or I needed right now.

What if Coach found out? What would the guys say? All the reasons I'd had not to get involved with Peyton were still there, only now I had a million more. This morning was a wake-up call. We were playing with fire, and we were lucky to escape with only a singe.

Peyton deserved better than me, though she'd never admit it. She was too good. Too kind. Too addicted to her hopeless causes. She took them in at the ranch all the time, trained them up and loved them enough so they were rehabilitated. But I wasn't a stray dog or a wounded horse. Love and a firm hand wouldn't save me. I was a walking time bomb, and I couldn't put her at risk anymore.

I reached into my pocket. "Actually, Lauren, there is something you can do."

Her grin was instant, if not malicious, as I withdrew my phone and sent a text to Peyton.

PEYTON

FAIRFIELD ACADEMY CONCESSION STAND 12:52 P.M.

The whole dang morning had been a blur.

After seeing the words "not pregnant" on my pee-stick, I'd assumed the day would be amazing. We'd dodged a huge bullet, and now an entire summer stretched before us—no school, no baseball, no gossiping classmates to hide from. Justin and I were never closer... or we were never closer up until last night. If we could just get past this, the summer ahead promised endless days of laughter and kisses, and nights filled with even more. We'd just have to be more careful.

But Justin was acting so weird. I understood him freaking out over the unknown; heck, I turned into a snotty, crying mess myself. But now that we knew I wasn't pregnant, that we weren't having a baby, the freak-out should've ended. Right? Twenty-four hours ago, Justin would've twirled me around that bathroom, kissed me senseless, and made plans to meet up later. Today's version acted like he couldn't run away fast enough.

What was his deal? Did he *want* a baby? Even as I thought it, I knew he couldn't, not after his big speech about his own parents. And we were *fifteen*. The second we read the words, we should have been celebrating.

So why does it feel like we're breaking up?

I shoved the question away and pushed through the gym door. It didn't make sense, and that was why it didn't matter what Justin wanted to tell me, or why he'd asked me to meet him at our spot. I was going to remind him exactly why it was our spot. The concession stand was where we shared our first kiss... my first ever kiss. It was where I started falling in love with him. And even though he hadn't said the words, I knew the truth.

Justin loved me, too.

Yeah, we were going to be fine. We just needed to clear the air and move the heck on.

With determination singing through my limbs, I picked up the pace.

Not for the first time, I cursed my weakened limbs. If it weren't for GBS, I could move faster, even run like I used to. My limp was almost gone, though, and if I kept at it, really hard, my speed would return. Now that I knew I wasn't pregnant, that's all I'd do this summer. Focus on regaining my strength.

That, and get Justin to admit to his feelings.

Grinning, I lifted my face to the sun. It was June in Texas, so it was hot as Hades, but the rays felt good on my skin. Like a promise of good things to come. The smell of recently mowed grass filled my senses and I kicked off my sandals to feel the smooth blades beneath my feet.

The baseball diamond was deserted. It was weird to see because even when the team didn't have a game, the bleachers were always filled. People read or dozed in the sun. They hung out and texted or made out. But today, the second the dismissal bell trilled, everyone beat a path to the parking lot. School was out for summer... and the entire field was now our playground.

Anticipation kindled under my skin and I hoofed it a little bit faster.

A minute or so later, I was a few feet away from the concession stand and I caught a glimpse of green fabric near the edge of the building. While in theory, it could've been anyone, only one guy filled out his uniform polo like that. *My* guy.

"Hey there, sexy!"

I was giddy. We were alone and I could call him whatever I wanted. I could run, or, in my case, walk very fast into his arms and kiss him senseless right here, in plain sight of the bleachers and parking lot, and no one would know.

Summer was going to *rock*.

Only, Justin didn't turn and throw his arms out. Instead, he stiffened. Strange, since he texted me, asking me to meet him here... and even weirder because he still had yet to face me.

My feet slowed of their own volition. It was as if they knew what I'd yet to admit. Saw what I was refusing to see. Because now that I was closer, despite my rapidly slowing steps, and even with Justin's head still turned, I could clearly see his profile.

Along with the bright pink lipstick stain emblazed on his left cheek.

I staggered forward. My hand slapped across my mouth as the peanut butter crackers from the vending machine threatened a comeback. *No*. Justin wouldn't do that. Not to me. He wouldn't cheat. Justin loved me. I knew he did.

Only, the proof was damning. Not only the lipstick stain, but the muffled giggle. Lauren Hays ducked beneath his arm, stepping out from behind the building with a little grin like she was embarrassed. I wasn't fooled. She made a production of wiping her bright pink mouth and said, "Oh hey... Peyton, is it?"

I didn't answer, didn't nod, and she continued on, a picture of innocence. "Don't mind us. Just had to give my man a proper summer send off. We didn't think anyone was around."

I had no words.

I had no emotions.

I simply stood there, staring at the couple before me, in complete and utter... nothing.

Oh, my brain still functioned. It reminded me that Lauren had staked her claim in January. That she'd spent the entire semester baking Justin cookies and decorating his locker, attaching herself to his hip before and after every game. The entire student body believed they were together, but each time my insecurity got the best of me and I got the courage to ask Justin about it, he'd swear he wasn't interested.

My brain screamed he was a big fat liar. That I was nothing but a fool.

"As you know, it's my job to service his needs," Lauren said, sliding her hand along his shoulder. Justin knocked it off, shooting her an angry look, but she just grinned. Then she looked at me. "Especially if no one else is."

"That's enough," Justin growled, pushing her hand away. "Knock it off."

Lauren looked shocked. Her eyes grew wide and her mouth fell open, utter confusion replacing her previous gloat. I should've found satisfaction in that, but I didn't. I was too busy acknowledging that she clearly knew who I was, what Justin and I were to each other, and that I was the only one in the dark.

Finally, Justin turned. He took a step toward me, his face twisted in... what? Remorse? Shame? I didn't know and frankly, I didn't care. He'd proven his point loud and clear by asking me to meet him here—I was nothing to him.

A sob built in my chest, shaking my shoulders, and I lifted my hand in a wave.

"Peyton!" Justin called my name, over and over, his voice strained with emotion.

But I was already gone.

SATURDAY, MAY 31ST

1 Week until Graduation

♥ Senior Year

PEYTON

GALVESTON BEACH HOUSE 11:00 A.M.

My suitcase is open on the bed. I toss another shirt inside, and Mi-Mi reaches in to fold it. She shares a glance with Aly, who then turns to Gabi, a surprising tagalong in this Operation Keep Peyton Busy. Kara, bless her heart, is wearing double sensor bracelets in the living room, watching Aly's and Mi-Mi's babies so they can talk me down from the ledge.

"You're *sure* you don't need anything?" Aly asks, giving me a hopeful look. "I could head down to the kitchen and grab a plate of snacks—I made a batch of dark chocolate chili brownies this morning. I think I even surprised myself. You liked them, right, Gabi?"

She nudges her best friend in the side, and Gabi rolls her eyes. "Excuse her. In her mind, chocolate cures everything, but in this case, she ain't wrong. They really are good."

I smile, grateful they're trying so hard. "Thanks, but no. I'm not really hungry."

Aly sighs, like she can't believe anyone would turn down chocolate, and I toss a pair of shorts into my case.

When I stormed up from the beach, she and Gabi were sitting on the stairs talking. They took one look at my tear-soaked cheeks and Justin hot on my trail and went full-on grizzly. While Aly threw her arms around me, Gabi threw her hand in Justin's face, telling him to cool his jets, then they both hustled me up the stairs. Kara and Mi-Mi joined the rescue team somewhere between the first and second floors, and after closing the bedroom door behind us, Mi-Mi let loose a shocking string of curses.

I think I love them all.

"I texted Brandon and he said we can take you home as soon as he gets back from the game. He also said to tell you they won." Aly smiles as she hands me my pajamas, hoping the news will cheer me up. It doesn't. I mean, I'm glad Dad's team won. I'm happy they're headed to the championship. But *cheered*? Sadly, it's gonna take a lot more than that.

Dropping my PJs inside my suitcase, I give the messy room one final search and then zip it up. Everything else here belongs to Lauren.

My stomach churns, and I inhale deeply through my nose. I still can't believe what an idiot I am. Falling for it—falling for *him*—again. They must be laughing so hard right now.

The bedroom knob turns and for a split second, silly hope blooms in my chest. I imagine Justin waltzing through the door, coming to fight for me and tell me that what I clearly saw didn't happen. Spew the same old song and dance he's been giving for the last month. Not that I would believe it, but it's nice to think he would try.

But it's not Justin who walks through the door. It's worse. Way worse. It's *Lauren*.

"What the hell are you doing here?" Gabi growls, stepping in front of me. She folds her arms across her chest and I admit even I'm a little intimidated.

But not Lauren. Nope. She sighs like she's bored, like she's seen this act a million times, and says, "Last I checked, this is still my room. And she and I have to talk."

She shifts her gaze to me, and all the hurt and anger that's built over the last three years boils to the surface. Laying a hand on Gabi's arm, I gently move her aside.

"Talk?" I repeat with a scoff. "What could you and I possibly have to say to each other? You've already won. Bravo. You've got Justin. I hope the two of you are very happy together."

Hands shaking, I tug my suitcase off the bed, having a total out of body moment. I don't do this. I don't get angry in public, or even speak my mind—not when it's counted, at least. But I've imagined doing so plenty. Each time I relive that moment freshman year, I try for a different outcome. Sometimes I imagine going off like a lunatic. Other times, I've gone for quietly strong and confident. But that's only ever been in my head. The living, breathing reality makes my stomach churn, and it's quite possible I'll throw up.

But I go for it anyway.

"Frankly Lauren, I think you two deserve each other," I say, yanking the handle on my case. "You're both lying, manipulative, spineless assholes, and I don't need that kind of energy in my life. Now, if you'll excuse me..."

Shockingly, Lauren has taken what I have to say up to this point, leaning against the wall holding her bedazzled car seat and nodding slowly. But now that I'm obviously done, she continues blocking the door while turning to Aly. "Think you can give us a minute?"

One look at Aly and it's clear she doesn't approve. Gabi, either. She laughs like the request is ridiculous, and from the hate-fire Mi-Mi's directing Lauren's way, the phrase, "if looks could kill" has new meaning. But I'm curious.

Lauren and I don't chat. I can't think of a single time we've even held a conversation. I'm about a half hour away from busting out of this place, and the only other time she'll have to see me is graduation on Friday. Other than FACS, we don't share any classes, so we won't share an exam room. The papers we turn in to Coach Stasi next week serve as our final exam.

So, why hold me up? What does she have to gain? Or, is she here to simply rub it in?

What can I say, I'm an inquisitive girl.

"It's fine." I nod at Aly's not-so-subtle look of "are you for real?" and say, "I can handle her."

I stop short of adding that there's nothing more she can say to hurt me, because that's not quite accurate. People don't fall in and out of love instantly. The broken pieces of my heart still beat for Justin. It's pathetic, but it's true. If Lauren chooses to go into specifics of their relationship, it will gut me for sure... but then, a part of me needs to hear it.

It's the only way I'll truly get over him.

Gabi makes a V with her fingers, swinging it from her eyes toward Lauren and back again in the universal symbol for "I'm watching you." "We'll be right outside."

Mi-Mi squeezes my shoulder on her way out, and Gabi gives me a chin lift, which I'm pretty sure is "good luck" in Gabi-ese. Aly hesitates at the door before offering a small smile of support, and quietly pulling it closed behind her.

"Nice guard dogs you got there." Lauren sneers as she walks over to the vacated window. "Everyone just loves you, don't they?"

I withhold the pity-party, not wanting her to have the satisfaction, and go for bluntness. "Why are you here, Lauren?"

Her lips flatten into a thin line and she moves aside a wisp of thin curtain, feigning interest below. "You know, I had to hold Justin off. He was ready to storm in here, go all caveman and throw you over his shoulder if he had to, so you would listen. I thought it'd be better if we talked this out, girl to girl."

She can't be serious. Are we supposed to negotiate visitation rights? In my opinion, she can have him. "I have nothing to say to you," I tell her honestly, but when she swings me an amused look, I feel my cheeks burn hot. "Nothing *else* to say, I mean."

"Well, suit yourself. I have plenty." And, with that, she strolls toward her bed and plops onto the mattress.

For a long moment, she doesn't say anything else, she just sits there watching me roll my suitcase back and forth along the hardwood floor. The inhuman sounds of breathing floating up from the car seat ratchet up the tension. My leg muscles twitch, and the insides of my cheeks ache as I mutilate them into hamburger meat in effort to keep from speaking up. But I refuse to budge or break the stand-off.

I've already said what I needed to say. More than I ever thought I would. Now, it's her turn.

Lauren's gaze zeroes in on me. "Nothing happened," she finally says. "Either time."

"Wait... what?" So much for not talking. Shaking my head, I reach a hand back and guide myself onto the bed. "I don't understand. What game are you trying to play here? I saw what I saw—*both* times. Despite what you may think, I'm not a freaking idiot."

Yes, that's exactly what I've been calling myself, but she doesn't need to know that.

Lauren sighs. "I never said you were. I know what you saw three years ago. You saw exactly what Justin and I wanted you to see." Her words bring an itch to the back of my brain, like something I'm supposed to remember. "That kiss behind the concession stand? It was staged, Peyton. I kissed his cheek, but that was it. Justin didn't kiss me back and he never touched me..." She winces a bit and corrects herself. "Well, not until junior year. But by then, you two were long over."

I stare at her, open-mouthed, words no longer making sense.

"I won't pretend I care about what happened," she continues, grabbing a purple squishy pillow she'd brought from home. "But Justin asked me for a favor, and I'm not in a habit of telling that boy no." She winks, like we're sharing a secret, and I fist my hands in my lap. "Anyhoo, he said he needed you to *think* he cheated, but the second we got to the ball field, he got really weird. Fidgety and looking green. Honestly, I thought he'd call the whole thing off. But that's when you showed up, so, I gladly played my part."

She squeezes the soft pillow in her hands. "Now, admittedly, I had my own reasons to break you two up, but, whatever. I kissed him. On the cheek. And sadly, that's all it took for you to buy it." She smiles like she's proud—typical Lauren behavior. But I catch the flare of shame in her eyes.

"How do I know you're not lying?" I ask.

Honestly, I want to believe her. I mean, *of course* I do. Believing means I wasn't pathetically blind in the past. It means I didn't miss Justin cheating on me right under my nose.

But, it also means that he set me up, that he lied to me, and that he hurt me on purpose.

"Damn girl," she says with a laugh, "my lipstick wasn't even smeared! I mean, I'm *good*, but I'm not that good. If we really went at it, I would've had pink crap all over me. It wouldn't have been pretty." Then with a wicked grin she adds, "But it *would* have been hella fun."

Like an old movie, I watch that reel rewind in my mind. I freeze frame it on Justin's face, and note the pink lipstick imprint on his cheek—but his lips... his lips are stain free.

How did I miss that?

I blink my eyes to clear the memory, and a thousand questions take its place.

"Then why? Why go through all that trouble? Why not just tell me he didn't want to be with me anymore?" I widen my eyes, totally lost. "And then... what, did he start to change his mind? Why?"

"All excellent questions," Lauren says, dropping the smile. "Things you should ask him." Her face turns serious as she tosses her pillow back at the head of the bed and pushes to her feet. "I figured you wouldn't even get to that point, though, if I didn't first tell you the truth."

She grabs the handle of the car seat and sashays toward the door—really, there's no other way to describe her walk—and I find my voice just as her hand closes around the knob. "Lauren?"

When she turns to look at me, I shrug. "Why tell me anything? You and I aren't friends."

"No," she answers. "But Justin and I *are*. He's a good guy, one of the best, and he deserves to be happy. For some crazy reason, he gets that with you."

Leaning her back against the wood, she tilts her head to the side and says, "Look, I'm not claiming we never hooked up. We did, often, but not until last year. It never really meant anything, other than blowing off steam. But he never... not once... looked at me the way he looks at you." She taps her palm against the door. "The way he's *always* looked at you."

I can't help but laugh softly at the slightly mystified look on her face. For all of Lauren's shortcomings, and Lord knows the girl has many, she's honest to a fault. I can almost respect that.

Glancing toward the window, I lift my chin and say, "And just now, out there?"

"Simply a hug between friends," she says, somewhat wistfully. "I got a call from home that made me sad, and Justin found me. He knows a bit about it, so he offered his shoulder.

That's all." Holding up three fingers, she vows, "Girl Scout's honor."

At her playful smile, I let out a breath, feeling the fight leave with it.

The misunderstanding today is on me. I saw Lauren and Justin together, read into it what our pasts dictated, and jumped to conclusions. I can admit when I'm wrong, and I truly believe that's what happened—this time.

As for freshman year, I'm convinced Justin didn't cheat. But Lauren's wrong when she says nothing happened. He lied to me. He purposefully set out to hurt me, and whether he got cold feet at the end or not, that's exactly what he did. Because of his choices, and because of that pain, I turned too early to the one place I felt I belonged and lost yet another thing I loved. Racing.

He owes me answers.

Nodding to myself, I stand from the bed. "I need to find Justin."

Lauren opens the door for me and steps back, motioning for me to pass. As I cover the distance between us, I know we'll never be friends. We're two *very* different people, and beyond the whole Justin drama, I don't like the way she treats people. Plain and simple. But today, she helped me. She didn't have to, but she did.

Stopping in front of her, I hold out my hand like a dork. "Thanks. I appreciate... this."

Lauren looks down with a smirk and awkwardly gives my hand a shake. "Make him happy, yeah?"

I don't say yes. I don't know what the future holds for us, and after that confession, Lauren deserves honesty. What I do say is, "I hope you find *your* happiness, Lauren."

She smiles softly and looks away, and I set off to find Justin.

JUSTIN

GALVESTON BEACH HOUSE 11:42 A.M.

Peyton flies out the door like Cerberus the three-headed dog is chasing her. She swings her gaze from side to side, hopefully looking for me, and I wipe my hands on my board shorts.

"Nothing happened," I call out, and she skids to a halt. I wait until she finds me hiding in the gazebo, and once she does, I say it again. "Nothing happened with Lauren. Either time."

She nods and says, "I know."

Her voice rings with the quiet calm that comes from knowing the truth—but it's also laced with hurt, and that keeps me from feeling any better. I'd hoped that hearing what really happened back then would make a difference; that it'd be enough for us to build on. But clearly, she still needs answers, reasons for the *why*, and she deserves them, too.

Peyton steps into the gazebo and gives it a cursory glance before pinning me in place with her eyes. "Lauren told me about the setup freshman year." I swallow as she takes a seat across from me on the circular bench and fists her hands around the seat. "Why would you do that?" She lifts a shoulder in confusion. "I just... I can't wrap my brain around it, Justin. Did I do something wrong? Did I push you for too much? What? Help me understand why you would do that to me."

"Because I was an asshole," I say, leaning my head back against a plank. Her mouth pinches at the past tense description and I huff a humorless laugh. "Okay, I'm still an asshole."

263

Damn, this went a whole lot easier in my imagination. I've had three years to think this through, to choose the perfect words to explain my stupidity. But right now, seeing her stare at me with eyes filled with hurt, I have nothing. Just my heart with her name on it, and too many years of regret.

I scrub a hand across my face. "I panicked. It's no excuse, I know, but it's the truth. I warned you I sucked at relationships. I made a mistake, Peyton, and the second I saw your face that day, I knew it. But by then, it was already too late."

"Why not just talk to me?" she asks, leaning forward on the bench. "Before *or* after. You could've told me you were panicking. Hell, I was, too! We would've figured it out together. Even if we decided to stop seeing each other, it would have been better than... than what you did. How that felt? God, Justin, I hope you never have to feel that. It destroyed me, and I can't help thinking that if you had just come to me—"

"I was in love with you."

I take a breath and give her an apologetic shrug. "I was in love with you, and too chicken-shit to say it, but I was. And I knew you loved me. If I'd told you that I thought we needed a break, that I'd almost ruined both our lives and that I thought moving on was what was best for you, you would've tried to talk me out of it."

"Damn straight," she admits, nodding her head.

"And I would've let you."

Across the street, my uppity neighbors walk outside. Every time I see them, they're fighting, and judging by their raised voices and stiff movements, today's no different. It's no wonder they get along so well with my parents. I've had nothing but sucky examples of relationships my whole life. Even my grandparents, who loved me as best they could, slept in separate rooms. It's insane that I ever thought I could make it work with Peyton back then.

But now... now I'm smarter. I've felt love from Carlos's family. They treat me like their own. Brandon's mom and even Aly's parents welcome me and show me what true love is like. I also have Coach. He's taught me what a man looks like, how he acts and holds himself. I only wish I could've known these things earlier. It would've saved us both so much heartache.

Once my miserable neighbors are tucked inside their Benz, I say, "Sunshine, you had me wrapped around your little finger. If we were going to break things off, and I really thought we should, I needed it to be *your* decision. I had to make it good enough that you wouldn't ever want me back... because I was weak... I still am, when it comes to you. I knew it was only a matter of time until I realized how much I needed you and begged for forgiveness."

Peyton doesn't give me the smile I hoped for. She just keeps watching me, staring into me with those big, blue eyes, and I lean forward on my elbows, needing her to understand.

"I had to keep you safe," I say. "I was terrified I'd mess things up. With you, with your dad. I know I hurt you, and that my methods were stupid and unforgiveable, but I did what I believed was best. Peyton, you've always deserved better than me..." I clasp my hands and look at my feet. "A guy who couldn't see past his own shit to hold you when you were scared out of your mind."

Fuck. I really was a dipshit. There are so many things I'd go back and redo if I could, but that day... that day trumps them all. As I sit here, stewing in the mess I made of things, Peyton's orange toenails appear next to my bare feet.

"You were scared, too," she says, sinking on the bench beside me. "We were *fifteen*, Justin. You're excused from not handling it perfectly. Or, well, handling it at all."

She bumps my shoulder softly and I tilt my head to face her, smiling ruefully at the slight dig. Her eyes are sad as she tightens her mouth and studies me.

"You used to say that a lot, you know. That I 'deserve better.'" Tentatively, she reaches out, brushing hair off my forehead, and a pulse of energy zings across my scalp. "Now that so much time has passed, do you still think that?"

"No." I release a sigh. "I know you *deserve* better. I'm just too selfish to care."

We sit quietly after that, Peyton absorbing my words, me hoping they make a difference. A small smile begins to bloom across her mouth, and though I'm terrified to read into it too much, I slowly stretch my hand out, linking our pinkies.

"Where do we go from here?"

Peyton scoots closer, our hips now touching as she stares at our entwined fingers. "Next week is graduation," she says softly. "If you go pro, you'll leave for who-knows-where, and your entire life will be baseball." She raises her eyes to mine. "It's the way it is and I'd never hold you back from that. But that's not how you build a relationship. Long distances rarely work and I've already lived my life on hold... I won't do it again."

The statistic we learned in the "Mate Selection" section of our project springs to mind, like an annoying Debbie Downer: less than twenty-five percent of couples make it if they don't live in the same area.

I can't handle losing Peyton again. I barely survived the first time. When we get back together—*when* not if—we're sticking for the long haul. Marriage, babies that don't require a battery pack, the whole shebang. I never wanted it before but I do now—but only with Peyton.

Yeah, we're young, but we'll take our time. Graduate college and do it right.

But this girl is it for me.

An electronic cry snaps my head toward the front door where Gabi stands holding Justin Jr.

"Sorry to interrupt, but y'all need to do something." She cranes her neck away from the robot baby like the crying disease is contagious. "This thing is possessed. I've tried everything I can think of, but it doesn't want a bottle or a diaper, and it doesn't need to be burped. I surrender. There's a reason I avoided FACS. Babies and I, we don't mix."

Peyton laughs under her breath and curls her pinkie around mine one last time before severing contact. "Sounds like it needs to be rocked. I've got this one." She pushes to her feet, and a mild panic stirs within my gut.

We haven't settled anything. I don't know where we stand, if we're back together, if we have hope of doing so in the future, or even if she wants me. If she forgives me for my hurtful, boneheaded mistakes of the past.

As she pads past me, I grasp her wrist and ask, "Are we okay?"

It just scratches the surface of my questions, but for now it'll do. Peyton takes a breath before answering, only ratcheting up my anxiety.

"Yeah," she finally says, her guarded eyes searching mine. "We're good."

I nod, slowly, glad to hear the words, and release my grip. She walks out of the gazebo, and I continue to sit here, watching a lone bird in the driveway eating some seed Aly threw out earlier, and working through a thousand questions that have no clear answers.

WEDNESDAY, JUNE 1ST

Aftermath

♥ Freshman Year

PEYTON

SWEET SERENITY RANCH 5:05 P.M.

"I'm the world's biggest idiot.*"* I laid my head on Oakley's strong, reassuring back and sighed. This was what I'd been reduced to—an openly sobbing, snotty mess, crying on my horse's back because I was too afraid to face my friends.

Pathetic didn't even cover it.

It was only a matter of time until Faith or Cade found me. So far I'd been lucky. Mama was so swamped with work she didn't question me when I said I wasn't feeling well. Instead, she pulled Faith in to helping as soon as she arrived. As for Cade, he was running late for his shift for the first time in his life. Clearly someone somewhere was on my side, but I knew my luck was running out. Once Faith's shift was over, she'd come out here and find me, just like she always did, somehow sensing my distress. She'd take my hand and bring me back to my room where we'd hide out with chocolate and Zac Efron movies like we did whenever my illness got to be too much.

But Cade would push for answers.

He'd always been a good friend to me, but over the last year or so, he'd taken protective to a whole new level. All it would take is one look at my splotchy, swollen face, and he'd demand to know what happened. Once he pulled the entire story from me, I knew he'd take off after Justin. I didn't need that. I didn't even *want* that. All I wanted to do was forget.

I lifted my head and laughed. "Do what scares you, huh, girl?" I ran my hand down Oakley's side. "God, what a crock. Look where that's led me so far... hiding from my family and friends, and crying here alone." Annie's ears pricked forward and she nickered softly. "Sorry, girl. You know you're awesome company."

Honestly, for years now, Annie Oakley had been my closest friend. Sure, I had Faith and Cade and even Trevor to some degree. I had the kids in my homeschool co-op and at church. But it wasn't the same. A special bond forms between a girl and her horse, a bond only animal lovers can truly understand. Oakley could read me without words. She felt my moods, seemed to know when I needed to ride fast and furious, or take it slow and easy. Riding her is where I found my joy.

Losing that was the cruelest blow GBS ever dealt.

When I first got sick, everyone looked at me with fear in their eyes. They had no answers, no way of knowing if and when I'd ever return to normal... and what a weird word, "normal." Today, most people looked at me and assumed that's what I was. I conversed and ate on my own, I had an entire semester of public high school behind me. Only my occasional limp would tip off a stranger that I'd ever been sick at all.

But I wasn't *normal*. I wasn't whole. Riding Oakley grounded me. Rodeo was my home. Other than my family, it was where I belonged, a place where I shined, and it had been ripped away from me. A piece of my soul was missing, and after today, I *needed* it back. Just this once, I needed to do what I loved, because if I didn't, I might just lose myself altogether.

A shiver of excitement danced down my spine as I realized I'd made up my mind. I latched onto that feeling, wanting to drown out the heartache, and walked around to look Oakley straight in the eyes.

"Wanna ride, girl?"

I didn't need Justin. I didn't need any guy. All I needed was to ride. The saddle was my rock, and it hadn't failed me yet.

Oakley pranced in her stall, and a grin, the first in hours, stretched my cheeks.

My therapists were wrong. Sure, they'd worked miracles, were creative in tailoring my sessions to prepare me to ride again, but I didn't have to wait. I could do it now. Hippotherapy proved it, and I very rarely lost my balance on a treadmill anymore. They were being overly cautious, and I got it. It was their job. But mine was getting back on Oakley.

The entire time I saddled her up, I kept an ear trained for footsteps.

Dad coddled me like a toddler. He listened to everything my therapists said, and if he caught me now, he'd freak. Luckily, though, he was still at school. As for Mama, she was elbow deep grooming a family of dogs checking out. A big part of me wanted to share this with her, but in some ways, she was worse than Dad. She wanted me to ride again, even encouraged me, but she refused to believe that I could handle it now. That the doctors didn't know everything. It hurt, too, because she knew how this felt. She grew up on this ranch; the need to ride flowed through her veins every bit as much as it did mine.

Once Oakley and I were ready, I grabbed the reins. My grip was still off, my muscles not quite responding like they used to, but I could make adjustments for that. We breached the entrance to the barn and another thrill of, "holy hell, I'm going to do this," shot through me.

With a click of my tongue, Oakley and I made our way to the open field.

"Hey, Peyton."

I nearly jumped out of my skin. Throwing a hand onto Oakley's back to steady myself, I turned and watched as Trevor yanked out an earbud and lifted his chin toward me. "I thought you couldn't ride yet."

Here's the thing... I hated lying. I hated it *almost* as much as I hated not riding. But even this small distraction from my goal let other things seep through my filter: fear that maybe I wasn't ready; memories of this morning; Justin's cruel betrayal this afternoon.

Lying was my only solution.

"Got the green light yesterday," I replied. "Just couldn't wait another second."

"I hear that," he said with a nod, already lifting his earbud to replace it. "It'd be the same with me and golf. Congratulations."

That was all it took. Trevor sort of lived in his own world half the time, and today, I was grateful for it. He shoved his earbud back in, bobbed his head, and headed for the doghouse. I hesitated for a second, worried he'd mention this to Mama, but then, this was Trevor I was talking about. If he told her hello it'd be a mouthful.

Breathing deep with relief, I continued on.

I wished I'd brought some music. The quiet was too... quiet. It let me think too much. Every footfall brought another whisper. Of Lauren's thinly veiled taunts. Of Justin's agonized voice, calling my name. Of my therapists saying I couldn't ride yet. That my muscles were still too weak.

That's probably what Lauren thought I was, too. Weak. Justin must as well or he wouldn't have hurt me the way he did. But I'd show them. I'd show them all.

At the field, I rolled my neck back and forth. I breathed deeply, in and out, and put my hand on the saddle horn. I could do this.

Up on Oakley's back, I stared out at the miles of open field ahead, ready to prove just how strong I was. I took the reins and wrapped them around my forearm. That gave my slightly weakened fingers more control. I sat up tall and clucked my tongue.

"Let's ride, girl."

We started at a trot. My hips rocked back and forth in the saddle and tears pricked my eyes. I was finally home.

Nothing compared to this feeling. Getting it back this summer would keep me sane. Nudging Oakley's flank, I urged her on, needing to feel the wind whip across my face. Needing to listen to sounds muffle under the pounding of hooves. I needed to lose myself.

I was so consumed with pushing my limits that I didn't hear the tires on the road.

The rhythm of the ride enthralled me so much that I didn't hear Cade calling my name.

But Mama did.

Suddenly, they both appeared yards in front of me, eyes thrown wide with emotion. Cade's was filled with confusion, and Mama—her head jerked to the side as panic overtook her features. I shook my head, not understanding what the big deal was... and then I saw it.

Rusty, our feisty boarder dog with energy to burn (and a nasty habit of running free on our property) had gotten loose. He was currently bolting right for us.

I didn't have time to think.

Oakley's head perked up, her feet shifted, and she took off, headed in the wrong direction. Spooked horses weren't anything new around here, but I was rusty. And my muscles didn't cooperate.

I tried to check her, but my grip was all wrong. Oakley threw her head in the air, took the bit in her teeth, and charged. Straight toward a fence.

I attempted to control her with my knees, tried to steer her away from the rail. But my hips were weak and my legs couldn't hold on. As a last-ditch effort, I sat back and deep within the saddle... but it was too late.

Unable to keep my balance, and with Oakley running scared, I fell. Hard.

Pain exploded everywhere, especially in my wrist, and my ears rang with Mama's screams. Someone ran down and grabbed Oakley. Trevor appeared to corral Rusty. Cade dropped to his knees beside me, the pity in his eyes confirming what I already knew.

My body had failed me, in the worst possible way. I wasn't strong.

And I never would be again.

WEDNESDAY, JUNE 4TH

Almost Free

♥ Senior Year

JUSTIN

SWEET SERENITY RANCH 4:00 P.M.

I'm sitting in my Jeep, watching Peyton like a psycho stalker. I can't help it, though. She's riding again, rounding the third barrel on the course like a pro—a slow pro, but a pro without fear, and a proud smile curves my mouth.

The selfish ass inside me would love to think I did that, that I helped her trust herself and find her strength. But she would've gotten there on her own eventually. Peyton is so much stronger than she ever gives herself credit for. I, on the other hand, am the one needing direction.

The graduation machine is in full force, and because of it, Peyton and I have barely talked. We finished our FACS paper on Monday, said "hi" in passing between finals, and sent a handful of meaningless texts before we both crashed from exhaustion. But I still have no clue where we stand, and time is flying by so fast it's starting to blur. Friday night we graduate, and then it's Peyton's exhibition and the championship game on Saturday. Suddenly everything seems to be coming to a head, and hell if I know where that even is.

A sharp *rap* on the window scares the shit out of me. Some stalker I am—I have zero sense of my surroundings. Hand to heart, I shift in my seat, and find myself on the other end of Cade's guarded gaze.

Awesome, just how I wanted to spend the day. With a sigh, I yank open the door and step onto the steaming ground. "Cade."

He ignores me, his eyes shifting to Peyton. "She looks good up there, doesn't she?"

"She does," I agree, feeling my muscles tense. His stupid cowboy hat shades his eyes and I can't get a read on him. What's his angle now? Feigning aloofness, I lean back against my door. "I reckon she'll be at full speed in no time."

Internally, I shake my head. *Reckon*? Apparently, country is contagious.

Cade's eyes cut to me. "That's on you."

My head rears back in confusion and I try to remember what we were even talking about. "Huh?"

"Her riding," he explains with a nod that tips his hat. I'm trapped in a damn western. "You helped her when I couldn't. She's up there on that horse because of you."

I'm too shocked to respond. In fact, my thoughts race as I search for possible motives or hidden meanings behind his words, but I find none. Cade's face is resigned and almost even friendly. The muscles in my shoulders relax a fraction.

"I was here the day she fell," he says, gently kicking my rear tire with his boot. He turns and rests his back against the frame. "We were damn lucky that it was only a wrist fracture. But I'd never seen Peyton so devastated." His throat strains with a swallow. "About a year later, I asked her why she pushed so hard that day. Why she went against what her therapists told her and rode Oakley."

I don't like where this is going. Warning signs are blaring but I ask anyway, "And what did she say?"

Cade looks at me. "That you two had broken up." He lifts an eyebrow. "I hadn't even known you were together."

I scrub a hand over my face as my world crashes to a halt. "No one did," I manage to croak. "Faith knew, but..."

"That girl knows everything," he finishes for me, and I nod once, feeling the bile rise up my throat.

God, I'm a schmuck.

It doesn't take a genius to put the pieces together. Peyton fell and broke her wrist the same day I broke her heart. It was almost poetic in its utter shittiness.

I bang my head against the window and Cade glances back at Peyton.

"It probably would've happened anyway," he continues. "She's always been a spitfire. Stubborn as hell. If y'all breaking up hadn't pushed her, it would've been something else."

"Maybe," I admit. "But it wasn't something else, was it?"

Cade turns, leaning his shoulder against the Jeep so he can face me. "Look, I'm not here to start anything or make you feel like shit. I just thought you deserved to know the full story. CC and I may not be together anymore, but I'll never stop being her friend. I'll never stop looking out for her."

"What are you getting at, man?"

"I want to know what your plans are," he tells me. "The draft is next week and I still don't know where your head is. Are you going pro or are you headed to college? Do you want to be with Peyton or not? I know it's none of my business, I get that, but the girl's been through enough. For the last three years, she's been locked in a shell, and I'd hoped to be the one to get her out. But it's not me... it's you. It's always been you. Just look at that smile on her face."

I follow his gaze to Peyton riding and, sure enough, her huge smile is back.

As if he's reading my thoughts he says, "It's not just her smile, either. She's back on a horse, too. Hell, *she's* back. I don't want to lose her again or see you break her."

He doesn't say, "like you did before," but I get the point, and the implication hits me like a two-by-four. "That's the last thing I want to do," I tell him, my legs suddenly weak. My head falls back against the Jeep and what feels like the weight of the world presses down on my shoulders.

Cade studies me for a beat, then pushes away from the door and adjusts his hat. "Good," he says. "Then I guess we're on the same page." Glancing back at the main house he asks, "You coming inside?"

I swallow past the lump of terror in my throat and shake my head. "Nah. I better get going. Need to clear my head, you know?"

Cade nods slowly and taps the hood of my Jeep. "See you around, Justin."

SATURDAY, JUNE 7TH

Freedom!

♥ Senior Year

JUSTIN

FAIRFIELD ACADEMY BASEBALL FIELD 12:42 P.M.

"Damn, it's good to have you back, kid." Carlos falls onto the open spot of the bench next to me and smiles his cornball grin. "Playing without you sucks, straight up, so don't even think about using that big old head of yours to stop a run today, you hear me?"

"I hear you, dumbass."

I elbow him in the ribs, but really, I'm stoked to be back.

It's not the first championship game we've played together, but it could be the last if I decide not to go to A&M. I don't want to forget a single second. Not the sun's scorching rays seeping through my cap, or the sting of sunblock in my eyes. The smell of dirt, grass, and hotdogs—a scent combination forever linked with Fairfield—and the crazy cheers of our frenzied home crowd.

The only thing missing today? Peyton screaming insults after a bad call.

I understand why she's not here. Today's the exhibition ride at the Round Rock rodeo and that's where she *should* be.

If I'm honest, as much as I love this game, I can't help wishing that's where I was, too.

Out of habit, I glance at her usual spot in the stands, and spy my father seated there instead.

"Holy shit."

I blink, unable to believe my eyes, but he's here. He made it. He actually got off his ass and came out to a game. Of course, my brother is here, seated on Rosalyn's lap, but I never would've expected my dad to show. A well of emotion builds in my chest, surprise and happiness, even affection... an emotion made even more pathetic once I notice who's sitting beside him. The area scout for the Toronto team that's been showing so much interest.

"Got a bird in the stands?" Alan Richard teases, taking a load off on my other side. He's a former Fairfield player now in the pros, and Coach asked him to come out today for inspiration. He lifts his chin toward the bleachers. "You're staring awfully hard over there. Either it's a chick or someone who owes you money."

"My dad," I reply, watching as Carlos does a double-take in my peripheral. "Chatting up a Toronto scout."

"Ah." Alan nods sagely. "I heard you got a lot of buzz going. You shouldn't be too shocked to see a scout hanging around."

"Not shocked at all." My voice is tight, even I can hear it. "Just... an observation."

Despite what I said, it sort of is hard to believe that I have this much attention on me. I mean, I'm grateful. Having options is amazing, and I'm in a position every player wants to be in. But I can't help feeling annoyed.

"Can I ask you something?" When he looks at me, giving me the go-ahead, I say, "You ever have any regrets about your choice?"

Alan sits back and sighs. "No. I weighed every option I had, thought it through, and in the end, chose the best path for me. There's no right or wrong answer here. It's about following what your gut tells you. For me, it was a farm team, working my way up. I got damn lucky. I have friends who are still back there." He takes off his cap, shoves his hair back, and then replaces it. "What about you? Where's your head on the whole thing right now?"

I shrug. "Torn, I guess. With the draft, I know about the shitty salary after the signing bonus, but I have a trust fund from my grandparents, so I'm not sweating that. It's not really about the money for me."

"So what is it about?"

I plant my cleat in the dirt, unsure how to answer that. Honestly, it's about tons of things. Making Coach proud and not disappointing my teammates. Wondering if Peyton and I have what it takes to last. It's deciding between getting an education now, or striking while the iron's hot, and hell, it's even about my dad, and what he's always expected from me. No way am I pouring all that shit on Alan.

So, Carlos answers for me. "It's about a girl."

I elbow him in the ribs and he smirks. Alan chuckles next to me.

"Something tells me it's a bit more than that," he says, turning to face me. "Listen, Carter, I'm not gonna tell you what you should do. But I wish someone had been around when I was in your place, someone who'd been in the same predicament, so if you want some advice, I'll give it to you."

Right about now, I'm dying for someone to tell me what to do, to make the decision for me. I look at him and say, "Dude, I'm all ears."

"Get a college education." He says it straight out, shocking the shit out of me. "Get your experience that way, and skip out on the low A and Rookie Ball crap. No one prepares you for that, man. The long bus rides to small towns, the bad food, and shittier fields. The completely empty stands. Some people get lucky. They draft high and advance quick, but for many, that's simply not reality."

Carlos leans forward. "What if he gets hurt, though? What if he blows his knee out in college and tanks his career."

"It's a risk you run, getting injured and missing your shot in the draft," Alan admits. "But it doesn't mean you'll never play professional ball. You'll heal up and earn your shot another way. Better to blow your knee in college, and have that education to fall back on, than out on a crap field with no one watching."

Carlos and I exchange a look. I know what he's thinking. He's headed to A&M, the same place Peyton is, and the same place I already signed my letter of intent. He'd love it if I stayed in state, and I admit, the pull to play more with my best friend is huge.

"For me," Alan says, "I was drafted high and the bonus money was life changing. My family needed that money, and it was impossible to say no. But if money's not an issue for you, and you can play ball either way, you're in a totally different position. The love of the game comes with either option, man, so it boils down to one question."

I can't help but smirk at the theatrics. "Oh, yeah? And what's that?"

"What are you chasing?"

What are you chasing?

The question rattles in my head. It shakes loose memories and thoughts I didn't even remember having. What am I chasing? I glance back at the crowd and lock eyes with my dad.

I can answer that.

PEYTON

ROUND ROCK EXHIBITION 4:15 P.M.

"*Welcome* to the Round Rock Kick-off to Summer Rodeo!"

The announcer's voice is tinny as it cracks over the loud speaker, but the crowd goes berserk regardless. The energy ripples through me, bringing chills in its wake, and I beam so wide my face hurts.

"I'm proud of you, CC." Cade squeezes my left hand, Faith does the same to my right, and together, we take in the insanity unfolding around us.

"I have to go check in for my event," he says, "but I'll be back as soon as I can. Faith knows to record your ride if I miss it, or I'll eat all the Reese's Peanut Butter Cups in the doghouse kitchen."

Faith extends a pink, sparkly fingernail. "You wouldn't dare. You mess with a girl's candy, you mess with the girl. And duh, *of course* I'm recording it. My bestie is a real life cowgirl. I have an entire vlog dedicated to rodeo fashion and terminology."

"Dear God, your poor viewers," I tease, winking at Cade. "Don't you worry about me, just go kick some saddle bronc ass."

My exhibition ride is part of the opening kickoff, but the day is jam-packed with other events, too. While we were dating, Cade put his own rodeo career on hold, only doing the occasional local event even though he loved it as much as I did. I never asked him to give it up—he decided to step back on his own, saying he knew how hard it was for me to be around this world. And I let him. It only goes to show how much better we truly are as friends than a couple. He deserves to be out here, chasing his dreams, so it makes me happy to see him getting back in the saddle. Like, *literally.*

Grinning at my cheesy pun, I release Faith's hand so I can throw both arms around Cade. It's only awkward for a second before he closes his arms around me and hugs me tight.

"Good luck, Donovan."

"Same to you, Williams."

We're both smiling when we step back and say goodbye, still us even if we're not together. Our friendship was always the best part of us anyway, and if we lost that, I'd be devastated.

Faith and I stand around, checking out the potential competition, when a tall brunette with a clipboard walks up to us. "Peyton Williams?"

My heart jolts but I somehow manage to find my voice. "Yup. That's me."

"Time to come on back and get ready." The woman smiles kindly and winks in a motherly sort of way, then heads off to find her next rider. I turn to Faith, already in the midst of a mini-freak out.

"Oh, crap, am I really about to do this?" Blowing out hard, I concentrate on my breathing and attempt to calm my racing heartbeat. It's currently pounding in a rhythm to match the stampede happening in the center arena.

"Girl, you were born to do this," Faith replies, bumping my hip. "And you look freaking *amazing.*"

Knowing this is the ultimate compliment my friend can bestow, I check my laugh and say, "Thanks. If the crowd awards style points, I'll be sure to mention you in my thank you speech."

The brunette catches my eye again as she nears the gate and I release another breath.

"Time to get my ride on."

It helps that Faith and Mama will be in the stands cheering for me. It'd be nice if Dad was here, too, but today's the championship, and I told him there was no way he was missing it—he couldn't miss it anyway, but I didn't want guilt eating him up.

Only one face is absent that I really wished were here, but he's with Dad, and I haven't heard from him in days. I have no clue where things stand with Justin. We cleared the air, we apologized, we scored an A as a married couple, and survived a weekend of pseudo-parenting. But the future remains one big blur.

I go to close the gate behind me, and Mama appears, running up with a strange smile twitching her lips. She yanks my phone out of her bag and says, "I felt it vibrate and thought you might like to see the message."

I take it from her hand, curious what could make her look so weird. When I glance down, I get it.

It's a text from Justin.

Ride it fast and ride it well. Go on pretty girl and give 'em hell.

My chest swells with emotion and I close my eyes, suddenly in love with technology. No, he didn't say the words, but I feel his love anyway. He thought of me, in the middle of the big game, and that means everything.

But... what does it mean to *him*?

Gah. Why couldn't we do this years ago? Hash things out, discover the truth. Maybe then a future together wouldn't seem so impossible.

When I open my eyes, I find Mama watching me with a knowing expression. "Go," she says, lifting her chin in the direction the brunette disappeared. "They're waiting for you."

I hand over the phone and close the gate, hiding my blush behind the slats. Justin's text didn't exactly reveal anything. Lately, I get misty-eyed over cereal commercials.

Graduation, reclaiming a lost passion, and breaking up with your boyfriend tend to do that to a girl. Mama's probably chalking my reaction up to that.

It's not until my back is turned and I'm halfway down the tunnel that she calls out, "Don't think you're not spilling everything when the ride's over, missy!"

I laugh and twist around, busted but happy, and blow her a kiss. Then, I head off to get my horse.

SATURDAY, JUNE 7TH

New Beginnings

♥ Senior Year

PEYTON

ROUND ROCK EXHIBITION 4:32 P.M.

My pride over my impending exhibition ride sours when I spot the girls hanging around out back. Girls I used to compete against, like Lexi Greene, waiting to go out and ride for *real*. They're here for the main events of the day: barrel-racing, breakaway roping, pole bending, and girls cutting, just to name a few. All events I used to compete (and kick ass) in. Seeing them again, smiling as they catch me up on all their successes, is a bitter pill to swallow... but I do it.

I do it because I'm here, I'm back in the arena, and they haven't seen the last of me.

The same brunette from before, a woman I've since realized is Ty Reynolds, an amazing rider on the circuit, comes up and tells me it's my turn. "Have fun out there," she says, and I smile at the simplicity of that. *Have fun.*

"Thanks," I reply. "I think I will."

Ty walks with me as the announcer talks about Sweet Serenity Ranch, our new rodeo school, and goes over my prior stats in the circuit. As he does, I lock eyes with Lexi, who's standing near the entrance.

The two of us used to be rivals. Every event, we seemed to trade who was the best. Secretly, I enjoyed the extra push she gave me, used it to fuel me in training, but I liked it even better when I beat her on a run.

Lexi narrows her eyes, her lips pursed, and as she curls a long strand of blonde hair around her finger, I wonder what she's thinking. Is she glad I'm back? Does she wish I'd stayed away? It's not until she lifts her chin and her lips twitch the slightest bit that I know.

That almost smile gives me the extra shot of confidence I need, and it acts like a boost of adrenaline.

This exhibition ride isn't about impressing anyone with my speed. I don't have to go fast. The other riders haven't, adding flare in the way of showmanship and personality, rather than hard riding.

But that's not me.

Ty nods me on, and I take a deep breath. Then... I take off.

Oakley's with me from the start. She remembers every movement, every cue. As we enter the arena, we're fully in synch, sharing one mind, moving our bodies as one. The sunbaked dirt and popcorn scent welcome me home as the dust circles around the air, coating my tongue. A brief moment of panic comes as we approach the first barrel, but we fly around it, easy as breathing.

Triumph courses through my veins as we circle the second barrel and I throw my head back in a laugh.

How could I have waited so long to feel this again? The rush is indescribable. The joy, uncontainable. I hear Mama and Faith screaming my name as I thunder past the front row of the stands at the completion of the course, the wind catching my vest emblazoned with Sweet Serenity's logo.

I think I did us proud.

Oakley and I make our way to the alleyway, and I lean over to whisper, "I love you, girl." The perk of her ears says she loves me, too.

I ride past the other riders, feeling my chest expand with each bit of praise they throw my way. Soon, I won't need the compliments. I won't seek out accolades. One day, I'll be confident in my ability again. But right now, I'm soaking up every drop of their praise like a crusty old sponge in the ocean.

Signs direct me to the area I'm supposed to drop off Oakley, and when I hop off her back, I find Lexi waiting for me, leaned against a column.

"I'm impressed," she says, fiddling with a blade of hay. "Glad to see you still have it in you. I'd hate to kick your ass on the circuit if it wasn't a real battle."

I laugh, one, because I'm pretty sure she's messing with me, and two, because even her old taunts can't steal my joy.

"Huh. Well, if memory serves, I'm pretty sure I beat you out for all-around cowgirl the year before I got sick," I remind her sweetly. "I have no doubt I'll do it again."

Lexi digs her tongue into her cheek, trying to hide her smile. It fails as badly as her taunt. She missed this rivalry every bit as much as I did. She raises her eyebrow in challenge and says, "Bring it, Williams."

"You can count on it, Greene."

I hand Oakley's reins over to the assistant on staff, and smile my thanks before turning back to my nemesis. When I do, I leave her with one parting thought.

"Enjoy the easy season, Lex, because next year, I'm coming for you."

JUSTIN

ROUND ROCK EXHIBITION COWBOY PROM 8:00 P.M.

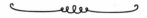

Damn, I feel like an idiot.

I catch a glimpse of myself in the glass door outside the building and shake a disgusted head. Cowboy hat, leather boots, and a black blazer my Gramps would've worn. I look like I went shopping in horse boy's closet, but when it comes to Peyton, there's not much I won't do.

Including, evidently, dressing like John Wayne.

I tug open the door and a wave of country music, Axe body spray, and the scent of leather engulfs me. So this is Cowboy Prom. Everywhere I look, couples are dancing, girls in fancy dresses and cowboy boots, with guys in Wranglers and dress shirts. It's like a whole other world.

I smile politely at the couple nearest me and maneuver around them as best I can, searching for her. Getting through the game was hard as hell once I made my decision, but I did it. Our team scored another win for Coach Williams, and I had just enough time to grab a shower and track down Cade before driving up here.

Deciding whether or not I can trust him is tricky, but it looks like the guy shot me straight.

While I don't see Peyton, I do spot Cade near the long table of food. He's chatting up a tall blonde who looks vaguely familiar. I hate to be a cock block, but this blazer is scratchy, the hat is annoying, and I need to find my girl.

"Hey, man," I say, effectively interrupting his conversation with the blonde. Cade shoots me a look and I shrug. "Have you seen Peyton?"

The girl looks me over before dismissing me. I bite back a laugh, vaguely impressed. As idiotic as I feel, I'm pretty confident I'm rocking this cowboy crap. She must have it bad for horse boy.

Sure enough, she places her hand on Cade's arm, leaving it there as she steps closer and says, "See you on the circuit."

Cade's totally obvious as he checks out her ass, watching her go.

"Was that necessary?" he asks when she's out of sight. "I can't catch a break with you around. First Peyton, now Lexi. You love keeping girls away from me, don't you?"

I shrug again, not denying it, and he sighs as he looks me over. "Nice duds, by the way. You almost look legit."

I flip him off. "So where is she?"

"Last I saw Peyton, her mom had her talking with potential students for their school."

I nod, glad to hear that things seem to be turning around, and say, "Hey, thanks again for sending the video of her ride. I appreciate it."

It's Cade turn to shrug as he says, "You deserved to see it. You helped make all this happen, and I'm man enough to admit that. Besides, Faith shot the video and she's the one who sent me your number."

A new song begins, a slow song about whiskey, if my ears are working right, and I chuckle to myself. The ode to beer I wrote one particularly bad night could hit gold if I turned it into a country song. Maybe lyric writing is in my future.

The crowd in front of us parts, and I finally catch a glimpse of Peyton. Cade follows my gaze and says, "I take it you've decided what you're doing."

I nod, my mouth suddenly parched from the sight of her. "That's why I'm here."

She hasn't noticed me yet, so I take a moment to drink her in. She's absolutely gorgeous. She always is, and her dress clings in just the right places, but it's her face that almost brings me to my knees. Her eyes are brighter than I've ever seen them. Her skin glows. And a smile as big as the stupid belt buckle I'm wearing spreads across her mouth.

Confidence looks damn good on her.

Peyton laughs with the old man in front, and jealousy tightens my gut. It's dumb, I realize that, but I want to be the reason for all of her laughs. She shakes her head, smiling, and her gaze drifts over to me. She instantly freezes.

I've had girls check me out before. It's an ego boost, especially when it's a girl you're into, but this is Peyton, and I'm not just into her... I'm in love with her. And I'm standing here in a ridiculous outfit that itches.

A flush brightens her cheeks, which I'm assuming is a good thing, and her eyes widen as she whispers something to her mom. She excuses herself from the old man and as she makes her way toward me, Mrs. Grace looks over and sends me a thumbs-up.

I head out to meet her halfway, and we meet toward the edge of the dance floor, couples surrounding us on either side.

"Wow, you look—"

"Congratulations on—"

We laugh and take turns motioning for the other to speak. I win when I say, "Ladies first," and feel a drop of sweat glide down my temple. Damn these hats are hot.

"Congratulations on the win today," she says, her blush deepening. "Dad called us earlier. I'm so happy for you, Justin." Then she tilts her head, sort of closing one eye, and asks, "But... how are you here? How did you even know...?"

"Cade," I answer, nodding toward him behind us. He lifts his cup in the air and I turn back to Peyton. "He also sent me a video of your ride. You were incredible out there."

Peyton beams. "It *felt* incredible! I wasn't supposed to go that fast, it was only an exhibition ride. But, no guts no glory, right?" She bites at the corner of her lip and glances at her feet. "Uh, when Dad called to congratulate me, he mentioned they had a ton of scouts out there today. Looks like your draft position is all but guaranteed."

I shift closer and wait for her to look back up. When she does, I say, "Too bad it doesn't matter."

An adorable squiggle forms between her eyes, even as hope fills them. I take her hand, needing to get away from the *Footloose* crowd, and lead her to the far wall where we can talk easier. I need to make sure she hears me.

When we reach a semi-secluded spot, away from any speakers, I say, "I realized a few things today."

"What sort of things?" she asks.

"Things like I'm tired of letting my father dictate my life," I reply. "Wondering when he'll remember he has an older son. Getting into baseball to begin with just so he'd notice me, or care."

She takes my hand, her eyes filled with compassion, and I shake my head, kicking myself again over how much time we've wasted.

"Sunshine, I've been so busy chasing the idea of being drafted that I never bothered to stop and ask myself why. It's never been a money thing, or even a love of the game thing—I already agreed to play for one of the best organizations in the SEC."

"But what about playing professionally?" Her eyes shift between mine. "Isn't that your dream?"

"At one time, it was," I say, threading my hand through her hair to cup her neck. Her skin is so soft beneath my fingers.

292

"And in four years, as long as no injuries get in the way, I can still enter the draft. On my terms, not some elaborate, attention getting way to earn my father's respect." I brush my thumb across her jaw and lower my voice. "Plus, this way I'll have a degree and can chase my other dream while I'm at it."

Peyton drops her gaze to my mouth. "You calling me your dream, Carter?"

"Nah." I grin and say, "I was talking about my writing. Having you next to me is strictly a bonus."

She laughs at that, throwing her head back and lighting up the whole damn room like she did when I first met her. The day she flipped my entire world off its axis. The couples dancing nearest us stop and stare, and I gape right along with them.

"God, I missed that laugh."

A mix of pleasure and embarrassment stains Peyton's cheeks and she glances away as the whiskey song transitions into another slow beat. The restless itch I've felt all year flares again beneath my skin, and without hesitation, I pull her in my arms... right where she belongs.

Something inside me sighs in relief.

Steering us deeper into the shadows, I press my palm against the curve of her spine. "On the drive up, I wrote another poem," I say, swaying us softly to the music.

She glances up at me. "Oh yeah?" she asks, batting her lashes. "Inspired by anyone I know?"

"Just some girl who drives me crazy," I reply, earning a playful pinch to the waist.

Peyton holds my gaze, not pushing, but clearly curious, and I tuck a curl of strawberry-blonde hair behind her ear. "It's not written down yet or anything. I mean, I just got here. But if you want..." A strange concoction of nerves and nausea explodes in my stomach and I swallow thickly. "I can tell it to you. You know, if you'd like to hear it."

My heart pounds harder than it did earlier when we won the game.

Peyton has read my stuff before. She flipped through my notebook that weekend over Easter, and over the course of our relationship, I texted her a handful of poems. But I never read them to her. I never had to say the words aloud. Even that day out by her barn, I purposefully kept my face averted so I couldn't see her face.

What if I'm not good enough? What if she thinks I suck but is too nice to say it?

Freshman year, I couldn't have handled that. Truthfully, I'm not that sure I can handle it now, either, but I'm here, prepared to stare straight into her eyes as I share my most honest, naked thoughts about her, about me, about the two of us together.

It's absolutely terrifying.

Peyton wraps her hand around my wrist and says earnestly, "I'd love nothing more."

I nod as I soak in the stark sincerity in her eyes, and I inhale a deep breath, prepping myself for exposure. This is by far scarier than staring down a no-hit pitcher. This is me, the real me, on display for the one person who matters more than anything.

Exhaling the fear, I remind myself it doesn't have to be perfect. That *I* don't have to be perfect. This isn't my father... it's Peyton. She loves me, *truly* loves me, and it's okay if my poetry sucks. She'll love me regardless.

Sliding my hand up the slope of her back, I draw her close against me.

"I loved you then," I say, my voice shaking only the slightest bit on the delivery. I pause to collect myself and rein it in. "I love you now. I'll love you always, because you showed me how. You always see the best in me, and because of you, I'm the man I want to be."

Peyton's eyes fill with tears, shining bright with love and pride, and the last of my anxiety fades.

"You've taught me that there's so much more, that I don't need the mask I wore. I'm casting it off, ready to walk in the light. Being with you is the only thing that's right." I smile down at her, feeling the truth of that in my bones. "I'm through with being patient, I'm not doing it anymore. Peyton, you're the girl I'm fighting for. You're the prize I'm gonna win—"

Through her tears, she lifts an amused eyebrow, and I shake my head. *So damn cute.*

"I promise you," I continue, lowering my voice to a whisper. "I'll be the best I've ever been."

The last line is delivered against her lips as I wipe away a tear with my thumb. Then I rest my forehead against hers, my heart completely laid open. But it doesn't matter... it's always been hers anyway.

Peyton sniffles, her eyebrow still raised. "Prize you're gonna win, huh?"

I huff a laugh and feign annoyance. "It's poetic, woman!" I shake my head, rocking hers back and forth in the process, and grin. "It means you're worth it. That I know my work's cut out for me when it comes to you, but I'm signing on anyway. You deserve better, and I know it, but I'm ready to spend the rest of my life proving myself. To you, to your father, to anyone who tries to steal you away."

I lean my head back and give her a pointed look, letting her know no one was flirting with her on my watch, and she rolls her eyes with that cute little smirk on her lips. *Damn, I can't believe she's mine.*

"You'll never be sorry you risked your heart again on me," I vow, hoping she hears the ring of sincerity in my voice. I slide my hand across the silky fabric of her dress, over her waist and up her torso, resting it right over her pounding heart. "I promise you, I'll keep it safe."

She gifts me with a soft smile and says, "I know you will. And I'll protect yours. Nothing is getting between us again, Justin. I won't let it. Not even your stubborn assumption that I deserve better."

As the determination in her gaze fully sinks in, my eyes close with contentment.

I've never had anyone in my life I could keep. My grandparents hung around as long as they could, but I only got a few years. My mom never wanted me, my dad couldn't care less, and Annabeth... well, I won't even go there. As for the others, Chase is only a kid, Rosalyn is paid to be there, and Carlos, as much as he has my back, has his own thing going.

With girls, every relationship before and after Peyton has been transient. Blink and you missed it, no attachments. *Casual.* I did that on purpose, so no one ever got too close. No one could ever hurt me.

But with this beautiful, brave, brilliant girl in front of me, I never even stood a chance.

Peyton's smile transforms, growing wider until it takes over her entire face. The skin around her eyes crinkles, two small dimples pop, and true happiness exudes from her pores. My breath catches.

"Justin, that poem... I loved it. You have to know how gifted and amazing you are." She presses her open palm against her chest, over my hand that's still resting on her heart, and says, "I'm so in love with you that it physically hurts."

Her confession weakens my knees. By the grace of God I don't fall on my ass in front of the crowd, and instead tighten my hold around her waist. She slides her arms over my shoulders, circling around my neck, and I lift her off her toes, responding to that the best way I know how. Kissing her senseless.

Peyton's taste explodes on my tongue, and the word mine pops into my head. I repeat it over and over as I kiss her again and again and again, locking my greedy lips onto hers and · tangling our tongues together.

Mine. Mine. Mine. Mine. Mine.

My fingers thread through her hair, loving that she's wearing it down so I can feel the soft strands glide across my rough fingertips. She moans in the back of her throat and I grin, grateful for the shadows, and gently back her against the wall.

It's not until she's good and flustered and clinging to my shoulders, breathless, that I lift my head. Gasping for breath myself, I brokenly whisper, "Peyton Williams, I'm crazy in love with you."

I slide my nose against hers, tilting my head to brush her lips once, twice, three times before saying, "You're not my dream... you're my *everything*."

Peyton's eyes fill with love, happiness, and awe as her mouth forms a smile nothing short of dazzling. Lowering her gaze to my lips, she tugs my head down and says, "*More*."

Grinning like I just won the damn lottery, I happily comply.

ACKNOWLEDGEMENTS

What a journey this has been! When I first sat down to write *The Fine Art of Pretending* in 2010, I had no clue it would ever be finished, much less published. That writing experiment turned into nine published books—*nine*. It seriously boggles the mind. But *Fine Art* was my first book baby, and it was soon after I typed 'The End' that I realized there were more stories to tell in this world. Particularly Justin's story.

Luckily, many of you agreed, asking for more stories of these characters that I love so much. Your emails, your tweets, your messages, and your reviews made this book possible. Because truthfully? This book wasn't easy to write. In fact, it tried to kill me. Turns out, writing a dual point-of-view story with a dual timeline isn't for the faint of heart. I confused myself more often than not while drafting, but your enthusiasm and support for this book motivated me to continue. I'm so very grateful. Justin and Peyton may be my two favorite characters I've ever written, and their journey to discovering true strength and forgiveness is a story I believe that needed to be told.

So, first and foremost, I want to thank YOU! I hope this book was worth the wait and that you fell even more in love with Justin in these pages. I know I did!

That being said, *The Natural History of Us* wouldn't even exist without the help of several people. Here is where I will slobber over them all:

Melissa West and Cindi Madsen, I'd be a complete mess without you. You are my soul sisters, and you talked me out of my confusion so many times. Melissa, your spot-on notes made this book stronger. I love you girls!

If you love Justin's poetic soul as much as I do, we all have Megan Rigdon to thank. As my assistant, she read over multiple versions of this book as it was being created, and while doing so she was somehow inspired by my crazy mess of words to write poetry. Poetry that became the very snippets that Justin wrote in his journal and were shared within these pages. Megan, your friendship and talent lifted this book to another level. Thank you, sweet girl.

Staci Murden and Ashley Bodette, you continue your reign as the most incredible betas EVER! Thanks for putting up with my bazillion and a half emails and for believing in these characters so much. I don't know what I'd do without you.

Mindy Ruiz, author and pure ray of light that she is, has had a hand in every YA story I've written—then again, that's no surprise to anyone who knows Mindy. She's sunshine in human form, always willing to help with a gorgeous smile. When I mentioned needing an illness for Peyton, something that shook her confidence and could also maybe bring awareness to an important cause, Mindy taught me about GBS. Her incredible husband Mark's personal experience and testimony helped shape Peyton's journey, making it so much richer and deeper than it would've been otherwise. I'm in awe of this powerhouse couple and the incredible things God continues to do in their lives. It's impossible to find two stronger, sweeter people, I swear. Love you!!

Kim McKinney and Sandra Salinas... you are a GODSEND! Your knowledge of GBS and personal experiences of the rehabilitation process made Peyton come to life. You tackled my questions like readers, knowing what would make a great story, and you put up with my insane number of emails. Your suggestions added depth and life to this book. I can't thank you enough.

Katrina Tinnon, one of my fabulous Flirts, introduced me to Ty Reynolds who completely brought the rodeo to life in a fun way for me. Ty even has a cameo in this book! Ashley Erin, another Flirt and awesome author, jumped in with even more horse details, making sure I sound like I know what I'm talking about. YouTube videos only get you so far, you know? Kristen Humphry Johnson dropped everything to speed read this for proofing, saving my frazzled self. Casey Quinn, Melissa Brown, and Jessica Mangicaro helped with all things baseball, and Veronica Bartles brought her brownie recipes. I'm telling you, this book was a team effort!

The Flirt Squad chicas... so many of you will find your names in this book. Your enthusiasm and laughter are a gift on days when my brain hurts or I find myself stuck on the silliest things. Ali Byars, you blew me away with your sweetness when you chose to pass along your win in the 'become-a-character' contest along to your youngest sister. Ciara Byars, you chimed in with fun details to include, and Peyton's bestie Faith was born. Faith Byars, I hope you enjoyed this fun surprise! You were a BLAST to write!

A huge shout out to my incredible team, Suzie Townsend (super-agent), Patricia Riley (editor of awesome), Karen Hughes (managing editor genius), Danielle Ellison (title genius), Kelly Simmon (publicist of whoa), and Felicia Minerva (publicist of win). Thank you all for being in my corner—I'd be lost without you!

And finally, no book would be complete without thanking my amazing family. My husband, Gregg, surprised me with not one but TWO hotel weekends away to write, complete with massage breaks and chocolate, and he's always there to give advice on the male mind. My two beautiful daughters, Jordan and Cali, ask about my characters every day during homeschool lessons, proving they are still at the age where they think Mommy is cool (ha!). Cali, thanks for all the fun suggestions, in this book and so many others. One day that Mario Kart scene will make it in a book! Jordan, thanks for the incredible Lauren fan-fic! You're already an incredible author and I seriously cannot wait to see what the future holds. My mom, Rosie, and mother-in-law, Peggy, are my biggest cheerleaders ever, and it's because of my best friend Kim that I can write stories of true friendship. My support system is unbelievable.

Thanks for reading, friends!

ABOUT THE AUTHOR

New York Times bestselling author Rachel Harris writes humorous love stories about sassy girls-next-door and the hot guys that make them swoon. Emotion, vibrant settings, and strong relationships are a staple in each of her books... and kissing. Lots of kissing.

An admitted Diet Mountain Dew addict and homeschool mom, she gets through each day by laughing at herself, hugging her kids, and watching way too much Food Network with her husband. She writes young adult, new adult, and adult romances, and she LOVES talking with readers!